W9-BLZ-321

DATE DUE

UNCANNY

DAVID MACINNIS GILL

GREENWILLOW BOOKS
An Imprint of HarperCollins*Publishers*

HarperCollins
PUBLISHERS
Since 1817

This book is a work of fiction. References to real people, events, establishments, organizations, or locales are intended only to provide a sense of authenticity, and are used to advance the fictional narrative. All other characters, and all incidents and dialogue, are drawn from the author's imagination and are not to be construed as real.

Uncanny
Copyright © 2017 by David Macinnis Gill

www.epicreads.com

The text of this book is set in 12-point Adobe Garamond Pro.
Book design by Paul Zakris

Library of Congress Cataloging-in-Publication Data is available.
ISBN 978-0-06-229016-8 (hardback)

17 18 19 20 21 PC/LSCH 10 9 8 7 6 5 4 3 2 1
First Edition

GREENWILLOW BOOKS

FOR PATTI

UNCANNY

You hang by a slender thread,
with the flames of divine wrath flashing about it,
and ready every moment to singe it and burn it asunder.

—JONATHAN EDWARDS

PART ONE

AT A TIME OF GREAT AWAKENINGS

CHAPTER ONE

THIS morning, I awoke to a dead girl standing beside my bed, peeling strips of skin from her arms. I closed my eyes, told myself it was a dream, and made her go away. It wasn't the first time I had dreamed of her. She had visited me every morning for the past two years, starting the day after my dad was murdered.

Even before her appearance, my whole life had been haunted by dreams. Maybe it was because I lived in a hollowed-out town, a thighbone wasteland with its marrow sucked dry. A river crawled through it, sneaking past high-spired churches and bullfinch halls, under murky catacombs with ghosts waiting for someone to wake them and hear the secrets only they could tell. Or maybe it was because I was that someone and their secrets were waiting for me.

Before I learned about secrets and ghosts and deep dark bowels beneath our feet, I was an average girl with above-average grades who loved poetry and hockey and the dichotomy of that. As I sat in Tom's Pub with my ma and little sister, Devon, I tried to forget my bad dreams and concentrated on stuffing a slice of pepperoni pizza into my face.

Then the kitchen doors blew open, and my best friend, Siobhan, burst through, holding a birthday cake.

A cake that was on fire.

So was Siobhan, who had stuffed lit candles into her long black braids.

"Surprise!" she screamed. Which was followed by Ma and Devon, yelling, "Happy birthday, Willow Jane!" Which was followed by me wanting to crawl under the table—I was a backstage kind of girl with crippling butterflies, not a diva who basked in the limelight.

"And now!" Siobhan clapped a frosted hand over my mouth. "We must sing 'Happy Birthday' to the birthday girl! Because she's a girl! And it's her birthday!"

"Let's not," I said.

"Shh, my sweet." Siobhan stuck a finger to my lips. "It's not every day a girl turns sixteen! Right, Devon?"

"Right!" Devon sniffed the air. "Did ja know your head's on fire?"

"Your head's on fire," Siobhan said sarcastically, then sniffed. Her eyes popped wide. "Again?"

She had braided her wild, staticky black hair into pig-tails, and she wore faded overalls with a black Bruins tank top. Her manic mood, like an airborne virus, had spread to Devon, who needed mania like a kid with ADD needs a double shot of Red Bull.

I licked my fingers and doused Siobhan's braid candles, then sighed heavily and closed my eyes. The last thing I wanted was a sweet sixteen, but Ma wanted one for me, and I desperately wanted Ma to be happy again.

"Just get it over with," I said.

"*Um, dois, quatro!*" Siobhan sang. "Everybody, sing with me!"

She belted the first sour notes and then was joined by a chorus of regulars singing at the tops of their lungs, louder than the volume of the six big-screen TVs showing the Patriots game. "Happy birthday to you! You smell like a monkey—"

"And you look like one, too!" Devon shrieked.

The air was filled with blue-gray smoke and shouts of well-wishing. Tom's regulars hadn't forgotten Michael Conning. The pub walls were papered with photos of singers, and my dad was pictured in a lot of them, flashing *that grin* and cocking his head just so to let his green eyes glitter. The oldest photo captured a curly haired guitar player in his youth, a soon-to-be one-hit wonder. The most recent showed a faded folk singer playing for his supper. But that was before the shooting, and I wasn't interested in his pictures anymore.

"Let the spankings commence!" one of the regulars called.

"First one of you lays a hand on my daughter," Ma yelled and shook her fist at the guy. "Is getting a shiner to show for it!"

The crowd laughed, raised their glasses to us, then turned back to the game.

"You guys?" I pleaded. "Could you possibly be more embarrassing?"

"Yes!" Siobhan waggled her artfully unplucked eyebrows. "We really, really could and in ways even your advanced intellect couldn't imagine."

I looked to Ma for sympathy, but she wasn't having it. Maggie Mae Conning was what Southies called a mere slip of a woman, but beneath multiple layers of sweaters beat the heart of an old-school mother superior. I had inherited her dimples, petite frame, and unruly flame-kissed hair, but not her personality. Ma was the crispy skin of a toasted marshmallow, and I was the soft, gooey center.

"You oughta see the look on your face, Willie!" Siobhan planted a sloppy wet kiss on my cheek. "Never saw it coming, did ya?"

Well, yes, I thought. I did.

In middle school my friends called me the Trivia Jedi because I knew the answers before the teachers finished asking the questions. I ruled games like Words with Friends and Scrabble. I would've won the spelling bee, too, if I didn't forget how to breathe in front of a crowd. So when Siobhan made a grand entrance with my surprise sweet sixteen cake, I wasn't surprised. I knew exactly what flavor (double chocolate with jimmies), what color icing (white), and what I would wish for when Devon demanded I blow out the candles.

"Willow Jane!" Devon yelled over the din of the pub. "They're melting! Hurry up!"

Another thing I knew? The candles would relight as soon as I blew them out. That didn't take clairvoyance—Siobhan had been pulling the same trick since third grade.

"Pull your head outta your ass, Conning!" Siobhan said, growling like our hockey coach. "There ain't time to make it look pretty!"

"Knew you'd say that," I said, but still let the flames burn.

Siobhan was right. My head was firmly anchored in my ass, metaphorically speaking. This morning, I had woken to waffles with maple syrup, delivered by Devon on a platter with a plastic red rose and a card written in crayon, the implement of choice for second graders. The rest of the day I had spent reliving bad memories, paying no attention to the priest at church, forgetting to take communion and getting a withering look from Ma instead of a paste-tasty wafer and a sip of sour wine.

I had sleepwalked the six blocks to Tom's Pub and had eaten the pizza because refusing it would alert Devon to my ennui. Nobody loved malaise like my little sister. She would pounce on a foul mood with the gusto of a kitten attacking a ball of yarn.

Truth was, I'd been dreading this day for months.

When Siobhan and Kelly O'Brien, my other but not quite best friend, first suggested a party, I had totally nixed it. Sweet sixteens existed to give girls yet another way to compete. Just on philosophical grounds, I opposed them, and reality check? A widow raising two kids in Boston couldn't keep up with the Joneses—nor the O'Briens.

My plan not to plan was dashed, though, when Ma got a sudden craving for pizza, even though she had a wheat allergy and tomatoes gave her heartburn. And it couldn't be just any pizza. It had to be Tom's, and we had to eat precisely at 3:00 P.M.

Because I was woolgathering, as Ma called it, I barely noticed Kelly scoot through the front door. Her hair was pulled into a ponytail, and she wore a peacoat over a knee-length dress. Kelly was, like Siobhan, almost a foot taller than me. Her face was all cheekbones and dimples, and she had a cleft chin, which Siobhan had dubbed the Butt Chin. She waved at me and Siobhan, who shot her a dirty look.

Later Siobhan would bust her for being the skid who's late for your friend's party, and Kelly would apologize profusely and swear to work on her recidivistic tardiness. Despite her poor grasp of time, Kelly was a trooper. She may show up late, but she would always show up, and she'd be carrying an apology in a beautifully wrapped gift bag.

"Willie!" Kelly swooped in and pecked my cheek. "Brought you a little something."

"You're a little something," Siobhan said.

"Get a new joke, huh?" Kelly said without looking at her. "Sorry I'm late. Hey, you waited to blow out the candles. How sweet."

"Woulda been sweeter," Siobhan said, "if you'd been here a half hour ago, you big skid. Y'know, like you promised?"

"I'm here now," Kelly said and sniffed. "You set fire to your hair *again*?"

"Willow Jane," Ma said. "Make a wish before the frosting catches fire."

Part of me had been waiting for my dad to magically walk through the door, but no amount of wishcraft could accomplish that. He always promised that no matter what, he'd be there for me. For us. "I've got your back," he'd say. Who had my back now?

Still, I closed my eyes and whispered a wish. It brought back the memory of my fifth birthday, when Ma decorated the house in a *Three Little Pigs* motif, and I pretended to be the Big Bad Wolf.

"I'll huff and I'll puff and I'll blow your house down," I whispered, then exhaled every molecule of air in my lungs.

The lights went out.

Not just the candles but the lights in the pub, along with the streetlights outside and the illuminated windows of the triple-decker across the street. In an instant the room turned black, and we were bathed in darkness until the sky boomed and lightning exploded in the heavens above.

CHAPTER TWO

THE blackout spread like a plague throughout South Boston, its tendrils spreading down the side streets, gathering on Broadway, and sweeping over the bridge until it covered all of downtown, and Boston went dark. The final light to shine was the spotlight on Faneuil Hall and the great gilded grasshopper weather vane that sat upon its ancient roof. Then that flickered out, too, and on the roof, the grasshopper blinked its bronze eyes and waited for fate to intervene.

Two beggars rounded the corner of Quincy Market. No, the grasshopper ruminated, beggar was not the right word. Vagabond? Bum? Homeless? Yes, they were called homeless now. The homeless men, one old and one younger, were dressed in cast-off clothing, and they were arguing. The grasshopper recognized their voices. The younger one had a name—Artie—and he had joined the service at eighteen and served a hard tour in Afghanistan, which had clogged his brain like a wet mass of hair and soap scum. After the army was done with him, his meanderings led him to Boston.

"What happened to all the lights?" Artie asked.

"The mayor forgot to pay the bill!" The second man laughed, then frowned when Artie didn't.

Artie shivered in a cast-off blanket as he ducked into a nook between Faneuil Hall's foundation and back steps. The wind off the harbor cut like a bayonet, and his only coat was a patched-up cardigan.

"You cold?" the second man asked. The grasshopper couldn't recall the second man's name, but he was born and bred in Providence, where he'd worked the scallop boats until a bad fall bent his spine like a question mark. "Wait till January. That's whatcha call some real winter."

Artie's teeth rattled so hard he bit his tongue. "I'll b-be gone b-by then."

"Gimme a cigarette."

"D-don't smoke."

"Found cigarette butts by your hiding spot."

"D-don't smoke."

"Liar. Saw you light up an hour ago." The second man had appointed himself unofficial Faneuil Hall grounds-keeper. He used a broomstick with a screw on the end to stab litter. He pointed it at Artie. "If you lie about smoking, you lie about cigs. Where's you hiding them?"

"I ain't got no smokes." Artie held up two fingers. "Scout's honor."

"You was a Scout?"

"Cross my heart and hope to die, stick a needle in my eye." Artie crossed his heart. "If I'm lying, may the man above strike me dead."

With a bone-rattling crack, the sky lit up, and a bolt of lightning shot down from the heavens, striking the second man dead.

"Wait!" Artie screamed to the sky. "I take it back! I never was a Scout!"

The dark air filled with wild static. Another strike hit the weather vane. The bronze grasshopper glowed bright orange for a few seconds. Then, with a grinding of metal on metal, the grasshopper began to grow. Inch by inch, it expanded until the weather vane bent. The grasshopper broke free and two bounding hops later, landed on the bricked courtyard. Its eyes glowed like a furnace, and its mouth was white hot.

"No one cares what you were," the grasshopper said in a deep—and deeply human—voice.

A third bolt flew from the sky, striking Artie. He fell to the ground, dead before his skull cracked on the pavers, and his spirit parted, shimmering like cellophane.

Then the grasshopper took another bounding hop and plunged into Artie's corpse. With a herky-jerky movement, the corpse sat and turned his head unnaturally toward Artie's spirit, the neck vertebrae popping like bones in a meat grinder. Artie's eyes fluttered, turned from blue to tarnished copper, then he rose and shed the patched cardigan and began removing the layers of tattered clothes.

"What the hell?" Artie's spirit said.

"The freshest kind," the grasshopper said. "Why does your corpse stink like fish? Did you never bathe?"

"My corpse?" the spirit said. "I'm d-dead?"

"Dead as the proverbial doornail, I'm afraid." He found a pack of cigarettes stuffed in a sock and tossed them aside. "I'm called Harken. Sorry to make your acquaintance under such tragic circumstances."

"But, but." The spirit tried in vain to pat itself. "I-I don't feel dead."

"No one ever does." Harken tossed aside the last of the clothing and stood naked in the howling wind, examining himself. "Not the best material, your body, but I've worn worse suits."

"That's me?" Artie's spirit said, staring into his own face. "You stole my body?"

"*Claimed* it, not *stole* it. I've also claimed your memories, but fortunately not your horrific body odor." Harken ran his hands over Artie's flaccid muscles, murmuring in a forgotten language. "This next part may be a bit . . . disconcerting, even to the dead."

Wild static filled the air, and a final lightning bolt struck.

When it cleared, Harken was resting with a hand on one knee, posed like a statue of a dying gladiator. His skin— red-hot slag that turned to thick black ash—crackled with current. He shook loose the ash, and underneath was flesh like alabaster marble. He had a strong chin, deep eyes, and thick dark hair that rose in waves on his head, and except for his torc, a braided bronze ring wrapped around his neck, he was nude. For a moment Harken's new body emanated waves of heat, then his molten eyes cooled, turning to the color of tarnished pennies, electricity dancing in the irises. He bowed his head and rubbed his face with his hands, and when he lifted his chin, he was human once more.

"I had a cleft in my chin." Artie's spirit reached out to touch Harken's torc, as if he were drawn irresistibly to some unseen fire. "Just like you do."

"Don't touch the metal," Harken said with cold command. "Its fire will burn even a spirit."

"Yes, sir," the spirit said and tried to salute.

"Don't salute me," Harken said. "I don't deserve your respect." He grabbed the cast-off clothing to cover himself. "This will do till I find better attire. It is damn cold, isn't it?"

"You're the prettiest man I ever seen," the spirit said.

"So I've heard. The first to compliment this face was a wicked woman who lured me from my home and plopped a changeling in my crib." Harken wrapped the sweater around his waist like a kilt. "So forgive me if I'm not flattered by the compliment."

"And you're just a kid," the spirit said. "I wasn't ever that good-looking. The ladies would've—"

"A handsome face is a curse!" Harken picked up the discarded blanket and used it to wrap the second man's corpse. Before covering the face, he closed the eyes with a gentle sweep of his hand and placed two coins on the lids. "*Dormit in pace.*" He shrouded the face and stood, wiping his hands. "On to business."

"But what about me?" the spirit said. "What happens to my body when you're finished with it?"

Harken had no suitable answer for him. He'd needed the man's body to build his own, much the way sand, straw, and mud were needed to build ancient tombs. He felt a deep kind of regret for the man, to have given so much of himself to service, only to have so little in return for his sacrifice. The war he'd fought had not taken his life, but it had taken the life he would've lived and given him a soldier's heart in return.

"You're done with this world and it with you." Harken pinched Artie's spirit like he would grip the string of a kite. "Come along. The ferryman won't wait forever."

"What ferry?" the spirit asked.

"The ferry*man*." Harken pointed to a MBTA bus idling at the corner. "He's made a special trip just for you. I have claimed your body, so I must help your spirit reach the afterlife. It is law, one of many those who pay penance must follow. Your friend, however, will have to find his own carriage to the afterlife."

"He wasn't my friend. Just pretended, to get my smokes."

"We can't always choose our friends, nor our fates," Harken said and involuntarily winced. A pretend friend was better than none. "Me, for example. I chose the wrong friends, and it's landed me in the service of lesser norns."

"What's a norn?" the spirit asked when they reached the bus.

"In your vernacular?" Harken rapped on the door. "A witch."

"Witches don't scare me, but the bus makes me puke."

"There are worse fates," Harken said and rapped again, "than a smelly bus to the afterlife."

The bus driver opened the door. He was a stone-faced man, and his eyes were like dun-white marbles. "No one rides for free, not even the dead."

"A penny for the ferryman." Harken pulled a mangled token out of thin air and pressed it into the driver's palm. He guided Artie's spirit to a seat. "This soldier was a decent man in life, though life was hardly decent to him, and he deserves to be warm one last time."

"Don't we all?" the driver said.

"Some do," Harken said, stepping back to the curb. "Others deserve a bad turn at the end of a long, bitter cold night. Or so the Fates have told me."

As the bus rolled into the darkness, he shivered from the cold and from the thought of what lay ahead. First order of business was to find some suitable clothes, then a meal for his empty belly and a pint or two to slake his gnawing thirst. That was the problem with going decades without a meal—you woke up starving. After the needs of his new body were met, he'd begin his service once again, by making sure the wicked creature he'd buried centuries before was still in her grave.

CHAPTER THREE

THE lightning bolt that awoke Harken had grown weaker when it reached Granary Burying Ground a half mile away. But the charge was strong enough to touch a certain casket in a tomb deep underground. The casket was four by six and two feet deep. The sides were carved from whalebone and inscribed with short poems, mostly in Latin and Greek. Engraved on the lid was the depiction of a woman at the gallows, a noose around her neck, an executioner stabbing her with a bodkin needle. The lightning dissipated quickly, and it would have done no damage, except that the casket made an almost imperceptible sizzling noise, like raw meat over an open flame.

Inside the casket, the Shadowless stirred.

Two lidless eyes rolled from the back of a skinless skull, and mummified lungs exhaled a mouthful of dust. Because no one knew about the tomb, no one knew when the Shadowless awakened from a forced slumber. No one heard when desiccated lips began to whisper, nothing but the worms crawling blind in the dirt. They began to writhe and twitch, and they fled inch by inch to the surface. But in the darkness they were still unseen, so no one thought it odd when dozens of crows and rooks began to gather from across the city, perching in the trees that dotted the burying grounds, filling the air with their harsh cries and devouring the fattened, juicy worms.

Several feet below, the Shadowless whispered, and the carrion birds stopped eating. They turned their heads in unison, listening like soldiers given orders. As one, they began to tear the ground with their beaks.

The Shadowless had lain in the casket for over four hundred years, unmoving, unspeaking, unhearing, unseeing. Now she peered into the darkness with something akin to hope. Now the shades were moving, and the Shadowless could hear sounds, not just of birds, but of humans. Humans who were happy to listen to the promises of treasure she whispered into the wind.

Then she raised her hand to the lid of her coffin and began to claw.

CHAPTER FOUR

SECONDS before the lights returned to Tom's Pub, I heard a voice shout, "Blood!" Then the pub filled with the hum of fluorescent bulbs and calls to turn on the TVs because it was the two-minute warning and the Pats were driving, for chrissakes.

Nobody noticed my spastic episode. Nobody except Devon, who never let the tiniest detail slip by. Ma said Devie had an eye for minutia, but the family therapists all diagnosed her with early-stage OCD.

"You're jumpy." Devon cocked her head just so. "Ma, Willow Jane's got the jumpies. Give her some meds."

We didn't mention Ma's meds. Not in the apartment,

not among family, and definitely not in a packed restaurant. After the shooting, Ma had suffered from depression, PTSD, and whatever the therapists needed to write down. She tried to hide it, but we had a tiny apartment, and when you cried yourself to sleep, your daughters knew. The therapists never could decide how to fix her, so Ma decided for them. "No more secrets, girls," she had told us when she cut the pills from nine a day to two. "From this day forward, we're a family again."

"I don't need Ma's meds," I told Devon, my tongue feeling like it was too big for my mouth. "I just. Just."

Blood!

Dancing red and blue lights seemed to wash over me. I heard a whoosh of air, then the shimmering sound of a xylophone. The notes warbled in my brain, and the room wobbled. The notes turned to whispers, and the whispers formed a voice, urgent and strident, the sound sharpening in my mind: "Come closer."

My body jerked. I grabbed the table and held on tight. "Whoa!"

"Willow Jane?" Ma held the cake knife ready to cut. "What's wrong?"

The price will be paid in blood, I thought, then steadied

myself until the feeling passed. After Dad died, I used to hear gunshots that woke me up, but our counselor said it was trauma, and they faded away. "Just got a little dizzy. Probably used too much wind blowing out the candles."

"You need more practice blowing," Kelly said and winked. "Too bad Will Patrick's not around."

"Will and Willow sitting in a tree," Devon said. "K-i-s-s-ing."

I covered Devon's mouth. "First, you know I hate that song, and second? We broke up Friday."

"What?" Kelly said. "Why?"

"He bought me lunch."

"But that's nice," Kelly said.

"At Uno Burger."

"I like their fries," Kelly said.

"And paid with coupons."

"A thrifty man," Kelly said.

"A cheap bastard," Siobhan said.

"And I had to order what was on the coupons," I said, "but I didn't want what was on the coupons because it comes with onions, and he called me a condiment snob."

"Onions are toppings," Siobhan said, "not condiments."

"Right? That's what I told him," I said, "and he made a

scene. Over a vegetable. I had to cut him loose. So no more k-i-s-s-ing, huh, Devon?"

"No more of this fresh talk at all," Ma said. "If I hear another word, you're all going straight to confession."

"But I'm Episcopalian," Kelly said. "I never confess."

"And I'm not anything," Siobhan said. "So I don't do sin."

"All the more reason. Here, stuff your faces with cake. Maybe that will shut you up." Ma deftly chopped the cake into eight sections. She dropped a slice on a party plate. "You first, birthday girl."

"Ma," I said, "you've got frosting on your fingers."

Siobhan grabbed Ma's hand and licked the frosting off. "Cat bath!"

"Guess it's true." Kelly forked up a bite of cake. "She *will* lick anything for chocolate."

Ma clapped her hands over Devon's ears. "Siobhan! Kelly! She's seven!"

"Seven and a half!" Devon said.

"Sorry, Mrs. C. Got carried away," Siobhan said and looked at the floor while Kelly smirked and nibbled on a frosted rose, not looking the least bit sorry.

Ma scanned the room, daring any of the regulars to

comment. "Surely your parents don't allow that kind of talk in their house."

"Allow it?" Kelly laughed. "They start it." Her parents were both professors at Northeastern, part of the wave of yuppie squatters gentrifying South Boston, and they didn't censor anything. "We talk about s.e.x. all the time."

"S.e.x. is sex," Devon said. "Spelling words doesn't work anymore, ya know. I'm not in kindergarten."

"Ahem," I said. "Can we stop with the moral corruption of my sister?"

"Sorry, Willie," Kelly said.

"Don't call me Willie," I said.

"Only I get to do that," Siobhan said.

"No you don't," I said.

"Can we eat now, Willie?" Devon asked.

"Dig in, Devie," I said. "I hope you like your cake with wax."

"And spit," Siobhan said.

"You didn't seem to mind a certain somebody's spit last week," Kelly said.

"Jeezum!" I said. "What's it with you two tonight?"

"Sorry," they both said, but they still weren't, so I had to be sorry enough for all three of us.

CHAPTER FIVE

THE street was dead when we left Tom's Pub. Decaying leaves swept down the sidewalk, pushed by a phantom wind. The air smelled of ozone and the harbor's oily, mossy odor of neglect.

"Close the friggin door, will ya?" somebody barked from inside.

I was still holding the door for my guests, who were walking off without me. I was woolgathering again, thinking about the voice I had heard.

"Sorry!" I said.

"Get your head outta your ass, kid!"

I wanted to tell him what he could do with his own ass,

but I wasn't brave or quick enough. Siobhan could fire off insults faster than Darth Vader could swing a light saber, but I was an Imperial stormtrooper of insults— slow on the trigger and missed the target every time. So I let the door swing shut and rushed to catch up with my party. Ma had the leftover cake, and Devon carried my gift bag. Inside was a vintage Battlestar Galactica lunch box and matching thermos from Siobhan and a frumpy wool scarf that Kelly had regifted because it reminded her of me.

"Movie starts in a half hour!" Siobhan yelled. "Move your butt."

"Yeah," Kelly said and shook her hips. "Move your butt!"

Devon started shaking her hips. "Move it, move it!"

Ma popped the back of her head. "Enough of that now."

"Ma-aa-aa," Devon said.

"Your mom's right." Kelly gave my sister a fist bump. "Stay out of trouble, kid."

"It's gonna hurt when you die," Devon told Kelly, who didn't seem to hear. Her voice was low and gruff, as flat as still water.

"Devie," I said, shocked. "Why would you say that to her?"

"To who?" my sister said, rubbing her eyes like she'd just got up from a nap. "I didn't say nothing."

I mouthed an apology to Kelly, who shrugged like, what's the big deal? "Siobhan, you guys go ahead, I'll catch up," I said and turned to Ma. "Thanks for the party. It was wicked awesome."

"You're only saying that to make me feel better," Ma said.

I kissed her on the cheek. Her skin was warm. "Did it?"

"From you, always. Wish your fa—" Ma began, then caught herself. Maggie Mae wasn't one for sharing her wistful in public. "It was nice. Wasn't it nice of Siobhan? She's a good friend, when she's not a bad influence."

Siobhan and I had lived on the same block since birth. In South Boston having the same address made you sisters for life. Kelly was a latecomer. Her parents moved in when she was three, so Ma always considered her an outsider. She still referred to Kelly as "that O'Brien girl." The last few weeks, Siobhan had picked up on the habit, too. There was something going on between her and Kelly, but every time I asked about it, Siobhan blew it off.

"Your presents are pretty." Devon peeked into the birthday bag and took out the scarf, pulling the receipt along with it. The wind caught the paper and whisked it down the street. "This is prettier on me."

"Know what? You're right." I wrapped it around her neck. On her, it wasn't frumpy at all. "You look ravishing, darling. It's yours."

"Yay!"

"I should've brought your gift to party," Ma said, rubbing her hands and getting the distant look that worried me. "What was I thinking? Mike would've wanted everyone to see it."

"No worries on the presents." I kissed Ma's wind-ruddied cheek. "Family time, that's all I need."

Ma frowned. "Always thinking of others, that's my Willow Jane," she said. "You girls behave yourselves. No phone calls from the police this time."

"We'll behave, Ma."

"It's not *you* I worry about. That O'Brien girl. So fresh. What a mouth."

"Kelly's okay, just a little loud."

"A little something," Ma said.

Siobhan wolf whistled. "We're gonna miss the T!"

"I've got to run." I blew them both kisses and jogged after my girls. The wind cut through my second-hand overcoat, and my bare knees rattled from the cold. "Coming!"

"You're not wearing leggings in this weather?" Siobhan said when I reached the corner, and we turned up Broadway toward the T. "Holy batshit crazy, Willow Jane."

Kelly wore her peacoat, and Siobhan had pulled a thick hoodie over her tank top. I was dressed in a formal white shirt, a black wool skirt, and black flats.

"Leggings don't go with this skirt." I pulled my overcoat tight. "What's crazy about that?"

"Nothing, nothing," Kelly said. "If you like dressing in uptight casual."

"You're an uptight casual," Kelly said.

"What's wrong with being uptight?" I said, and then added: "It beats being loose."

"Burn," Siobhan whispered.

"Willow Jane!" Kelly opened her mouth wide, pretending to be shocked. "I can't believe you said that! Come on, we're friends."

"See? I knew you needed to cut loose." Siobhan laughed and bumped my fist. "You keep too much bottled up, y'know?"

No, I don't. I wouldn't start cursing, and I wouldn't be freely exploring my sexuality, either. Kelly's parents let her do what she wanted, but I didn't have that luxury.

"So tomorrow in chemistry?" Siobhan said. "I'm going to be lab partners with your future husband."

"Which future husband?" I said, playing along as we passed C Street.

"The one from Dorchester. You'll like him. He's got his act together."

"Is his brain full of smarticles?"

"He plays hockey and has nice teeth. They sparkle like a million tiny chips of mica."

"Hockey and teeth," I said. "Checklist complete."

"In case you guys hit it off, what baby names have you got picked out?" Siobhan said. "Now that William's out of the picture. Unless you want to name your kid after a jerk face?"

"Ew. No," I said. "Kate, if it's a girl. If it's a boy, Harry. Charlotte if I have a second girl."

"If you have a second boy?" Siobhan said.

"Then there will a discussion with the husband about his chromosomal shortcomings."

"Oh my god, baby names?" Kelly interrupted, her eyes

the size of half dollars. "Willow, are you pregnant?"

Siobhan looked at me.

I looked at Siobhan.

We burst out laughing.

"What's so funny?" Kelly said. "You guys? Stop laughing at me! You know I hate that."

"Sorry," I said, "it's not what you think."

Siobhan grinned. "Yeah, you gotta have sex before you get knocked up."

"I thought you and Will had—seriously?"

"So baby names," I said, cutting her off. "You know, what we're going to name our kids, after college is over and our careers are established? That's the Life Plan."

"What plan?" Kelly said.

"The Life Plan," I said. "Capital *L*. Capital *P*. The one we started in middle school."

"Right," Siobhan said. "You gotta have it all laid out for when you get knocked up, Willow says. It's *très importante*."

"Very *très*," I said. "More *importante* than the husband."

"What the hell," Kelly said, "are you guys talking about?"

"The plan."

"What plan?"

"The Life Plan!" we said together.

"We've had it since middle school," I said.

Siobhan cut her eyes at Kelly. "All three of us."

"Oh, that. Seriously? Middle school?" Kelly rolled her eyes so far back, they turned white. "God, you guys. I swear, sometimes we don't even speak the same language."

No, we didn't and hadn't for a long time, since probably ninth grade, but Kelly never seemed to notice before. The Three Musketeers had become two, and Kelly was only an honorary member of the group, a Snickers bar alongside two chunks of whipped nougat. But she was still our friend, even if she and Siobhan were waging a silent battle.

Fighting the wind, we continued down the sidewalk toward B Street and an Urban Gourmet Market, the organic foods store, and then past a mini-mart with a sign that read Boycott Urban Gourmet!

"Awesome," Siobhan said. "Love that sign."

"What's wrong with Urban Gourmet?" Kelly asked. "I like their cheese."

"Their cheese? Their effing *cheese*?" Siobhan said. "It's a chain, and chains run the locals out of business."

I stared through the plate-glass window of Urban Gourmet at the middle-class white women in yoga pants squeezing organic avocados. They looked nothing like my ma, and their shopping baskets had no potatoes, no pierogi, no sliced white bread. If Daddy were still alive, he would barely recognize South Boston, any more than I recognized myself when my gaze shifted from the shoppers inside to my face reflected in the glass. I hadn't grown an inch since middle school, but my face was longer, more angular, and my hips were hippier. I felt like a little girl with her nose pressed against a store window, but a young woman was staring back at me.

"So what? They have good cheese." Kelly shrugged. "Good chicken, too. It's free range."

"You're free range," Siobhan said. "Just like Willow Jane's boyfriend."

"Ex-boyfriend," I said. "Heavy emphasis on the ex."

"I just don't get why you broke up with him," Kelly said. "He's superhot, and his mom has buckets of money. Also? Those abs when he plays shirts and skins in gym? Girl."

"Uh," I said. "Yeah."

"Oh, yeah, duh." Kelly smacked her forehead. "But you guys had like the perfect name mash-ups—Will-O."

"Wouldn't that be Will-Ow?" Siobhan said.

"No, Will-O, like Jell-O?" Kelly said. "Like Kimye and Bennifer but even more perfect."

"Or more jiggly," Siobhan said.

"Doesn't matter how hot he is on the outside," I said. "He's a huge jerk—"

"Douche," Siobhan said.

"—on the inside. He's looking for a hookup, not a girlfriend."

"Ahem. Best friend standing here?" Siobhan said. "Why've I not heard about this hookup-seeking behavior before now?"

Will Patrick and I had dated for about three months. The first couple of dates were cool. He was cool. This hot guy with a lock of hair that he flipped nonchalantly to the side when he laughed. He had huge charisma, and Kelly was right about him. He had longish blond hair and almost translucent blue eyes. He could turn out to be a supermodel or a sociopath.

Or both.

The more we dated, the more he started pushing me. We started out by kissing, and no lie, it was awesome. Then he started asking for more. When I would tell him no, he'd laugh at first and play it off like it was no big deal. "You're worth waiting for," he'd say. Then a couple weeks ago he started getting serious. The playfulness turned sour, and he looked at me like, well, like he was starving and I was a coupon item on a fast-food menu.

"Because it's so cliché, it's not even worth talking about," I said. "He just wanted to quote, get some of that sweet stuff, end quote. Can you believe it? He kept calling it sweet stuff, like my vagina was a cinnamon roll."

Kelly blew spit. "Like a *what*?"

"A cinnamon roll."

"Willow Jane." Siobhan blinked twice at me. "Did you just say vagina?"

"I say vagina all the time," I said, my voice rising in mock self-righteousness. "It's a body part. Just like ears, eyes, mouth."

"And penis," Siobhan said.

"Yes, penis, too. Penis is also a body part."

"Boobs," Siobhan said.

"That's a dysphemism, not a body part."

"Tell that to my bras." Kelly wiped her face and made sure no soda had touched her dress. "Your mom's right. We are a bad influence on you."

"You are a bad influence." Siobhan covered my ears

like Ma'd covered Devon's. "I only spell out p-e-n-u-s."

"I'm not seven." I pulled her hands away. "So you can stop protecting my virgin ears. You misspelled penis, by the way."

Siobhan said something smartass in reply. I heard her tone but not the words because they were washed away by the rush of an MBTA bus blasting down Broadway. The bus was awash in thick gray mist that curled in on itself, as if it were breathing, then exhaling. I peered through it at the swirling shapes of my friends crossing the street ahead of me, but I stayed put, my feet feeling like they had sunk into the concrete. The fog clung to me, damp and sticky on my skin. The hair on my neck stood up, and I had the sudden unmistakable sensation that someone was following me.

I gasped and inhaled a stinging breath, and I saw red and blue lights rippling inside the mist. The haunting xylophone sound returned for a few seconds, followed by a loud bam-bam-bam, as if a battering ram was trying to break through a door.

"Blood," the voice whispered.

What the hell? I snapped my head around, expecting to find someone looming behind me. But the street was deserted, except for an empty coffee cup blowing in the wind. I watched the cup bounce, then evaporate into the last remnants of the mist. My heart pounded again, and I felt a pain in my chest. Don't panic, I told myself, it's just a stressful day, and some old memories were seeping from the swamp I called a brain.

"Willow Jane!" Siobhan yelled from the corner. "Hurry up! The T's coming!"

The sound of her voice snapped me out of the spell. "It's just stress," I mumbled and ran on, trying to make as little sound as possible, unable to shake the feeling that something dangerous was stirring and I didn't want to disturb it.

CHAPTER SIX

THE Park Street T stop let out on the lip of the Common, right on Tremont Street. Up the hill was the Granary Burying Ground, and around the corner was the Orpheum Theatre, which was famously haunted by a variety of ghosts. But when I left the warm, oily air of the T station with Siobhan and Kelly, it wasn't to chase ghosts. We had tickets to see a digitally remastered version of *Nosferatu*. It was a birthday gift from Kelly via her dad, who knew I liked horror movies.

When we reached the street, a light rain was falling from the heavens and a three-block line was snaking from the entrance of the Orpheum.

"The hell is this line?" Siobhan eyed the crowd. "Effing half of Boston stands on line for a black-and-white movie? A *silent* black-and-white movie?"

"A silent black-and-white *vampyre* movie," Kelly said. "It's a classic, so yes, half the effing city is here."

"Half of effing Boston's a huge exaggeration." I calculated the number of people on line and compared it to the population of the Boston metropolitan area. "Less than one percent of the city is here."

"What percentage is that, Willie?" Siobhan said.

"Percentage of what?"

"Of the *effing* city," Siobhan said. "Meaning only those who are sexually active, which we assume is a significant percentage of younger adults and a disproportionate number of those over the age of forty, after which we all know there is no more *effing* to be had."

"You're so, so . . ." My brain fritzed, and I couldn't think of the right word, for the first time in my life.

"I broke Willie's marbles!" Siobhan cackled. "Wicked awesome!"

There was a plethora of words I could use to describe Siobhan. Impulsive. Indefatigable. Moxie. Formidable. I was running through the vocab list in my brain, trying to pick the perfect one for the moment, when my mind hiccupped. My whole body jerked, and I heard a singsong whispering and the fluttering of wings. I could smell the stink of decay on the air, the wet, fecund odor of organisms decomposing. My stomach turned, and I felt so queasy, I almost puked.

"You okay?" Siobhan asked when I leaned against a light pole. "Cause you're acting—"

"Speaking of wicked *and* awesome." Kelly unzipped her coat and produced a can of UFO, which she drank to be ironic. "A toast to Sam Adams. The dude who invented beer."

"Kelly," I said to divert Siobhan attention. "You're underage, and it's in public."

"What she said," Siobhan said. "Where's mine?"

"Sorry it's warm." Kelly produced a second can. "Had to keep it stashed during the party."

"Hell's yeah!" Siobhan grabbed the UFO. "Wanna sip, Willie?"

I waved off the offering. "You know I don't drink."

"That's why I only brought two," Kelly said.

"Only brought two of what?" a guy behind us said.

I turned to face Will Patrick, my ex-boyfriend. He was

six-one with sandy blond hair, blue eyes, and pink cheeks that practically glowed in the cold wind. He smiled, his gaze fixed intensely on my face. I could hardly look back at him, both because he was so handsome it hurt and because I had the sudden sensation that I was sprinkled with cinnamon and glazed with warm frosting.

"Hey, ladies," he said. "What brings you to this side of town?"

"Hey, hey, and hey," Kelly said. "Look who's here. What a surprise!"

Siobhan looked at me and rolled her eyes as if to say, *This is no effing surprise.*

"Really?" I said.

Kelly hugged Will Patrick and his friend Flanagan, who was smoking a cigarette, and Siobhan's eyebrows almost shot off her face. Will Patrick was yuppie spawn like Kelly, but Flanagan was old-school Southie. I was surprised to see him playing wingman.

"Saw your party on Snapchat." Will Patrick held up his oversized phone. "Kells posted something about a vampire movie, so here we are."

"Oh, it's *Kells* now," Siobhan said.

"I am so not interested in seeing you," I told Will Patrick.

"Who says I'm here to see you?" he said.

Burn.

Will Patrick's condescending smirk made me want to ram a hockey puck down his angelic throat. But keeping with my philosophy of never letting jerks see me sweat, I lifted my chin and steeled my eyes and refused to let my face betray the stinging hurt in my heart.

"What're you boys doing out on a school night?" Kelly asked them.

"Same as you, looking for a good time," Flanagan said. He wasn't the tallest guy in the world, but when you were barely five feet, every boy was a walking skyscraper. He wasn't bad looking, either, with a tangled mess of brown hair and a gentle face. Too bad he stank of cigarettes. "Sup, Siobhan. How you, Conning?"

"She has a first name, y'know," Siobhan said.

"Two of them," I said softly.

"So," Will Patrick said, "about that beer?"

"What beer?" Siobhan hid the evidence. "You see any beer, Butt Chin?"

Kelly took an ironic sip. "None in these parts, sheriff."

Flanagan laughed too loud. He finished his cigarette and ground the butt into the sidewalk.

"You should really pick that up," I said, pointing to a trash can three feet away.

"You should really mind your own business, uptight little bitch."

Siobhan turned on Flanagan. "What'd you call my friend?"

"I said, she's an uptight bitchlette."

"Watch your mouth, Flanagan." Siobhan pushed her beer into my hand. "If anybody's the little bitch here, it's you."

Flanagan stepped back. He was a small guy, and Siobhan was easily four inches taller, with a better right cross. She would squash him like a grasshopper under her Doc Martens boot.

"Hey, hey!" Will Patrick stepped between them and held up his hands. "We're all friends here. Flanagan, apologize for being an asshole."

"C'mon, man," Flanagan whined. "It's just Conning. You said she was just a—"

"Do it, Flanagan." Will Patrick nudged him. "Say you're sorry for being an asshole."

"Sorry for being an asshole, Conning," Flanagan mumbled.

"Her name," Siobhan said, "is Willow Jane."

"Yeah, a pretty screwed-up name," Flanagan blurted out, which earned him a punch. "Hey! What was that for?"

"It's a very pretty name." Will Patrick flashed his cherubic smile at me. "For a very pretty girl."

I shot him the bird.

He laughed.

I flicked a second finger, and he laughed even harder and winked, and then their plan became obvious. Will Patrick was trying to get back together, and he had somehow gotten Kelly to help him. Well, they could shove their plan because it wasn't going to work. Was it?

"Enough bullshit. What do you shitdoodles want?" Siobhan said. "Besides our beer?"

"You came to see the film. We came to see the film." Will Patrick winked. "Coincidence? Or kismet? Or fate?"

"Or beer," Kelly said.

"That, too," Will Patrick said, putting his arm around Kelly.

He co-opted her brew and took a long swallow. She giggled, and I felt an icy stab of jealousy. Will Patrick was a jerk, but he was my ex-jerk, and there were rules about exes and friends. One of those rules was your almost best friend was not allowed to flirt with your ex-jerk in the same weekend you broke up. Especially not in front of you. On your birthday.

Siobhan looked at me. "I can*not* believe he's showing you up like that. In public." She hooked my arm. "Come on, Willow Jane. You're not spending your birthday with losers."

"Hey, guys!" Kelly called. "Where're you going?"

"Back to Southie!" Siobhan decided without consulting me. "You want to hang with a douchebag, go ahead."

"I'm a douche?" Will Patrick yelled back. "No offense, but a player's got to play."

"Suck on that!" Siobhan fired her can at him. "No offense!"

Will Patrick spazzed and covered his face as the beer can sailed toward his head. It hit the light post next to him and sprayed suds in a rooster tail arc that soaked his crotch. "What the hell, man? Kells was right about you!" He shook the beer off his pants and stepped back, his heel caught on the lip of the curb, and he stumbled into the glaring headlights of the 43 MBTA bus.

CHAPTER SEVEN

WILL Patrick's body floated like a ghost, into the bus lights. His hands grasped helplessly for some invisible rope, but there was no lifeline for him. He was a dead douchebag the instant the driver laid on the horn and slammed the brakes. It was a useless effort. An eighteen-ton bus couldn't stop in time, and it would send Will Patrick to the afterlife as soon as its grille splintered his body.

"No," I whispered.

That's when Will Patrick truly froze. Not in a Snapchat snapshot way, but in the super slow-motion way that lets you see a bullet tearing through a balloon. His eyes were wide, the pupils dilated and reflecting the bus's headlights.

He didn't even react when I hooked my elbow around a guy wire for support, snagged him, and yanked him away from death's door.

His butt hit the sidewalk as Kelly screamed, face buried in her hands, and Siobhan's mouth hung open.

I staggered away and pressed a palm to my forehead. It felt like an ice pick had been rammed through my skull. The xylophone exploded in my ears, followed by the sound of banging, as if a monstrous fist was hammering on a door to be let in.

In a snap it was gone, and my head was clear.

Will Patrick sat on the sidewalk holding his chest like he'd had a heart attack, but I knew it was for effect. The others surrounded him, saying things that I couldn't hear. The crowd turned toward him for a few seconds, but it all had happened so fast, nobody else seemed to really under-stand. We were just a pack of kids screaming and behaving like idiots, and they were all too busy texting and tweeting and Snapchatting to notice that I had just moved faster than the Flash after a double espresso.

My heart was pounding again, but this time it was from an adrenaline rush. I had felt like this before, wind-ing up for a slap shot and watching the stick bend as it hit the puck. Except this time it was even more slo-mo and I hadn't just scored a goal, I had just saved someone, and every nerve in my body was firing.

Will Patrick got to his feet and screamed at Siobhan, "God damn! You could've killed me."

"Sorry, jerk face," Siobhan said. "I didn't see the bus."

"And you!" Will Patrick turned to me. "You saved my life."

He lifted me from the ground, twirling around so quickly my shoes flew off. He set me down barefoot, lifted my face to his, and kissed me. But it wasn't his kiss I was thinking about—it was how fast I'd moved, the way I wished I could've moved when my father was shot. When I only watched and did nothing.

Why hadn't I moved that fast before? Why had I just stood there paralyzed and watched the bastard pull the trigger again and again? Why did I save Will but let my father die? I felt hate welling up in me, like something stuck in my throat that I couldn't cough up, making me want to sink my fingernails into his soft, pretty face.

"No! I am not your cinnamon roll!" I pushed Will Patrick away and wiped my mouth. "I dump you, and you still have the nerve to kiss me?"

"Didn't see you stopping me, baby." Will Patrick laughed, wiped his own mouth, then punched Flanagan. "What were you're doing, just watching me get run over?"

"Bro, it happened wicked fast, and she moved like, like . . . damn."

Wicked fast.

Wicked.

Something wicked this way comes, I thought and wiped my mouth again. I felt sick to my stomach, like the birthday cake and pizza were a bad idea. I wanted to be home, on the couch with a cup of tea, my ma singing and hustling in the kitchen the way she used to. "Know what?" I said. "Life's too short for this crap. I'm going home."

"Hey!" Kelly said. "Don't go. Don't waste the tickets."

"Sorry." I flipped up my collar and started across Tremont. "But one bloodsucker's enough for one day."

Will Patrick hooked Kelly's arm and pulled her close. He pressed his lips against her ear, and she blushed the way she always did when impure thoughts crossed her mind. He had pulled the same trick on me, the sweet words, the invitation into his charming world of bad boy-ness. I felt another prick of jealousy and betrayal, but it passed quickly this time. I realized that it was all just an act, a well-rehearsed trick to make a girl think she was the center of his world. There was only room for one person in his world, though, and it was William Patrick Wilson III.

"Willie!" Siobhan loped across the crosswalk and grabbed my arm. "Don't leave me with those asswipes! Butt chin! Come with!"

"You guys!" Kelly took a lingering look at Will Patrick, sighed loudly, and then followed us. "Don't just walk off, for chrissakes."

I expected Will Patrick and Flanagan to say something smartass, but they were looking past us, pointing, along with the others standing on line. I turned to the massive trees that overshadowed the burial ground. A murder of crows lifted from the thick branches as one dark mass. They swirled above us, cawing to one another in hoarse grunts and deep rattles. The wind from their black wings touched my face, and the calls filled my head with noise, a roar that grew so loud that I clapped my hands over my ears and clenched my eyes tight. Then just like that, the sound was gone, and when I opened my eyes, the birds had disappeared into the night.

CHAPTER EIGHT

A half hour after leaving the theater I was in a window seat at Frank's Mini-Mart, sitting between the Two Towers, aka Siobhan and Kelly, slurping down double hot fudge sundaes. Our faces were reflected like ghosts on the glass. On the wall behind us, a big-screen TV was tuned to the Bruins game, which had been interrupted twice by a weatherman reporting a nor'easter forming off the coast.

Kelly licked her empty sundae dish and turned to watch the game. "God, I miss Tim Thomas."

"Tim who?" Siobhan baited her.

Kelly imitated a Southie accent, badly. "Only the best freaking goalie evah."

"Impossible," Siobhan said, and for her, the accent wasn't imitation, "as I'm the best freaking goalie evah. Which All Saints is gonna to find out this time tomorrow. Am I right?"

The three of us started for Beacon School girls' hockey. Kelly and I played defense, and Siobhan was goalie. She wasn't the fastest keeper in the scholastic league, but she had flawless technique and a knack for knowing where the puck was going. Our coach called it hawkey smahts. Siobhan was this close to a D1 scholarship, which was the only way she was going to a Public Ivy. Unlike Kelly, who had the grades and money to go to anywhere, she was a blue-collar girl. She lived with her dad in a duplex three blocks from us. As for me, no coach wanted a defender too short to reach her own cookie jar, so my career would end after high school.

"Best goalie ever?" Kelly said. "And I'm Brad Marchand." She flung her arms wide. Her hand knocked the ice-cream dish off the table, and she gasped as it fell toward certain destruction.

I grabbed the dish and in one fluid motion, returned it to the counter.

"Wicked save!" Siobhan applauded. "Couldn't have done it better myself."

"How did you move so fast?" Kelly said.

Wicked fast. Unnatural. "I just . . . got lucky. That's all," I said, then felt a weird tug, like a wire was hooked to my belly button.

"You're pale as a ghost." Siobhan touched my forehead. "Skin's clammy, too."

"It's the weird lights." I pointed to the neon green beer sign, then giggled compulsively. "You guys look like Hulk's little sisters."

"Since when do you giggle?" Siobhan checked my pulse. "Your heart's pounding."

"I giggle. I have giggled many times in my life."

"Name one," Siobhan said. "You're so uptight you could swallow a lump of coal and—"

"Third grade!' I snapped my fingers. "During the Christmas pageant I giggled for a solid minute."

"Because you were Rudolph and you forgot your lines," Siobhan said. "Then you cried so hard, your ma had to carry you home."

"It still counts." I tried to stand up and found my knees had melted like double hot fudge.

"Wullo?" Siobhan said, sounding as if she were underwater.

Her lips were moving, but the words were distorted. Siobhan's and Kelly's faces looked frozen, their mouths open, eyes half shut. It felt like I could reach out and touch their eyeballs before they blinked. Their breath was visible, and I could see every pore in their skin.

I turned to the TV. A thick black band rolled down the screen, like when you take a picture of a television with a camera. My science teacher said it was because TVs always had black lines running through them, but they moved so fast, the human eye couldn't perceive them.

Siobhan shook me. "Willow Jane!"

"It's the birthday cake," I said, snapping out of it. "Sorry, my blood sugar's just screwed up."

"Come on." Siobhan nudged Kelly. "Let's get Miss Sweet Sixteen back to the palace before she turns into a pumpkin."

"She looks more like a zucchini than a pumpkin," Kelly said.

"It matters why?" Siobhan said.

"Zucchinis are green."

"You're a zucchini."

Kelly rolled her eyes. "You said she was looking green, not orange."

"And I thought Willie was the literal one." Siobhan waited for Kelly to open the door, then steered me outside into the evening. "Butt chin, you okay to walk yourself home?"

"Like I'm going home," Kelly said, waving good-bye and blowing us a kiss. She pulled her phone out and was texting before she turned the corner.

"One day's she's gonna fall in a manhole," Siobhan said when we reached the crosswalk. "What's up, Willie? You're acting funny. Not funny ha-ha, funny strange."

"We live in the Hub of the Universe!" I said, arms wide. "What could possibly be wrong?"

She pulled me in for a bear hug that got me a face full of curly black hair. "Happy birthday, Willow Jane."

"Your hair still smells like charcoal," I said, picking a strand of hair out of my mouth.

"Cause I'll walk through flames for you."

"You lit your hair. It's not the same thing."

"It's even better! Cause sparklers!"

We said good-bye, and I turned for home. God, I was glad the day was finally over. It had been just a few hours, but I was shuffling like the walking dead up the front stoop, hoping for a quiet dinner and a night's sleep without nightmares.

I reached for the doorknob and heard the flapping of wings. In one quick movement, a grackle swept past me, so close I felt feathers on my cheek, and slammed into the window next to the door.

The glass shattered.

The bird fell to the sidewalk. It lay there, twitching, wings mangled, dusk dancing in its iridescent feathers.

"Poor thing," I said, but as I reached for it, the bird jumped up and with a flap took to the air. I stepped back, dizzy again.

The bird, the buildings, the street, everything moved in and out of focus, as I bent over and threw up the cake-and-pepperoni remains of the worst birthday ever.

CHAPTER NINE

"SERIOUSLY, bro," Will Patrick told Flanagan. "The voice said 'treasure.' Heard it loud and clear, just like my grandmother yammering in my ear."

"Clean out your ears then, because I ain't heard jack." Flanagan popped the first bottle of a sixer. "You owe me ten for the beer."

The movie at the Orpheum Theatre had long since ended. The crowd had thinned to a few stragglers hunched in the darkness against the cold. In the Granary Burying Ground, Will Patrick and Flanagan sat at the base of the Franklin family obelisk, backs to the deserted street. They'd scored a couple of six-packs by slipping a homeless guy ten bucks, plus an extra ten when he refused to turn over the goods.

"Goddamn extortionist," Will Patrick said. "I should've kicked his ass."

He tossed an empty bottle across the graveyard. It crashed against the headstone of Paul Revere and broke into thousands of pieces.

"Hey," Flanagan said, "you just defiled the grave of a great patriot."

"Yeah right," Will Patrick said but started tromping toward the grave anyway. "My history teacher said nobody ever heard of Revere until some dumbass wrote a poem. He made all his money as a silversmith. When he died, he had his silver hidden in his casket so grave robbers couldn't find it. Wait! That's it! Treasuuuuuuuuuu—"

With a crack the ground collapsed beneath his feet. One second he was standing, the next he was writhing on his back, nine feet below, covered in dirt, leaves, and chunks of the lid that had once hidden the hole.

"You total wad." Flanagan looked down into the hole. "What the hell?"

Will Patrick moaned and crawled to his feet, a sharp pain in his lower back bending him over. He raised a hand but couldn't reach the lip of the hole.

"You're in a freaking grave!" Flanagan crossed himself and spit. "Get out!"

"It's not a grave. These walls are stone. It's a tomb." Will Patrick snorted. "I'm a tomb raider. Ha-ha."

"You ain't gonna think it's funny when you see the goose egg on your skull." Flanagan turned on his cell phone light. A stairway led down into darkness. "Stairs? Seriously?"

"Follow the yellow brick road." Will Patrick laughed and started toward them, still hunched over.

"Hey!" Flanagan called. "Don't go down there!"

Will Patrick waved him off and disappeared into the shadows.

"Ten bucks says you piss yourself," Flanagan said. He knew he should follow but Grandmother had raised him Catholic, and even if he never listened in Mass, he knew doing belly flops with the dead was a bad idea.

For a few seconds his cell phone light continued to illuminate the stairway. Then, without warning, it went out.

"Yo!" Flanagan's voice echoed, but there was no answer, and there was no light. Seconds ticked off, but they felt like minutes, and panic formed in the pit of his gut. Something was wrong. He could feel it. Holes didn't suddenly open up in cemeteries, and you sure as hell didn't go crawling around them in the dark.

"Asswipe!" he stage-whispered into the blackness. "Answer me!"

"Boo!" Will Patrick shouted, jumping out of the darkness.

"Holy hell!" Flanagan screamed and fell backward into the dead leaves. He clutched his pounding heart. "Don't do that! I had too many beers for that shiz."

Digging his toes for purchase onto the stone wall, Will Patrick pulled himself from the hole and knocked the dirt off his pants. A goose egg was rising on his head, and a rivulet of blood trickled down his face to his neck, but he didn't seem to notice. "You're not going to believe what I found!"

"For real?"

"A casket covered in writing and pictures."

Flanagan let out a long burp. "Liar."

"What if the casket holds Paul Revere's hidden stash of silver? Huh? Huh?"

"You didn't look?"

"I tried. The lid wouldn't budge. You want to try?"

Flanagan had no desire to open some dead jackweed's coffin, but if there really could be treasure? "I'll get a crowbar and maybe a sledgehammer. Meet back here to open the bitch up."

"Sounds like a plan," Will Patrick said. "What time?"

"Midnight."

"The witching hour. I like it."

"*Sláinte.*" Flanagan raised a toast. "May the road rise to meet you, boyo."

"*Erin go bragh,*" Will Patrick said. "Or some Irish shiz like that."

"Watch your mouth about the Irish," Flanagan called back as he cut across the burying ground. "Or the road's going hit your pretty face."

A street cleaner rumbled down Tremont. Flanagan waited till its bright lights were almost past, then stepped on the low wall and vaulted over the iron fence. He looked up as a massive crow soared into the trees behind him. The bird landed on a thick branch and started preening. It yanked its feathers by the beakful and let them drop into the hole below. In minutes half its breast was plucked bare, as if it were molting, and its corneas had turned milky white like the eyes of an ancient blind man.

That's one fugly bird, Flanagan thought. His grandmother always said crows were an evil omen. Even though
he didn't believe any of the crap, he crossed himself just to
be sure, unaware that it had already marked him for death.

CHAPTER TEN

WHEN I got upstairs, Ma stood by the kitchen sink, peeling potatoes. She wore her cooking apron, a bright yellow frilly job with a red rooster on front. Maggie Mae Conning was magical with needle and thread, but she was a danger to herself and others when it came to food preparation, so she usually either left dinner to me or grabbed something from the frozen food aisle.

Lots of weird things had happened today, but none of them were as strange as seeing my mother cooking again.

"You're home early," Ma said when I came in. "Everything all right?"

"Everything's fine," I lied. "Just wasn't in the mood for bloodsuckers. Be right back."

I dashed to the bathroom to clean up, and when I came back, Devon was sitting quietly in front of the couch, cutting out paper dolls and arranging them on the oak floor. Our apartment had once been a grand home. Its ceilings were high and trimmed with crown molding iced with dust. The walls were last painted when I was six, and the sunflower yellow had wilted to pale ocher. The sloping floors were swept once a day and mopped on Friday. A bay window in the living room looked into the building across the street and down on the corner. Traffic, voices, and the oily scent of Silver and F Streets intruded when the windows were opened and were barely smothered when they were closed.

Our furniture was Early American Little Old Lady. The pieces were inherited from my late grandmother, who had lived a block away in an apartment that mirrored this one, but they couldn't be called antiques. That word implies that the pieces had once been expensive, designed by craftsmen, not modest furnishings that had weathered three generations of abuse by children, husbands, and pets. The only heirloom was from my dad's side—a curio cabinet in the corner of the dining room. It was so old that the glass had begun to run, like water frozen in time.

"You're cooking dinner?" I asked. Cooking had been my job since the sixth grade. "I thought you had a dress rehearsal? Everything okay?"

"Isn't that what I just asked you?"

"Seriously, Ma."

"My, aren't we the little mother?" Ma smirked and shook her head. "The actors were grousing about rehearsing on Sunday, so the director threw a tantrum and told the bunch of them to go home and thank God they had jobs."

"You're not fired?"

"Fah! Who'd make the costumes?" She pointed to a bag of vegetables on the table. "Start peeling. Pizza's nobody's idea of dinner."

I sighed in relief. She hadn't been let go again. Since Dad died, she'd had trouble holding down a job.

"I'll be happy to help."

"Before you do." She took a wrapped box from the top of the fridge. "For your birthday."

The paper was plain silver, and the red bow was a stick-on. Ma never cared much for wrapping, even Christmas presents.

"What is it?" I asked.

"Open it and find out," she said while I plucked the bow and ran a finger through the cellophane tape. "Times are hard, so . . . well, you know. I didn't want to give you some useless piece of crap, you know?"

"You shouldn't have," I said.

"Yeah, I shoulda, and it shoulda been better."

Ma never got nervous, and she almost never apologized. There was an edge in her voice that was both an apology and a hope that I wouldn't be disappointed. No matter what was inside, I was prepared to love it.

I pulled the wrapping off and set it on the table. Inside was a cherry box no bigger than my hand. I had seen the same box on Ma's dresser since I was old enough to walk. It sat between her jewelry and a silver-framed portrait of her mother. The only difference was that the wood had been freshly oiled, and my initials were carved into the lid and gilded with gold paint.

"The set designer did the carving in trade for me taking in his suits." She rubbed her hands, concentrating on her swollen knuckles. Four decades of sewing had taken its toll on her joints. "Your dad's ma gave me those for a wedding present because Connings never have girls. Since you're sixteen now, I thought . . . well, you know, time to pass the torch back to the Connings."

My heart skipped a beat. Yes, I'd seen the box every day, but I could count on one hand the number of times I had been allowed to marvel at the contents. The gold hinges creaked when I pushed the lid open. Twin thimbles lay in a nest of red velvet. They were white porcelain, hand painted with blue and yellow flowers and green foliage. The bottom of each was wrapped with a gilt *Gitterwerk* band made of fourteen-karat gold. Ma once told me they were made in the 1750s in Meissen, Germany. They had been in the family for hundreds of years.

"Ma," I said and sniffed. "They're beautiful."

"You like them? The gift's okay?"

I set the box on the table and took her hands in mine. "Best birthday present ever."

"You're just saying that. What teenage girl wants old thimbles?"

"Hush. It's perfect."

I threw my arms around her. I could feel her spine and the sharp edge of her shoulder blade. Ma needed a cookie. For a second or two, she let the hug linger, then she gave my back two quick thumps, the signal that the display of affection had gone too long.

"Here," she said after extricating herself, "let's put them in the curio. No use hiding your treasure."

She swung the cabinet door open and set the thimbles on the shelf next to the egg box. She paused and tilted her head, considering the placement of the box. She reached for it, and I gasped.

"What?" she said.

"The dust!" I said, snatching a hand towel from the rack. "Look at how much built up in just a week."

With practiced ease, I hip checked Ma and pushed the egg box aside. I went after the dusty shelf like a sparrow chasing a worm. I kept Ma away by keeping my hip between her and the cabinet, then moved on to the next shelves when she gave up and returned to the kitchen.

I turned the boxes just so, then closed the cabinet. "Ta-da," I said, shaking out the hand towel. "Perfect, right? What do you think?"

"I think you ate too much cake." She reached for the old cookie tin where she hid the Christmas fund and pulled out a yellowed envelope. "From your father. He left it with me, in case . . ."

Her hands were shaking when I took the letter from

her. Scrawled on the front in faded black ink, in my dad's own hand, were the words *To My Darling Daughter on the Occasion of Her Sixteenth Birthday.* My hands started shaking, too, and I ran a fingernail under the flap, breaking the crumbling glue, but Ma stopped me.

"He meant for you to open it alone," she said, her voice cracking. She tucked it into my pocket. "Those were his very words, *alone*, and you know how Mike was about words. So after dinner, okay?"

"Words are magic," he always said. "How long ago," I said and cleared a lump from my thumb, "did he write this?"

"Ten years ago, when you turned six." Ma pressed a finger under her nose to stop her tears. "It's almost like—like—"

Like he knew he was going to die.

Chapter Eleven

MA really meant the alone thing, but the instant I tried to sneak off to my room to read, there was a sharp knock at the door.

"We don't want any!" Devon yelled.

Another knock.

"Who can that be?" Ma looked down her nose. "It's dinnertime."

"I'll get it." I put the note in my pocket, expecting it to be Siobhan, who liked to drop by when her parents were going at it, but I saw the landlady's nose in the peephole. Her nose meant trouble.

"Sorry to keep you," I said after slipping into the

hallway. "We're making dinner."

Miss Haverhill, as she insisted we call her, had inherited the house from her great-aunt when I was thirteen. She was tall with long, wavy tresses and a handsome face. Her skin was Sleeping Beauty pale and thin, like an alabaster sculpture, and the air that wafted from her clothes carried the odors of licorice and anise.

"Sorry to wreck your dinner," Miss Haverhill said, but her tone indicated she wasn't. "The rent's due."

When Haverhill's great-aunt owned the house, she would let the rent slide, knowing that Dad would catch up when some money came in. She died, and her niece took over, and she laid down the law.

"Already?" I nervously peeled the paint on the door casing. "Ma doesn't get paid till next week."

"Next week's next week." Miss Haverhill poked her nose at my face when I refused to meet her eye. "Rent is today. Let's talk to your ma."

She tried to rap on the door, but I blocked her. "I'll get you the money. Promise."

"The same way you got it last month?"

"You—" I said. Somehow she knew my worst secret. "You heard about that?"

"Word travels."

"Louie told you?"

"A little bird did." She grinned through crooked teeth. "Bring me that egg, and I'll forget the rent. Next month's, too. Just remember the needle that goes with it."

The needle was the only thing I could give her. When I hocked the egg, I had pulled a long, thick iron needle from the egg and set it aside. "Louie said it was only worth a couple hundred at most."

"The scumbag's a pawnbroker," she said. "Give me the egg, and I'll not darken your door for two months straight. Three, if I don't have to ask again."

"Louie still has it." A little voice told me she was scamming me. Free rent was tempting, but that egg meant more to Ma than the thimbles, and I still planned to get it out of hock. "I can't just wave a magic wand and make him hand it over."

"You're a smart girl. Figure it out." She sniffed the air, then recoiled as if I had smacked her nose. "Is that stench boiled cabbage?"

"Good old New England food. Green beans, cabbage, boiled potatoes, and fiddlehead ferns."

"Ferns? Waste of a good houseplant." She started down

the steps, then paused. "It would be so sad if the widow Conning learned her own daughter had stolen her prized possession."

"You wouldn't!"

"Double-cross me, and you'll find out what I'm capable of." She started to turn, then she reached for the letter poking out of my pocket. "What's this? Cash?"

I smacked a hand over the envelope.

"Temper, temper." She wagged a manicured finger in my face. "Don't do something stupid and ruin your birthday."

She cackled, actually cackled. A minute later, her apartment door banged closed.

Her demand was impossible. Louie would never just hand over a valuable. My father used to use his services for "unwanted items," and the guy busted Dad's chops on every deal. How did she think a sixteen-year-old reeking of desperation could pry the egg out of Louie's sweaty hands? And why did she think I would turn it over to her for a couple months' interest? Better yet, why was a plain glass egg so valuable, and why did Miss Haverhill suddenly want it so badly? I vowed right then that I would get the egg back, no matter what it cost.

"Who was that?" Ma asked when I came back inside. I stuffed my letter in my book bag. *He meant for you to open it alone.*

"Just Siobhan." I hated lying, but when it came to paying the bills, telling little white lies came as easily as breathing. I kept telling myself it was for the best. "Needed help with math."

"That's nice of you," Ma said.

"Um hmm." I started clearing the table. "Hey Ma, want to read to Devon tonight?"

"I'll do the dishes." Ma gave my shoulder an affectionate squeeze. "It's your birthday, and Devon likes your stories better than mine."

"What about Dad's letter?"

"Later. It's bedtime reading for now. Want me to set aside some cabbage for your school lunch?"

My nose wrinkled. "Ew. Not if I ever want anyone to sit with me again."

CHAPTER TWELVE

"YOU'RE way old enough to read to yourself, you know," I told Devon when I found her tucked in and ready for bed. With her dark hair spread over the white pillow, she looked more beautiful than cute. She had Ma's fine features and Daddy's wry grin. She was going to break some hearts when she got to high school.

"So?" she said. "Ever tried telling yourself a story?"

"Touché." I opened the first page of *Owl Moon* and began to read.

"Not that one," she said. "It makes me think about Daddy, and that makes me sad."

"Yeah," I said and thought, *Me, too*. Nothing like a

picture book about a father/daughter bonding experience
to make you realize how unbonded you feel. "How about
The Monster at the End of This Book?"

"I am seven years old. I know the monster's Grover."

"Maybe, or maybe it ends differently this time." I made
a demonic-sounding laugh. "Maybe there's a monster that
eats the monster."

"I wanna real story. A once upon a time, but scary."

"Once upon a time," I began, "there was a fairy princess who dressed only in pink."

"No, a zombie princess!"

"A zombie princess who dressed only in pink—"

"Rags!"

"Who dressed in rags and loved with all her heart, the
prince of—"

"Not a prince! A thief! With one hand!"

"Who loved a thief with one hand—"

"Tell it in your scary voice. Bwahaha!"

"You're one weird little chick, you know that?"

"Hell's yeah I am!"

"Shh! Don't let Ma hear that mouth."

"Do the laugh!"

"Bwahaha!"

I laughed deeply, summoning the sound from my gut. It shook my whole chest and gave me a side stitch worse than wind sprints, but if it made Devon happy, it was worth it.

"Once upon a time," I said, "in a far, far away city called Toronto, a zombie princess stalked the land, dressed in a soiled wedding gown, seeking the prince who had left her jilted at the altar. The prince had many times professed his undying affection, only to turn his wandering eye to another, more wealthy duchess from the foreign land of Quebec. Heartbroken and inconsolable, the princess wasted away in the royal tower, refusing to eat or drink or bathe."

"Eww." Devon held her nose. "Stinky."

"Until like a whisper on the wind, the princess passed beyond the veil. But with her last, dying breath, she cursed the fickle prince and swore that she would one day crawl forth from her grave to bring her vengeful wrath down upon the prince and destroy all that his evil machinations had brought him."

"What's a machination?"

"It's an evil scheme," Ma said from the doorway. The light in the hallway behind her formed a halo around her tangly mass of red curls. "Willow Jane, you're going to give your sister bad dreams."

"No, she won't! Scary stories help me sleep. They give me something else to dream about."

Ma and I traded a look. Since the shooting, Devon's nightmares had become constant. To fight against them, she developed this bedtime ritual. She'd lock every door three times and check every window, even though most of them were painted shut. Then she would surround herself in bed with paper dolls and sing the same song over and over until she fell asleep. Her recent favorite had been "Will and Willow sitting in a tree, k-i-s-s-ing."

I inclined my head in a question to Ma. She sighed and nodded.

"Just one story," Ma said. "There's only so many zombies a mother can take."

Devon clapped and began forming the paper dolls in a circle around her. I remembered when I was little and Ma would read me a story and Daddy would tell one of his own. I wished I could be little again, cuddled under cool sheets and warm blankets, when the only monsters were imaginary and confined themselves to the space under my bed.

"Where was I?" I asked.

"Machinations. Wicked evil ones."

"Right. The princess is undead, and her love for the prince is undying. Vengeful but undying."

"Where's the thief?" Devon said. "I want a thief."

"Hold your water," I said. "Everything bad can't happen at once."

I started with another story but realized after a moment that Devon wasn't listening. Her head was tilted at an odd angle, as if she were hearing something in the distance. Her eyes glazed over.

"You okay?" I asked.

She rotated her head slowly back to me, lifted a hand to point at the heating grate, and rasped in a low, gruff voice, "That's where the dead girl hides when you're asleep."

CHAPTER THIRTEEN

KELLY exited the T at the Park Street station with two sixers, which she'd procured by trading her dad's cigarettes and twenty bucks to a package store cashier on Dot Ave. She had skipped curfew by telling her mother that she and Siobhan were cramming for a math test. Her mom had been against it until Kelly explained that Siobhan was flunking math and really needed the tutoring but was too proud to ask. Mom said it was kind to help, but she really liked the idea that her daughter was superior to her friends. Kelly sucked at tutoring, but she knew how to play on her mom's need to appear compassionate.

When she got to the Granary cemetery, she found Will

Patrick and Flanagan in the middle of the grounds, leaning on Franklin's obelisk and sharing a smoke. They were hard to pick out at first—the spotlights on the hotel across the street cast long, thick shadows. Her eyes had trouble adjusting to the difference between light and dark.

"You guys were freaking invisible," she said, pulling down her hoodie and peering at them. She swung her backpack off. "Who's thirsty?"

"I'm parched," Will Patrick said. "Couldn't refuse my invitation, huh?"

Truth was, no, she couldn't. Will Patrick was too damn sexy cute to resist, even if he had just broken up with her old friend—emphasis on the *old*. Willow Jane was cool, though. She'd understand, and if she didn't, *c'est la guerre.*

Flanagan yanked a beer from her backpack, twisted the cap, and got a face full of foam. He held the bottle at arm's length, then sucked half of it down. "Ah," he said, "that's the stuff."

Kelly clicked her tongue. "Sixteen years old, and you're already looking at liver damage."

"Eighteen years old." Flanagan nodded the bottle at her. "And you can kiss my ass."

"You've got a nasty mouth." Kelly spat into her palm

and rubbed his face with it. "Somebody needs to scrub it clean."

He didn't try to stop her. "Knew you wanted to swap spit with me."

"Ew," she said. "Not on your life!"

"Knock it off, bro." Will Patrick pulled a crowbar from his duffel. "Kells, follow me to the tomb."

"It's really a grave?" Kelly asked. "I thought you were just screwing with me."

Will Patrick walked to the far left section of the cemetery, then jumped straight into a black hole. "Not just a grave, a *tomb.*"

"Holy shit!" Kelly switched on a yellow utility flashlight. "It really is a tomb! How'd you guys find it?"

Will Patrick held up his arms to catch her. "Would m'lady care for a hand?"

She wasn't so sure about jumping into a dark tomb, but there were worse things than a cute guy waiting with open arms. "Which way now?"

"Down, obviously," Will Patrick said and took her hand.

With Flanagan following, he led Kelly deeper into the ground. They turned left into a stone-walled room. Her flashlight fell on a casket. It was a plain rectangle, more like a sarcophagus, with a heavy lid covered in symbols and pictures.

"Jeezum," Kelly said, bumping her head on the low ceiling. "That's a real casket."

"With a real dead person inside." Will Patrick flashed an empty smile, and it made her blood run cold. He held up a crowbar. "Want to see her?"

"Her?" Kelly said. "How do you know it's a her?"

"Who cares? Step aside, ladies." Flanagan yanked the crowbar from Will Patrick's hands and attacked the lid, chipping off chunks of stone. "We ain't got all night."

"Stop defiling the casket," Will Patrick said, his voice hollow. "You'll pay hell for that."

"As long as the devil takes Visa." Flanagan laughed. "I'm good."

"Wait." Kelly said. Then something caught her eye. "Hey, there's words on the lid." She held the flashlight up and began reading. " 'You cannot hear the Shadowless when her breath is in your ear. You cannot see the Shadowless.' There's more, but I can't make it out."

"Who gives a rat's ass about some poem?" Flanagan said. "All I want is treasure."

"It's not a poem." Kelly crossed herself three times and spat over her shoulder. "It's a curse."

"I've got more spit if you need it," Flanagan said.

"Don't mock me!" Kelly slapped his shoulder. "Just 'cause you're too damn stupid to be scared!"

"Calm the hell down," Flanagan said, pushing her away. "It's just a joke."

"It's . . . It's not a joke. Will Patrick, tell your asshole friend the poem's not a joke."

Will Patrick stared at the casket lid. "The girl has been given leave to go," he said in the same hollow voice.

"Yeah, if you're so freaked out, go home," Flanagan said. "We don't want your ass to get cursed or anything."

"Up yours, Flanagan. And yours, too, Will Patrick. Thanks so much for sticking up for me." Kelly ducked and backed into the wall of the tomb. "Can one of you jerks give me a hand up?"

Flanagan glanced at Will Patrick, who stared straight ahead. "She came to see you, asswipe." Then he rolled his eyes and gave Kelly a boost until she climbed out of the hole.

"Thanks," she said, looking down at him.

"Whatever," he said.

"Go ahead then, jerk. Open the casket and see what happens."

"Like I said," he said, turning his back on her, "whatever."

"Been nice knowing you." Without a backward glance, Kelly pulled her hoodie tight against her face, thinking that if she were to look back at the tomb, it would be the last thing she ever did.

CHAPTER FOURTEEN

TEN minutes after church bells struck midnight, I opened my bedroom door and peered down the hallway to make sure the coast was clear. Ma wasn't a night owl by nature, but designing and making the costumes for the revival of *The Crucible* had kept her working late into the night.

Miss Haverhill wanted the egg, and Louie still had it, until tomorrow evening, when the loan was due. If I could come up with the money, I could get the egg out of hock. Fate or kismet was in my favor, because Ma had just hours earlier given me the means to get the money—the thimbles. After dinner I did some Googling and found out the Meissens were more valuable than I ever dreamed. One almost like mine had sold for eight thousand at auction last month. If I could pawn a thimble for one-tenth of the auction price, I could keep the egg and make rent. I would worry about getting the thimbles back later. Ma would call it borrowing from Peter to pay Paul, but what else was a girl to do?

I tiptoed to the living room, opened the cabinet and picked up my birthday gift. Inside the case were two thimbles. The white porcelain almost glowed in the light from the streetlamps outside, and the gold glinted as I pushed one onto my thumb. It slid on easily, but when I tried to remove it, it popped like a cork and left a stinging red cut just below the nail.

"Jeezum," I said and rubbed the sore spot. Who knew a thimble could be lethal?

"The price to be paid in blood!" someone screamed, an electric pain arced up my hand, and I could taste metal on my tongue. My eyes closed, and I was lying prone in darkness, my hands crossed over my chest, a shroud covering my face. A casket. I was in a casket, buried deep in the ground, and I had lain there for hundreds of years, waiting, waiting for this moment. I heard a splintering crack, and light flooded in, blinding me, and the muttering returned, louder this time and growing more loud until the voices reached a crescendo and someone called my name.

"Willow?" Ma said. "Willow Jane?"

When I opened my eyes, she was standing next to me with a tissue pressed against the cut on my thumb. Blood bloomed through it, and I was surprised how I bled. The thimbles were in their case. She must have put them back.

"Hey, Ma," I said.

"Poor girl." She steered me to the couch. "Sleepwalking again. It's been two years, hasn't it? Since your father—"

Was murdered.

"—died. Here, keep pressure on the cut while I get the Mercurochrome."

It wasn't really Mercurochrome: The stuff was banned before I was born. Ma wasn't one to change, even when the small brown bottle she returned with was clearly labeled "Iodine."

"This won't hurt a bit," she said.

"That's a lie." I sucked in air when the antiseptic hit the wound. "We both know it burns like molten lava."

"Saying it helps me feel less guilty." She wrapped a Band-Aid around my finger. "When was your last tetanus shot?"

"Eighth grade. When that goon cross-checked me into the bench and the refs didn't even call a penalty."

"Tsk. You nurse injustices far too long. That's the Conning in you." She rubbed the worry lines between her eyebrows. "Ever since the party, you've seemed a little bit off."

"Just a headache." It was true. I had been fighting a headache since the party. "No big deal."

"Those headaches worry me." Ma closed the cabinet. "The sleepwalking, too. An aspirin for you, then straight back to bed."

"Yes, Mother dear," I said, kissed her on the cheek, and headed to my room.

But while Ma was in the bathroom getting aspirin, I ran back and swiped the thimbles. Seconds after I slid between the sheets and hid the thimbles under the mattress, she came in with a bottle of aspirin, a glass of water, and a pair of tailor's scissors.

"Take two," she said.

I was surprisingly thirsty, and the water burned, it was so cold. Maybe I really was coming down with something.

I eyed the scissors suspiciously. "What are those for?"

"Your headache." She tucked the scissors under my pillow. "Sleep on these, and your pain will be gone like magic."

"If I sleep on those," I said and removed the scissors, "I'll need stitches."

"Steel's the best thing for a headache, my grandmother always said."

"There's no scientific evidence that sleeping with steel does anything. The same with magnets, runes, and charms."

"There's more in heaven and earth, Horatio, than your philosophy allows," she said. "Know who said that?"

"Shakespeare. In *Hamlet*. Hamlet was telling his friend to have an open mind."

"Might I point out that Shakespeare put ghosts and fairies in his plays."

"There's no scientific basis for those, either."

"Not everything can be explained with science, missy."

"Name one."

"Love."

Really? "Love is the accumulated effect of endorphins flooding the brain due to chemical responses in another human being."

"Leave it to my daughter to explain love like a chemical formula."

I put the scissors on the nightstand. "Leave it to my mother to eviscerate me in my sleep."

"Good night, my treasure. Sweet dreams," Ma said. She turned out the light and shut the door, and that's when my nightmares really began.

CHAPTER FIFTEEN

"I thought fear's supposed to make girls horny." Flanagan pulled the crowbar out of the casket. The corner of the lid had broken off, revealing a dark space but no treasure. "It's open. You want first look?"

Will Patrick grabbed the crowbar and swung it over his head. The bar slammed into the lid, and a chunk fell into the darkness.

"Why the hell did you bust it up?" Flanagan said. "You were just whining about me doing the same thing."

"The Shadowless needs to breathe," he said, slack jawed, and dropped the crowbar on the ground. His gaze was fixed on the casket, where an unnatural light glowed between the cracks, illuminating a tattered shroud.

"I knew it!" Flanagan peeped inside. "Just a pile of dust and rotted bones! Next time you wanna hunt for buried treasure, leave me out."

"The bones are the treasure."

"Up yours. I've got work in six hours. I'm out of here."

"You do not have leave to go," Will Patrick said, his voice low and ghostly.

Flanagan grabbed his crotch. "Leave this, jagoff."

He climbed to the surface, but when he grabbed a tree root to pull himself up, the root snapped, and he fell hard on his back. He lay gasping on a mound of fecund earth and worm-eaten leaves.

"Oh hell," he rasped. "I think I cracked some ribs."

Snap!

"Will?" He jerked his head toward the noise in the darkness. "Damn it!" Somebody was watching him. No, he told himself, it's just a squirrel or a chipmunk or some bird. Nothing to be scared of. The T station in Roxbury was way more dangerous than a bunch of worm-eaten corpses.

He heard a footfall and looked up at Will Patrick's face. "Dude! Don't sneak—"

Will swung the crowbar, and the claw shattered the bones of Flanagan's temple and tore off a chunk of ear. The force of the blow snapped his neck so violently two cervical vertebrae splintered, but Flanagan felt nothing but the sensation of floating. He blinked into the darkness and saw the dim streetlights reflected in hundreds of tiny yellow eyes.

Crows.

Thousands were roosting in the dead branches above, not making a sound, as if they were silent sentinels keeping watch. Then, with a cacophonous crescendo of screams, the birds cried out and took flight, claws out, beaks wide and sharp, screaming for blood.

His blood.

A shadowy figure appeared, a tattered shroud covering its face. The shadow raised its desiccated arms and wrapped its rotted, sinewy hands of gristle and bone around Flanagan's throat. The words Kelly had read came back to him: *You cannot hear the Shadowless when her breath is in your ear.*

"Help me," Flanagan whispered, but his voice was lost in the fury of the birds' attack.

They swept down on him, screaming and pecking,

sharp beaks and talons ripping into the soft flesh of his face. In the distance the bells of the Park Street Church tolled half past the hour, and Flanagan's screams mixed with the sound of the ringing notes.

PART TWO

WONDERS OF AN INVISIBLE WORLD

MALLEUS danced through the shadows down the path between the graves of Abiah and Josiah Franklin, a yarn necklace tied around her bony neck. Her feet padded on the gravel path, making almost no sound. Streetlights seemed to wash over and off her shroud like water on oilcloth as she left the cemetery and turned down the road, an internal compass pointing her toward the lights in the southern sky. They drew her like a beacon.

A-hunting, she would go.

CHAPTER SEVENTEEN

THE doors of the dive bar blew open, and two hefty bouncers, who had just used Harken's head like a battering ram, tossed him toward the street. His face skidded over the dirty sidewalk, and he landed on the asphalt on Tremont Street between two parked cabs.

"Not so pretty now, huh?" the smaller bouncer yelled. "The tooth fairy's gonna be real good to you tonight."

"Pretty is—" Harken crawled to his feet. "—as pretty does." He put up his dukes like a bare-knuckle brawler. "Ready for another go, gentlemen?"

"Come back in here again," the second bouncer yelled as Harken knocked dirt from the shirt and jeans he'd scrounged, "and you'll get a real beating."

Harken cupped a hand and spat an incisor into his palm. His face was skinned, and his left eye was puffed and purple from the left hook the bouncer had been lucky to land. One of his ribs was broken, too, but he wasn't sure if it was from a punch or from being kicked by the three college boys whose girlfriends he'd flirted with.

"I've had worse beatings from crippled fishwives." He held up the bloody tooth. "I've paid for my supper, and I plan to eat it."

"All you can plan on eating," said the smaller bouncer, "is the curb. Curb service. Get it?"

"I'm familiar with the phrase." Harken rolled up his sleeves and cracked his neck. "And you, gentlemen, are about to learn that I give as well as I get."

An hour before dawn, Harken awoke in a church courtyard to the sound of screaming. He leaped to his feet, fists ready. He looked around wildly for the source of the sound and found nothing but the stray gray cat that had been curled up next to him. It raised its hackles and hissed, fangs showing.

"Damned cats," he said and sighed, allowing his

borrowed body to relax. "Why is it always cats?"

He ran a hand through his black hair to straighten it, then rubbed his neck and stretched. The vertebrae he'd cracked had healed nicely in the hours since he left the bar on Tremont triumphant, if he could call eating a cold steak while the two bouncers and the three angry boyfriends took the naps he'd given them a victory. He'd gone into the seedy dive looking for food—being locked in a bronze grasshopper for almost thirty years raised a scorcher of an appetite—but part of him had been spoiling for a fight. He'd woken up angry, but even an old-fashioned donnybrook had done nothing to take the edge off.

Harken's bruised skin had changed during the night. It was now covered in tattooed symbols that began at the back of the neck, wound around his shoulders, and flowed down his broad chest and arms. The symbols were marred by deep-creased scars from a hundred battles great and small. Not all the scars were old. Some of them were as fresh as the new day dawning, but in the patchwork of runes and glyphs, words and pictures, it was impossible to tell. Harken's body told a story, but like him, it was impenetrable. He had lived nineteen years and four months by his reckoning, but it had taken almost four hundred years to do it. That's what came of being in the service of the wicked.

Harken slipped off the leather jacket he'd procured from one of the bouncers and pulled a borrowed crimson hoodie over his head. He'd gone twenty-nine years without a meal, and last night's steak was long gone. Already his body had burned through the food, using the fuel to heal his wounds. He stood and flexed his arms. There was a gash across his chest, a superficial cut from some glass that had almost healed. He ran a broad palm over the thick chest muscle and pushed hard, so hard he grunted. The black lines of the tattoos seemed to glow like his copper-colored eyes.

He yawned, then heard another scream, this one louder than the first. The cat hissed again and bounded into the blue-gray light as a murder of crows descended on the courtyard. They washed over the church steeple and filled every nook and cranny from the windowsills to the iron fences to the power lines that stretched to the street.

"Wicked birds," he said. "Where's a cat when you need one?"

But there was nothing funny about the birds, not the way the flock of crows and rooks and magpies seemed to be

moving west toward the Granary Burying Ground, where
Harken had long ago buried his own secrets.

He, it seemed, had not been the only creature reawak-
ened last night.

It was no more than fifteen minutes later that Harken
emerged from an alley. His hood was pulled low to hide his
face, and he made sure that traffic had passed before walking to the corner and crossing the street.

He slipped between the iron gates and headed down
the path to the graves of a former merchant and his family,
all of whom had lived long lives and died wealthy, only
to take eternal rest in graves atop a secret tomb. Wind
whipped the branches, sending the leaves to the ground.
They tumbled ahead of him and stopped at the hole in the
earth where the merchant's grave had been.

Beneath a canopy of half-naked trees, Harken could
see the chunks of dirt and pieces of mossy lid cast aside.
He could see dead crows and carrion on either side of the
hole. He could see the body of a young man swinging from
an ancient sycamore, a noose tied around his neck, both
thumbs sheared from his hands.

"Not another killing," Harken whispered. "After so
much time."

Then he could see more and more and more, looking deep into the past and across the wide ocean to Scotland and its capital. There, as a lad of ten years, he stood with a crowd at Castlehill, separated by a deep ravine from Edinburgh Castle, which was perched high above them on Castle Rock.

Hiding in the shadows of three tall poles raised upon a platform, Harken had watched as three confessed witches were marched through the crowd. They were led by a haughty minister, who had shoulder-length wavy red hair and a thick mustache. He wore a frock coat, black stockings, and buckled shoes with sturdy heels.

They were followed by the executioner, a taller spidery man dressed in black and dun who carried a cudgel and a torch. A week earlier a young woman named Gillis Duncan had confessed to witchery and had accused Harken's mistress and two other women of also cavorting with the devil.

"Mistress," Harken whispered as the women marched past.

Her shoulders were thrown back, chin held high. She wore a gown of red velvet, and her dark hair flowed behind her like a horse's mane. Although her dress was torn and stained with dried blood, she looked as regal as always. The other two women had fared less well. They wore blood and sweat-stained smocks, and their hair was caked with filth. They walked barefoot, and each of their stumbling steps left a bloody print on the path.

Under a writ of James VI of Scotland himself, soldiers had taken the mistress in the night, binding her hands before she could fight and carrying her to the dungeons. She and the other accused had been put to torture and pinned to the prison walls in the witch's bridle, an iron muzzle with four sharp prongs that dug into their soft mouths.

After a day, their spit turned to blood, and their tongues swelled until they gagged for breath. After two days, they were ready to confess anything, just to be free.

Now the crowd closed in on them, pressing in like a weight, spitting and cursing.

"Back!" the executioner bellowed and raised the cudgel and torch. "Else ye'll be getting the same!"

The crowd fell back. Harken ducked around shopkeepers and tradesmen, fishwives and horse traders, all smelling of hemp rope, pitch, tar, and flaxseed oil. Their voices were shrill and full of excitement. A witch burning stirred their blood as much as a battle or a holiday.

The wavy-haired minister led the condemned up wooden steps to the platform. He chanted a prayer as the executioner tied the first two to their stakes.

The executioner grabbed Harken's mistress. He yanked her bound hands above her head, cinching the rope around the charred skin of the stake. Then she laughed, and he stopped cold. She spoke softly, laughing again, and the executioner hastily bound her torso and arms to the stake, then quickly withdrew.

"Mistress?" Harken whispered to no one. All along he assumed she would escape the soldiers. That she would trick them or kill them, then simply walk out of the dungeons. He never thought that she might actually burn.

The thought gave him a thrill. To be free of the mistress! To no longer be forced to find other norns for her to kill! To finally return, perhaps, to the arms of his mother. His real mother, whose face he no longer remembered, except in dreams.

"Confess!" The minister stepped forward, screaming into their faces, "Confess your sins before God and man!"

The first woman, her head hanging low, confessed. As did the second, and the crowd went mad, screaming, "Fire!" and "Burn!"

The minister came to the mistress, his face bloodred from screaming, but she met his eye and held it. His voice shook as he tried to yell again. It came out so soft and raspy Harken barely heard him say, "Confess your sins, woman."

"Where shall I begin?" The mistress seductively licked her ruby lips. "I have poisoned the king's children with gut of toad, cat's feet, and an old man's toe cuttings. And I've thrice danced naked with the devil in the king's own court."

The angry crowd gasped, and Harken felt the flicker of hope go out, never to be rekindled.

"Harlot! Heretic! Unclean!" the minister cried out. "Woman, how dare you!"

"How dare I what?" The mistress laughed, still seductive. "You called upon me to confess, and I did."

"Peace!" he screamed, but there was more fear in his voice than anger.

"You want peace?" she said, almost cooing. "Then unbind my hands, and I'll give you peace like no other." She laughed again, but the sound died when the minister swept open his frock and pulled out a pair of tailor's shears. She twisted violently, freeing her hands from the bindings and raising them toward her mouth.

The minister grabbed a handful of her dark mane and opened the shears. "A woman's hair," he screamed, "is a temptation in the eyes of . . . God?"

Harken felt a strange buzzing noise, and lightning split the sky. It struck the platform where the minister stood, the very spot exploding with light and splitting all ears with sound and filling the air with the stench of burnt flesh.

Coughing and eyes burning, Harken stared in awe through the thick smoke. The other two women were still tied to their stakes.

But where the mistress had stood, the minister now slouched, dead, bound by arms and torso to the stake. His long red curls lay at his feet, shorn to the scalp.

Blood dripped from the stubs where his thumbs had been.

"Witchcraft!" came the cry. "Murder!"

"Mistress?" Harken whispered, stepping toward the platform. The mistress was gone.

But not for long. After she had escaped her execution, the mistress found Harken wandering the town. They fled Scotland for Germany. In Würzburg the mistress became a witch hunter herself, an irony that delighted her. When the witch trials ended in Europe, they'd crossed the sea to the Massachusetts Bay Colony and had begun the witch hunting again—until Harken betrayed her and had put an end to her hunting forever.

"How long does forever last?" Harken whispered, rubbing the copper coins in his pocket, his mind returning to the cemetery and the boy hanging from the tree.

The Park Street Church bells tolled the hour. On the steeple, lit by arc lights, a flock of blackbirds perched silent as a tomb, waiting for something or someone to come. They did not caw or beat their wings or preen.

The bell tolled again, chasing the flock into the sky. There, in the cold air above the bay, the small flock joined with other, larger flocks, the way that streams become creeks become rivers that run wide and deep into the sea, becoming a superflock of ten thousand birds whose sheer mass and density blotted out the sky.

"Bloody hell." Harken looked down, down into the tomb, down into the abyss. "Bloody, bloody hell."

The casket was empty.

"The Shadowless has risen," Harken said, and as rain began to fall, he turned and ran for his life.

Chapter Eighteen

EXHAUSTION finally carried me to sleep. At first I was restless, vaguely aware that the bed was too hard and the air was too dense. A thought to open a window flickered past, but it was replaced by the sepia-toned dream images of the gravestones of the Granary, a flock of crows circling in the air above, and a dead man curled up in the front seat of a city bus, clutching a token in his half-open palm.

He opened his eyes, dirt black orbs flecked with white, and walked toward the exit, where I was standing. A scream formed in my mouth, and I backed against a seat, but the dead man shambled past me. He pressed the copper into the driver's hand. The door opened onto the shore of a brackish river, and he walked toward the water until he was swallowed by the swirling mists.

The door began to close, but a hand forced its way in and wedged the panels open. Will Patrick walked up the bus steps in his school uniform, a navy blazer, white button-down, and khakis. His black loafers were caked with mud, and he flipped his bangs from his forehead, eyes on me, licking the corners of his mouth.

"You cannot ride," the driver said.

But Will Patrick ignored him and turned toward me.

I backed up, and his gaze trapped me in the aisle, so that I couldn't flee. My legs shook, and my knees gave out. If I hadn't been holding the pole, I would've fallen.

Will Patrick smiled and began to sing "Will and Willow swinging in a tree, k-i-s-s-ing."

He laced his fingers through my hair and tilted my face up to his, his soft lips pressing warm on mine, his breath sour like turned milk. His skin was stretched taut over his skull, and he tasted like sewer gases, but the kiss never ended. I screamed at myself to fight, but I was paralyzed, unable to run or even pull away as his corpse sucked the life from me.

Mist swirled from Will's mouth, and I was swallowed up by it. My hands closed into fists, and I felt something round and cold in my palm. I opened my hand, and the coin hit the floor. It rolled away, copper glinting in the light, a penny for the ferryman, like the token the dead man had held.

"No!" I screamed and squeezed my eyes shut. "Leave me alone!"

When I opened my eyes, Will Patrick was gone. It's just a dream, I told myself. Wake up. You can leave any-time you want.

But I couldn't. The door was open, but my feet wouldn't move, and I would not wake up.

"What you do want from me?" I screamed.

The answer came as a knock from the back of the bus, tapping on the glass like Miss Haverhill's sharp knuckles on the apartment door. The window cracked, and the mists seeped in, bringing a strangling cold with them. The glass frosted over, and a sheen of crystals formed. It crept toward me, and I shivered both from the cold and from the knocking.

"I'm not afraid of you." I lied through chattering teeth. It's a dream, I told myself. You can wake up. Just open your eyes. But my eyes were open, and my arms were pressed against my belly to fight off the chill.

The rapping became a hammering, a steady beat, growing louder, shaking the safety glass, the metal frames bulging with each strike, then shrinking, and bulging again when the hammer fell. The sound echoed through the empty bus, and I covered my ears and bent over. Then with a terrifying blow the window behind me exploded, and I screamed.

"Leave me alone!"

Shattered glass lay on the seat behind me, and the cold mist still oozed inside, but it was silent. I shuddered and said a silent prayer of thanks.

Then the whispering began. Children's voices, light as air and sweet, though too ethereal for me to make out the words. I leaned closer to the ruptured window, straining to hear. The whispers turned to singsong, turned to a familiar tune, a familiar voice.

"Will and Willow sitting in a tree . . ."

"Devon?"

She appeared in the seat next to me and said, "The shadow people watch when you sleep."

"What?" I said. Something caught my eye. I looked

past Devon at the dead girl standing right behind her, a cold hand reaching for my sister's hair.

"No!" I said, just as boom! a devastating clap shook the bus, and the rest of the windows blew out.

I ducked and ran for the exit, but the door slammed shut, and the one remaining piece of glass, the windshield, turned white with frost. The knocking began again, then a persistent, insistent rapping that shook the frame until I stood bolt upright.

The dead girl was beside my bed, staring at me with Mercurochrome eyes and flaxen hair, her mouth as dark as an open grave. "The shadow people watch you sleep."

"What do you want from me?" I said, shutting my eyes. I rocked back and forth, counted down from a hundred, and when I opened my eyes again, she was gone.

I held up a hand to block the sunlight streaming through my windows. That's when I saw two things at once—a dozen blackbirds perched on my sill and blood dripping from a cut in my thumb.

The scissors! Ma must've come back and tucked them under my pillow, and I'd stabbed myself in my sleep. I wiped the blood on my pillowcase and flung the scissors at the floor. With a thunk, the sharp points stuck in the wood. The noise frightened the birds, and they beat the window with their black wings.

"Holy crap," I whispered, staring out at a miasma of black feathers.

Thousands of starlings, grackles, and blackbirds filled the trees, the roofs, and even the sidewalks. They roosted on cars, trucks, road signs, power lines, and handrails. The birds screamed and whistled, trilling a guttural racket that made my skin crawl.

"Ma! Come look!" I called.

But the flock took off, rising in a crescendo of feathers. I grabbed a white button-down and a pleated green tartan skirt, my Beacon School uniform, the frumpiest collection of fabric in the universe.

"Come look at what?" Ma called back.

"Ma!" I rounded the corner to the kitchen, zipping my skirt and stuffing Dad's letter in a pocket. Ma never smiled until her second cup of coffee, but her sleepy face was much better than the dead girl's. "Did you see the birds outside?"

"I heard them." She stood at the sink, washing dishes and watching the street below. "What a noise! It could wake the dead."

"It's called a superflock," I said. "We studied them in

AP bio. Wicked cool, huh?"

"Wicked, yes." Ma wiped her brow. "Birds are an ill omen. Mark my words."

"Oh, Ma," I said. "It's just birds, for chrissakes."

"Watch your mouth," Ma scolded but without much gusto. She was keeping watch on Devon at the corner bus stop. "Like your dad said, words are dangerous weapons in the wrong mouth."

"Speaking of dangerous," I said. "Could we stop with the lethal objects under my pillow? We're playing All Saints today, and now I've got to play with a gash in my thumb."

"That's nice," she said.

"So is Devon still there?" I said while slapping together a peanut butter and fluff sandwich. "Or did the birds carry her off?"

Ma pushed the curtain aside. "Still there, standing behind that nose-picking Flanagan boy. That one's trouble, just like his big brother."

"You can tell that from one nose picking?" I took a bite, leaving teeth prints in the peanut butter. "Most ladies read tea leaves, but not my ma. She sees the future in the boogers of little boys."

Ma swatted me as I twisted the bread bag closed.

"Boogers and body functions, it's no way to talk."

"Next to Siobhan, I'm a saint."

"Next to Siobhan, Whitey Bulger is a saint."

I grabbed my book bag. "Nobody's ever taken Siobhan for a mobster."

"Give her time."

Time! I checked my watch. If I hurried, I could hit the pawnshop on the way to school. I retrieved the thimble case from my room and slid it in my book bag, between my lunch and a copy of *The Crucible*.

"Jimmy Flanagan!" Ma yelled out the window. "Don't dare touch my baby with that finger!"

"I'm leaving!" I called. "I've got the All Saints game, so I can't pick Devie up from aftercare. Okay?"

"Who's the mother here?" Ma said. "It's chilly out. Take a sweater."

"It's Boston. It's always chilly out."

"Your mouth won't be so fresh when you catch cold."

"Viruses cause colds, not the weather." But to make her happy, I grabbed my school sweater from her leaning tower of sewing scraps. "Happy?" I said, pulling it over my button-down.

"You've snagged a thread." Ma dried her hands on the

apron. "Let me get that."

"No, I'm good."

I opened the front door, ready to make my escape, but Ma was too quick. She grabbed a crochet hook and in a blink was bearing down on my chest.

"No touching the boobs!" I clapped a hand over the loose thread. "Give me the scissors. I'll cut it."

"Cut it?" Ma tsk-tsked me. "What've I told you about never cutting a thread? One snip—"

"And the whole thing unravels," I said and curtsied. "I yield, m'lady. Do with me as you must."

"You watch too much TV."

"I read books. The book is always better."

Ma pulled the thread back into place. "All fixed. Now lean down here and give your old mother a kiss."

"You're thirty-eight." I pecked her cheek. "That's not old."

"I feel sixty," she said, rubbing her swollen knuckles. "Those needles do their damage. Did you read your dad's letter yet?"

I patted the envelope in my pocket. "Running late, so I'll read it at school."

"A letter from your father should be read in his home."

I started to argue but had to admit she was right. Ma went back to the sink to dry dishes, and I carefully tugged Dad's letter from the envelope. The back was blank, though when I looked more closely, there seemed to be lettering on it, but it was too faint to read. I flipped the paper over and read the greeting, "Dearest Sweet Willow."

Tears welled in my eyes, and a knot as hard and round as a Tootsie Pop formed in my throat. Ma had warned me to read it alone. Now it was too late. I pressed my wrist against my lips and tried to read the next lines:

"I write this on the eve of your sixth birthday with you snug in your bed, your belly full of cake and soda pop and your heart full to bursting with the love of friends and family. You are reading it on the night of your sixteenth birthday, and as the letter was given by your ma, I was not there to share it with you."

"Oh my god," I whispered and covered my mouth. "It sounds just like him." My eyes clouded with salty tears. He knew. He knew somehow that he wouldn't be alive, and it was like he was reaching out from the afterlife. "Ma," I said, starting to show her the letter, even though she had told me I couldn't.

But she didn't hear me. Outside on the street a truck

horn sounded. Brakes squealed, and metal hit metal with a hollow, echoing thump that made my blood run cold. Nothing good ever came of a noise like that, especially when the silence that followed was shattered by my mother's heartrending cry.

"Devon!"

I dropped the letter on the coffee table, rushed to the bay window, and threw the curtains aside. A crowd was gathering on the sidewalk and street, where my little sister lay still on the pavement, a pool of blood spreading under her head like a dead dove's wings.

CHAPTER NINETEEN

"NO! No! No!" As I vaulted down three flights of stairs, I pictured Devon's face, cold, bloodless, and serene as if she were sleeping. Or maybe not sleeping.

Don't say it! I yanked open the heavy front door. Don't even think it!

My legs carried me down the sidewalk to the corner. I was barely aware of horns sounding and people yelling to call 911. I saw a Civic resting on the sidewalk, a dent in the front fender. The driver, a girl in a BC hoodie with cell phone in hand, was beating her head against the steering wheel, crying hysterically. A crowd, watching in silence, had gathered around Devon.

I lowered my shoulder to plow through them.

"Devon!" I yelled, dropping to her side. I checked her wrist for a pulse and felt nothing but the fading warmth of her skin. "You wake up right this instant! You're scaring Ma half to death! Devon!"

A siren squawked, and the crowd parted. Red ambulance lights danced on Devon's black curls, and her pale skin flickered pink, then white, pink, then white.

"Step aside!" the EMTs yelled, their doors slamming, their radios squawking, too. They'd come to help, but what could they do?

"Oh, Devie." I touched her cheek. "Please. Don't be dead."

"Miss," an EMT said, putting a hand on my shoulder. "Move aside."

I moaned and covered my mouth, tasting blood and something metallic, unsure if it came from my tongue or the cut on my thumb. I felt the sudden shock of vertigo, and the air turned ice cold. The breath was sucked from my chest, and I was floating in space, not moving, not breathing, suspended by a phantom string. An electric chill went up my spine, and my tongue tasted like iron, just before everything went black.

A moment later the light returned, and I opened my eyes. My right hand was covered in blood. I splayed out my fingers and took a closer look.

No, not blood.

Chalk.

Red chalk.

"Willow Jane?" Devon sounded very far away, as if she stood at the bottom of a deep well. My baby sister, dressed in the blue coat and matching cap Ma had knitted for her last Christmas, fixed her eyes on me, then said in a gruff voice, "Daddy says you woke the dead girl up."

"W-what?" I said. "What dead girl? Devon?"

She blinked three times. "That's my name, you big ginge," she said, taking a piece of red chalk out of my hand. "Why're you using my school supplies?"

I swept her into a bear hug, swinging her around so hard her shoes almost flew off. "Devie!"

"You're choking me," she said through my sweater.

My sister wasn't dead. Not even hurt. "Sorry!" I pulled back, and chalk dust rubbed onto her coat. "I'm so happy you're alive!"

"Why wouldn't I be alive?"

"Because that . . . car . . ." Ten feet away I saw the Civic resting on the sidewalk, a dent in the front bumper from where it jumped the curb. The girl in a BC hoodie was tapping her head against the steering wheel, crying but not hysterically. A small crowd gathered around her, asking if she was okay. "Hit . . . you?"

Devon cocked her head like I'd lost my mind, which wasn't far from the truth. "Did you drink too much coffee again?"

"Yes! That's it!" But I hadn't had a drop.

"My bus is here." Devon pointed to the yellow Blue Bird across the intersection. "Lemme go, before I have to sit by the booger eaters."

With a quick hug I let my sister go. She waved as she climbed the steps.

"Keep your phlegm to yourself, Jimmy Flanagan!" I yelled, and all the kids looked back at me. Yes, I was a weirdo, but my sister was alive, and they could just deal. It was normal for nerdy Willow Jane to act abnormal, right?

What the hell was going on? I looked up to the third floor of our building. The kitchen window was shut, like it had never been opened, and Ma was nowhere in sight.

My relief quickly mutated to confusion. Before the vertigo hit, Devon had been dead, but when the spell was over, it was like the Civic had never hit my sister. But I had seen it with my own eyes, felt Devon's breath slip away.

Was it all my imagination?

How did imagination explain my chalk-stained palms?

My eyes moved to the pavement, where I saw red letters written in my own hand:

You must not wake the Shadowless
When she sleeps within her bed.
But kiss the lips of the Shadowless
And the morning finds you dead.

CHAPTER TWENTY

BY the time Harken reached the corner of Silver and F Streets, his head had cleared, and the wild panic from finding the Shadowless gone was fading. So she had escaped: Her body was a rotted corpse. How much damage could a walking corpse do? But in the dark part of his mind, he knew the answer. A weak Shadowless was stronger than any human.

He stopped to catch his breath and to pull the crimson hoodie tight against his face. He zipped up the leather jacket, stuffed both hands in the pockets, and bowed his head. The Connings' house was just around the corner, and it would take only a few seconds to confirm that the family was safe. Then he could get far, far away from Boston and the ghosts that haunted it.

But when he rounded the corner, he was surprised to find people milling about a damaged vehicle, which for some reason was parked on the sidewalk near a pack of schoolchildren. He paid attention long enough to decide the commotion didn't concern him before noticing a petite ginger girl who was rubbing chalk off her hands. She then ran down the sidewalk, and he thought she looked vaguely familiar. That didn't concern him, either, and he would have walked on, except for an overwhelming sense of déjà vu, a sensation so strong it made the hair on his neck stand up.

Something strange, he thought. "Excuse me!" he called to one of the men near the car. "Might I beg a moment of your time?"

"Can't you see I'm busy?" the man replied. He was wearing a khaki uniform, and his name tag read "Reed Barker."

"Reed Barker, I have your name." Harken touched the bronze torc on his neck and commanded, "Tell me what happened here."

"Girl hit the curb," he said. "Coulda sworn she was

gonna hit the kids, then bam! She veers right and nails a parking meter instead."

"Very curious," Harken said, caught Reed's eye, and put a finger to his lips. He stepped back into the crowd and dissolved like smoke.

Reed blinked three times, then shrugged and returned to the accident, where he began giving advice on how best to move the wrecked Civic.

Harken moved through the crowd, listening. The other gawkers were as confused as Reed. For some reason they couldn't explain, they all had expected the car to hit the children. One woman called the police by pulling a device from her pocket and punching merrily on it.

I must have one of those, Harken thought, and promptly picked one from the pocket of a man in a business suit, along with a penknife and a wallet. He dropped them into his own pockets as the man walked away oblivious.

"Some things never change," Harken said.

He would need transportation as well. His gaze fell on a fire department standpipe, where someone had chained a weathered Harley. He pulled out the penknife and picked the bike's chain lock while everyone went about their daily business.

"Ma!" a ginger-haired girl called up to a third-floor window. "Come look! You're not going to believe this!"

Harken walked to the corner and read the poem written in chalk again. "'You must not wake the Shadowless,'" he whispered. "Too damned late for that."

But the poem had to go.

He borrowed a cup of coffee from a bystander and poured it on the sidewalk. The liquid hit the chalk and washed it in bright red rivulets down the gutter. When the evidence was gone, he returned the empty cup to its owner.

"Thanks," he said.

The bystander gave him a blank look as the ginger girl rushed by. Harken's eyes met hers for a glimmer of a second, and her eyes widened with a glimpse of recognition. Then she looked past him, as if he weren't there. Stunned, Harken turned to watch her go. There had been none of the usual shenanigans—no blush, no fawning over his looks. It was as if he were a telephone pole or fire hydrant. He felt a flash of annoyance and embarrassment. No one ever walked by him when he wanted them to stop, especially a young woman.

"Excuse me!" the girl said, pointing at the sidewalk.

"What the hell?" he said under his breath, and felt a

strange tug when she bent over the puddle and tucked a curly strand of hair behind her ear and turned her chin just so, a gesture that made her fair skin look almost translucent.

Harken pushed the hoodie back and ran a hand through his hair. He fixed his eyes on her delicate face and said in a low voice. "Miss, might I beg a moment of your time?"

"No," she said flatly and hardly gave him a second glance. "Ma! Ma!" she called out. "Where'd the chalk go? The poem, it's gone."

"How should I know? All I see's a puddle," a woman— the mother—called from the porch. She held the door ajar, using it like a shield. "Willow Jane Conning, I've got no time for shenanigans. Dress rehearsal's tonight, and Mr. Parris's gained ten pounds since the last fitting."

"Willow Jane," he whispered. Now he understood why she looked familiar—she had Michael Conning's eyes. "I have your name."

"But Ma! The poem was right there," the girl said. "Devie said I wrote it."

"You've taken too many checks to the head," the mother said as she shut the door. "Off to school."

The girl stared at the puddle of coffee in disbelief until

the arrival of the 8:05 bus caught her attention. "Too many checks to the head, my butt," she mumbled, threw her book bag over a shoulder, and crossed the street to board.

Harken waited until the bus pulled away, then returned to the Harley he'd unlocked. "A Conning *girl*," he whispered. A female born to the Conning line, the first in more than four hundred years, and he had discovered her on the same day the Shadowless had risen from the grave. "A beauty, too."

As he started the motorcycle, the fear that he'd squelched came back with a double fury, burning brighter and hotter than the metal that had formed his body. This was no chance, no coincidence, no happenstance. This was the Fates acting against him, those cruel bitches. Then in a heartbeat, his thoughts crystallized, and he knew what he must do.

If he wanted to live, Willow Jane Conning had to die, and to kill her, he needed magic.

CHAPTER TWENTY-ONE

LOUIE'S Pawnshop was an average hole-in-the-wall Boston pawnshop. Lots of spare tools stuffed on shelves. Jewelry under the glass counters. Guns locked behind barred racks, the kind of place where dreams went to die. It was the last place a nice, underage girl like me should've been, but it was the only chance I had left.

Louie, the owner, was just an inch taller than me but weighed twice as much—at least. His hair was long, and he tucked it behind his ears. He wore a pair of glasses on a silver chain like an old-maid librarian, a white dress shirt with sweat stains in the pits, and baggy khakis with frayed cuffs. The place had a stink all its own, like the thick, greasy air of a short-order diner.

It's just business, I reminded myself at the counter. Don't take it personally. That was Dad's philosophy when he haggled with pawnbrokers. He changed from Dad, with his soft, crooning voice and twinkling green eyes, to Mike Conning, with the attitude and fast talking to match.

"Got something that might interest you," I said.

"Yeah?" Louie sucked powdered doughnut sugar from his fingers. "I'll be the judge of that."

"Judge this." I carefully placed the wooden box containing the thimbles on the counter. "They're Meissen. How much?"

"What? No good morning? No hey, Louie, how's it hanging?"

"Never, ever will I ask you how's it hanging because that's just TMI. How much for these?"

"What's the rush?"

"Late for school." I also wanted out of there. Louie was wicked sketchy and gave me the creeps. "I'm here to square the debt on my egg."

"What egg?"

"Don't futz with me, Louie." My dad liked the poetry of *futz*. It got the meaning across without being so offensive.

"The loan on the object in question was thirty days, right?" He checked the fake Rolex on his plump wrist. "Your thirty days are up, let's see, in eight hours and fifty-seven minutes, so forget about the egg."

"I said, don't futz with me." I reached for the thimbles, but he batted my hand away.

"Don't touch me," I said.

"Don't get cranky." He scooped up the thimbles and flipped a jeweler's lens over his glasses. "The thing's a work of art. A friggin' work of art."

"Told you so."

He looked up, his eye magnified. "Too bad I ain't no art dealer."

"They're the crown jewel of thimbles. Worth a lot of cash. A *lot* of cash. Get it?"

"You ain't exactly sub-tile, so yeah, I get it."

Louie spent a minute inspecting the goods with his googly eye. I crossed my fingers behind my back and said a little prayer to St. Nicholas, the patron saint of children, thieves, and pawnbrokers. Daddy said the art of nego-tiation was knowing how badly the other person wanted something. A minute later Louie proved he had the same philosophy.

"For this thimble," he said, sucking his teeth, "I can give you maybe a hundred."

"A *hundred*? As in dollars?" I said. "Are you nuts?"

"One-fifty, max." He set the thimbles down. "One seventy-five for both. That's being generous."

"I'll trade you straight up," I said. "The thimbles for the egg."

"How stupid do I look?"

I almost made the mistake of telling him. "Come on, Louie." It sounded like begging, and I hated to beg. "I owe four hundred bucks on the egg, right?"

"Four hundred seventy-two dollars and sixty-three cents. Don't forget the interest."

"Forget *you*." I cupped a hand over the thimbles. "I'll take my business elsewhere."

"Where else they gonna let some underage kid pawn junk like this?" Louie clapped his hand on mine. "One call about stolen goods, and the cops'll slam you in juvie."

"I didn't steal them." I knew Louie was bluffing. Everybody knew he fenced stolen goods, and he wasn't about to invite cops into his shop. "My ma gave them to me."

"What's your mommy gonna say about you hocking

family heirlooms?" He reached for his phone. "She at home or working at the Shubert?"

"I want four hundred."

"Two hundred."

"Three."

"Two-fifty." He grinned, loving every minute of torturing me. "For both the thimbles. That's what I call a gift, and it's also what I call my final offer."

I ran the numbers. No matter how I added it up, Louie came out on the winning side. I still owed him $220 and change. How was I ever going to come up with two hundred bucks by the end of the day?

"Forget it," I said.

"Walk out that door," he said, "and I cut my price in half."

"But I'll still owe two hundred bucks. How am I going to come up with that?"

"Two hundred's better than three and a quarter," he said. "But hey, I'll make you a deal. If you don't get the two hundred, I'll cancel the loan on the thimbles. Even stephens."

What choice did I have? "You should be ashamed," I said.

"I am. Very."

"You're a lying sack of crap."

"What? Liars can't feel shame?"

"Crap can't."

"I'll pretend you didn't say that." Cackling to celebrate his victory, Louie put the thimbles back in their wooden box. "That leaves you two hundred twenty-two sixty-three dollars short. The remainder is due at seven P.M. tonight, or else the egg goes on eBay."

"Don't you dare sell it on eBay," I said. "It's been in my family for centuries."

"Centuries, huh? That's a good run." He locked the thimbles in the display case. "Too bad it's over."

"Not yet," I said over my shoulder. "I'm getting my egg, come hell or high water."

"Tough luck, sweetheart. The forecast is for sunshine."

CHAPTER TWENTY-TWO

HARKEN parked the Harley on Dot Ave and walked a half block to the magic shop on the corner. With Malleus free, he had to act quickly, or he would be lost in the Shadowlands like that boy. What was that adage, there are fates worse than death? Having Malleus feed off his spirit for eternity was the worst fate of all. But ridding himself of his duty to the Connings was proving more complicated than he had hoped. The plan had seemed easier when the Conning in question wasn't a slip of a girl with eyes like spring water.

He pushed the heavy oak door open. An iron bell clacked, and he felt a rush of heat and smelled a fragrance like licorice. The store was filled with toys and games, books and other strange merchandise for sale in gaudy packaging—not the kind of goods he'd expected. He scanned the windows to make sure he'd not been followed, then closed the shades and turned the OPEN sign to CLOSED.

"Isn't this a magic shop?" he asked the clerk, an older teen with pale skin and black lipstick. It felt like a magic shop. Smelled like one, too, that unmistakable scent that he had followed here.

"A magic *trick* shop," she said with her back to him, her voice dripping with ennui. "We sell tricks and costumes. There's no such thing as real . . . magic. Oh my."

Harken smiled—his ability to vex was as strong as ever apparently. Then he inhaled deeply. There was real magic in the air. "Might I speak to the proprietor?"

"You mean, the manager?" She touched her throat lightly and dropped the crystal ball she'd been pricing. It shattered at her feet, but she didn't seem to notice. She inhaled deeply. "You smell amazing."

"Thank you, but it's dangerous to get close to me. I didn't catch your name?"

"Veronica. Veronica Hannigan."

Harken smiled and noted the blush rising from her

neck and the quick dilation of her pupils. Her nostrils flared, and a bead of perspiration formed on her lip, but he had no time for this, not with Malleus free. "Is this manager a norn?"

"A norn?" she said and bit her bottom lip.

"The manager. She is a norn, correct?"

"Oh, no," the girl said. "She's a Remember. Remember Marie Haverhill." He read her name tag. "Veronica Hannigan, I have your name." He touched the torc on his neck, then fixed her with a gaze, and the girl's jaw went slack. "Be a good sport and lock the door?"

"I need to lock the door," she said dreamily, then turned the lock.

"Thank you," he said. "Where might I find this Remember?"

The girl pointed to a door marked No ENTRY.

"Have a rest, Veronica," he said, "and thank the stars there's nothing special about you."

The room in the back of the magic shop looked ordinary. Harken saw that the shop sold only gimmicks—sleight-of-hand card tricks and cheap toys meant to amuse children. True magic was sterner stuff, practiced only by norns and other cunning folk, and it left a trail of indelible marks that anyone could see, if one knew where to look. Magic also left a smell in the air. Seven sticks of anise were burning in a vase on a cluttered desk.

He took a step, and the floor emitted a high-pitched squeal—a protection ward.

"Show yourself," he said into the void.

He didn't really expect a response, so when silence greeted his request, he walked around the room, kicking aside boxes and crates. There were no other runes, not even a warding spell.

Foolish, he thought. "Show yourself, norn. I won't *ask* again."

Seconds ticked by, and he glanced at the large clock on the wall, a Black Forest cuckoo clock carved in the shape of a buck's head, with two dead birds hanging upside down on either side of the cuckoo.

"I see you like my clock," a woman said behind him. "It's a *Jagdstück*, meaning "hunt piece," from the Black Forest. You should hear the sound the cuckoo makes. Very unique."

"I despise birds," he said, turning. "Especially false ones."

The woman was younger than he'd expected. She had

alabaster skin and high cheekbones hidden behind an iridescent veil. Her neck was long and graceful, as were her hands, which emerged from the ends of her gossamer sleeves and extended when she bowed. She was tall, almost as tall as Harken, and she smelled of oranges and allspice and a glimmer of tobacco.

"Veronica was right. You are very pretty." She reached for him but drew back as if she'd been stung. "But dangerous, too. You move like a great cat on the hunt. A cat with interesting spots."

"My spots are none of your business. How is your magic, norn?"

"Strong enough to see the warding symbols inked into your skin. Enough to sense your temptations."

"But are you strong enough to resist them?" he said, fixing her with his gaze.

"A girl really could get lost in those eyes. If she let herself." She threw her head back and laughed. "What is your name, familiar?"

No, she could not have his name. Names had power. "What's yours?"

"They named me Remember so I would forget nothing."

"They call me Harken. I had another name, but it was lost."

She smiled slyly. "Whom do you serve?"

"Those far greater than you."

"Smelly and bitter and proud," she said. "Not the best mix."

"Remember Haverhill." He caught her eye and tried to hold her. "I have your name."

She laughed, a soft, tittering sound. "I'm not so easily vexed as a shopgirl. Tell me what you seek or leave."

"Freedom," he admitted. "To be unbound from my service. I have faced the abyss for my masters, but I will *not* do so again."

"You made a pact?" She clucked her tongue and circled him. "Signed it with your own blood?"

He held out his hand. A thick, bulbous scar ran the width of his palm. "Proof."

"Fool! Vain, ambitious fool," she whispered. "You've been given a gift, and you want to squander it!"

"What use is a gift if you aren't alive to use it?" It was no gift to face the Shadowless again, not after he had betrayed her. He'd seen what tortures she used on innocents, but that was nothing compared to what she'd do to him. He feared only one thing, and she was walking the earth. "I must be free! Now!"

"Free to be mortal again? To throw away immortality?"

"To die a natural death."

She shook her head. "I can't help. The only one who can unbind you is you."

"You're talking in circles," he said. "How do I unbind myself from the useless, quarrelsome family I serve?"

She picked up a stick of incense and blew softly to redden the ember. "Do you think it's so easy to change your fate? To cast a few spells and unweave your life tapestry?"

"If it were easy," he said, "I would've done it centuries ago."

"What about the family you serve?"

"I pledged my service before I understood how . . . mundane they are. I was promised more."

"Changing one's fate is possible," she said. "But it comes at a cost, a very high cost, and will leave a stain upon you."

He was already stained by his crimes, and what good had it done? What did another mark matter? "I don't give a damn."

"I see that you don't," she said. "What do you have for payment?"

Harken delved into his pocket and pulled out a handful of antique subway tokens. "Pennies for the ferryman."

Remember threw the veil from her face, and her youthful complexion began to crackle like weathered paint. Hand shaking, she examined the treasure in his palm, then cocked her head. "How did you get them?"

"Take as many as you like, in trade for answers."

She pinched her lips. "Norns spend decades searching for just one of these coins, and you offer a handful. Do you understand their value?"

"Do you?" he said, shaking his hand so that the coins rattled like tin bones.

"Three," she said, voice trembling. "I take three coppers as payment. Enough for the future, the past, and the present. And I require one more thing."

"What?"

"A memory."

"Of what?"

"Where your service began."

"Coppers are my payment."

"Great norns cannot do great magic on coppers alone," she said. "It's takes emotions, too, which you damn well know. I'm called Remember for a reason. Give me a memory, and I'll help you."

"Be careful what you wish for, norn." Harken rubbed his forehead with the heel of his hand and touched the bronze torc around his neck. Then he sighed and said in a low voice, as if he feared being overheard, "When she found me, I was a small boy playing in the barnyard of a highlands farmhouse. I was full of life and laughter, my black curls bouncing as I ran from the stalls to the fence, herding eider ducks and geese while my mother watched.

" 'Watch for the wee ones, now,' my mother said.

"I lined up the hatchings and marched through the grass, the birds honking and quacking behind me, laughing and giggling. Then my mother's soft hands lifted me high into the air, and I felt like I was flying. It was my first memory of my mother. It was also my last.

" 'Be a sweet lad now,' my mother said. 'The horse will be wanting her breakfast, too.'

"While Mother tended to the animals, I felt a warm zephyr blowing through my hair. I could still feel the sensation of it on my shoulders, still see the dirt on my hands as I bent down and made cakes in the mud.

"That's when I heard it whisper to me like bells in my ears. I lifted my head to listen. The sound of the bells grew louder, and I dropped the pies back into the mud. Through long grasses I wandered, following the chimes. I don't know how far I went, but there was a hill and a lone tree in the distance. After a while I thought I heard my mother calling my name, but she was drowned out by the music.

"I inched closer to the tree. The music turned to a voice, and it spoke to me, honey sweet. 'Harken to me, my wee child. Hear my voice.'

"I walked onward, closer and closer to the tree, until I broke free of the high grass. All that mattered was the voice that came from the beautiful lady sitting against the trunk. Her hair was black, like mine, and cascaded over her shoulders. She wore a flowing crimson velvet dress that seemed to swallow her. She stretched her arms and smiled as brightly as the sun above us.

"I hesitated because the limbs above her were full of birds—grackles, sparrows, crows, and magpies—all perched in the branches, their eyes trained on me, following my every move.

" 'Sweet child,' the woman said, 'listen to my voice. Come sit on my lap, and I will tell you a story.'

"I took a tentative step forward, but still I hesitated. Then she smiled again, as if her eyes held a secret, and then she held out a honey tart.

" 'For you,' she said, and my hesitation was gone.

"I dived into her lap, and snatched the treat from her hand, greedily eating it, the honey, the sweet honey running down my chin.

" 'More?' I said.

"She laughed and ran her fingers through my hair. 'Soon,' she said. 'What beautiful eyes you have, blue like the seas of Denmark. Not even the Three Norns could resist them.'

"I barely heard her. My thoughts were only for another treat and how I might get one.

" 'Are you an angel?' I said. 'Or a fairy?'

" 'An angel I am not,' she said, laughing. 'Nor am I a lady of the fae, but if ye dare to kiss my head, a treat you'll have to the end of days.'

"She kissed my cheek, and I slept. In that moment I lost all yearning for my mother, the barnyard, and the ducks and goslings that had followed me around. I wanted only another treat, and if this dear lady with the beautiful face and long black hair would give it me, then I was willing to do anything. Anything she asked."

"And did you?"

"Yes," he said after a moment, "until she asked too much."

"A very powerful memory, familiar." Remember carefully plucked the coppers from his hand, then placed two glass vials on the table, one brown, one clear. "To be free of your promise, you betray someone you love. Can you do that?"

"I can." He held the brown bottle to the light. A betrayal would be nothing to him. He loved no one, and he could remember no one ever loving him. "What is this? Tea?"

"Aqua Tofana," she said without looking up from the coins. "Giulia's own recipe, death in two parts. The brown vial sedates the victim, and the clear finishes them off. It will set you free, if you are willing to pay the price."

"I'll pay whatever is necessary."

"Even if the price," she said, pulling the veil over her face as one eye rolled back in her head, "is your soul?"

CHAPTER TWENTY-THREE

THE Beacon School was housed in a four-story brown-stone near downtown. The front had a patch of green lawn, with a flagpole in the middle, and wide, sweeping stairs up to four huge oak doors, like something from a cathedral. The back of the building was plain, with tall windows and a rickety fire escape that likely would collapse in a strong wind.

The building was much older than the school. It was built in the 1870s with a gift from the Boston College of Surgeons. The top three floors were wood and plaster, with sweeping staircases and high transoms. The basement was dank and moldy, a former morgue where medical students practiced on cadavers and stray animals alike. Rumor had it that the first dean paid grave robbers, and supposedly there were still jars of specimens in formaldehyde hidden behind the steel doors that blocked entry to the basement. The ghosts of the dead lingered below, looking for the bodies that had been stolen from their graves.

It made for a good story to scare the freshmen. None of it was true, though. The basement was full of cleaning supplies and broken furniture, and the only thing left of the old morgue was a room with a tiled floor where the Zamboni was parked between games. The basement and the ice rink were connected by a short tunnel. I had passed it hundreds of times after practice on the way to the locker room, and it was no more haunted than the free-range chicken aisle at Urban Market.

I arrived at the school gates, a ten-foot-tall fence made of iron and topped with sharp spikes, fifteen minutes late, which Siobhan reminded me of by texting, **Do you know for whom the bell tolls?**

It tolls for me, I texted. **Again.**

I sprinted down the dimly lit hallway, hit the brakes at my classroom, and almost kissed the floor. Years of scooting around on ice with knives strapped to my feet helped me keep my balance. I righted myself and stopped at the door labeled "US History: SAXON." Through the glass I could see my AP teacher, Mrs. Saxon, pointer stuck in hand, showing a PowerPoint about *The Crucible*.

The Beacon social studies department believed in teaching history through literature, so it felt like we had English twice a day. Since Ma was doing costumes for the Shubert's revival of *The Crucible*, my family had lived and breathed the Salem witch trials for weeks.

Saxon had spent four classes lecturing about the Communist hysteria of the fifties and Arthur Miller's attempt to draw attention to it. Why couldn't we just read the play? Or better yet, go watch it? Who even thought reading a play was a good way to appreciate it? Did people study screenplays instead of watching the movie? Shakespeare was right when he wrote, "The play's the thing."

Thankfully Siobhan, who was wearing thick-framed glasses and a kerchief to tie up her hair, like a myopic Rosie the Riveter, was sitting near the door. Saxon always locked it after the tardy bell. If you came late, you had to knock and wait, then recite from an important work. Yesterday I had recited the Preamble, which was enough blessings of liberty to last a posterity.

I tapped the window and mouthed, Let me in.

Siobhan shook her mop of black hair, no.

I nodded, yes.

Siobhan pointed at Saxon. No.

I shook my fist. Yes!

Siobhan stuck out her tongue.

I made a kissy face, then imitated a guppy by putting both hands beside my ears and crossing my eyes. Siobhan laughed and mimed applause. She held a finger up, waiting for an opportunity, then sprang for the door.

I slipped inside as Saxon's voice droned, "Inspired to write the play by the House Un-American Activities Committee, led by a certain senator from Wisconsin. Does anyone know his name?"

Shoes in hand, I slid into an empty desk. "The weirdest thing happened," I whispered to Siobhan. "Devon was—"

"Miss Conning," Mrs. Saxon said. "Detention for your second tardy, unless you'd like to say the Preamble?"

"I'll take Classroom Punishments for two hundred, Alex." I stood and began reciting the tardy passage. "You cannot hear the Shadowless when her breath is in your ear. You cannot see the Shadowless when she raises up her shears." What the hell? How did that come out of my mouth?

"Salty!" Siobhan whispered and gave me a surreptitious fist bump.

"That is not," Saxon said, like each syllable was imprinted by a tax stamp, "from the Constitution."

"It's not?" I said. "But that's the way they did it on *Schoolhouse Rock*."

Siobhan started to sing, "We the people—"

"Be quiet!" Saxon said. "Now, do you or do you not know the senator's name?"

"Me?" I said.

"Is there another Willow Jane in this classroom? On this planet, for that matter?"

"Well, I am pretty unique," I replied tartly. Where the hell did that come from? Since when did I get salty with a teacher?

"I sincerely doubt that," Saxon said flatly. "Answer the question correctly, and I'll forget the detention."

"Uh." I glared at Siobhan, mouthing, Help me! "Um."

Siobhan shrugged, as if to say, Why're you asking me?

"I know the answer, Mrs. S." I mimed tugging a hat onto my head. "I just need a minute to put on the ol' thinking cap."

Saxon tapped her foot. "With each passing moment, I

grow less interested in anything you have to say."

"That's what her husband said last night," Siobhan said to take the heat off me, and the room erupted with laughter.

"Out!" Mrs. Saxon screamed. "To the dean's office, Siobhan. I've had enough of your mouth!"

"That's what he said," Siobhan said.

Saxon whacked her lectern with the pointer stick. "That will be quite enough!"

"That's what he said," Siobhan said, "when she offered him seconds."

Mrs. Saxon snapped the stick in half. "In all my years in the classroom, I have never—"

I jumped up and announced, "Joseph McCarthy!"

"What?" Mrs. Saxon said. "What did you say?"

Siobhan was just trying to protect me, so I couldn't let her get kicked out. She and the dean of students were literally on a first-name basis, and he'd warned her that one more "episode" with Mrs. Saxon would earn her three days of OSS and no D1 scholarship offers. She couldn't get suspended, not with the game against All Saints coming up. She was our only chance of winning. And she was my best friend. My only true friend.

"The name of the senator was Joseph McCarthy," I said quickly. "Arthur Miller wrote the play as a modern protest against the actions of the House Un-American Activities Committee, likening its actions to witch hunts. By the way, McCarthy was a senator, so he didn't actually chair the Un-American Activities Committee, since it was in the House."

"Wicked," Siobhan whispered. "Somebody's been cribbing off teh Wikipedia."

I snapped my fingers. "Just call me Wicked-pedia, bitches!" Oh my god, what have I done? Bitches? Why did I call them bitches? Ma was going to kill me. The dean was going to suspend me, too. I had never even been to the dean. Ever. I rubbed my face, stunned at my own stupidity. "I wish I'd just answered the stupid question."

The words had barely escaped my tongue when I heard the xylophone noise and colors swirled like a rainbow toilet flushing in my brain. The fabric of reality whipped around and around, and I found myself slipping into my desk.

It was déjà vu all over again.

Mrs. Saxon faced the class. "Miss Conning, nice to see you've shown up. Detention for your second tardy. Now, do you know the senator's name?"

"Me?"

"Is there another Willow Jane in this classroom? On this planet, for that matter?"

"Um . . . no?"

Saxon crinkled her nose. "Answer the question correctly, and I'll forget detention."

It was as if somebody had hit the rewind button on reality. I was really getting a do-over? I glanced at Siobhan, who gave no indication that something weird was going on.

"Joseph McCarthy." I squinted at the too bright lights. "Arthur Miller wrote the play as a modern protest against the actions of the Un-American Activities Committee, likening its actions to witch hunts."

"Somebody's been cribbing off teh Wikipedia," Siobhan said.

This time I kept my mouth shut. No *wicked*. Definitely no *bitches*.

"I'm impressed, Conning," Mrs. Saxon said. "From your grade on *The Scarlet Letter* test, I assumed you only read *SparkNotes*. Now class, back to the PowerPoint."

Her voice trailed away. What had just happened? I was no stranger to déjà vu, but this, this was totally different.

It didn't just *feel* like I'd experienced this before—I *knew* I had.

"Hey, you okay?" Siobhan whispered. "You look like you saw a ghost."

Because I did.

Myself.

"Can I get an aspirin?" I whispered. "My head's killing me."

"What about water?"

"I don't need no stinking water."

It was a lie. I was so thirsty I could drink a whole gallon. Siobhan dug two tablets from her purse and put them in my palm. There was a red, angry bump on my thumb. I touched it, and a jolt of electric pain arched up my arm. The aspirin tumbled from my hand and rolled under a bookcase.

"Stop!" I whispered.

The aspirin stopped on edge, unmoving. So did everything else: Siobhan, the other kids, even Saxon. Everything she had written—the week's vocab words, the day's agenda, a list of due dates for assignments—had been erased from the whiteboard. In its place were large red letters. They were turned at crazy angles, some backward, as if the writer had been blindfolded and dyslexic.

And if you feel the Shadowless
When she blankets you with chill,
Do not accept her cold caress—
For the Shadowless will kill.

It was just like the poem on the sidewalk—this time in marker instead of chalk. I picked up an eraser and wiped out the first line of the poem, just like it had been removed from the sidewalk.

But you weren't the one who washed it off then, I thought. At the time I'd been so freaked out by Devon that I missed that little detail. Someone else had seen the poem. Someone else knew about it. Knew about the Shadowless.

Knew about me.

CHAPTER TWENTY-FOUR

TWO long, bony fingers groped beneath the cabinet. With a soft clink they found the object they sought, a sewing needle several inches long. As the hand withdrew the needle from the darkness, it glinted in the sunlight streaming through the windows of the magic shop.

"I believe," the strange customer said, holding up the needle, "that you may have dropped this."

A sign behind the register read Do NOT TOUCH COSTUMES WITHOUT GLOVES. The Magic Shop was the only place in South Boston that custom-tailored authentic costumes, and Veronica, who had come into work feeling hung over even though she hadn't been drinking, preferred that customers make appointments for fittings in advance. She especially didn't like strangers dropping in unannounced, like the weird one here now, wearing a stained trench coat and a dirty fedora pulled low. At the customer's feet lay dozens of pins, which Veronica had dropped when she turned and shrieked.

The empty pin box still clutched in her hands, Veronica winced. "T-thanks," she said, but didn't mean it.

"Nothing delights us more than chaos."

"Delights?"

The stranger smiled through broken teeth and black gums, sending a shiver down Veronica's spine. She quickly grabbed a U-shaped magnet to clean up the pins. Should she call Remember? She was taking lunch at home, trusting Veronica with the shop, which she hardly ever did, but Remember usually dealt with the really freaky customers, and Veronica stuck to the awkward magician wannabes. Maybe if she just took her time cleaning up the pins, the freaky guy would leave? Or was it a woman? Who could tell with that outfit?

The stranger examined a bolt of red silk, rubbing the fabric with fingers tipped with broken, yellowed nails.

"Hey!" Veronica grabbed a pair of white gloves. "Don't

touch the fabrics. The oils from your skin will ruin them. They are pretty expensive, and you don't look like—"

The stranger turned, slowly and deliberately, like a corpse twisting in its grave. "You will find our skin is quite . . . parched."

Veronica, pressing a black lace sleeve to her nose, backed away until she was safely behind the counter. "Can I show you a costume? Sexy vampire? Slutty werewolf?"

"We seek . . . an egg."

"So yeah, this is a magic slash costume shop? We don't sell eggs."

The stranger stared into Veronica's eyes, and she felt herself getting colder. Goose pimples rose on her skin, and she shivered. Her eyes rolled back. Her mouth went slack.

"It is an unusual egg," the stranger said, her voice sounding like it was underwater. "A *special* egg, with an iron needle the length of one's hand—a bodkin."

"A needle?" Veronica said dreamily. "I might be able to help you find one."

"It would be a coveted possession, an heirloom passed through generations."

"My boss works with a few expert seamstresses," Veronica said, opening a ledger on the counter.

The stranger slapped a necrosed hand over the page. "I do not seek a few!" she snapped. "I seek only one, an artist with the needle, one with an . . . uncanny touch."

"Uncanny?" Veronica said. "I don't know of anybody like that."

"Liar, liar, flesh afire." The stranger grabbed Veronica's arm and inhaled deeply. "The nornish stink perfumes your skin." The stranger sniffed again. "Would you care to keep it?"

"Keep what?"

"Your skin."

Veronica wanted to say yes, but she couldn't find the word. Her mouth wouldn't open, and her tongue wouldn't move. She desperately wanted to run, to flee this horrible creature and disgusting stench, but something held her in place.

"Speak."

"My friend who's big into cosplay? She hires this one lady." Veronica pointed to a line on the ledger. "She does period costumes, hand sewn, if you're interested. My friend swears she works magic with a needle."

"We have no interest in magic," the stranger hissed. "Only in the needle."

"Y-yes." Veronica quickly scribbled the address on a scrap of paper. "I think she's the one you need."

"Pray that she is." When she opened the door, the iron bell made no sound. "Else we shall return and bestow even more gifts upon you."

The stranger snapped two bony fingers and turned away.

Veronica ran to lock the door. She had taken only three steps before she gagged on something lodged in her throat.

A foul odor made her lungs burn, and she fell into a violent coughing spell that dropped her to her knees. Eyes stinging with tears, she crawled to the door and flipped the lock. *Safe,* she thought, before a furious itch began in her nose. She rubbed her face, an attempt to scratch what couldn't be scratched. Her eyes watered fiercely, and mucus poured from her nostrils, dripping off her chin onto her black lace shirt. So much that she gagged and coughed, then sneezed.

A mass of black mucus and blood landed on the floor. Veronica leaned close and examined it, not believing it had come out of her body, until the mass buzzed and spread four veiny wings. She screamed and tried to back away. Her boot heels slipped as she tried to stand, leaving long marks in the tile. Her fingers found the lock.

It wouldn't turn.

The thing grew larger. More wings sprouted, and the shop filled with buzzing. A dozen moths hatched at once, followed by a hundred, then a thousand, until it was a swarm. The swarm took flight, and Veronica covered her face with her hands to ward them off. The girl didn't interest them. The silk did, and they descended on the bolts like a biblical plague, consuming the fine fabric like blowflies devouring a corpse.

CHAPTER TWENTY-FIVE

"WAS that bizarre or what?" Siobhan followed me into Mr. Pearce's AP English classroom. "Did you see her fire the pen at me? Saxon's totally lost it!"

Honestly, I hadn't seen Saxon throw the pen or anything else. I remembered erasing the board and walking back to my seat. After that the room spun, and I woke up to find everything in a shambles and Saxon screaming that she wasn't paid enough to put up with our BS. She had stormed out a minute before the bell, leaving the class too stunned to talk. That lasted about ten seconds, then the room erupted again, and we all started talking at once.

"Totally bizarre," I said, sliding into the middle seat of

the center row and taking out my homework. It was one of many bizarre things, and they just kept piling up. "Oh, crap."

The letter. I had left my dad's letter on the coffee table. In the confusion after, I had left for school without it—and without reading all of it. It was going to drive me crazy not knowing what else he wrote.

Siobhan sat in the seat behind me. "What's wrong?"

"My homework!" I said. "I did most of it Friday and then forgot about it. I usually go over my planner on Sunday, but with the party, I didn't."

"Did somebody say party?" Kelly dumped herself into a desk next to Siobhan. "Couldn't have been you losers, since you guys totally bailed last night. Wait till you hear what happened!"

Actually, I really had forgotten my homework. Mr. Pearce had assigned twenty vocab words over the weekend. I had fifteen done. Maybe if I worked through a couple before the bell . . . I got down to work, then looked up at Kelly and said, "Can I borrow two hundred dollars?" It just popped out, like the cork on a bottle of skunky champagne.

Kelly did bat an eye. "I spent my allowance already, but if you return the scarf I gave you, it's worth three hundred plus tax. The gift receipt's in the box."

"But," I said, "it was a present."

"So? I always return re-gifts and buy what I want." She waved a hand, like it was nothing. "You guys want to hear what happened or not?"

Siobhan pulled her pop bottle glasses down her nose. "You jerks probably just paid some homeless dude to score a six-pack and sat on the Common drinking it."

"So not true." Kelly scoffed. "We drank it in the cemetery."

"Underage drinking with dead people." Siobhan rolled her eyes. "What a wicked pisser that is."

"I know, right?"

"Sarcasm, Butt Chin."

"Know what?" Kelly said. "I'm not even going to tell you what happened."

"Guys, please," I said, a little too harshly. My mind was racing. If the scarf was worth that much, then I was saved! After the game I'd take the bus home, return the scarf to Neiman Marcus, then catch a bus to Louie's. It would be tight, but it was doable. Yes! No! The receipt had blown away when Devie opened the bag. "Dammit!"

"Somebody's grumpy," Kelly said.

"I'm not grumpy," I said.

"Maybe it was having her sweet sixteen ruined by jerk-face assholes," Siobhan said.

"Don't be so hard on yourself," Kelly said. "You might be a jerkface, but not an asshole."

"Ha freaking ha," Siobhan said.

"Seriously." Kelly's voice dropped low and well, serious, along with an unfamiliar quake of fear. "Some stuff happened last night, and Willow Jane, there's something I need to ask you."

"Just a sec," I said, scribbling furiously.

"Like what stuff?" Siobhan snapped. "Got something to get off your chest, Kells? Other than Will Patrick?"

Kelly's face turned whiter. "What—what about Will Patrick?"

The bell rang, and Mr. Pearce closed the door. "Attention, inmates! Pencils down! Hands in the air! You guys had all weekend to do twenty vocab words, so if you didn't finish, may the Lord have mercy on your souls."

Mr. Pearce was in his early thirties and a huge fan of prison movies like *Cool Hand Luke* and *The Green Mile*. His room was, air quotes, The Block, and when you got sent to the dean, you served time in, air quotes, The Box.

He called it thematic teaching. Siobhan called it a blatant and pathetic attempt at being, air quotes, cool.

"Pass your papers up!" Pearce said and hit Start on his laptop.

His PowerPoint on the importance of comic relief in *Macbeth* was met with a chorus of boos.

"Bubble, bubble, toil and trouble." Siobhan cackled behind me. "Only Pearce could make witches more boring than Julius Caesar."

"Seriously, Willow," Kelly whispered. "We need to talk."

The lights dimmed, and the LED projector cast a warm blue glow over the room.

Time.

My constant nemesis.

I passed my incomplete paper to the kid in front of me, one of Will Patrick's douchey bros.

"Got one for the Box, Mr. Pearce!" Jerk Bro called me out. "Conning didn't finish her homework! Dead girl walking! Dead girl walking!"

"Be quiet," I whispered.

"You wish!"

"I wish," I said, snapping my fingers, "you'd just shut it!"

Something yanked on my belly button, and I felt my

stomach twist into a knot. A gurgling sound came from Jerk Bro's throat, and click, he stopped talking.

He wasn't the only one. The room, which had been filled with the shuffle of papers and the whir of the projector fan, was silent. Euphoric giggles rose in my stomach like tiny bubbles.

"I'll take that," I said, grabbing my paper from Jerk Bro's rigored fingers.

In the dead silence I raced through the words, quickly filling the rest of the page. "Finished!" I said and raised my paper, expecting time to thaw.

But it didn't. Kelly's face was still frozen, her eyes at half-mast, and Siobhan was holding a lock of black hair in mid twirl.

The room was a graveyard.

No one moved.

No one spoke.

No one breathed.

They're all dead, I thought, but knew it wasn't true. They were just very, very still, ships stuck in the doldrums. Then from the hallway I heard a knocking sound, a periodic rapping noise like the one from my dream, testing every door as it moved methodically down the hall.

Something was coming.

Coming for me.

I covered my ears and pressed my eyes shut, then slid under my desk. The knocking grew louder and closer, and like a little girl hiding from monsters under her blanket, I stayed as still and quiet as a mouse, praying the noise would pass me by.

The knocking stopped. The old wood door shook, and the brass knob rattled. Above it, the glass transom was open to let in the air. It let in a smell, too, potent and earthy like a fresh grave, along with a voice that I recognized.

"Willow Jane?" Will Patrick called softly. "Open the door and let her in or bad things will happen."

"Get the fuck away from me!" I screamed.

"Bad things will happen, Willow Jane," he said, then crooned in a ghostly voice. "Willow, Will-ow Jaaaane."

I buried my face into the crook of my arm. The room swam, and a xylophone murmur filled my ears, before it turned into the whispers of my dead girl calling from the bottom of a dark well, "Come drown, come drown, come drown."

"Willow Jane," Mr. Pearce bellowed. "Conning! Back in your seat!"

"Huh?" I said, my brain full of voices.

On the board, written in letters of red ink, was another verse:

And if you feel the Shadowless
When she blankets you with chill.
Do not accept her cold caress
For the Shadowless will kill.

"That's your handwriting, Conning! In permanent marker!" He swiped the whiteboard to prove it. "Out of my classroom!"

"Willow didn't do anything." Siobhan protested. "She was sitting right here the whole time."

"Of course you would be involved, Siobhan," he yelled. "To the Box! Both of you!"

He stood shaking, waiting for us to gather our things. I'd never been kicked out of class. I wasn't sure what to take, so I packed everything and followed Siobhan like a child.

"Come with me, young Padawan," Siobhan said as we left. "Now you will know the power of the dark side. And if you're lucky, there'll be cookies."

CHAPTER TWENTY-SIX

"DEAD girls walking!" Siobhan danced into the dean's office, which was on the bottom floor of Beacon Hall. "Hey, Jaybird. Miss me?"

Mr. Johnston, dean of students, was in his early sixties, with salt-and-pepper hair. He wore a white button-down, khakis, and scuffed loafers with no socks. His nickname had followed him from Boston Public, where he'd worked thirty years before coming to Beacon.

I hung back, clutching my book bag and wondering if I had lost my mind.

"Good morning, Miss Ferro," he said. "What was your crime this time?"

"Crime?" Siobhan plopped into a chair and propped her red plaid Chucks on his desk. "I'm innocent, I tell ya. Filthy rotten screws."

"Mr. Pearce wouldn't think his prison motif was so clever," Jaybird said, "if he had to listen to all the bad James Cagney imitations."

"James who?"

"The actor you're imitating so horribly."

"No shit?" Siobhan snatched a snow globe from his desk. It was one of twenty, all depicting different cities— New York, Chicago, San Francisco. She was holding Phoenix. "It doesn't snow in Phoenix, by the way."

Jaybird confiscated the globe. "What's the charge?"

"Writing on the board without a license," she said.

"Thirty minutes of wiping tables at lunch," he said, handing down the sentence. "Go back to class and behave."

"What about my co-conspirator?" she said and pushed me inside. "Your turn, nerd girl."

I waved. "Hi."

"Hello, Willow Jane," Jaybird said. "Did you need something?"

"Mr. Pearce sent me," I said quietly. It was my first visit to the Box, and I didn't know the drill. "I wrote on the board and told this douchebag guy to shut it."

"If you told a guy to shut it," Jaybird said, trying to hide a smirk, "then he deserved it. So thirty minutes of wiping tables at lunch with James Cagney here, and we'll call it even."

"Yes, sir," I said and shook his hand.

He gave me a quizzical look, and I felt like it was the most awkward thing possible, so I yanked my hand away and in the process, swatted the closest snow globe and sent Salem MA falling toward the floor. It turned end over end, the witch inside tumbling with her broomstick through the scattered bits of snow. My hands were faster than my mind, though, and I snatched it out of the air.

"Save us," the globe whispered. "Before the shadows fall."

"What?" I said.

"I said, nice catch." Jaybird took the snow globe and set it on his desk. "Got it at the witch museum. I'd hate to see it broken."

"Me too," I said and clumsily picked up my book bag. "It's bad luck to mess with witches."

CHAPTER TWENTY-SEVEN

SIOBHAN was waiting for me by the stairs. "So what happened?"

"Same sentence as you. I can't believe he let us off that easy," I said as we walked back to class.

"I can't believe you said douchebag," Siobhan said, "in front of the dean."

"I did not say douchebag."

"It rolled right off your tongue like a little nugget of poetry."

"I made nuggets?" I covered my mouth and stopped short. "Oh my god! I don't even remember nuggets. I need to apologize!"

Siobhan grabbed my arm, steering me back to class. "No matter how many tables you have to wipe or toilets you have to scrub, never apologize, not a single time."

"But."

"No buts."

"But."

"While we're on the subject of butts," she said and her voice turned serious, "there's something you need to know."

"What's wrong with my butt?" I cocked my head and waited, hoping it was good news for once.

The day had been weird enough without Siobhan confessing some secret sin. Not Siobhan. After Dad died, she was the only person I could depend on. She was my rock in a stormy sea, but if I ever told her that, she'd make fart noises and pretend not to hear me.

She lowered her voice. "It's about Butt Chin and Will Patrick."

"What about him?" I drew back. "I dumped him. So who gives a shit about him?" I paused. "Is that the right kind of attitude? Too forceful?"

She took me by the shoulders. "That skank Kelly, our friend? Our effing friend and teammate? She was with him last night."

"No, she left with us."

"Yeah, and then she snuck out and met him and that jerk Flanagan at the cemetery to drink a few cold ones. Guess what time she got back home?"

"I'm not guessing."

"Guess."

"I'm not guessing."

"Guess!"

"Midnight!"

"Guess again."

I cut her a look and folded my arms. "I'm so not in the mood for this."

"Four A.M. Four in the morning. Her neighbor told this girl who told me. Can you believe that? And she had the nerve to chat away in Pearce's class like nothing had happened. Does she not know the rule? Thou shalt not screw your friend's ex. Oh my god, I want to punch her in the face. I swear, if she was on All Saints, I'd slew-foot her till the ice busted her ass."

"Were," I said in a faraway voice. The news was supposed to make me mad, but all I felt was sadness. Kelly was my next best friend, not my rock like Siobhan, but still a friend. If I couldn't trust her not to betray me, who could I trust? Was anyone really, truly my friend?

"Were what?"

"If she *were* on All Saints, not *was*."

"Seriously?" she said, all cranked up. "Your friend betrays you, and you correct my grammar?"

"What time did Will Patrick get home?"

"That's just it," she said. "He didn't go home. In first period he shows up late, dressed in filthy clothes like he'd been sleeping on the ground. This girl I talked to says he looks stoned."

"Will Patrick doesn't do drugs."

"And friends don't date friend's exes. He's in chemistry this period. Let's go find him."

She took my arm, but I locked my heels. The thought of seeing his face made my guts clench. Don't set eyes on him, I thought. The crows will see you. "Not now. We've got to get back to class."

Siobhan started to argue, but she was stopped by a sudden rush of green skirt and button-down Oxford cloth that slammed her against the wall.

"Dude!" she said and pushed Kelly off. "What the hell?"

"Sorry! Sorry, but holy Jeez!" Kelly said. "Did you guys hear about Flanagan?"

"Him, too?" Siobhan said. "Damn, girl, you get around."

Kelly drew back like she'd been slapped. "Huh?"

"What happened to Flanagan?" I asked, something telling me it wouldn't be a good answer.

Kelly's hands were shaking. "He's dead."

"No way!" Siobhan said. "You're lying."

"I'd never! It's on Snapchat," she said. "There's pictures and everything. You know that the cemetery, the one on Tremont?"

"The one you snuck out to last night?" Siobhan said.

"Right. That one," Kelly said, not caring that she had just confessed. "Me and Will Patrick met him there last night. They'd found this tomb, and they said there was treasure in it."

Siobhan shoved her phone in my face. "It's true! Look!"

The picture of the tomb made my head spin. I could smell the earthy malodor of damp ground and the decaying tang of mold. It clung in the air like foul perfume, and it reminded me of the cemetery where my dad was buried. I had smelled that odor before, in Pearce's classroom when Kelly came in. That's why Will Patrick smelled like damp earth. He had spent the night in an open grave.

"Yeah, I see the hole," Siobhan said. "But no dead guy."

"Nobody takes pictures of a dead kid," Kelly said. "They found him in it. That's not enough for you?"

Her breath smells like raw sewage, I thought, and it made me want to scratch her eyes out. My hands closed into fists, and I took a step toward her before recoiling, horrified at what I was about to do. "Guys?" I said, my stomach twisting. "I'm definitely going to hurl."

Siobhan pressed a finger against the bottom of my nose, a trick that hockey players used to keep from barfing on the ice. "Breathe. It'll pass."

It didn't pass. I leaned over and exhaled and opened my hands. They were marked with half moons from where my nails had dug into my palms. The urge to claw Kelly's eyes out had passed, but the stink hadn't, and it was growing by the second.

I had to leave.

Siobhan looked at Kelly. "You're hiding something," she said. "I can see it in your eyes. You look guilty as sin."

"What are you, psychic?" Kelly said.

"You and Will Patrick were in that cemetery with Flanagan, and you didn't get back till four. What took you so long to get home?"

"It's not passing," I said.

"Four?" Kelly shook her head. "It was before that. I don't know shit about Flanagan. I—" She blinked twice, then ran for the exit, calling over her shoulder, "Left something in my car! I'll be back!"

"Breathing's not helping," I said.

But Siobhan wasn't listening. "I was just baiting her, but wow! She's scared out of her mind. I'm definitely going back to tell Jaybird." She dropped her backpack. "Watch this for me?"

"What about class?" I rasped.

"Kelly's gone full psycho," she said. "That comes before AP English."

Dead girl walking, I thought, but didn't know how close to the truth it was.

CHAPTER TWENTY-EIGHT

WILL Patrick walked across the parking lot, head down, hands in pockets. The wind blew his blond hair from his face, turning his cheeks so red that he looked even more like a cherub. What he was thinking, though, was nothing angelic. He had awakened at the bell in a pool of his own drool with his dirty hair matted to his moist ear.

Mrs. Rosalind was standing over him, and the rest of the classroom was empty. "Late night?" she said.

"Huh?"

"I said, late night? You're looking rough, Will. Did you sleep in those clothes?" Mrs. Rosalind asked and waved away the odors wafting from his hair. "Did you even go home last night?"

"Yeah," he said, but realized that he had no recollection of it. He remembered jumping into the tomb with Flanagan and Kelly, then the sound of a bell ringing and chairs scraping. The space between was blank. No, not blank. It wasn't empty at all. It was filled with swirling, poisoned mists, bitter cold, and the violent whispers deep in pain. "No, wait. That's not right. I spent the night with my boy Flanagan."

"Flanagan? Isn't that the boy who died?"

"Died?" he croaked. His throat was hot and inflamed, and the word turned to dust in his mouth. "No, no, I just saw him."

"Maybe it's another boy with the same name? It breaks my heart when a young person passes away." Mrs. Rosalind turned away as her students started filing in. "Jacob! Taylor! Stop throwing paper!"

Will Patrick reached for his backpack and realized it wasn't there. He patted his pockets. His car keys were in the left front, and clumps of dirt fell out of the back pocket when he pulled out his wallet to check for cash and his ID. Both were still there, though his wallet smelled of mold. He sniffed his pits and gagged.

What the hell happened to Flanagan? he wondered as he

pushed through the knot of girls trying to enter the room, then stumbled into the hallway on half-numb legs. What if somebody had snitched about the treasure hunt? What's going to happen when the cops showed up at the front door? His mother was a lawyer, for chrisssake. She would get him off, but he hadn't done anything. Flanagan was the grave-robbing thug, not him.

He ached for a beer. There was a six-pack hidden in his car trunk in case of emergencies, so instead of going to his next class, he took the back stairs that led to the student parking lot. He threw a hand up to block the blinding sunlight and stumbled toward his spot.

Beer. He needed beer and a change of clothes and a shower. But mostly, beer. He was so lost in his yearning that he walked right past a man in a dark hoodie.

The man fell in line behind him.

Will shuffled through his key ring until he found the right fob. The trunk popped open, and he was reaching for the six-pack when the hooded figure slammed the lid down, pinning Will's hand.

"Fuck!" he yelled. "Dude!"

Harken put a finger to his lips, and Will Patrick fell silent. "Got a light?"

"I don't smoke, sir."

"The nicotine stains on your fingers say you do." Harken inhaled deeply. "So does the scent of tobacco on your clothes."

"Do I know you?" Will Patrick blinked slowly. His brain was trying to place Harken, who seemed awfully familiar. "You a cop? Because I've never smoked a day in my life."

"You're a rotten liar." Harken grabbed Will Patrick's shirt and removed a crumpled pack of cigarettes from his pocket. "And if you aren't careful, you're going to be a dead man."

"You can't kill me for a couple cigs."

"This isn't about cigarettes." Harken pushed the lid down, and Will Patrick grunted. "I've half a mind to let you suffer the same fate as your friend. The one I found hanging this morning in the burying ground."

"Flanagan?" Will Patrick's face blanched, and his Adam's apple bobbed as if he'd swallowed a hot ember. Flanagan's screams filled his ears. Flanagan, lying on the ground, his throat torn out, blood gurgling from it.

"You fools had no inkling what you unleashed, did you?" Harken pushed Will Patrick hard against the bumper. "That boy is dead, and you'll be next. That's how the Shadowless pays for treasure."

Treasure. They'd been hunting treasure. Him, Flanagan, and Kelly. That's right, she'd been there, too. "Please, you have to help me."

"Do I?" Harken stared hard into Will Patrick's eyes. Shadows moved in them, deep in the pupils. "You wouldn't want the help I can give."

"She's coming for me," he whispered. "Hide me, please."

"That's not a terrible idea." Harken punched Will Patrick's jaw, and the light in his eyes went out.

Harken rolled Will Patrick into the trunk. He tucked his elbows and knees inside and stuffed an emergency blanket under his head for a pillow. If the boy were lucky, the Shadowless would only kill him. So young, so arrogant, and so ripe for the picking. He had once been just like this boy, brash, handsome, thinking that the world was his oyster, but the oyster belonged to the Shadowless, and so had Harken.

Why this boy? Why now? He was too old to lure from his crib and too ordinary to ever make a good familiar. No time to wax philosophical, he reminded himself. This was just an unfortunate coincidence—it had nothing to do with him or the family he served.

Before he closed the lid, Harken confiscated Will
Patrick's student ID. The photo looked nothing like him.
Will Patrick's hair was different and longer, and his face
was moon shaped, while Harken's was angular and lean.

"Close enough in a pinch."

The next step was to find the Conning girl, then keep
her under his thumb while deciding the best way to pro-
ceed. The vial of Aqua Tofana was in his pocket, awaiting
the perfect moment. He felt an unfamiliar pang of guilt.
The thought of killing her made his stomach lurch. He had
sworn to defend the Conning family, and the Fates had
special punishments for oath breakers. Nothing they could
do, though, terrified him as much as the thought of the
Shadowless's punishment for his betrayal.

"Damn," he said and dropped the car keys in the trunk.
He slammed the lid. It popped open, and he slammed it
harder. "Damn! Damn! Damn it!"

Overhead, a roll of thunder shook the air. Harken
looked at the sky, then checked his stolen watch. The storm
was coming, and if he didn't act, it would consume him,
too.

Chapter Twenty-Nine

ON the wall of the Beacon School cafeteria, a seventy-two-inch plasma television hung next to a large clock showing the time: 12:01 P.M. Lunch always began at noon sharp, and at the faculty's request, the television was tuned to the local news. It was the teachers' not so subliminal way of exposing us to current events. The lead story was about the cops "still investigating the death of a local boy whose body was found in Granary cemetery this morning."

Flanagan.

He really was dead. We had heard about it all morning, but with social media, you never knew if it was a hoax or a rumor. When your face was on TV, it was as close to the truth as it could get.

Flanagan.

I dropped my book bag on a table and sat down. My shoulder muscles were tied up in knots, and my stomach was tighter than a noose. How had the day gone so wrong so fast? Flanagan was dead, Kelly was acting guilty as sin, and I was seeing and hearing things that made me doubt my sanity. I rubbed my thumb and stared at the clock. It was already past noon, and so far I had no plan for getting the egg out of hock.

"Hey baby sweetie honey darling." Siobhan dropped her stuff next to mine and opened a container of juice. She chugged half in one gulp. "Ah, just the healthy dose of vitamin C, carbs, and fluids I need to kick some All Saints ass. Am I right?"

"Right."

She held up a fist. "I said, AM I RIGHT?"

Without much enthusiasm, I tapped it. "Right as rain."

"Damn right, you mean. Right as rain makes no sense. Rain doesn't have hands."

"It's an English idiom, and right means straight or going in one direction. Rain is straight down."

"Unless the wind is blowing. And only you would know that."

"Right as rain," I said because word games were the least of my worries today.

The camera switched back to the anchor, who gave a brief update on the day's hottest news story, the death of James Flanagan of Dorchester. Now the whole of Beacon School knew his name. Some rumors said he was attacked by feral cats, and others said he'd been stabbed. There was also the rumor that Will Patrick had been involved. He'd been acting weird in chemistry, then he'd disappeared. His car was still in the student lot, which I could confirm by standing on my chair and looking out the windows. There it was, his dad's old Beemer. It was nicely appointed for a cliché.

"Willow Jane." Siobhan looked up from her grinder. "Why're you standing on the chair?"

"It's terrible," I said, sitting down. "Poor Flanagan."

"Sucks, doesn't it? I read online that it was just a freak accident." Siobhan, always the pragmatist, added, "Or something."

"But we knew him. And he died."

"Yes, we met him, but shit happens," she said, trying

to sound harsher than I knew she felt. "Let's talk about All Saints, which is who we need to be concentrating on."

I touched my head. My scalp felt sore, like I'd been brushing my hair against the grain. "Okay. All Saints."

"Siobhan knows best."

"Hey, losers." Kelly plopped down next to me. "What does Siobhan know best?"

"Hey, Kelly," I said, not wanting to be rude but unable to hide my hurt feelings.

"What do you want, shitburger?" Siobhan didn't share my need for politeness. "Find that thing in your car?"

"Car? Oh, yeah. That. Sure, I got it." Kelly flashed an innocent smile that wasn't fooling anyone. "Did you call me a shitburger?"

"She didn't mean that," I said.

"Hell, yes, I meant it. Don't go nicey-nice with her. She went out with your ex before the spit had dried on his lips, then lied about it to our faces."

"Ew," Kelly said. "Way to be graphic."

"Too graphic," I said.

"Way to stab your friend in the back."

"You guys, it wasn't like that." Kelly took a long sip of

Diet Coke. "Okay, maybe it could've been, but Will Patrick was acting all weird, and the cemetery was supercreepy, so nothing happened."

"Except something did happen," I said. Maybe it was the way Kelly angled her head or the way her eyes kept darting from me to Siobhan to the floor like a little bullfinch with no place to perch. "Tell us about it."

"I can't. My brain is fried."

"Tell us," I demanded. No, commanded.

Siobhan shot me a WTF look. I shrugged and nodded at Kelly, who was playing with the tab on her drink.

"Did you hear about Will Patrick coming to school hung over and dressed in dirty clothes?"

"Sort of," I said.

"He was stumbling around like a stoned zombie," Siobhan said.

"Except he wasn't. Stoned, I mean." Kelly took another sip. "He was possessed."

Siobhan burst out laughing. "Possessed by beer maybe."

"Shh," Kelly said, stealing furtive glances around the cafeteria. "You guys will think I'm crazy."

"We think you're a shitburger with extra sauce."

"Well, not with extra sauce," I said and felt bad for

Kelly. She was clearly upset and not in her usual look-at-me way. This wasn't some drummed-up drama. She kept preening her hair, and her gaze darted from me to Siobhan, then back again. "Hey, it's okay," I said. "I'm not mad about Will Patrick. Tell us what's going on. Sisters before misters, right? You can trust us."

"The guys found a tomb, right?" Kelly said. "Down some steps, there was this casket with all sorts of pharaoh pictures and weird writing carved into it."

Runes and hieroglyphs, I thought. To ward off evil. Or to keep it inside.

Siobhan huffed. "You saw this alleged casket?"

"Yeah, but it was dark."

I put a hand on Siobhan's arm to get her to cool it. I meant it when I said Kelly could trust us. "What did they do in the tomb?"

"That's what's so stupid. Will Patrick thought there would be treasure inside, so he and Flanagan opened the casket." She crushed the Coke can in her worried hands. "Surprise, no treasure, just a mummy. Not even a good one. Just bones wrapped in a rotten old sack."

"A shroud?" I asked. "They used to lay a shroud over the dead before they were buried."

"So there were bones," Siobhan said. "That's why you chickened out?"

"I never saw the bones, okay?" Kelly shrugged. "Will Patrick Snapchatted me pics."

"Let's see these alleged pics," Siobhan said.

"It's Snapchat?" Kelly said. "The pics don't save?"

"They do if you turn Save on."

"Well, I didn't, so effing sue me!" Kelly sobbed and hid her face. "I think Will Patrick might have killed him."

"Holy hell," Siobhan said.

"He didn't do it," I said, still confident. "Someone else"—*the Shadowless*—"did."

I winced at the sound of my voice. It rang in my head like a church bell. My knees turned liquid. A droning noise filled my ears, and a rip opened in my vision—a series of alternating red and blue triangles, the aura of a migraine. Please, not a migraine, not before the All Saints game.

"Yo, Willie!" Siobhan snapped her fingers. "Stop zoning out and answer me."

"Huh?" I said, trying to focus. "Answer what?"

"I said, where'd this poem come from? Kelly took one look at it and freaked."

"What poem?"

"This one." Siobhan turned my chin toward the table. In block letters I had written:

You cannot wake the Shadowless
When she sleeps within my bed.
Kiss the lips of the Shadowless
And the morning finds you dead.

I scrubbed it out with my sleeve, and the letters disappeared. "It's dry erase." I sighed, relieved.

"What's with you and the slam tagging? Did you join a nerd gang behind my back?" Siobhan said. "What's the Shadowless?"

"Just," I said. "Just some poem."

"Well, your poem scared Kelly, and she bolted. Again." Siobhan slung her backpack over one shoulder. "I'm going on a shitburger hunt. Come with?"

"The dean said we had to wipe tables."

She pointed at the full cafeteria. "Kids are still eating."

"Hang on." I stepped onto my chair and looked out the cafeteria window at the student parking lot, checking again for Will Patrick's car. A guy in a hoodie was standing near the rich kids' cars. He was tall, and even from a distance, I recognized his face. My eyes lingered for a second. We had met before—the guy who had bumped me on the sidewalk.

Then he looked up at the cafeteria window. He knows me. And I know him, I thought, and promptly puked on the floor.

CHAPTER THIRTY

WHEN they got me to the infirmary, I had vomit all over my shirt and in my hair as well. Siobhan told the nurse I was "wicked sick" and demanded she attend to me immediately. After she reminded Siobhan who the medical professional was, the nurse changed my soiled shirt, wrapped my hair in a towel, and gave me a quick exam.

My fever was 101 degrees, and my body was wracked with chills. I was muttering. The nurse decided I had the flu, but a while later, she did a more thorough exam and found my wounded thumb. The skin was inflamed, red and hot and full of pus.

When she tried to clean it, I sat bolt upright and

screamed. "Stop! Stop it! Get out of my house!"

Siobhan caught me by the shoulders and gave me a hard shake. "Willow Jane," she said, "you're dreaming. Lie back down."

I looked at her blankly. "I am?"

"Some dream, huh?" Siobhan guided me back to the thin mattress. "Want to tell me about it?"

I tried to recall the details, but the dream slipped from my mind like a fistful of sand. "I don't remember."

"Probably for the best," she said. "You have some weird ass dreams."

"Language," the nurse said. "Come on, let's have a look at that thumb. How did you hurt it?"

"Cut it on a pair of scissors."

"Helping your ma, huh?" Siobhan said as the nurse coated my thumb with ointment and wrapped it in gauze. "You working on the Pilgrim costumes, too?"

"No," I said. "She stuck scissors under my pillow to fight a headache."

"Did she now?" The nurse scoffed, drawing the curtain around us. Her voice became a formless mass of sounds. "Never paid much mind to superstitions."

Siobhan gave me a kiss on the forehead. "I'll be back

after geometry. I need my best defender for the game, so get better or else."

"Love you, too," I said, the words sticking to the roof of my mouth like peanut butter.

After Siobhan left, I lay still and quiet, hoping to rest, but my brain had other plans.

"It's blood," I whispered. "Blood's the price of magic."

A prick of pain stabbed my thumb, and I felt something warm ooze down my palm and tickle my wrist. I unwrapped the gauze and found that the wound had ruptured. A silver filament stuck out of it—two inches long and glittering in the fluorescent light.

"What the hell?" I said and squinted at it. Then my eyes fluttered, and I fell into a restless sleep.

"I'm ba-ack!" Siobhan threw open the curtain, and I stuck my hand under the sheet. "Got your ma on the phone," she said. "Feel like talking? Geometry totally sucked, beeteedubs."

I took the phone. "Hello?"

"The nurse called and said you threw up." Ma wasn't one to stand on ceremony in a crisis. "Are you sick?"

"Just something I ate." I forced myself to sound perky.

I was so not feeling perky: Perky was the vertically opposite angle of how I felt. "How the cafeteria passes health inspection, I do not know."

"Can you finish the day?" she said. "The cast's doing final fittings tonight, and I can't get away."

"No problem. We've only got two more classes left."

"Ahem." Siobhan pointed to the clock on the wall. "One more class. Fifth period's almost over."

Seriously? I mouthed. "Ma, I better run."

"You're okay?"

"I'm okay."

"Really okay?"

"Trust me."

"I do," she said. "But a mother can still worry."

I handed the phone back to Siobhan. "Have you seen my sweater?"

"Uh, it's covered in puke?" She threw a sweatshirt on the bed. "I borrowed this from lost and found."

"Beggars can't be choosers, I guess," I said and slid my arms into the sleeves, then glanced at the clock. Five till three. Only four hours left till Louie locked up his pawnshop.

"So that jacked-up thumb?" Siobhan said. "How's it

going to feel in hockey gloves?"

"I played with a broken thumb once, remember?" I said, wobbling from the bed. I was going to need a lot more armor than hockey pads to survive this day. "Where's the nurse?"

"On break. I promised to watch you." Winking, Siobhan pushed aside the curtain, then held the infirmary door open. "Glad you're feeling better. You worried me."

Except I wasn't better. There was definitely something terribly wrong. And not just with me. There was something wrong with a boy getting killed in the cemetery. Something wrong with Will Patrick walking around like a stoner zombie. Something wrong with Kelly being scared of her own shadow. There was something wrong with the way things smelled. With the way light turned colors. With the voice in my head that was haunting me, whispering over and over, "The dead watch you while you sleep."

PART THREE

SINNERS IN THE HANDS OF AN ANGRY GOD

Chapter Thirty-One

THE world had been at war for three days when Remember Haverhill was born in Verdun, a village near Luxembourg and Belgium. She had learned to walk in trenches and wore a gas mask before she had cut all of her teeth. Her father was a Red Cross doctor from England, her mother a farm girl who turned to caretaking when there were too many wounded for the field nurses to keep up.

By the time Verdun was free of war, a million men had suffered there. The fields around Remember's home were choked with their bodies, the night filled with their ghosts. She spoke to the dead, these boys come so far from home to die in muddy trenches, killed by men who were themselves just boys, and she learned how to eat their souls.

Her first was a horseman's boy from Birmingham. There was a field hospital next to her grandfather's farm. She had followed her mother to the tents one pretty spring day when the fighting was at its fiercest. A boy called out to her, and she turned in time to see a mist begin to rise from him. Laughing, she toddled over, reached out a hand, and, as if her fingers were sipping straws, drew the mists into herself.

In later years she would try to find the words for what eating the first soul felt like. It was sweet, she would think, like fresh milk but powerful, too, like pale cognac. There was a smell, too, spun sugar or perhaps plums. Whatever it felt like, it was powerful, and it made Remember feel stronger than a grown-up. The next two months, she haunted the field hospitals, extending her fingers to all the dying boys. The hospital staff began to think of her as a death omen. When a soldier was about to go under, Remember was at his side.

It wasn't until the war had ended and a new war spread throughout France that she had a chance again to feast. With Verdun destroyed, her family boarded a steamer out of Belgium bound for the United States. The promises of the New World were still music to the ears of war refugees, and her mother hoped to find a place where Remember could grow up, far away from the lines of white crosses that marked the western front.

Something else went with the family on the trip. It turned out to be the most deadly enemy of all, and it did not carry a knife or gun. It was so tiny it could not be seen, a virus called Spanish flu. It started out in the trenches, killing as many soldiers as bullets did, and after the war it spread to the survivors and then to the innocent civilians.

By the time the ship was halfway across the ocean, the passengers were overcome. Once again, Remember was surrounded by the dying. As before, she knew when a ghost was about to leave the body, and three times in as many days she drank. The souls gave her power beyond belief. Made her strong. Made her bold. And that was when she was found out—by an old crone, a toothless peasant dressed in rags who chased her to the ship's deck to confront her.

"How did you do it, child?" the crone demanded. "Tell me your secret. Or I'll tell everyone yours."

There was something dangerous in the eyes of the old crone. She was bent, both her nose and her spine, and the skin on her hands was like yellow parchment. But she was strong. Remember tried to wrestle free, but it was the woman's eyes that held her. Eyes that knew what Remember truly was, because she was a norn herself.

Remember couldn't allow that. She stabbed the old woman with a pocketknife, then pushed her overboard. When the alarm bells rang, Remember just stood at the railing, sipping the old crone's soul.

Her family settled in Andover, and she learned to hunt other norns, stalking them for weeks, sometimes months, before she took their lives—and their power. Their magic made her stronger. Made her beautiful. Kept her young. But it made her hungry, too, and Remember's hunger was never sated for long.

She first saw the stone egg one night in a bar, where Michael Conning was bragging about it to his friends. She was working as a waitress, and when she served them, she'd felt the magic in the obsidian, like waves of heat rising from baked asphalt. She knew instantly that it was the most powerful artifact she had ever encountered, and she had to have it. She had always lusted for more magic, more beauty, but this stone of Michael Conning's was more magical and beautiful than anything she could imagine. But before she could speak to him, the bar closed, and he was gone.

It took months to track Conning to his triple-decker in South Boston. It took even longer to ingratiate herself with the landlord, pretending to be her long-lost niece. When the landlord died suddenly of a fall on the slippery back stairs, Remember was bequeathed the property, and she began her long and winding attempt at capturing the stone. Norns were not disposed to come at things head-on, and magic was offended by directness. There were laws to follow, paths that had to be taken, and courtesies that had to be upheld.

Even before her "aunt" died, she had introduced herself to the family in 3A and confirmed that Michael Conning lived there. And as it turned out, he owned a curio cabinet covered in warding spells so potent, she was only able to come within a few feet of it. But she got close enough to see a box that held a powerful object.

One day she used chocolates and a simple hunger spell to coax the younger daughter into opening the box and giving her the stone egg. As she gloried in the alchemic possibilities, Michael Conning had come home and caught her in the act. He banished her from the apartment, and her hopes were dashed. Without his leave she could never enter 3A again. On that day Michael Conning had signed his death warrant. It had been a trifle for Remember to arrange for his murder, an end he had richly deserved.

Ding! Ding! The front bell rang, pulling Remember out of her memories. She jumped at the noise, and the potion sloshed out of the pan and scalded her hand. "Gods damn it."

The bell rang again, following by a loud pounding.

"Hold your water!"

But the visitor kept knocking.

Wrapping her hand in a dish towel, Remember stalked out of her apartment and down the hallway. The scalding pain intensified with each step, and the house was suddenly filled with the odor of rancid meat.

The lights in the foyer flicked.

She faced the door, a tall, looming thing made from oak a hundred years ago with a lead crystal transom. It was four inches thick and had to weigh hundreds of pounds. When her burned hand finally found the knob, the strength to open it was gone, and she could only call through the open transom, "What do you want?"

"We would like to enter," the caller said, a voice that made Remember's blood run cold.

"You can't—"

The knob turned, and the door swung open, easy as pie. But pie wasn't easy, Remember thought, not easy at all. Cake from a mix, that was easy. She laughed, and pain bit her in the side.

A figure in a trench coat and a raggedy fedora stood on the porch, the collar turned up to hide the face. Behind the silhouette, a murder of crows had returned to the corner of F Street and Silver. They filled every free nook and cranny from the windowsills to the rooftops. They settled on power lines and wires, anything that allowed them to perch. The cable line that ran parallel to the triple-decker became so burdened, it had begun to sag with their weight.

"Do I know you?" Remember said.

"We are called by many names. The Shadowless will suffice."

It's her! Remember thought, gasping. The one that Harken feared! How did she find me?

"Will you give us leave to enter?" the Shadowless purred.

"Not on your life!" Remember slammed the door shut and turned to run.

The front door flew open, and a gust of gelid wind blew

down the hallway. The walls seemed to breathe, and the floors convulsed, the subfloor popping loose from the floor joints and the wooden slats rippling like keys on a lunatic piano.

"If not on our life," the Shadowless said, "then on yours perhaps?"

"Get out of my house!" Remember screamed, shaking the knob on her apartment door. It spun in her hand, and the catch refused to release. "I didn't give you leave to enter!"

The Shadowless moved impossibly fast, her fingers closing on Remember's throat. The air turned frigid. Remember's breath froze in it, and her vision wobbled, drawing in and out of focus, until it turned white. Death was coming, and there was nothing she could do to stop it.

"Please," she gasped, "I've done nothing to hurt you. Leave me be."

"You have lovely hands," the Shadowless said, her putrid lips touching Remember's cheek. "Would you like to keep your thumbs?"

CHAPTER THIRTY-TWO

THE Shadowless lifted Remember and shook her like a hollow doll. "Open it."

"What?" Remember said, woozy from shock. The Shadowless had pulled her up two flights of stairs to the Connings' apartment, and the stump that used to be her thumb was bleeding like a dripping spigot. "Open what?"

"The cabinet." The Shadowless tossed her across the room. "Open the cabinet and give us the box inside."

"If I do that, please don't hurt me again."

"Give us the box."

"Master, there are wards that will scour my flesh."

"GIVE US THE BOX!"

Remember did as she was told. The glass in the cabinet shook when she opened the door, her flesh burning from the wards that had been placed on it. She screamed, but the sound seemed to evaporate, and the Shadowless paid no heed to the bare bones and oozing blood on the backs of Remember's hands.

"Here you are, mistress," Remember said, holding the box aloft as if making an offering. Blood dripped on her face and ran down her cheek.

"Fool. If we could not open the cabinet," the Shadowless hissed, "how could we open the box?"

"But the wards on the box are too strong. I—"

"The stronger the magic, the stronger the wards!" the Shadowless screeched. "That is how wards work, you prattling fool! Open it!"

"Yes, yes." Skin searing even worse than before, Remember obeyed. When she saw the indentation in the velvet, she held the box up again. She swallowed hard. "It's empty."

"No!" The Shadowless slapped the box away. With a banshee scream, she snatched a dining chair and threw it into the cabinet. Wood exploded into thousands of splintered pieces, and glass shards scattered across the floor. A thick iron needle rose from the debris, spun wildly, then fell back into the pile.

"Conning! Deny us the egg, and we shall deny you every scrap of peace. You shall be ripped apart as Elizabeth flayed the Babingtons! You shall hang as we hanged the witches of Salem Village. No one you know, no one you love, shall live!"

She attacked the couch and chair, ripping the stuffing out like a butcher gutting a slaughtered pig. She rendered everything in sight, hell bent on bedlam, until she turned back to Remember and pulled the shears from her shroud.

"You! You know! It is written in your gaze! Where is the egg?"

"The Conning girl, she has it," Remember whispered.

"Where is this Conning girl now?"

"At school. St. Mary's. Over on Fifth." Remember coughed. "I can find her. Please, mistress, spare me."

Remember crawled across the floor, furiously gasping for breath. Her ears were ringing, and her eyes watered like a stream. The Conning girl didn't go to St. Mary's anymore, she remembered that. Willow Jane went to some high school now. The name escaped her, but the fact that the apartment door stood open did not. Her knees were raw, and she couldn't catch her breath. She'd be damned, though, if she'd be slaughtered like a farm animal without a fight.

"Do you not sense it, little one?" the Shadowless said, sniffing like a hound that had caught the scent of its prey on the wind. "The blood of the Uncanny is in this house."

"The Uncanny," Remember whispered. "An old wives' tale . . ."

"Do we look like an old wives' tale?" the Shadowless bellowed.

"No, mistress, I— Mercy, please."

"This *is* mercy." The Shadowless's laughter filled the room as Remember's left eye rolled back into her head. "The price of magic is blood. First yours, then the Uncanny's, and so Malleus the Usurper shall rise again!"

CHAPTER THIRTY-THREE

BY the time the bell rang to end the day, Kelly had cut two classes, smoked three cigarettes, and had a long crying fit in her car. Her head pounded like jackboots had stomped her skull, and when she looked in the rearview, puffy, bloodshot eyes and mottled skin looked back at her. She had skipped lunch but still had no appetite, only a ravenous thirst that a liter of bottled water hadn't quenched. The All Saints game was about to start, and she yearned to run to the locker room, but that would require leaving the friendly confines of her VW, and the distance between the lot and the rink seemed too wide and perilous to cross.

In the warm haze inside the car, she drifted off to sleep, wondering where Will Patrick was. Not that it mattered.

Only sleep did.

CHAPTER THIRTY-FOUR

"WHERE the hell's O'Brien?" Coach boomed as we jumped on the ice for the warm-up skate. "Captains! Get over here!"

Our captain and assistant captains did a lap and joined Coach by the bench, while the rest of us ran drills. All Saints took the ice, and Siobhan drifted to the net so we could run the butterfly drill. Coach was still reaming them out about not accounting for all players, his face the color of Harvard crimson and spit flying from his mouth, when Siobhan stepped out to let the backup goalie take a few shots.

"Coach is wicked pissed," Siobhan said to me as she

adjusted her leg pads. "Wouldn't want to be them right now, huh?"

"I wouldn't want to be Kelly when he finds her," I said, pinching the tape on my stick. I'd been lost in thought when I taped it and had done a crappy job. Too late to fix it now. "Wonder where she is?"

"Probably off shopping. Or drinking with Will Pathetic."

"She wouldn't do that," I said. "Not when there's hockey."

"Like she gives a whiz about hockey anymore."

I was about to argue when Coach whistled a new drill. Siobhan got back in the net, and I skated to my spot and smacked the ice for the puck. *Get your head in the game, Conning.* I lifted a wrister halfheartedly, worried where Kelly might be and what trouble she had gotten herself into.

CHAPTER THIRTY-FIVE

KELLY awoke with a start. The day had ended, and the sky was dark. Lights flickered in the upper two floors of Beacon, and the student lot was cast in shadows. Only one other car remained, parked fifty feet away.

How long was I asleep? she wondered. The dash clock was blinking 12:00, and her phone battery had died, damn it.

The game had started right after school, and now it was dark, and it must be half over. Coach would kill her for missing it. Maybe he'd even kick her off the team, a thought that should have terrified her but only made her smirk. What difference did it make? It was just a stupid game.

She sighed and opened the door, expecting the dome light to come on. It didn't, and when she found the keys in the ignition, not in her purse where she'd left them, she figured the battery was dead. Sure enough, the starter only clicked.

Kelly giggled. It wasn't funny, so she giggled again and slumped back against the seat, wallowing in a not unsatisfying malaise. She was too tired to get up, although she felt a strong desire to run screaming across the parking lot. Maybe she had hit her head or maybe she had caught the stomach bug that made Willow Jane splatter the cafeteria with puke. Her joints ached, and when she turned her head too fast, she felt a rush of vertigo and heard a wobbly sound—wobbly, flobbly, wob.

Just rest here for a while, she thought. You're too stupid to walk alone.

Bare knuckles rapped the window. She was too tired to jump, even if the sound startled her. Her head lolled to the side, where she found the pallid face of a disheveled Will Patrick pressed against the glass. She hit the button to roll the window down, then realized the power was dead, and so was Will Patrick.

His flesh had turned to paste, and his mouth was a

ragged maw where his lips had been sliced off. Dried blood and spittle were caked on his jaw and neck, and his left ear hung from a thread of skin. If exhaustion hadn't rendered her helpless, Kelly would have screamed, especially at the dead pool eyes that stared blankly at her, as Will Patrick clawed at the handle, trying to get into the car. She shut her eyes tight and recited as much of the Lord's Prayer as she could remember.

Then, as abruptly as he had appeared, Will Patrick was gone.

Kelly finished the prayer, and when she opened her eyes again, she found nothing but a smear of spit and blood on the window, dotted with chunks of what she hoped wasn't skin. She realized her lip was bleeding and dabbed it with her tongue. The blood tasted salty, and she guessed that she'd bitten it while praying.

"You hunger for the taste of your own blood," the Shadowless said, sitting beside her in the passenger seat. She wore a trench coat that stank like a butcher shop, and when she shifted her weight, a pair of tailor's shears poked from the sleeve. There was blood on the blades, fresh blood, which made Kelly think of Will Patrick's lipless mouth.

No more kissing for you, Will Patrick, she thought and

giggled. "You killed him. And Flanagan."

"We have punished many boys. What are a few more?"

"What did you do to Will Patrick?" she said.

"When we found him," the Shadowless said and smacked her lips, "the boy said he was thirsty. You are as well?"

"I'm not," Kelly said, covering her mouth and lying. "Not thirsty at all."

"We only hunger, and now the boy shares our hunger, too."

The Shadowless pulled her trench coat wide, revealing rotted skin and decayed bones. In her chest cavity, pink tail entwined among the ribs, was a rat the size of a house cat, foaming at the mouth and hissing.

The rat launched itself at Kelly.

Kelly caught its thick body and held it at arm's length. It chewed through her fingers, ripping out chunks of skin. "Get. The hell. Off me!"

Anger and terror fueled her, and she slammed the rat into the window. Its neck snapped, and it fell to the floor dead.

"You took its life," the Shadowless said. "Now you must devour it."

"But it's a rat. I can't eat a freaking rat. You can't make me eat *rat*."

"We do not make a human do what we want. We make the human *want* to do it. If you will not eat the rat, then you will do something for the Shadowless instead."

Kelly stared at the dead animal twitching on the floorboard. She squeezed herself against the door, pulling on the handle, but the door wouldn't open. There was no escape.

"Serve the Shadowless, and you will not eat rat."

"What if I refuse?" Kelly said. She was so thirsty.

The Shadowless smiled. "The boy refused. You saw what became of him."

"What?" Kelly said, her mouth dry. So, so parched. "What do I have to do?"

"You know a girl. The daughter of a seamstress."

"Willow Jane? You want me to get her?"

"It's not the girl we want," the Shadowless hissed. "We want what the girl loves most."

CHAPTER THIRTY-SIX

THE next time I looked up, the scoreboard read HOME 3, VISITOR 2. With Kelly out of the lineup, Siobhan had stood on her head to keep us in the game. When the announcer called, "One minute left," in the third, I had the puck on my stick and Coach was screaming out orders.

"Puck possession!" he bellowed. "Puck possession! Time and space!"

I skated the puck into our defensive zone and nodded to Siobhan, who'd taken fifty-two shots and let only two sneak in. The All Saints captain, a winger named Radcliffe, jumped out on a line change and rocketed toward me.

Head on a swivel, I thought. Play the hips, not the

~232~

puck. Quick feet. Wheels. Win the battle of time and space. I retreated to the corner. Draw her closer. Closer. When she was six feet away, I did something totally crazy: I handed her the puck, then stepped aside. Her eyes big as saucers, she caught an edge and slammed into the glass. The puck bounced back into play, but Radcliffe didn't.

Now! Skate hard! I grabbed the biscuit. Dangle! Time and space!

And broke into open ice.

The All Saints goalie was skating toward their bench, and their net was wide open. Head on a swivel! If I put a slapper between the pipes, the game was over, baby! I wound up and—

"Time out!" Coach bellowed. "Time out, ref!"

WTF?

The ref whistled and made the signal. Both teams skated to their benches. I looped behind Siobhan and gave her a push to the bench.

00:57 left in the game.

"Nice move on Radcliffe." Siobhan pulled off her helmet. Her face was soaked with sweat, and she stank like a pound of moldy corn chips. "See her face? She was all like, whaaa?"

"Yeah," I said. "But I had an open net!"

"Bring it in!" Coach clapped his calloused hands. His face was the color of a rare steak. "You know the drill, ladies? Soon as the puck drops, they pull their goalie. Whoever wins the draw, no icing, so don't shoot on their net unless you clear the red line first. We don't need a face-off on our end against six shooters. On three."

"One-two-three," we shouted. "Go, Beacon!"

But I had *an open net*!

"Teams! On the ice!' the ref shouted and skated to the circle.

Our center took the draw. On the drop, she planted a shoulder in the All Saints center and won the puck back to me. The safe play was to take it behind our net to invite their forwards to chase.

Don't be safe, I thought, seeing an opportunity I couldn't pass up.

The All Saints winger had tripped. She lay on her back, legs in the air like a turtle flipped on its shell.

Be great, Conning.

I raced up the boards and across the red line. My stick went back for the shot. I swung an instant before Radcliffe hooked my skate, and the puck slipped away.

"She tripped me!" I yelled at the ref.

"Play on!" he shouted.

00:42 on the clock.

Radcliffe skated into our zone. She lined up for a slapper, and our center dived across the ice, taking the puck off her chest. It bounced right back to Radcliffe, who flicked a quick wrister on net.

Siobhan blocked it with a sliding split save.

The rebound popped out to me.

00:11.

Eleven seconds to glory.

As both All Saints defenders closed in, I zigzagged almost to mid ice and threw the puck at the empty net. It landed on its edge and playfully rolled past the crease, then hit the boards on the back wall and felt flat, unmoving, mocking me with its stillness.

The ref whistled. "Icing!"

"Conning!" Coach screamed. "Get your head outta your ass!"

"Sorry!" I yelled and skated to our face-off circle. I bumped Siobhan's glove. "Sorry. My bad."

"No worries," Siobhan said. "Today I own these beotches."

"Don't get cocky, kid."

"Telling a goalie not to get cocky is like telling a fish to ride a bicycle."

I shook my head and lined up for the drop. "That's a terrible analogy."

The ref whistled and fired the puck at the ice. Slamming sticks and elbows, the centers clashed like gladiators hungry for blood. The puck squirted free, and their center kicked it backward. It rolled right to Radcliffe. She wound up for a monster slap shot.

I saw the shooter's stick flex as the blade hit the ice. The shaft shattered, and the puck rocketed toward the goal as chunks of carbon fiber and tape flew out in all directions.

"Oh, shitburger," I said.

The shot whistled past Siobhan's outstretched blocker. It rang like a chime on the crossbar and bounced into the crease. Siobhan spun and dived as the puck rolled over the line, an inch from the tip of her glove.

The ref extended his arm. "Goal!"

The horn sounded, and just like that, our victory was gone. Cheers erupted from the All Saints bench, and Coach pointed at the scoreboard, screaming that time had run out before the shot. I knew he was wasting his breath.

The puck had crossed the line with one second left.

One lousy second.

All Saints rushed to center ice and made a pig pile, throwing gloves and sticks into the air. I'd never seen a team so happy with a tie.

"Conning!" Coach screamed, his mug blood red with fury. "This one's on you!"

It was. It was all on me. I had let the whole team down. "Wish I could have a do-over," I whispered.

The last horn became a steam kettle in my skull, and a series of blue and red triangles ripped through the center of my vision. The droning became louder and louder as the rip became a black hole surrounded by colored light.

At center ice, the All Saints players jumped out of the pile. Gloves and sticks flew into their hands, and they skated backward to our end of the ice. The ref skated backward, too, and I ducked as his blades passed by me.

His hand went up.

The whistle left his mouth.

The puck rose from the back of the net, bounced away from the crossbar, then slowly floated until it was inches from Siobhan.

"Stop!" I said.

The puck stopped. It hung *right there* in midair, suspended as if dangling from a piece of invisible thread. No one else moved—not the ref, not the players, not even Coach, whose spray of spittle hung from his twisted mouth.

The clock showed 0:02.

"Holy time warp," I said.

My thumb hit my stick, and I felt a stab of pain. The hard bump was inflamed again, boiling red and angry, with a thin silver filament emerging from the middle of the abscess. And I didn't care. I was happy, the ecstatic I-got-what-I-wanted-for-Christmas happy that makes you want to twirl around and belt out lyrics from "Happy" at the top of your lungs.

Which I did.

Because I was.

Giddy like a New Year's reveler drunk on Asti Spumante, I skated over to the dangling puck. I lowered it three inches, angled Siobhan's blocker a pinch, and skated back to my spot.

"Go!" I yelled and . . .

Nobody moved.

The players were still as statues on the Boston

Commons, staring blankly into an abyss that only they could see.

"I said go, dammit!"

I looked at the real clock. Its hands were frozen in time.

Time. It was all about time. And my thumb. My thumb was the key.

I put the digit, which burned like it'd been cauterized with a white-hot needle, up to my lips and licked.

My neck made a cracking sound, but then I realized it wasn't me—it was the stick shattering in Radcliffe's hands. Ping! The puck rang off the crossbar. It flew over the goal and into the glass.

"No goal!" the ref yelled.

I grabbed the rebound. Their defenders rushed me hard. They hacked at my stick, my hands, and my legs all the way to the boards, but I didn't drop the puck until the buzzer sounded.

Coach whooped as if we'd won the Stanley Cup, and my teammates tackled Siobhan. My attention, though, stayed focused on the clock. Real time hadn't stopped at double zeros, and the minutes kept ticking by.

CHAPTER THIRTY-SEVEN

FIVE minutes later, the rest of the Beacon School Lady Lanterns were in the locker room in various forms of dress and undress, celebrating. I sat on the bench, my uniform in a pile on the floor, my wet gear stuffed into the locker. I'd tied my hair into a pony and was pulling on a pair of sweats.

"I say All Saints, you say sucks!" Siobhan yelled. "All Saints!"

"Sucks!"

"All Saints!"

"Sucks!"

"Willie!" Siobhan yelled at me. "All Saints!"

"Tried really hard, too?"

"Boo!" she jeered, and the team fired their wet towels at me.

I made no effort to avoid the onslaught. The game was over, and I had other obligations. Last night I had gone to bed as a fairly normal teenager, and just now I had stopped time and then reversed it and changed the outcome of the game. To quote Siobhan, what the frickdoodles did I do?

Just get the egg, Willow Jane, and go from there, I thought. But I can change things. I can make them like they never happened. A conversation. A game. Maybe even more?

Should I, though? All Saints tied that game fair and square, and I cheated to win. Maggie Mae Conning never raised no cheaters. Could I wish to redo the do-over?

"Yo, bender!" Siobhan plopped beside me, totally naked and smelling shower fresh. Her hair hung like raven feathers over her shoulders. "Cheer up! We just kicked ass. Well, I did. You mostly just witnessed my badassery."

"That's me." I forced a smile. "Your badass witness."

"This whole Will Pathetic and Kelly thing, huh? That's why you look so down?"

"Totally." That and a dead kid named Flanagan. How

could she just shrug stuff off? I put on my jacket and checked the time again. "Text me if you hear anything?"

Siobhan pulled sweats and a hoodie from her locker. "Want to grab a few holes at Dunks? I'm in the mood to celebrate, and only fat and sugar will satisfy."

"Rain check? I have to be somewhere before seven."

She sniffed the air. "No shower?"

"No time," I said and headed for the exit.

"Basking in your own stink! Next, you'll be manspreading on the T. Conning, I'll make a man of you yet."

"God, I hope not," I said. Every man I'd known had let me down. It would be a miracle if I ever found one who didn't.

Miracles happen every day. Maybe today was that day. If I could turn back time to win a hockey game, why couldn't I do the same thing to Louie? I rubbed my thumb, and an idea of how I could retrieve the egg from the pawnshop popped into my head. It was brilliant, positively brilliant—and illegal.

My cell phone rang. "Hey, Ma."

She shouted in my ear, "Rehearsal's running superlate, and Mr. Parris still can't get his shirt buttoned. Can you be a dove and rescue Devon from aftercare?"

"I'm really pressed for time."

"I can't be in two places at once," she said, on the verge of losing it.

"Don't worry about Devon." I wanted to ask if she had taken her meds, but that would make it worse. "I've got this."

Her reply was drowned out by the sound of hammering, then the line went dead. I jammed my phone into my pocket. If the bus was punctual, I could make the pawnshop with fifteen minutes to spare. All I needed was a little divine Providence to make the bus run on time.

Ha.

Like Providence was ever on my side.

CHAPTER THIRTY-EIGHT

THE back door of Beacon School opened, and a shaft of light sliced the darkness. A mop bucket exited, followed by a mop handle, then a pair of hands so large and leathery, they could pass for catcher's mitts. The hands belonged to a middle-aged man with drooping, rheumy eyes. The name embroidered on his jumpsuit was Pete. It was a spare jump-suit that Pete kept in a broom closet. No one had noticed that the real Pete was sleeping in the corner of the same closet.

The man who was not Pete dumped the mop water, then tossed the mop back inside as the buzzer sounded to end the hockey game. The Conning girl would be getting off the ice now, and when she left the school, Harken would be outside, waiting to follow. He had spent the last few hours masquerading as Pete, watching and listening, and he was convinced the girl was more than she seemed. He had dismissed her sidewalk poem as trivial, but other signs persuaded him.

The birds. Blackbirds everywhere, with enough ravens and crows to make murders.

And the girl. He had heard her in the infirmary, crying out in her sleep. Then the nurse had said something about her thumb being infected, and a shiver had cut right through him. When he was watching the hockey game from the wings, he felt a strange tug in his stomach. He had looked up to see her shimmering.

Lesser norns did not shimmer.

Harken tossed Pete's coveralls into the Dumpster. The lights in the school parking lot were so dim, he had no worry of being seen. The whole lot was deserted, except for the car that belonged to that Will Patrick boy.

"Poor bastard," he said, walking toward the car. "He's still inside."

The BMW was parked far away from the building. It looked abandoned, sitting all alone in the darkness, just beyond the light. Harken gave the trunk a tug and felt something wet on his fingers.

"What the hell?" he said and smelled his hand. "Blood."

The blood had congealed like jam. The trunk lid was scarred with a dozen long gouges, three of which cut straight through the metal and the lock. He lifted the lid and cursed.

The trunk was empty.

"Where have you gone, you little bastard?" But Harken knew before the words left his lips that the boy hadn't gone anywhere.

He plucked the flashlight from the built-in BMW tool kit and shone a light on the pavement, searching for more blood. There! The droplets glimmered like sanguine raindrops. He followed the trail until it dead-ended beside a cluster of utility buildings. The largest was labeled "Lawn Equipment." When Harken wiped the dirt from a window and aimed the flashlight inside, he found a variety of mowers, hedge clippers, and grass trimmers.

"Damn it," he whispered. "Not here."

He followed the diminishing trail to the next building. It was labeled "Theater Arts," and on the frame was a large smear of blood. He shouldered the door open and peered inside. In the middle of the room was a dark circle. The circle was smeared into the dirt, and there were clear signs of a struggle.

No, he thought. Not a struggle.

An attack.

Harken swept the darkness with his light. The beam illuminated two lumps of material in the dirt. He nudged them apart with his toe, revealing two strips of flesh caked with blood and dirt.

"Lips," he said. The boy had lost his mouth. Probably had said the wrong thing at the wrong time. If his lips were here, where was the rest of him?

Harken found the body a few yards from the hut, in a bare patch of ground under a massive oak tree with long, spreading branches as thick as a man's leg. A length of hemp rope swung from one of the sturdiest branches, and at the end was a noose. The noose was wrapped around Will Patrick's neck.

The boy had been handsome when the day started, but the Shadowless wasn't one to let beauty go unpunished. As Harken had guessed, the boy's lips were missing. His face was bruised, and his dark eyes bulged in their sockets. His body twisted on the rope like a weather vane in a storm.

If there was anything the Shadowless liked better than lopping off body parts, it was watching a corpse twist in the wind.

He couldn't let the poor bastard swing. He lifted the body and dug the noose out of the swollen flesh of his neck, then lowered the corpse onto his shoulder. Rigor mortis was setting in, and carrying him was like toting a slab of heavy marble. He returned to the theater arts shed and set the boy on the ground. From a box labeled "Props," he removed a sheet and covered Will Patrick with it. The white shroud made the body less horrific and hid the swollen head and blood-speckled face, but it didn't change what the Shadowless had done.

In old Salem Town he had helped the Shadowless hang more than a dozen people. That was four hundred years ago, but he had looked into the dead eyes of every victim and still could hear their screams. Especially the children. They haunted him the most.

"You'll not be haunting anyone," he told Will Patrick, and removed two coppers from his pocket. He pushed the boy's eyelids shut, thankful that she hadn't cut those off, too, then placed the coins over the lids. "A penny for the ferryman."

UNCANNY

The sheet began to shimmer, the fabric resonating with silver light. The light took a human shape. At first, there were no legs or arms, but as the ether thickened, the features hardened, and the spirit became Will Patrick.

"Why do you summon me?" he said in a flat, harsh voice.

"To send you to the afterlife," Harken said. "It's part of my penance to the Fates."

"The afterlife is forbidden. The Shadowless has designs for me."

"What plans?"

"The Shadowless does not share her schemes with servants. I must wait until she has use of me."

"She's already used you enough, boy," Harken said. "Take the tokens and let the ferryman do his work."

The spirit threw back his head, wailing, a high-pitched keening sound that belonged more on a Scottish heath than in a school in Boston. "She will give us treasure. Treasure beyond all imagination."

"Seeing as you're dead, how will you spend your treasure?"

The spirit shimmered, uncertain.

"That's what I thought," Harken said. "Listen, why is

Malleus interested in Willow Jane Conning?"

"The Shadowless does not reveal her plans," the body said.

"No more lip out of you." Harken put a foot on the corpse's chest. "The Conning girl was your friend, and she's in danger. There's not much hope for your soul if you turn down the coppers, but if you help her, you might not spend eternity in damnation."

The shimmering shadow lost substance, and the ether spread out in a thick fog. Harken felt it move through his body, sending a cold shiver down his spine. The temperature had plummeted, and when he exhaled, he could see his breath in the air.

"The Shadowless hunts the girl who knows no future and no past."

"No past and no future? That's—"

"The Shadowless hunts the girl who knows no future and no past."

"Does she think that Conning is the girl?"

"The Shadowless hunts the girl who knows no future and no past."

"Tell me!"

"The Shadowless does not share her secrets."

"Neither do I." Harken threw back the sheet and removed the coppers from Will Patrick's eyes. The lids popped open, and empty sockets stared up at him. "I take back my gift. Go to whatever hell will have you."

The fog thickened for an instant, then melted into the ground, a whispered voice lingering. "Hell is empty, and the devils are here."

Chapter Thirty-nine

I ran down the front stairs and sprinted to the student parking lot, which was on the back side of campus, near the rail yard. The lot was totally deserted, except for two dark cars and a white kidnapper van with LARRY'S LOCKSMITH stenciled on the side. In a pool of harsh light I saw two guys standing by the trunk. One of them was Mr. Johnston. The other was a middle-aged guy with gray coveralls, jimmying the lock.

"See this?" the locksmith said. "Looks like somebody took a butcher knife to it."

"Just get it open," Mr. Johnston said.

The trunk popped. "There she goes," the locksmith

said. "Just stuck, not lo—Jeezum Crow, will you look at that blood?"

"Oh, hell." Mr. Johnston dialed his phone. "I'd like to report a possible assault."

"*Possible* assault?" I crept toward him, full of trepidation. "That's Will Patrick's car. Where is he? What happened to him?"

Jaybird held up a hand, but I scooted around him to see for myself. He covered the phone and said, "Larry! Get her!"

The locksmith moved in front of me. He wasn't big enough to block my vision, though, and I got a glimpse of the empty trunk. It was bathed in blood.

"The Shadowless," I heard myself say. The Shadowless had done this, just like she had killed Flanagan at the cemetery. They had disturbed her grave. So had Kelly. Was she dead, too? Is that why she wasn't at the game? "I need to call Kelly."

"Hold on now." The locksmith tried to grab me. "You need to stay right here till Jaybird says it's okay."

"No!" I shouted, surprising myself.

Jaybird reached for me. "Willow Jane, we need to talk."

"Got to catch me first!" I yelled and took off.

✗ ✗ ✗

I reached the bus stop two minutes before the bus was due to arrive. Panting, I dropped onto the graffiti-covered bench. A light rain began to fall, illuminated in the head-lights of passing cars and trucks. Rain. Of course.

My ex-boyfriend was dead, and it didn't even bother me. No, it bothered me, but it wasn't a surprise. Since I could turn back time, could I go back far enough to truly change the past? Could I keep Will Patrick from dying? Could I help my friends?

I called Kelly's number and got voice mail. "Hey, Kells. It's Willow. Give me a call. If you can." *If you're not dead.*

I hung up and waited for the bus. One minute late. One minute ten seconds late. I watched each second tick by, feeling more and more panicked, until I felt the hairs on my neck stand up.

Someone was watching me.

I searched the shadows through the rain-streaked glass but couldn't see anything but rush-hour traffic. The end-less line of cars made me feel even more alone. Even more vulnerable. "Step into the open!" I yelled, feeling way more brave than I felt. "Leave me alone or I'll call the cops!"

In the miasma of loud rain and bright headlights,

I saw a dark figure, face hidden by a hood, sitting on a motorcycle. My hands started to shake, and my mouth went dry. I pressed into the corner of the shelter, knees under my chin, trying to make myself small. The bike's headlight flicked on, and high beams blinded me. I raised my phone to shield my eyes, but the light seeped through my fingers like a milky veil.

Blood will have blood, I thought, but it wasn't my voice. It belonged to a man, a man whispering in the darkness. *Blood will have blood.* My hands started shaking, and the air seemed to freeze around me. I buried my face in my knees and wrapped my arms around my legs, trying to fight a violent, fevered shiver.

"Leave me alone!" I screamed.

Then I heard the sweet music of air brakes, and the 10 bus swung to the curb. Heart pounding, I jumped from the shelter. The door popped open with a hydraulic hiss, and I ran up the steps.

"Stop. You paying or not?" The driver pointed at the fare box. "Nobody rides for free."

"Right, right," I said and dug out my CharlieCard. "Sorry."

The bus lurched out into traffic, and I tucked a strand

of wet hair behind an ear. The seats were all taken, except for the back. I didn't want to go to the back.

"Take a seat," the driver barked. "No standing in front of the white line."

As I walked down the aisle, I watched out the windows. The road was full of cars and trucks. Their lights reflected on the rain streaming down the windows, mixing with the red, yellows, and greens of traffic lights. It was hard to tell one vehicle from another and impossible to spot a motorcycle. Maybe I had just imagined it, I thought as I swung into the last seat. What if I was just freaking out over nothing?

My phone pinged, and I screamed. Passengers looked up. I turned away from them, embarrassed, and checked the screen.

My heart sank.

The time was 6:45. Fifteen minutes to closing, and there was no way I could pick up Devon at aftercare *and* make it back to Louie's.

Siobhan. She lived close to Devon's school. Maybe she could give me a hand.

"Hey," I said after she answered, "you're not close to home, are you?"

"Out with the team, scarfing doughnut holes sans you.

Nom, nom." She chewed in my ear. "Where'd you go in such a hurry?"

"Which store?"

"Down on Dorchester. Why?"

It was on the opposite end of South Boston, too far away to help. The bus stopped at a light, and I looked out the window. A motorcycle was idling in the next lane over. The driver wore a hood. His face was hidden.

"I repeat, why?" Siobhan said.

"Call me crazy," I said, "but I think there's a creeper stalking me."

"Stalking you at school?"

"On the bus."

"There's a creeper on the bus with you?"

The hooded rider stood on the pegs and craned his neck, trying to see inside.

I slid behind the seat. "He's following the bus. On a Harley."

"A Harley?" Siobhan asked. "The bus is way faster than that."

"You're not taking me seriously!"

"Sorry, Willie," she said. "But you have been acting kinda batshit crazy."

Then I saw the sign for Louie's Pawnshop shoot past.

The time was 6:52.

Eight minutes till the witching hour, I thought. Devon had waited this long, so she could wait a little longer.

"Talk later! Bye!" I pulled the stop cable and shoved the door open. An alarm chime rang, and the driver started yelling, but I hit the sidewalk and sprinted like the hounds of hell were nipping at my heels.

CHAPTER FORTY

"LOUIE!" I yelled when I burst into the pawnshop. "I'm here for the egg!"

The cowbell over the door clanked. Louie looked up from his laptop, then snapped it closed. "Look what the cat drug in," he said. "Don't tell me you came for the egg."

"I came for *my* egg."

"Got *my* money?" Louie laughed at his witty retort.

"No," I said. "But you're going to give it to me anyway."

"Yeah?" Louie coughed and almost brayed in my face. "Why's that?"

I leaned across the counter and jiggled my eyebrows. "Because I wish I'd never sold it to you."

The corners of Louie's mouth twitched. "You don't say."

"I really wish," I said and contorted my face like a toddler sucking on a lemon, "that I had never sold it to you."

Louie scratched his belly and burped. "I dunno what you're up to with the dancing face thing. Maybe your brain's gone sour."

"I SAID—" I raised my voice as if calling on a higher power. "—I WISH that I had never sold you that egg!"

"Yeah, well," Louie said, cleaning the wax from his ear, "if wishes were horses, we'd all be winning at Suffolk."

I puckered my toddler face again. My wishes had been coming true ever since I blew out the birthday candles. Why wasn't it working now? "I wish you'd shut up."

"And I wish you'd get your twitchy face out of my sight." He checked his watch. The second hand and the minute hand had already swept past seven. "Closing time, kid. Get lost."

"This is *not* how my plan's supposed to go!" I sucked on my sore thumb. "Dammit, Louie! Give me that egg!"

"What egg?" Louie pushed the laptop further away. "You mean the one that'll belong to me in, oh, two minutes and change? The one locked in my safe in case some psycho gets ideas about stealing it back?"

"Come on, Louie," I said, my voice softening. "Don't make me beg."

"Gee, my heart breaks for you, sweetheart." Louie popped open the laptop and showed me an online auction page. The bid was $15,892.00. "Now your precious egg's going to belong to username BennyHannah12 or Qwertyxqr99. Depending on who forks over the cash."

"Give me back my egg, you lying sack of crap."

He smirked. "*My* egg."

"We had a deal—money and the thimbles for the egg." I grabbed a golf club from a plastic elephant-foot umbrella stand. It was a Fat Bubba model with a club head as big as a man's fist. "Don't make me hurt you!"

"You weigh less than a yard gnome soaking wet, and I'm supposed to be intimidated by this violent display?"

I swung the club, but momentum took me too far, and I only managed to hit the floor. The oversize head broke off, leaving me with a crooked metal shaft. "I'm not paying for that," I said.

"Here, take the stupid thimbles and get out!" He waddled and shoved the thimble case at me. "You got ten seconds to get outta my face!"

The thimble case went in my book bag, and I waved

the broken club at him. "Or what? You're going to hit me?"

"I don't hit little girls. I got scruples."

"Since when?" I said and paused, thinking of something to grind his gears. "Fat boy!"

There was murder in his eyes and heart. "Don't call me fat, you little witch!" Louie growled and rushed me.

I swung. The bent club hit his gut and bounced off, and Louie wrenched it from my hands. Moving fast for a guy one powdered doughnut from a cardiac arrest, he steered me to the exit.

"Let go!" I yelled and tried to bite him. "I wish you'd let go of my arm!"

"Keep wishing, sweetheart." He pushed me onto the sidewalk and belly-laughed when I slipped and hit the wet pavement. "Stay out until you learn some manners!"

The door slammed, the cowbell clanged, then Louie locked the deadbolts and turned his sign to Closed.

CHAPTER FORTY-ONE

LOUIE turned the pawnshop lights out and waddled back to his office. He was breathing heavily and could feel his pulse pounding in his temples. His ears were itching, and when he felt them, the skin was hot to the touch. It was the kid's fault. She had got him all wound up. His pain management guy said stress could kill you faster than a heart attack.

He should've closed up early. That would've fixed her little red wagon, but no, some sick part of himself wanted to wait till the second hand and the minute hand ticked from 6:59:59 over to 7:00 so when the kid came begging at the door, he could tap on his wristwatch and shake his head mournfully, while all the time laughing inside.

Mike Conning had always treated him like something to be wiped off the sole of his shoe, not like a legit businessman. Maybe that's why Louie wanted to keep the egg, to laugh at that curly headed ginger one last time. When he sold it on eBay in a few hours, the first thing he'd do was buy a bottle of cheap Irish Rose and pour it all over the bastard's grave.

As soon as he reached his desk, Louie popped two pills and washed them down with spit. He collapsed into the chair, which listed to one side. A minute later, he felt good enough to slither from his seat to the shag carpet. He crawled under the massive metal shell of a desk and retrieved a wooden box from his safe.

It didn't look like much, the egg. It was an oval hunk of obsidian, about the size of a kid's fist, rough cut and dull, with curved ridges. There was a hole at either end where something had pierced it. It smelled like mold.

He flipped open his laptop and smiled. Sixteen grand and the chance to piss on Michael Conning's grave? It didn't get any better than that.

Louie stroked the egg. "Ow!" The surface vibrated like it was flowing with current, and he snatched his hand back.

He licked his fingers and tasted sulfur.

What the hell? he thought, and then he felt another zap, this time in his arm. It sparked up to his chest and seized so tight his breath caught. He groped for the phone and somehow hit the speaker button. A dial tone came through the speaker, loud and insistent. He gagged and felt his eyes bulge.

A heart attack. Through the thickness in his brain, the thought formed, followed by the realization that the next grave he visited would be his own.

That's when Louie heard whispers coming through the phone. He heard a voice, then laughter, and the great weight that had been bearing down on his chest fell away. He leaned close to the receiver, then realized that the voice was not coming from the phone but from the egg, and it was calling him by name.

CHAPTER FORTY-TWO

LIGHTNING danced through the heavy black clouds that hung over St. Mary's School. When I got there, the parking lot was empty except for a dark green Saturn station wagon, which belonged to Miss Frances "Frankie" Wilhoite, Devon's teacher's aide.

Aftercare had officially ended at six thirty, and almost everyone had gone home. The only light in the building's windows came from the third floor, where I imagined that Devon had helped Miss Wilhoite tidy up. Devon would be waiting with her lunchbox in hand while "Frankie" texted her "special friend" to explain that she'd be late for their "dinner meeting," again.

Outside, another bolt of lightning lit the sky. The school building was illuminated in a flash of white light as I ran across the parking lot. I had failed. Ma was going to be heartbroken. What a crappy, crappy daughter I was.

I stumbled through the rain, tears of frustration streaming down my cheeks, while a church bell tolled the half hour. Seven thirty. It was hardly even dinnertime, so why did it feel like the day—and my life—were coming to an end?

At the door I paused to shake the rain from my hair, then glanced over my shoulder.

A single headlight turned into the parking lot.

"Oh, shit!" I yanked the door open and ran down the hallway. I hit the stairs, taking two at a time, then leaped to the next landing and slammed into a tall figure blocking the way.

"Ahh!" I screamed.

"What's wrong with you, child?" the janitor said. "Why're you here this late?"

"Mister!" I grabbed his arm. "You have to save me!"

"From what?" The janitor tried to take his arm back. He might as well have tried to extricate himself from a bear trap.

"A stalker!" I pointed at the stairwell. "Following me!"

"Nobody there," he said, then peered into the darkness. "A storm's coming, and wind makes this old building moan and groan like it's full of ghosts."

I looked down into the abyss. Like he said, nothing. Maybe it was just the wind. "Sorry." I sighed. "It's been a really, really weird day. I better get Devon before the aftercare teacher feeds her to the wolves."

"Devon Conning?" he said. "That girl, more likely she'd be teaching the wolves to sit, fetch, and play dead. Room three-two-two. To the left."

"Got it." I ran upstairs to the third floor and made a wrong turn to the right, completely oblivious of the shadow slipping from the blackness below.

CHAPTER FORTY-THREE

"SORRY I'm late!" I told Miss Wilhoite. "Ma sprang this on me at the last minute, and I had a hockey game and—"

"What." Miss Wilhoite slung her purse over a shoulder and walked right past us. "Evah."

"Don't worry," I called after her. "We'll lock up!"

"She's really mad," Devon said.

"I can see that," I replied. "She probably has a life."

"More like a hot date. With a guy named Matthew she met at Fenway. He 'accidentally' spilled her beer while 'Sweet Caroline' was playing. She says it's the most 'romantic thing' a guy ever did for her."

"Really? Ever? That's sad," I said. "Wait. She *told* you this?"

"She texted it. When she types, her lips move. I think Matthew is in trouble."

"What? Why?"

"She said he was naughty. Twice."

"Stop reading grown-ups' lips." I collected Devon's backpack. "There's a bad storm brewing outside. Let's go before it hits."

"Yuck!" Devon covered her mouth. "What's that awful smell?"

The classroom door slammed, and the lights flickered, brightened, then died.

"Willow Jane!" Devon screamed. "Why'd the lights go out?"

"The school forgot to pay its power bill?" I teased, but a chill went up my arms.

Devon pointed at the door. "It's the dead girl who smells like wet newspaper."

"There's . . . nobody there." I squeezed Devon's hand, trying to hide the fact that I almost peed my pants.

Outside, the whole street was lit up. The windows and the orange sign shining over the fire exit gave the room its only light.

"Got all your stuff?" I said quietly. My hands were shaking. "It's time to go."

We snaked our way through the maze of tables and chairs. We had to move slowly, too slowly for the panic rising in my throat.

A long shadow crossed the frosted glass—the silhouette of a hand.

"Shh!" I peeked under the door and saw a pair of shoes caked with mud. The air smelled like sewage.

"Open the door, Willow Ja-ane. Will and Willow kissing in a tree . . ."

"Kelly?" I eased the door open and peeped through the crack.

Kelly's pants were as muddy as her shoes, and her hair was a fright wig of mud and dirt. Her cracked and bleeding fingers were thick with dirt. The same moldy stink wafted from her hair, and when she opened her mouth to talk, she exhaled sulfur.

"Open the door," she said. The voice was Kelly's, if Kelly spoke in a dead monotone full of menace.

"You're covered with crap." I waved Devon away from the door "Have you been gardening?"

"Will and Willow swinging from a tree," she sang.

"H-A-NG-ING." Then she thrust her hand between the door and the frame, peeling off a thick layer of skin. Underneath, there was no blood, just brackish mud. "Do you want to hang, Willow Jane?"

"Stop singing the freaking song!" I yelled, blocking the door with my hip.

"Will Patrick hanged." Her hand disappeared, then came back. "And he wanted it. The way he wanted you."

She rammed the door so hard it slammed into my face. My lip squirted blood, and my eyes gushed with tears. She shoved again, and I tripped, my head hitting the floor. It was cliché to say you saw stars, but damn the clichés, I did. When they faded enough to make out the face above me, I expected it to be Kelly's.

"Get up, you big ginge." Devon fanned me with a copy of *Highlights*. "You're such a klutz."

"What happened? Where's Kelly?"

"Moldy Kelly crawled away," Devon said. "After she kissed me."

"Kissed you?" I started to get up, but my legs went numb, and my feet slid out from under me. "What the hell?"

"Are you drunk?" Devon said, worry on her face.

"Please, Willow. You're starting to scare me."

I groaned and closed my eyes, wishing like frickdoodles to be curled up on the couch with a hot-water bottle and reruns of *Gilmore Girls*.

Devon slammed the door hard enough to shake the frame, then dashed to her desk and returned with a handful of paper dolls cut from construction paper. She lined them up on the floor across the doorway.

"That will stop her," Devon whispered as she snuggled up to me.

"Hope so," I said, but I knew it wouldn't.

The door hinges creaked, and a pair of shears as long as my forearm pushed the door open again.

A drop of something fell from the blades.

Another drip followed.

Then a third.

Blood will have blood.

"It's the Shadowless," I whispered.

"You said her name was Kelly."

"Shh! The person at the door is a very bad stranger." Devon knew about stranger danger. Her teachers had drilled it into her head since kindergarten. "We need to go."

I pulled her toward the fire exit in the back, but she locked her heels.

"Don't make me," she whimpered. "The man who killed Daddy came from there."

"The fire exit? No, sweetie, that was another place, not school."

Devon pointed to cubbies in the back of the classroom. "Ricky H hides there when he throws a fit." Her eyes seemed to turn to glass marbles. "But don't worry," she said. "She can't kill . . . you."

"What's that mean?" I said and felt a shiver.

"What's what mean?" she said, shaking her head. "You're so weird."

I'm not the only one, I thought, as we crawled to the cubbies. Maybe it was a great place for Ricky—he was apparently small enough to fit into a cubbyhole—but we were unprotected.

The door inched open, and long, spidery fingers followed the shears.

"The janitor's under the stairs," Devon said. "That's where the moldy girl stuffed him."

"That's it! We're taking the fire exit!" I grabbed Devon's hand and pulled her to the fire exit. I slammed the panic handle, but the latch didn't release. "Jeezum! What else could go wrong?"

Devon pointed out the window. "There could be a stranger on the fire escape."

"Not funny." I braced my feet firmly on the floor, squared up like I was taking a check, and hit the emergency handle with everything I had.

The latch held.

The classroom door swung wide, and the creature without a shadow stepped inside. She moved slowly, as if savoring the moment. Her face was bone white and angular, her eyes iodine.

"Yesterday, upon the stair," she sang. "We found an egg that was not there. It was not there again today. Oh, wish, oh, wish, the egg would stay."

She raised the rusted tailor shears. The blades opened and closed with a screech.

"May we see," she wheezed, "your thumbs?"

Devon screamed, and the emergency door blew open, and the stranger bounded inside. He moved so fast he was a leather and blue jeans blur. I barely caught sight of his face before he swept Devon into his arms and turned for the fire escape. He put my sister down and returned for me.

"Willow Jane! Come with me!" he yelled, grabbing my coat and lifting me off the ground.

My world was turned upside down—again—and all I saw was that muzzle flash in the dark movie theater and Dad's head snap back. Then there was screaming, and the exit door flying open, and a shaft of bright light arcing over us. My hand was pressed against Dad's chest, blood pouring through my fingers, and I was crying for somebody to please help him.

I had seen things happen in slow motion before, like the puck at the game or the bus almost crushing Will Patrick, but watching this guy move wasn't like that. He was strong—a dark slick of fluid motion and power. When his hand wrapped around my arm, it felt like jaws had closed on it. Then blink fast he eased up.

"Let go!" I smacked his hand away. My knuckles flared with pain. "I can effing walk!"

He pushed me outside, slammed the door, and wedged a steel bar between the handle and the fire escape. "Do exactly as I say!" he said. "She's coming for you, and that bar won't hold for long!"

I popped him in the mouth with Devon's lunchbox. His head snapped back, and I pulled my sister to me. "Get away from us!"

"I damned well saved your life!" He wiped his mouth with the back of his hand. "This is the thanks I get?"

"I said back off!" I swung the box again. "You don't know who you're messing with!"

He knocked the lunchbox aside. "You're Willow Jane Conning, orphaned daughter of Michael Conning, son of Eric Conning, descendants of Josiah Conning of Salem Village, Massachusetts. The imp beside you is your sister, and your lives are in danger."

"That, that thing?" I said. "Is after Devon?"

"No, little idiot," he said. "That thing is after *you*."

Thunk! The tips of the Shadowless's shears struck the fire door, rending the metal like soft cloth.

"Malleus!" The stranger rapped on the door and yelled at the creature, mocking her. "Let's see you chop your way through that, you pus-filled pile of rot! You rump-fed bulbous pustule!"

Thunk! Thunk!

The shears hit the door.

"Temper, temper!" he yelled, mocking her, which didn't seem like a smart idea.

While he spewed, I led Devon down the escape. "Come on!" I whispered.

We were almost to the next floor when the stranger vaulted over the railing and dropped to the landing in front of us. "Stop running from me!"

"Go, Devie!" I bodychecked him into the building. His head snapped back, and his teeth clacked together. "Stay away from her, asshole!"

"It's *Harken*, not asshole!" He shook his head and flexed his jaw. "Stop attacking me! I'm trying to protect you!"

"You got a funny way of showing it!" I gave him another hard shove. My bad thumb caught on the railing, and I howled with pain. "Damn it!"

"What fresh hell is this?" Harken caught my wrist and peeled my fingers away, revealing a huge, throbbing ulcer choked with blood. "This is bad. Very, very bad."

"I know that!" I said. "It's my effing thumb!"

Above us, the steel door ripped loose from its hinges and went hurtling into the night. The Shadowless stepped onto the fire escape. "Surrender the egg! Or be gutted like a butchered hog!"

"She means it," Harken said. "Come with me or you die."

"Come with me or you die?" I said, feeling oddly confident. Or obstinate. "What's this, *Sophie's Choice*?"

"Maybe you can't trust me." Harken pushed me ahead. "But you know damn well you can't trust *her*!"

Our shoes clanged on the metal risers as Devon and I pounded down the stairs. I didn't look up for fear of finding the Shadowless at our heels, holding the shears like a butcher knife. "Blood!" she shrieked. "The price will be paid in blood!"

I stumbled on a step and would've fallen if Harken hadn't caught me. Devon and I reached the drop ladder and clambered on as Harken kicked it free. It shot away with us, stopping five feet from the ground.

"Jump!" Harken barked.

"I don't like hiiiiiii—"

He shoved us and slid down after. "That should buy some time!" he said. "Follow me!"

I looked up at the Shadowless, who was standing, just standing, on the fire escape. I caught a glimpse of her paste-white face and black pool mouth. Then she screamed, and the night was filled with the cries of thousands of birds. I clapped my ears, deafened by the sound. Tears rolled down my cheeks, even though I wasn't crying.

Another scream, and the Shadowless leaped from the landing. Her long coat fluttered like wings, then she seemed to disintegrate, as if the night had opened up and swallowed her whole. Just like that, she was gone.

"Willow Jane!" Harken yelled, pulling Devon along. "What part of 'or you die' don't you understand?"

I followed them, running toward the Harley parked twenty yards away, praying that the Shadowless wouldn't materialize from thin air in front of us.

When we reached the bike, I looked him dead in the eye. "What just happened? Who the hell *are* you?"

His copper-colored eyes locked with mine for too long, then he smirked, and the spell was broken. "Don't stand there like an idiot!" he said. "Get on!"

"I'm not riding a motorcycle."

"You. Are. In. Danger!"

"What danger?" I said. "From that thing or from you?"

"Damned stubborn Connings." He pulled off his jacket and draped it over Devon's shoulders. He swung her gently onto the seat in front and then started to pull off his crimson hoodie, exposing rock-hard obliques dotted with white scars, and I felt something tighten in my own stomach when he handed the hoodie to me. "Put this on."

"What do you think you're doing?" I protested.

"Giving you a sweater," he said. "You're shivering, a

symptom of shock. It will keep you warm."

"It's a hoodie. And keep it," I said. "You're just wearing a shirt."

He noticed his bare belly and tugged at his shirt. "Right."

Did I see a flash of embarrassment?

"You're pretty," Devon told him. "So's your tummy. Willow Jane likes your tum—mmm."

I clapped a hand over her mouth. "Is this a rescue or not?"

"It was," he said, "but now I'm having doubts!"

A crow the size of a condor dived at us, claws extended, wings beating the air, talons ready to rip me to shreds. Before it could, thunder rolled across the sky, and lightning lit us up like a new dawn, and the crow fled.

"Get on the bike!" Harken yelled. "Now!"

"Why are you afraid?" Devon asked. "It's just a bird."

"When Malleus the Deceiver is involved, little one," Harken said, revving the engine, "there's no such thing as just a bird."

CHAPTER FORTY-FOUR

THE sky dumped hail the size of marbles onto the street. Harken weaved the Harley through traffic, riding bumpers and nicking side mirrors, trying to outrun the storm. He whipped in and out so fast I felt the air being sucked from my lungs. Colors ripped past, and sounds bled together, but we couldn't outrun the ice that pelted us, stinging our faces.

I tried to hang on, struggling to make sense of what had just happened. My arms were wrapped around him, one hand locked on my wrist and the other pressed against his chest. His shirt was soaked with rain, and I could feel his muscles right through it, the tendons working as he steered, the heat from his body. I pressed my head between his shoulder blades and felt him breathe, slow and steady, like this was just a joyride.

Then I remembered the white face.

The death rattle voice.

The wicked sharp scissors dripping with blood.

And my separate peace was gone. "Whose blood was on the scissors?" I yelled, but before he could answer, I heard a weird buzzing sound and looked up.

Birds.

A swirling, dazzling cloud of noise that widened and thinned, then turned toward us.

"Look out!" I yelled.

Harken swerved as the swarm swept past, and birds splattered the windshield of a delivery truck, leaving a smear of blood and guts. The driver yanked the wheel, and the truck sideswiped the bike, slamming us into a parked car. The bike whiplashed, and Devon flew over the handlebars.

"Devie!"

I saw my little sister skid along the pavement until she lay still in a pile of hailstones.

"No!" I beat Harken on the back. "Stop!"

I heard a rushing noise and saw nothing but white. The city was gone. The street was gone. Only a white sidewalk remained, where I stood in front of Urban Market's plate-glass window.

"I'm losing my mind," I said, blood trickling from both nostrils.

A crack made of ever-growing blue and red triangles opened in my vision, and pain poured through the crack. The pain grew brighter and fiercer until I curled up in a fetal ball, moaning.

And then, it stopped.

The wind.

The sound.

The light.

The pain.

Stopped.

And I was standing on the sidewalk. Facing a shopwindow, a finger on the glass, where shaky letters spelled out, *Do not accept her cold caress. For the Shadowless will kill.*

"Hey, ya big ginge." Devon tugged on my sleeve. "That's the same poem."

"It is?" I wondered how she got here but wrapped my arms around her anyway. "I'm glad you're not dead anymore."

"Why's everything so white, Willow Jane?" she whispered. "It hurts my eyes."

"I'm sorry. I just. Just . . . Can you see that?"

The window looked like the surface of a winter pond, dappled with crystals of ice that sent ripples through the glass. A pinprick of light glinted from the center. It grew lighter and brighter as it expanded. The light was hypnotic, and it held me in its spell.

Devon walked toward the expanding fissure, laughing and raising her hand to the mist that rose from the frosty glass. Her fingers sank into it, and instantly the light changed. White turned to sickly green, and the ice melted around her wrist. A sulfur-infused stench drifted from the hole, an odor so strong my stomach heaved.

"No!" I screamed. "Stop!"

She turned and smiled. Her eyes were vacant and dark, and she covered her mouth with a hand and giggled, a lilting, high-pitched sound that sent a shiver through me. I leaped across the sidewalk and reached for her, hearing laughter. My face appeared in the glass as a blur of red hair and porcelain skin that transformed into a bone-white skull and a row of jagged teeth.

The Shadowless, I thought. She's come for me.

But it wasn't me she reached for.

"Devon!" I snatched at my sister's coat, catching

nothing but air. She seemed impossibly far away. "Don't go with her, Devie! Stay with me!"

Like an antique doll rotating its head, Devon turned. Her face was a blank, glistening slate. "The dead girl wants to play."

My blood ran cold.

Kelly's reflection appeared in the window beside mine. She wrapped an arm like a tentacle around my waist, pressed her body against my back, and put her cheek against mine. She stank of dirt and rot, and when she thrust her lips to my ear, I thrashed against her embrace. But she held me too fiercely, laughing with quiet ferocity, and pulled me away from the window.

A long, bony hand covered Devon's mouth. "Treasure for treasure," Malleus said. "The clock ticks, Uncanny. The clock ticks."

Then they were gone.

"No! You can't leave! I can make you come back!" I bit my thumb and tried to pull out a gossamer thread. "Damn it, work! I need you to work!" I bit down again. All I got was skin. "Come on, stupid thread!"

"Uncanny tricks won't work in the land of shadows," Kelly said, mocking me.

"No!" I gasped. It was the only sound I could manage, a weak, impotent noise, as insignificant as I was.

"Submit," Kelly said. "Submit and be free."

An ill wind flowed in from the bay. The air blew straight through me, and I felt Kelly's teeth on my earlobe, tugging and tasting my skin.

"Devon and Willow swinging in a tree," she sang, "H-A-NG-ING."

Then she stepped through the window and was gone. Without a sound, she was gone. The rippling glass solidified, the fog dissipated, and I alone was reflected in the glass.

Above me, the clouds had parted, and the dark sky was pocked with silver stars. I stared at them dumbfounded, until Harken, the street, and the world came back in a rush of color and sound.

I stepped off the sidewalk, and Harken caught me before I could fall into oncoming traffic.

"Steady there!" he ordered. "Willow Jane, where is your sister?"

"Devon is gone." I heard myself say. "To the place of shadows."

PART FOUR

MAN KNOWS NOT HIS TIME

I woke up on my living room couch covered with the hand-stitched throw that Ma had given Devon for her sixth birthday. It smelled like bacon and my sister's shampoo. I inhaled deeply, then sat up with a start.

"Devon!"

The apartment was a shambles. The place had been ransacked, and the curio cabinet was demolished, a pile of glass and splinters. Our family heirlooms had been smashed and ground into the floor, destroying generations of family history, destroying us.

All of it was Malleus's doing, Harken had said when he brought me home. That monster had been in our house.

She had invaded our home and taken my sister. Why? What did she want from us? I dashed from room to room in sheer panic, feeling like a wild animal in pain with no way to make it stop.

"Willow Jane, I've put a kettle on." Harken sat at the kitchen table with the egg box, the iron needle, and two mugs. "Join me. We have business to discuss."

"Where's my phone?" I said. "I'm calling the cops."

"There," he said in a low voice. "But you will not be calling the police. Sit, please."

The *please* didn't sound like a *please*. Before I could argue, the kettle whistled, and he got up for it. I grabbed my cell phone but couldn't enter the password. Numbers were alphabet soup, my eyes were roasted marshmallows, and my tongue felt like a wad of chewing gum. And there on the coffee table was my dad's letter. Right where I'd left it, unread.

"Willow Jane." Harken stood two feet away from me, just stood, but I could feel heat emanating from him. "We are running out of time."

"Potty break!" I said, tucking the letter under my shirt. "Be right back!"

He said something in reply, but I was moving too fast

to care. I ran past the bathroom and slammed through my half-open door. It rattled in the frame when I kicked it shut and threw the bolt. I plugged in my phone and ducked into the closet to open the letter.

When I was a little girl, I used to dream that there was a door to Narnia in the back of my closet. My dad would read me a chapter a night, and many mornings, Ma found me sleeping among the winter coats, sucking my thumb, and talking about magic. She didn't like it a bit. Dad, though, he always said there nothing wrong with a little magic in the darkness. That was a long time ago, and I had forgotten about magic in the winter coats.

Dearest *Sweet* Willow:

I write this on the eve of your sixth birthday with you snug in your bed, your belly full of cake and soda pop and your heart full to bursting with the love of friends and family. You are reading it on the night of your sixteenth birthday, and as the letter was given by your ma, I was not there to share it with you. I pray that your day was filled with joy and that you've not missed the old man overmuch. For my part, I've not missed you at all, because St. Peter and I will be drinking buddies by now, and he will allow me the window seat to look down upon my sweet Willow anytime I like.

This letter isn't a hello from your dad, but a word of warning. Soon, today or tomorrow, you will meet a young man. He'll have news for you, and you must listen to it very closely. Don't fear him, for he's come to do you no harm. Though he might seem a bit touched, you'll know in your heart that all he says is true, and you'll know a peace like no other. Odd things have been happening to you, and perhaps you think you've gone mad yourself. I wondered the same thing when he found me.

On the back of this paper, you will find words that only you can read. Set them to memory and set them to heart, so that they will serve you well hereafter. Remember that words are magic, and so is she that speaks them. Take care of yourself the way you take care of others, and all will be well.

Your Loving Father,

Michael Danvers Conning

"All will be well," I repeated. Hadn't Harken just said those very words to me? *You will meet a young man. He'll have news for you, and you must listen to it very closely. Don't fear him, for he's come to do you no harm.*

I flipped the letter over. The page was blank. The surface was scratched up, as if it had been written on with a dry calligraphy nib. There were no other marks and certainly no words to memorize. I turned the letter back over, and at the bottom, under a folded edge of paper, a postscript: *I hope you will be there for your ma and sister, as I hoped to be there for you.*

Someone knocked on the closet door, and I started. "How did you get in here? The door's locked."

The closet door opened, and Harken stood there, arms folded. "It was locked, and now it's not. Take my hand."

Don't fear *him*. Fear him? Give me a freaking break, Dad, what kind of daughter do you think you raised?

"Either walk to the kitchen," he said, "or be carried. Your choice."

"Touch me," I wanted to say, "and lose some teeth. Your choice." But my dad had never let me down. I prayed this wouldn't be the first time and took Harken's hand. He pulled me up so quickly, I gasped. His skin was hot, and even though his jaw was set, the mischief was still in his eyes. He held my hand for only a few seconds, but when he let go, my skin felt cold.

I stalked past him to the kitchen and sat down. I smoothed out the letter, my hands shaking, and tried to sort out the conflicting emotions that had turned my brain to stew. "How did my dad know about you?"

"That's a long story." He poured the tea, first my cup, then his, with absolute precision, then took the chair opposite me. "And the clock is ticking."

The clock is ticking, Uncanny. Long story or not, I knew I needed to hear it. "My father wrote this when I was six," showing him the letter. "He knew I would meet you. He knew it would be today. He said, *Odd things have been happening to you, and perhaps you think you've gone mad yourself.* Yes! Exactly! Don't pretend you can't read that!"

"I can't."

"It's right in front of your face!" Then I gasped. "Oh! You can't read?"

"I can't read it," he said and held the paper to the light. "Because there's nothing written on it."

I took it from him. "Yes, there is! Right here!" Where the page had been blank before, faint lines appeared, ink seeping into the scratches that I'd noticed before. The ink darkened and spread. The lines became letters, and the letters became words, and the words became a poem:

You must not wake the Shadowless
When she sleeps within her bed.
But kiss the lips of the Shadowless
And the morning finds you dead.

You cannot hear the Shadowless,
When her breath is in your ear.
You cannot see the Shadowless,
When she raises up her shears.

And if you feel the Shadowless
When she blankets you with chill,
Do not accept her cold caress—
For the Shadowless will kill.

To end the sleep of Shadowless,
Weave silver 'twixt her eyes,
Cut gossamer threads with sparks coalesced,
Then the Shadowless shall die.

"The poem!" I waved the letter like a victory flag, a warm sensation flowing through me, a mix of joy and relief. "I'm not crazy! My dad wrote the poem. For *me*."

"And he gave you implicit instructions to trust *me*." He sipped from his cup and stared at me from under his eyelashes. They were really long lashes, as black and thick as his hair. Devon was right: He was very good-looking. Not pretty like Will Patrick but handsome. "Drink. Tea helps."

"I'm a coffee girl," I said. "How old are you again?"

"It depends on how you count years." He smirked and took my hands in his, rubbing them gently with his thumbs, and the warmth spread over my wrists and up my arms. "I've lived nineteen years, four months, and twenty-six days. If you told me I seemed older, you wouldn't be the first. Nor would you be wrong."

It was suddenly very warm in the room. I felt a knot in my throat. I wanted to pull away, but his touch was warm and comforting, and it had been so long since anyone had tried to take care of me. After Dad died, caring for Ma and Devon became my job.

"No matter what age I am, I know what I'm doing, so listen to everything I tell you." His voice was calm and firm, and it made me calmer, too. "It is the only way to get your sister back."

I pulled away and folded my hands in my lap. "I'm listening."

"Drink."

I took a sip of tea, then downed it all at once and winced at the aftertaste. "Bitter," I said. "So I have a bazillion questions about—"

He held up a hand. "Hear me out first. Let's start with your thumb. When did it start festering?"

"This morning, when I used magic to save Devon's life."

"It's not magic per se."

"It was magic."

"No, you're not a norn. Also known as cunning folk, sorcerers, and witches."

"So I'm a witch?"

"Not witch, not a norn. You can't do magic."

"Black magic then."

"Hell's bells, you Connings do love to argue," he said, sounding annoyed but looking amused. "Let me explain it this way: All norns can do magic. Lesser norns have lesser magic, often called talents. Greater norns have, well, greater magic. The most powerful norns, the Three Fates, have the greatest magic—the ability to control the past, present, and future. Then there are the Uncanny like you. No one's really sure *what* you are."

I'm not really sure what I am, either, I thought. "It sure *feels* like magic."

"It's called glimpsing. Your ears will ring with a loud noise," he said. "Your vision will go swimmy, and you'll black out. When you wake up, some terrible event that just happened will not, in fact, have happened. That's a glimpse, not magic."

"Like when I moved the puck in our hockey game?"

"You moved a what?"

"A puck, duh. When Siobhan missed the save and I hit rewind and moved the puck ever so slightly. Don't look at me like that, okay? I know it's cheating, I just felt responsible because I screwed up—why do you keep shaking your head?"

"You couldn't have done that."

"Whatever. I did it. I moved the puck, and we won the game."

He rubbed his fingers together as if polishing an unseen coin. "You've had other glimpses?"

"The first was when Devie died." I pointed out the window. "This morning on the street corner, right in my arms. Then, poof, she was alive. Then she died again after she fell off the motorcycle."

"But Devon didn't fall off." Harken looked at me, his face expressionless. "Did she?"

I bit my lip and scratched at a stain on the Formica table. He seemed a little unsure of himself, and I liked it better when he was confident. It made me doubt myself less, and I wanted to believe that he could really bring Devon home.

"That explains a great deal," he said. "I thought you were a lesser norn like your father and his fathers before him. Then I saw you shimmer at the hockey game, and I knew you were—"

"Weird?"

"Special."

"I've never been special a single day of my life."

"You've been special your whole life. Until yesterday, you didn't know it."

"And look what it cost me," I said "My friends and my sister."

"Malleus wants treasure, not Devon," he said. "I can

work out a trade. But we have to tread carefully. The Shadowless is frightened."

"She didn't look afraid to me."

He tapped the egg box. "She wanted the object from this case."

"It's a family heirloom, not an object." An heirloom that I had pawned for rent money. I felt like a bad version of Jack trading the cow for beans, except there were no magic beans to throw out the window. "Why does she want it so much?"

"There's something I would like to show you," he said. "Close your eyes."

Trust him. "Whatever," I said and did as he asked.

He touched my face. "Concentrate on my voice."

"It's kind of hard not to, since you're talking."

"Do you make everything difficult?"

"I'm a Conning?"

He went silent, and I tried to concentrate on not talking or thinking about how long his eyelashes were. Then he whispered again, low and deep and soothing: "In 1692," Harken said, "Tom Burroughs became jailer of the Salem Town dungeons. Old Tom had lost most of his eyesight, a good deal of his hearing, all of his teeth, which was why the court tapped him for duty."

Hard as I tried to comply, my eyes just wouldn't stay shut. His own eyes were closed, and he was touching a bronze necklace hidden by his hoodie. The metal glowed irresistibly, and I reached out to touch it. The instant I did, his eyes flew open, and he groaned, "No!"

But it was too late. One second, I was looking into his copper-colored eyes, and the next, I was staring down on a very old building covered with dead leaves and a dusting of snow.

CHAPTER FORTY-SIX

IN the pitch black of midnight, the Hanging Man walked under a canopy of trees, wind whipped the branches, pulling the fall leaves to the ground. They tumbled along a muddy road and through the gate to Salem Jail and stopped at the feet of a sleepy jailer.

"Jailer," the executioner whispered.

Old Tom leaped to his feet. "Who goes there?"

"Malleus the Hanging Man," the executioner replied.

"You're about late this evening, sir," he said. "'Tis almost upon the witching hour."

"The midnight bells have yet to toll. Has our apprentice arrived with the rope?"

"He never did," Old Tom said. "I've seen none of his face."

"How could you, when you've seen naught but the inside of your eyelids? Unbar the door."

Salem Jail sat near the North River and was built of massive oak timbers hewn by hand, measuring twenty-two yards in width and ninety-three yards in length. It was surrounded by a fence, usually unguarded, meant more to protect the prison from animals than to keep prisoners inside. To escape meant execution if captured, so it was seldom attempted, and once a prisoner escaped, where in the hostile wilderness was a good saint to go?

Old Tom opened the door and grabbed a torch from the sconce. He lit a second lamp, cupping the ember to shield it from the quickening wind. The smoke drifted toward the Hanging Man, and Malleus stopped abruptly.

"Keep the torch to yourself," Malleus said. "Our eyes are at home in the shadows."

"This way, if it please you," Old Tom said, holding a torch close. The yellow light cast shadows in the deep craggy lines of his toothless face. "The Reverend Mather has come a-town," he said. "He'll be watching the hangings on the morrow. Forgive an old man for speaking plain, but the Conning girl. How can judges send a child of six years to the gallows?"

"The devil may take a child's soul as easily as any."

"But an innocent girl, sir."

"All earthly creatures are born in sin, are they not? Were you not? Should we ask the Reverend Mather to be a-watching you next?"

The curiosity drained out of Old Tom's face as he led Malleus into the common room, where four prisoners were held. One stayed in private quarters, wealthy enough to pay for a decent room. Two others were locked into small cells, the roofs too low to let them stand. The jail was frigid in winter, broiling in summer, and infested with lice, rats, and darkness.

"A prisoner weeps," Malleus said. "Is it the child?"

"No, a woman distressed. I'll hush her, sir."

"Nay, do not. Tears make their own sort of music."

The sobs came from the fourth woman's cell. The door stood open, as she had to stand, being too poor to provide for straw bedding.

"She has to beg a drink," Old Tom said. "Judge Hathorne allows that thirst helps a confession."

As they passed by the cell, the woman moaned for mercy. "Water," she said.

"Nothing for you," Old Tom said, directing Malleus to a narrow hall that led out of the common room.

"Leave us," Malleus told the jailer. "Do not return, no matter what you hear. Take the torch with you."

"You'll see naught a foot in front of your face, sir."

"We are at home . . . in the darkness."

"As you wish, sir," the jailer said, seeming glad to be dismissed.

Malleus turned away and removed her mask. She shook loose her long hair, which cascaded over her shoulders. It was rich and black, the color of midnight, the locks like the finest silk. When she had been a weaver of possibilities, she'd used her own hair instead of thread, plucking strands when she needed them, knowing that they would grow back when she slept.

"You're a woman?" the prisoner whispered.

"Masquerading as a man," Malleus said. "For only men are permitted to use the noose. Do you like our face? Beautiful, is it not? But beauty is the greatest deceiver, and power is the only bed worth sharing."

"Harlot!" The parched woman slammed against the

bars. She took hold of one bar and pulled, her spindly arms bulging, groaning with the strain, face bloodred with effort. "Deceiver! Murderer!"

"Be still now," Malleus said, and the woman fell silent.

Malleus held a silver cup to the woman's face, collected the tears, and drank them like mulled wine.

"Oh how sweet the taste of bitter, bitter tears," said a young man from the dark corridor.

Malleus shook the last drop into her hungry mouth. "Ah, you have come at least."

"You mean at last."

"Do we?"

Malleus grabbed his face and held it ever so close to the torch. Pitch spat at his skin. His name was Harken, a boy she had found wandering and made her familiar. The villagers knew him as the pretty simpleton who went farm-to-farm selling brooms. They let him into their homes, and there he always found what he was seeking—lesser norns whose power Malleus could consume.

"Is he not handsome, prisoner? So fair a face and yet so dark a heart? Good thing he wears a hood at the hangings, else the maids of Salem Town would go even more mad with lust."

"Do you lust only for tears now, master?" Harken asked. "Have you so quickly forgotten the child? Did you not say the blood of a callow Uncanny was the sweetest of all?"

"Do not mock us, Harken. You are our familiar, and you serve at our pleasure, *for* our pleasure."

Harken bowed low. "Then follow your humble servant, master. I know what you enjoy the most."

He led her down another corridor, this one more constricting and darker than the first. He reached the end and unlocked the cell with practiced ease, though he had no key. The door to this cell was hand-hewn oak, thick and heavy, held up by iron barrel hinges.

The door swung open, and Malleus entered.

On a pallet of loose straw, a flaxen-haired girl lay. She had bedding and food but was kept in irons. At first she seemed to be sleeping, but her breaths were short and ragged, and she coughed pitifully.

Malleus bent down and pricked the child's thumb. She licked the blood from the wound and shuddered. "The taste! The power! Like honey mead on our tongue. Oh, how long we have searched for a child like this! With her blood, we shall become as strong as the Fates! They will know our strength!"

The child mewled, like a frail kitten curled in a ball, dying in a dark, dank cell, alone.

"When you die, sweet child," Malleus said and licked again, "you will go to a special place, where you shan't be troubled by dreams again . . . eh?" She sniffed and recoiled. "Familiar, what have you done?"

"Betrayed you, master." Harken slammed the cell door. "Or should I say, m'lady?"

"Prattling fool! Why can't you leave me—oh."

Malleus rose, hand drawn back to strike her servant, but when she turned, it was to find three women in white robes instead.

"Greetings, Sisters," she said. "Skuld, how fair your face. Urth, how . . . wise you look. And Verth—"

"Hold your tongue, deceiver," Urth said. "No more of your lies will we hear."

"Lies?" Malleus said. "I have told no falsehoods."

"We shall become as strong as the Fates!" Urth said, repeating Malleus's boast. "Familiar, bring forth the pressing board. Let confession be pressed from her lips."

"M'lady, there are no such boards at hand." Harken turned to the cell door. He pulled the pins from the iron hinges and lifted the heavy door off its barrels. "This one will have to serve."

Malleus fell to her knees. "Mercy!"

"Mercy was asked by every lesser norn you slayed," Skuld said. "You granted them none and stole their souls. Why should we show it to you?"

"Stop!" Malleus grabbed the flaxen-haired child by the throat. "Here lies a norn, a child full of great magic. If you loved the cunning folk so much, then let us go, and her life will be spared."

"Do you think us fools?" Urth said. "Her blood is tainted. She is bound to you, and even in death, her spirit will be yours to feed on."

"Accept your fate," Skuld demanded.

"We will suffer no poisoner to live."

"No?" With a twist of her hands, Malleus snapped the child's neck, then bit her own thumb to expose a shimmering thread. "Too late! She is dead, and I shall escape you yet."

But before Malleus could bite the thread, Urth grabbed her hand. "Sisters! Bind her! Let her be Unmade!"

As Verth pinned her to the ground, Skuld drew the thread out of the Shadowless's thumb. She pulled yard after yard, wrapping it like a skein around Malleus's outstretched hands. With each inch of gossamer lost, Malleus struggled less and less, until she lay unmoving.

"Familiar," Urth commanded, "the pressing board!"

"M'lady," Harken said and let the heavy oak door drop on the Shadowless.

One by one the Sisters stood on the door. The wood groaned from their great weight, and one by one Malleus's ribs cracked.

"Familiar, let her be shorn," Skuld said.

"No!" Malleus wailed. "Not our beautiful hair!"

"Yes, mistress," Harken said and used Malleus's own shears to chop her hair to the scalp. Where the shears sliced her skin, the blood sizzled, and thick pus oozed out. Then, when Malleus could stand the torture no more, the Sisters demanded her confession.

"We confess!" Malleus cried. "We have killed hundreds of lesser norns to take their power. You have Unmade us, now spare our life!"

"Confession may save your life," Urth said. "But your sins demand a blood price."

"The price to be paid in blood," Skuld said.

"And your heart made stone," Verth said.

"Harken, my child," Malleus pleaded. "Please. What promises the Sisters have made, I shall reward you the same and twice again."

"You cannot promise a clear conscience," Harken said. "Nor cleanse a twice-rotted soul."

At the Sisters' command, Harken cut out Malleus's heart and plunged an iron bodkin through it. The heart turned as hard as a diamond, as black as coal, and with that act of betrayal, Harken sealed his fate.

CHAPTER FORTY-SEVEN

I jumped as Harken pushed my hands away from his neck. The room seemed brighter than before, and I felt more calm. My thoughts had stopped winding round and round like thread on a bobbin.

"Wow. That's one cool magic trick," I said. "Don't tell me it's not magic."

"Oh, it's magical enough," he said and tried to smirk, but his face wasn't having it. "But not your magic and not mine. How . . ."

"How what?"

"Why did you touch the torc?"

"Is that a thing? Oh, you mean I wasn't supposed to?"

"It was *supposed* to kill you, like it does—"

"Oh, hell."

"—every other creature that has made contact with it."

"And it didn't kill me."

"No, it did not."

"That's good, right? The Fates gave it to you, so maybe it means that they like me?"

"The Fates don't *like* anyone."

He picked up his teacup and stared at the leaves in the bottom, as if there were answers hidden in them. I started to take a sip, and he lunged across the table and grabbed my mug.

"No!" The stoneware shattered in his hand. "You've had enough tea for one evening."

"Hey! That was my favorite mug."

His demeanor changed, along with his expression, and I could almost see him sorting things out. He stared at the broken pieces of the mug, rubbing his chin. Then he leaned toward me, still brooding, until he was uncomfortably close—uncomfortable in a good way that made me feel flushed and warm. "Sorry I broke your favorite," he said.

"Nah," I said and actually laughed before pulling back. "I'm just giving you shit. It came from the dollar store."

He smiled.

Trust him, my dad's words whispered, and in that moment I decided I could. "So what happened to the casket after that? How did you end up serving my family? Wait, the jailer called that little girl *Conning*."

"The child would be your great-aunt. Eleventh great-aunt, if I recall correctly."

"She died?"

"The jailer took her body and buried her in a pauper's grave."

"And you helped that monster kill her?"

"I did no such thing!"

"How many Connings have you killed?"

"None!" he said and looked truly hurt by the question, which made me trust him even more. "I vowed to protect your family!"

"You call this protection?"

"I helped Malleus hunt norns," he said. "I admit that, but I drew the line at killing children. The Fates gave me laws to follow: Guard Malleus's grave. Send the dead to the afterlife. Protect the Conning family. Train any Uncanny born of them. I buried Malleus's casket in a secret tomb, and if she was discovered, I was to rebury her." He snapped his fingers. "Too late for that now, eh?"

"You did this when? Every generation?" I said, looking at him sideways. He looked completely truthful, which made me question him. Guys were always most devilish when they looked like angels.

I reached for his cup to carry it to the sink, and he reached for my hand.

I let him take it.

"I rose every time a Conning reached age sixteen," he said before letting me go. "To tell the same story I just told you. I warned them to guard the egg with their lives, to never take it out in public, and never let a stranger touch it. Exactly that, nothing more."

"Right," I said and scoffed. "And I'm—"

"An interdimensional being capable of manipulating time." He picked up the egg box and turned it over. He had graceful hands, but they were marked with scars on the knuckles. He'd been a fighter and maybe still was. I watched his hands moving, the muscles and tendons and the scars. "Which idea is more fanciful?"

"I'm a Doctor Who without a Tardis," I said. "Point taken."

"The egg your mother kept in this box," Harken said.

"It's Malleus's heart, black as coal and turned to stone."

"Seriously?" I said. Just because it was so weird, I had to say it out loud. "Her heart?"

"Yes. You saw what happened when I cut it out. It was your family's job to protect it, and it was my job to protect your family until it was time."

"Time for what?"

"Time for you to quicken, I surmise. The Sisters were never definite on that account."

"So you're winging it?"

"Does it matter? As long as you save your sister and destroy Malleus."

"Oh, is that all?"

"You can do it, Willow Jane." Harken took my cold hands again, warming them up. "With my help."

Words caught in my throat. I wanted to pull away, but his touch was so comforting, I could feel tendrils of famili-arity wrapping around my brain.

Harken held up the iron needle. "Show me your thumb."

I hid my hand behind my back. "That's exactly what the Shadowless—"

"Call her Malleus. Giving evil a name lessens its power."

"—said when she stuck those wicked scissors—"

"Shears."

"—in the door. Why did she want my thumbs?"

"She collects them, like hunting trophies, and wears them tied around her neck."

"Around her neck?"

"I should have kept that detail to myself. Hand, please."

"I *like* my thumbs."

"Notice there are no appendages dangling from my neck."

He caught my eye, and I relented. "Don't get crazy with that needle."

Harken gently took my hand again. The heat flowed up my arms to my neck and into my blushing cheeks. He was definitely working some magic, though I couldn't fathom why he was wasting his sparkle ponies on me.

"How do I start this time turning?" I said. "Instead of, y'know, making wishes on my putrid thumb."

"If you will stop asking questions, I can show you."

"Does it require any body parts or sacrifices? We're Catholic, so we're not into that."

"No sacrifices. Be still, please."

"Who else knows about this secret magic club of yours?"

Another, deeper sigh. "If it will shut you up . . . Humans don't believe in norns. Lesser norns are looked down on by greater norns, who lord over the lesser and try to gain more power by practice, manipulation, and dumb luck."

Even though my debate team brain told me to keep arguing, my heart knew there was a grain of truth to it. All my life I'd felt out of sync with the world. "What about my type of norn?" I asked.

"Uncanny are very bossy and bullheaded, but they are not norns."

"Ahem?"

"Worse, they show very few signs of power until their sixteenth birthdays, when they cause all sorts of mischief. Once trained, however, they can be very powerful."

The idea of being very powerful appealed to me. Powerful girls didn't get plowed on the ice. They didn't get bullied by teachers. They didn't lose their fathers. But could I be powerful enough to face Malleus, though? "What about those Sisters?"

"The Fates do not concern themselves with affairs of norns or humans, only with the weaving of time."

"They concerned themselves with Malleus."

"She broke the rules so badly, they had to."

"And I can move through those threads? How far back?"

Harken wrinkled his brow, then understood exactly what I was getting at. "It's impossible to save your father. Once a spirit is ferried away, it is out of reach."

"How do you know for certain?"

"Because you wouldn't be the first one to try it," he said, digging the rusted needle through a pocket of pus, then drew out a sliver of thread.

"Holy frickdoodles, that hurts!" The sliver glistened in the light like a metallic filament. "Wait! The thread is *growing* in my skin?"

"It's gossamer, not thread. Imagine it as a metaphorical manifestation of chronology. It allows an Uncanny to control time."

"Been there, suspended that twice," I said. "A metaphorical manifestation of chronology? Seriously?"

"Imagine time as being woven one strand of gossamer at a time on an infinite loom," he said. "As each thread is woven into place, it's still fluid. Until a new thread is woven over it, the weaver can break the thread and twist in a new strand to reweave it. But when the thread is woven into the fabric, time becomes locked into place, and it can no longer be changed."

"My sweaters unravel all the time."

"That's knitting, not weaving. A seamstress's daughter should know better."

I smirked. Of course I knew the difference. I just liked giving him shit. It was almost as much fun as feeling his touch . . . *Willie*! I yelled at myself in Siobhan's voice. *Get your head outta your ass*!

"Rule number one about gossamer," he said. "Never cut the thread. Only break it."

"Why not?" I asked.

"If you cut the gossamer, time will unravel, and you'll be lost within it."

"So I'll die?"

"Worse. You'll become Unmade, like Malleus when the Sisters wrapped her in her own gossamer. She's cursed to live forever but can no longer glimpse. Rule number two: Never glimpse the same moment twice. Rule number three—"

"You have lots of rules."

"Number three: Never raise the dead."

"Why not?"

"Even an Uncanny can't pull a spirit back from the veil, and then you have a reanimated corpse on your hands," he said, drawing out the thread.

In a blink I became the only moving thing in the room. "Are you just screwing with my head," I said and waved a hand over his face.

"You know, Harken," I said, "you're cute, in a tattooed bad boy sort of way. Too bad you're so obnox—"

Something warm hit my lip. I touched the spot with my finger and drew away a spot of blood. My nose was bleeding again. "Damn it," I said, dabbing it with my thumb. Like wax melting, the gossamer filament dissolved, and Harken was animate again.

His eyes widened at the blood pooling in my hand. "The sink!" he yelled and spun me around. "Now!"

I leaned over the drain. Blood dripped like a leaking faucet. "Don't just watch me. Do something."

"Right." He twisted a piece of paper towel and stuffed it up my nose. "This is going to hurt."

"Ow! Jeezum!" I tried to lean back. "No kidding it hurts."

"Nosebleeds are serious side effects," he said. "If you glimpse too long, you'll bleed out."

"This sucks." I spat a clot of blood and mucus into the sink. "Maybe I'll pass on the whole Uncanny thing."

"It's your destiny to be Uncanny," he said. "Your

quickening caused a disruption in the fabric of time and space so powerful, it caused Malleus to stir in her grave."

"You're joking. Tell me you're joking." I tried to gently pull out the paper towel, but it stuck. "I let Malleus out? It's my fault Devon got taken? And we're standing around talking and not going after her?"

"Chasing after Malleus is always a bad idea," he said. "We will get your sister back—you still have the heart."

"Not anymore," I said, feeling stupid and defeated and small. "We needed money, so I hocked the egg. It's locked up in a pawnshop safe, waiting for that dipweed to close a sale."

"Providence is on our side then," he said. "We'll have to retrieve the egg before the pawnbroker can sell it."

"Hello? It's locked up in his safe."

"Locks," Harken said, smiling gleefully, "are meant to be unlocked. Before we retrieve the egg, there's something I have to do."

"Like what?" I said, with a flash of anger that surprised me, and I remembered the words I'd said when Devon was taken. "My sister's in the place of shadows. What's more important than keeping your vow to protect us?"

"Trust me." He caught my eye and held it for several

seconds, then touched the torc. "Willow Jane Conning, I have your name. I need you to sit on the sofa and wait there until I return."

His words coalesced in my brain. I tried to force him out, but it made my head hurt. The only way to stop the pain was to obey him and take a seat on what was left of the couch, which seemed like the best idea ever.

"I'm sorry," he said with regret in his voice. He caressed my cheek with backs of his fingers and drew his thumb to my chin. He held it there for a few seconds, like he didn't want to go. "You'll be safe until I return. Then we'll rescue your sister. I promise. Cross my heart and—never mind, that's probably not the best vow to make."

"Where are you going?" I said, staring at the carpet, although I meant to say, Sorry for what?

"To arrange for the exchange, the egg for your sister." He picked up the long iron needle and stuck it in the lapel of my coat. "For safekeeping. And stay away from the tea. You've had quite enough for one night."

With a quick bow, he was out the door, leaving me sitting there, watching dust fall to the carpet.

CHAPTER FORTY-EIGHT

SOMETIME later, my phone buzzed. I read the message from Siobhan but didn't answer. My fingers seemed too far away.

A minute passed.

A new message: **Effing answer me!**

Siobhan seemed angry. My fingers felt closer, so I typed: **I know.**

She replied: **Your house. Fifteen minutes. Be there or ass will be kicked.**

That made no sense, so I typed: **Whose?**

I put my phone on the couch cushion and wondered whose ass Siobhan was planning to kick. Her ass-kicking list was very long. It was taped to the mirror behind her door. I wondered if Kelly was on it for missing the game. My mind was still processing the idea when the laughter began.

It began as a giggle. It sounded like the crystal bell ornament from our Christmas tree. The light, tinkling sound that made me pause. I cocked my head and listened, waiting for it to return. For a long moment, there was silence, interrupted only by the muffled noises of voices on the sidewalk and traffic on the street. I could hear the refrigerator humming and the slow, endless, drip, drip, drip from the bathroom sink.

Drip.

Drip.

Drip.

Blood will have—

Drip.

Drip.

Drip.

—blood.

"Stop!" I stumbled to the bathroom, a hand on the wall for balance, and twisted the handle until the dripping ceased.

"Willow Jane," Devon said softly, and I whirled around, sure she had crept up behind me. Only bare walls and cold white tile greeted me.

I'm losing my mind, I thought, and the laughter floated up from the heating grate. It was louder this time, more sharp and metallic and singsong.

"Will she? Will she?" the voice sang inside the air duct.

I dropped to hands and knees in front of the grate. "Devon? Is that you?" Could she be inside the house? Could she somehow have escaped from the Shadowless? Or was it a trick? "Answer me, please."

More laughter, longer, high pitched, followed by singing. "Will she? Will she? Will Willow be hanging? Will she? Will she? Will Willow be hanging from the willow hanging tree?"

"Devon!" I yelled.

The singing stopped.

Then, "Will and Willow swinging from a tree."

"Shut up! Just shut up!"

The voice was still.

"Devon! No! Don't go! Don't leave!"

I threaded my fingers through the grate and tried to yank it off. It was an inch thick and buried into the tiles with heavy brass screws. I braced my feet against the wall and heaved. Something sharp sliced my fingertips, and I screamed until my voice gave out, crying for my sister to answer, but all I heard was giggling.

There's nothing scary about the sound of your sister laughing unless you're in the house alone.

CHAPTER FORTY-NINE

FOR the hundredth time in the last couple hours, Siobhan looked at the words *call ended* on her phone. She licked her lips, wondering when was the last time Willie had hung up on her. Ninth grade? Middle school? It had been a long time, maybe even never. She was too polite to cut a call short. Kelly would for sure, Siobhan herself had dropped calls probably a hundred times, mostly because the caller was some guy who turned boring and who has time for boring? Willie? Never.

But Willow Jane Conning hadn't been herself since her sweet sixteen, which Siobhan realized hadn't been all that sweet. Your dad getting murdered on your birthday kind of screws up the rest of them. She had hoped that a kickass party would erase some of the yuck, but then, when they were eating cake, she saw Willow Jane staring at the pictures of her dad on the wall, and Siobhan had kicked herself for letting Mrs. C choose Tom's Pub. The idea was to exorcise the ghosts, not eat cake and ice cream with them.

In psych class she had read about victims of violent crime burying their emotions as a way to cope with grief, then later a traumatic event opened the door, and the feelings came out. The party! Instead of helping Willow, she had screwed her up totally!

"It's all my freaking fault."

She was about to hit Redial when her phone buzzed. Kelly's photo popped up.

"Yo, Kells," she answered. "What's up with your skank self? Coach's so pissed you're going to be skating suicides till you wish you were dead."

"Siobhan?" Kelly's mom said.

"Oh, hey, Mrs. O'Brien. You're using Kelly's phone?"

"Have you seen her?"

"Kelly? Um, no, not since lunch. She totally bailed on hockey, so—"

"She has gone missing, Siobhan. When she didn't come home after the game, we called her cell phone, and the assistant principal, Mr. Johnston, answered it. He found it in the trunk of her car."

"In the trunk?"

Mrs. O'Brien kept jabbering on and on about personal responsibility and consequences and bad influence and how they had just about reached the end of their rope with this latest manifestation of oppositional defiant disorder when Siobhan's phone blew up. Text after text flooded her home screen, along with Twitter and Tumblr and even Facebook. They all said the same thing:

Will Patrick's dead.

Suicide.

Will Patrick's dead.

Hanged himself.

Will Patrick's dead.

A photo—a cut noose—popped up on Snapchat.

Hanged himself.

Suicide.

Suicide.

Suicide.

"Mrs. O," Siobhan said. "I gotta go." She hung up

and texted the news to Willow Jane: **Jeezum Crow. Will Patrick's dead! He hung himself!**

She hit Send.

The message status changed to Read.

Siobhan stared at the screen, waiting for the message bubble to show she was typing a reply. "Come on, Willie, you read the damned thing. Answer!"

In Dunkin's dining room, the other hockey girls and a couple of cops looked over at her table. She tucked a tuft of crazy-curl black hair behind her ear and pointedly ignored them. Then their phones buzzed and binged, too, and the whole room turned bedlam. She heard screams and one girl crying and lots of OMGs, but her phone stayed silent.

A minute passed.

She typed, **Effing answer me!**

Sent.

Delivered.

Read.

No balloon.

Then.

A reply: **I know.**

"You freaking know?" Siobhan said and typed

furiously: **Your house. Fifteen minutes. Be there or ass will be kicked.**

Reply: **Whose?**

Siobhan started to type, as if that was a question, then paused and realized that she wasn't sure of the answer.

CHAPTER FIFTY

THE intercom buzzed twice. I pressed the button. "Hello?"

"Is your sister home?" Kelly's languid voice seeped through the speaker. "The Shadowless wants to play."

"Kelly?" I said, snapping out of it. "What the hell are you talking about? Where's my sister?"

The intercom went dead, and the front door downstairs banged shut. I heard footsteps on the stairs, fast and light, coming closer. On the landing and then outside my door. I reached up to turn the dead bolt, and fists hammered on the frame.

"Little pig, little pig, let me in." Then Kelly cackled and

slammed her eye against the peephole. "I see-ee-ee you."

Go away! I wanted to shout. But I made myself take a deep breath. "Kelly, where is my sister?"

"Open the door and let me in," she whispered. "And I'll tell you with my chinny-chin-chin."

"You can tell me with words, too," I said, using the calming tone therapists had used on me.

"Words are sharper than knives. Shall I carve my master's message into your belly?"

"Kelly!" I shouted. "You asshole! Tell me where Devon is, or so help me god, you'll regret it!"

"Yesterday, upon the stair," Kelly sang, "we found a girl who was not there. A doll of paper she became. Oh wish, oh wish, the girl would hang."

"Hang this!" I yelled.

I opened the door.

The landing was empty.

Laughter drifted down the hallway.

"Devon?" I stepped outside and saw a paper doll on the back stairwell.

More laughter, and I chased after it, past the doll and down the back stairs, which were too narrow and slick, and I fell on my butt at the bottom.

The laughter had stopped.

What now? I thought, rubbing my ass. There was a paper doll peeking from under Miss Haverhill's door. Keeping to the shadows, I crept to the landlady's apartment. I picked up the doll. Its head had been sliced off. I knocked quietly but frantically and whispered, "Miss Haverhill, I need your help!"

The door swung open, and I saw that the jamb had been shattered. Her apartment had been tossed, like ours.

I followed a trail of paper dolls to the bathroom. She had an old-fashioned pedestal sink and a claw-foot tub that looked deep enough to bury a body. The trail of paper dolls led to the tub, which was surrounded by a mold-crusted shower curtain that hung from metal rings on a bar suspended from the ceiling.

"Devon? Kelly?" I whispered and was relieved when neither of them answered. If only Harken were here, I thought, then, *WTF*? Michael Conning had raised his daughters to take care of themselves, not wait for some guy to do it. So I grabbed the shower curtain and threw it aside.

"Hell's bells," I whispered.

The tub was full of dolls. All of them paper. All of them with the heads cut off. *We found a girl who was not there. A doll of paper she became.* I dug deep, looking for my sister. When my hands hit bottom, I had found nothing but paper cuts.

Whoosh! A flash of movement in the living room. "Come back!" I called and left the bathroom, rushing toward it, almost reaching the entryway, when the door swung shut.

"Will she? Will she?" came a high-pitched voice. "Will she be hanging from the hanging tree?"

Oh god. My heart hammered in my chest, and I jumped into the front closet, breathing so hard, it sounded like an iron lung. The closet was deeper than I expected and black as pitch, except for the slit of incandescent light under the door.

There came a scuttling noise from the entryway, then something blocked my sliver of light. I squatted and backed away, bumping into winter coats behind me, until something meaty and cold touched my face.

I reached up. My fingers traced a set of knuckles, then touched the sticky stump of a severed thumb.

"Oh hell," I said as my boots slipped. My hands checked my fall, and then I felt something tacky, like honey or syrup or—

Drying blood.

"Oh bloody hell," I whispered.

I looked up at a face hidden by shadows, but I already knew who it was.

Miss Haverhill hung from the ceiling. Her throat had been ripped out.

CHAPTER FIFTY-ONE

"HARKEN!" I yelled, even though he was gone and even though it was a waste of breath. I kicked the closet open and fled the apartment. "She's dead! Miss Haverhill's been . . . been . . ."

"Murdered?" A septic voice drifted down the hallway. It slinked from the ornate heating vent, a creeping murk that scraped its snout along the peeling planks of the hardwood floor, licked my bare ankles, curled around my shoulders, and yipped softly in my ear, "Murdered most foul."

"K-Kelly?"

I managed to step away from the voice, but before I could take another step, the front doors flew open, and the corridor was filled with screaming birds beating their wings and attacking with jagged claws.

"No!" I kicked and screamed. "Let me go!"

Bounding through the cacophony on all fours, Kelly made a sudden leap and hammered my knees with her shoulder. When I went down, she clamped my hair with taloned nails and dragged me through the frenzied flock.

"I've come to fetch the mistress's egg." Kelly gave my hair a wicked twist. "Give it to me, and your sister will know a quick death."

Death? "She sent you for it? Harken said Malleus would trade Devon for the egg."

"I came for it." Her face was no longer human, nor was she. "The Shadowless does not bargain with lesser norns."

"But I'm not—"

"Liar!" Kelly dragged me back into the apartment.

I grabbed the doorframe and wrenched my hair from her grasp. I had already lost my father. If anything happened to Devon, I'd lose her and Ma, too.

"Let go!" I kicked her knee, and with a pop of ruptured ligature, her hold broke. I turned for the back stairwell, then realized: Kelly was my best chance of finding Devon. "Come get me," I said and crooked a finger, "if you want that egg."

Kelly shrieked, and I leaped up the stairs to the next landing. The sound of footsteps rose behind me, along with the swish of cloth and the stench of sewage. Where had Harken gone? Together the two of us could take Kelly out. Without him my only hope was to outrun her, then double back and try to jump her. Maybe lock her in a closet till Harken came back.

"Run, run as fast as you can," Kelly called. "Your Life Plan stops when you are dead."

Where was Siobhan when I needed a smartass retort? My nerves were firing, and I could feel my pulse sparking in my fingertips as I reached the third-floor landing and looked back. Kelly was taking the stairs on all fours.

She looked up at me and licked her lips.

"Oh shit!"

I dived into my apartment. In a swirl of dead leaves smell and dank air, Kelly followed me. Before I could shut her out, she stuck her arm inside. The door slammed on her. Bones cracked, and Kelly's forearm flopped at a ninety-degree angle.

"Ouch," she said, then laughed. "That's going to leave a mark."

I laughed, too, even though I was horrified.

"Give me the egg," she howled. "Or I'll take off your head!"

"You can't have my head!" I blurted out. "I'm still using it!" *Come on, Willow Jane. Think!* I pushed the door open so I could slam Kelly again, then saw my only hope. On the wall beside the opposite apartment was a fire extinguisher. Below that, in large letters was the warning "Break Glass in Case of Emergency."

If this wasn't an emergency, nothing was.

I hip-checked Kelly to the floor. I smashed the glass panel and yanked the extinguisher from the broken shards. My finger popped the protective plastic ring, and my hands squeezed the operating levers closed. I swung around, and carbon dioxide burst from the nozzle as Kelly appeared behind me.

A thick paste of yellow dust covered her face like a death mask. For a moment she froze, and I thought I had won. Then her black-ink eyes blinked open to reveal the liquid orbs beneath. Her mouth opened, and a long tongue flickered out, glistening red.

"Nice shot." She licked her lips. "What else you got?"

"This!"

I swung the extinguisher at her temple. Steel rang, bone

crunched, and she staggered backward, while I slipped past her.

But not fast enough.

Kelly clawed at my clothes and pulled me to the floor. She dragged herself onto my belly, pinning me down. I gasped for air—my chest caved in, wheezing like dying prey.

Kelly grabbed my face and sank her tattered claws into my skin. "May I have this dance?"

"I wish . . ." Do it, Willow Jane! I bit my thumb and tried to draw out the thread the way Harken had shown me. The filament slid between my teeth, and before I could seize it, Kelly jerked my hand away. "I *wish* you'd let me go!"

"If wishes were horses," Kelly hissed, "we'd be eating your guts for dinner."

"There's a thought," Siobhan said and caved in Kelly's temple with the extinguisher.

Kelly collapsed atop me, leaking blood on my cheek.

Siobhan rolled her off and pulled me to my unsteady feet. "Holy batshit sandwich!" she said. "I think I killed her."

"No," I said and bit my thumb. "She was already dead."

CHAPTER FIFTY-TWO

A few minutes after he left the Conning girl in a trance, Harken entered the T station at Dot Ave and Southampton Street. He followed the crowd of commuters into the entrance and slipped beside a young mother as she pushed her infant through the gate. The mother and the daughter went left, and Harken turned right, thinking of the Uncanny and gossamer and the powerful electric shock when the girl had touched the torc and wondering why it hadn't killed her and finding himself very . . . pleased . . . that it hadn't. What was he feeling? When did he start feeling at all?

No, he had no feelings. It was just the girl's power that

electrified him, nothing more. And how powerful was she? As strong as Malleus had once been? If the blood of a callow Uncanny child would have made Malleus strong enough to usurp the Three Sisters, how strong would Willow Jane's blood make her?

No, not Willow Jane. Just Conning. Just another in a long line of foolish, small-minded *lesser* norns.

Except there was nothing lesser about Willow Jane. He could no longer deny it or the foolishness of wanting to be rid of her. Be rid of her, he thought, scoffing at himself. He couldn't even use the correct word for it.

Harken moved to the end of the platform and leaned against the wall. The train roared past him, blowing wind across the platform. He dropped to the tracks, avoiding the electric current coursing through the third rail, and walked into the murk. The ground between the rails was littered with paper bags, empty cups, and smoked cigarettes. Harken was surprised. Was everything so easily discarded now?

Up ahead the tunnel split in two. The scent coming from the left was pungent and strong, and he knew that he was getting closer. He grabbed a piece of rebar and took a few practice swings. He had gone into battle with worse weapons, all for Malleus and her insatiable lust for power.

Harken followed the path of the tracks for a half mile. The rank stink grew stronger with each step, until he heard a squeal to the left. He heard a second one, followed by another, and he knew he had found his former mistress.

Illuminated by a shaft of light, Malleus held a plump rat to her mouth. Its long pink tail whipped about, and it attacked Malleus's fingers with sharp teeth. All of the rat's effort was wasted. There was no flesh left on Malleus's bones to gnaw.

"Having a snack?" he asked.

Malleus pulled back her desiccated lips and snapped her jaws shut. One last squeal, and the rat stopped squirming. She spat out the head and squeezed the body so that blood dripped into her mouth. A soft gurgle came from her throat, a moan of ecstasy. Then she tossed the carcass onto a pile of fresh bodies.

On the ground beside her, wrapped in a blanket, Devon lay unconscious. Her face was pale, as if all the blood had drained from her body, too. Harken held the rebar close, wrapping his fingers around the dirty cold metal.

"We knew you were here, familiar," she said. "We could smell you."

"I can smell you, too," he replied. "The stench of your rotting flesh. The stink of a thousand senseless deaths. Or perhaps it's just your breath."

Malleus slunk toward him, disjointed, disarticulated, like a wounded spider trying to walk on two legs. "No tender greeting for a long-lost friend?"

"You were my captor, not my friend," he hissed. "You stole me from my crib and left a changeling in my place." He extended the rebar and felt her ribs hit the tip. "One more step, and I'll bash whatever shriveled brains you have left."

"Have you come to rescue the poor waif as you *saved* her forebear so long ago?"

The insult stung, but his face was a hard mask. "I'm here to broker a trade."

"We make no trade—" Malleus ripped the rebar from his hands and tossed it aside. It clattered on the rails, throwing sparks, the sound echoing in the darkness. "—with traitors."

"I had hoped you might," he said, watching her closely, "let bygones be bygones."

"We are not the . . . forgiving . . . kind."

"It's not forgiveness I want," he said, edging closer to

Devon. How many children would he allow Malleus to take? He bowed his head to hide his expression and knew what he had to say. "It's freedom. Only you can give it to me now."

"Your fate was sealed when you nailed that damned casket shut."

"Then they yoked me to a clan of lesser norns. Three hundred years of servitude is enough."

"Fate is fate."

"You can change fate. For a price."

"Do you know the price, familiar? Are you willing to pay it?"

Harken pointed to Devon. "Give her back to her family, and they will give you the egg."

"Our servant is even now striking that bargain," Malleus said and pursed her lipless mouth. "What need do we have from you?"

"What only I can give," he said and reflexively touched the torc at his throat. "The blood of the Uncanny."

CHAPTER FIFTY-THREE

WHEN I got back to the apartment, I was shaking. Whatever bravery I felt fighting Kelly had seeped from my body, leaving me feeble with weariness. My next-to-best friend had just tried to kill me, and my real best friend had barely saved me. Now Kelly lay on the floor of the empty apartment next door, one of Ma's old sheets covering her.

"Jeezum!" Siobhan said when we went inside and locked the door. "What shitstorm landed here?"

My heart fell and soared at the same time. The glimpse had erased the fight from Siobhan's memory, but it was too short to hide the carnage Malleus had left behind. What was I going to tell Siobhan? How could I begin to explain the wreckage in the living room? The blood smearing my palms? Our dead friend?

"Hello!" I heard her say in her telephone voice. "I'm at my friend's house. Some assholes have busted in here and tore the place up. It's totally wrecked!"

"Put the phone down," I said, coming up behind her. She was listening to the operator and didn't hear me, so I took it away and pressed the End button. "No cops."

Siobhan looked at me, at the cuts and bruises on my arms and the streaks of mud and blood in my hair. "Oh my god, Willow. Your face."

"What?" I said, then gazed past her and saw myself in the hall mirror.

My eyes were so sunken, they looked bruised, and my face was pale as a corpse. My shoulders shuddered, and with a loud whoop, I started to cry, great sobbing sobs. Siobhan wrapped her arms around me and pulled my head to her chest. I kept crying, feeling like a statue of cracked porcelain, needing only one more tremor to shatter into a thousand pieces.

"Willow Jane?" she said after a moment. "Where's Devon?"

"She's gone," I said into the soaked cloth of her hoodie.

"The girls in the shadows took her away."

"The girls in the what did what?" Siobhan dropped her arms and stepped back. "Willie, what the hell's going on? Did something happen to your sister?"

The front door swung open. From the darkness of the hallway, Harken entered. He was wearing a sweatshirt with the hood pulled over his eyes. When he looked up, his eyes glinted in the lamplight, and his face had just a second to register before Siobhan knocked him out cold.

CHAPTER FIFTY-FOUR

"I don't have time for more questions," I told two Boston detectives. "I've got calculus homework and an essay to write."

"You're worried about homework," one of them barked at me, "at a time like this?"

"Willow Jane's wicked stressed," Siobhan told them. "Cut my girl some slack."

In the hour since Siobhan had knocked Harken out cold, the cops had arrived—thanks to Siobhan's first 911 call. I'd tried to do another glimpse, but the filament wouldn't come out, and then it was too late. Harken had been arrested, the SVU had arrived, and the BPD had escorted Ma home from the theater. Other than a couple of long hugs and whispers, she and I'd barely had the chance to speak. The detectives swarmed us, questioning me in the living room and Ma in Devon's. Our home had been invaded by blue Windbreakers, yellow caution tape, and silver fingerprint dust, the modern criminal version of a witch hunt.

The cops exchanged a look and told me to take a minute to compose myself. I made a production of opening the bay window and leaning outside. A gurney with Miss Haverhill's body slid into the mouth of an ambulance.

Siobhan joined me, and we watched them tuck my landlord away, cleanly and efficiently.

"Miss Haverhill was mean, but I should be sad for her, right?" I whispered. "But all I care about is Devon and Ma. Does that make me a bad person?"

"It's shock. They say we'll feel nothing, and then boom! it'll hit us all at once. That's what the school counselor told me when your dad . . . y'know."

"Yeah." I didn't mention Kelly, which made me feel a hard twist of guilt, even if she had tried to kill me.

An EMT shut the doors and gave the thumbs-up to the driver. The ambulance rolled past a woman with a brown pageboy haircut. She was dressed in blue slacks that matched a SVU Windbreaker. She wove through the crowd of cops, slurping coffee.

I opened the window and leaned out, the way Ma did when she spied on the neighbors.

"O'Connell, what's the situation?" the woman asked an officer, loud enough that I could hear. Why were cops always so loud?

"Hey, Bishop," O'Connell said. "Victim died of multiple stab wounds. Medical examiner says that both thumbs were lopped off with a sharp blade of some sort. They won't know what kind until they've run the body through the lab."

"Sharp blade, huh?" Bishop said. "What about the kidnap victim?"

The officer tapped his ink pen on the clipboard. "Name is Devon Renee Conning, age seven. Abducted from the residence. Command put a BOLO out, along with an Amber Alert."

She gave her empty cup to him. "The mother's here?"

The officer pointed right to the bay window. "Upstairs. Third floor. She's with the sister, Willow Jane Conning, our only witness."

"She talking?"

The officer shook his head. "When the first unit arrived, she was bawling like nobody's business. We made her calm down, but nobody's gotten squat from her since."

"What about our suspect?" Bishop looked at the squad car where Harken sat in the back seat. "BPD likes him for the murder?"

"Yeah," the officer said. "But he denies taking the kid."

When Bishop reached our apartment, I was sitting between Siobhan and Ma on the couch. Ma had been patient with the detectives questioning her, alternating between answering the same question over and over and casting furtive glances at me. The sand in the hourglass of patience had just about run out, though. It was two minutes after nine, and my temper was growing as short as my mother's.

"I'm done talking," Ma told the detectives, dabbing her eyes with a dishrag. "Go find my daughter."

Dad used to say that Ma was perfect for him because every balloon needs an anchor and without her he would just float away. Watching her at that moment, when the pills weren't working, when the grief therapy was just talk, and even when a long-hidden cigarette was pinched between her shaking fingers as she tried in vain to light it, I realized that an anchor wants a balloon as much as the balloon an anchor. Without Dad, Ma was just going to keep sinking until she reached bottom.

Maybe this was bottom.

"Hey guys," Bishop said to the detectives when she walked in. "There's coffee downstairs."

Her voice lilted like it was a question. It was a command, and Bishop was used to giving them. The detectives put away their minitablets and ducked under the yellow tape.

"Detective Bishop." She flashed her badge. "SVU. How're you holding up?"

"SVU." Ma scoffed. "Call us a regular Boston cop. They know how to deal with criminals."

Bishop tried to smile. "Mrs. Conning, the SVU has jurisdiction in all special victim cases, and I've worked a few myself."

I hopped up. "Know what you need, Ma? A nice cup of calming tea."

"I don't want tea," Ma said.

"Coffee then," I said, because I had to do *something* to take care of her.

Bishop asked one question after another. Ma answered none of them.

"Here you go," I said and put the warm cup in Ma's hands. "A nice cup o' joe."

She took a big swallow to make me happy, then gagged. "Tastes like cat piss!"

I pretended to take a sip. "Tastes fine to me." I gave it back. "Maybe I like cat piss."

"Such a fresh mouth," Ma said and walked into the kitchen. The cabinet above the fridge made a squeak, and I heard the familiar rattle of a pill bottle. *No more secrets*, Ma had said when she'd stopped needing the pills. *We're a family again.* My instinct was to stop her, to tell her that she didn't need meds to get through this. But she did, and if I was being honest, I needed her to take the pills. Tonight I needed to have secrets.

"Just a few more questions," the detective said when Ma returned. "To clarify some inconsistencies."

Ma blinked at her. Just blinked like she wasn't even in the room.

Siobhan cleared her throat. "Mrs. Conning's too upset for questions. She's been at work all day and doesn't know anything about that dead lady. She needs to rest, right, Willie?"

At first I thought it was a clever ruse to get rid of Bishop, but Ma's eyes were half closed. She was almost out like a light. Jeezum, how many did she take?

I patted her hand. "Time for bed."

"No, I need my baby home." She looked at me. I'd seen her look this frail once before. "I'm not moving from this spot till she walks through that door."

"Ma, the cops are looking for Devon," I said. "What good can you do if you're too exhausted to help? Siobhan, give me a hand."

"Yes, boss." Siobhan hooked Ma's waist and steered her down the hallway.

"Your mother's distressed," Bishop said. "Is there someplace you can go for the night? Family close by?"

"Devon and I are the only family Ma has," I said.

"A hotel then."

"No!" I said a little too loudly. "We're not leaving. The kidnappers might come back, and this time, I'll be ready."

"Don't worry, Jane," Bishop said. "We've got the suspect under arrest."

"My name is not Jane! It's Willow Jane Conning! And *that guy* you arrested did not take my sister!"

"Jane, you need to calm down," she said. "You can't

help your mother like this."

"Don't you dare try to handle me!" I stalked into the bathroom. "Leave my mother out of this, detective. She doesn't know a thing!"

I slammed the door and splashed water on my face. Maybe I did need to calm down a little.

"You're a terrible daughter," I told my reflection. I had let a widow with a missing child drug herself and left a dead body under an old SpongeBob sheet. "And a terrible friend."

My reflection nodded in reply.

"Thanks," I said and opened the medicine cabinet and took out a box of Band-Aids. I closed the cabinet door and glanced at the mirror.

I whirled around.

On the wall behind me, words were cut into the wallpaper, as if it had been attacked with a straight razor:

When the witching hour begins to bell,
Knock three times at the gates of hell.

Laughter floated up from the grate, and I lifted the toilet seat and threw up. It was the color of tea.

CHAPTER FIFTY-FIVE

"HEY, Siobhan." I ducked my head into the hallway and called to Ma's room. "Got a minute?"

"Michael?" Ma said in a dreamy voice, and my heart broke a little.

"It's just Willow, Mrs. C." Siobhan appeared, checked the hallway, and rushed over to the bathroom. "What's up?"

"Where's the detective?"

"She left. Told a cop to watch us. He's on his phone."

Excellent. It would make escaping easier. "Listen, can you watch Ma for me? Make sure she doesn't doing anything stupid?"

"Why?"

"There's something I need to do."

"Like what?"

"If I tell you, you'll try to stop me."

"Maybe I'll stop you anyway."

"This—" I stepped back so she could see the letters gouged into the wall. "—is what."

Her eyes grew big, and she tugged on her braids. "Then again, maybe I won't. Willie, what the shitbiscuit have you gotten into?"

As much as I yearned to tell her everything, I couldn't risk it. She was the only one I could count on, and I didn't want Malleus coming after her.

"Willie," she said. "Let the cops handle this."

"Like they handled it so far? They arrested the guy who's helping me find Devon."

"He was helping you?" She smacked her forehead. "And I knocked him out?"

"Like the badass you are." I checked my watch. "Crap! I've got to go!"

"You promised you'd spill." She blocked the way. "So spill."

"I made no such promise," I said. "And I don't have time for this."

"You can fill in the details on the way." She grabbed her coat from the bedroom. "I'm coming with."

"Like hell you are."

"I helped put your ma to bed so you could get rid of the cops. I've earned some fun."

"How did you know?" Of course she knew. Siobhan always knew. "This isn't fun, dammit! It's dangerous!" I tried to push by, but Siobhan held her ground like she was guarding her crease. Stupid goalie balance. "It's about saving Devon's life, for chrissakes."

"Like I said, I'm coming with," she said. "Devon's my sister, too."

"Siobhan, I'm scared to death, but I'm the only one who can fix this."

"Life Plan," she said, sounding un-Siobhan-like serious.

"What?"

"The Life Plan. You and me. Defender and goalie." She raised a hand for a fist bump. "You got my blind spot, and I've got your back. No matter freaking what."

"But—" I almost burst into tears. Wanted to tell her how much she meant. How much I loved her. Why because of that, she was staying right here. Where it was safe. Too many people were dying. Devon was gone. Dad was gone. She and Ma were all I had left, and if I lost her, *no one* would have my back.

"Michael?" Ma called. "The baby's crying."

Siobhan dropped an F-bomb and looked back at Ma's dark room. "Christ, how much did you give her?"

"Just one." I checked my watch again. "Please? I really have to go."

"Look at you, being all badass." She gave me a hug. "I'll take care of your ma, but I want full details later. Full details, missy, or we're dropping the gloves."

"Full details," I said and forced a smile. "Later."

Siobhan checked the cop in the living room to make sure the coast was clear. She waved me over to Devon's room, pushed the door to without letting the lock catch, then turned out the light. In the glow from the street-lamps, I opened a window to the fire escape, then climbed out into the night.

CHAPTER FIFTY-SIX

MY first goal was to spring Harken from police custody. When I got outside, he was still in the back of a squad car on F Street, handcuffed to an O-ring and looking like he could spit nails.

F Street was crawling with law enforcement. The whole block was jam-packed with police cars, blue lights flashing and radios squawking. The neighbors were watching from their windows, but nobody was allowed on the street. The beat cops had strung up yellow tape and set out the sawhorse barriers. You had to have a badge to get in out of the area, or you had to know how to stop time.

Using the nosy gawkers as cover, I walked along the yellow police tape until I was close enough to Harken's squad car to hear Bishop's voice. She was standing outside the car, the back door open, which was not standard procedure on any cop show I'd ever seen. "I'm not in any hurry," she said. "So I'll play along. Got a name?"

Harken looked straight ahead. "No."

"You're somebody," Bishop said. "I'm going to find who. Just like I'm going to find out why you kidnapped a little girl and cut off a woman's thumbs."

"I did not."

"Who did?"

"Not who, what."

"All right, what?"

"Evil." Harken snapped his head so that he stared right into Bishop's eyes. "Pure evil beyond your comprehension."

"Highly refined evil. Got it." Bishop waved to a nearby cop. "Time for that psych eval. He's talking about evil spirits."

As I waited for the right moment to act, I wondered if I should be doing this at all. Devon was in danger. Not TV danger but real danger. She could be dead already.

Don't think that, just don't, I told myself. She isn't Dad, who died for no reason. That was the worst part: He died for no reason.

"Here's goes nothing," I said and bit my thumb.

I tasted something metallic, and my teeth closed on a sliver of metal. The squatting detective froze like a mannequin.

Yes! I pumped my fist. I had glimpsed! On purpose! Two times in a row!

I lifted the handcuff keys from Bishop's belt, then cuffed her to the side mirror. I felt a pang of guilt because the poor woman was never going to live it down. She might even lose her job, but it was either the detective's dignity or my sister's life.

I unlocked Harken's handcuffs and dragged him off the seat. He hit the pavement like a dead weight, and I pulled him to the sidewalk and under the yellow tape.

"God, you're heavy!" I dragged him up a neighbor's driveway and hid him behind the trash cans. "What are you, stuffed with doughnut holes?"

My stomach began to churn, right before a wave of nausea hit. Time to end this glimpse before I got too sick and blacked out. I stuck a note in Harken's pocket, then circled down the alley back to my house, giving the cops a wide berth.

You better not run out on me, Harken, I thought and licked my thumb. The strand of gossamer melted on my tongue with a sudden rush of sound and lights, and I heard a crack like a gunshot.

"Hey," I said softly after calling Siobhan's cell. "If Ma's okay, there's something I need you to do. It's a matter of life and death. . . . That's what I said, life or death. . . . Yours if you don't shut up and listen."

CHAPTER FIFTY-SEVEN

TEN minutes later Siobhan was waiting for me at the Broadway T station. "Spill," she said.

So I did. As we swiped our CharlieCards and waited on the platform, I unloaded the whole sad tale. I kept waiting for her to laugh or call crisis intervention or worse, run away screaming. But when the next train came to a stop, she cocked her head and said nothing.

The doors opened, and we got on, welcomed by the familiar scent of body odor and motor oil. We found a spot at the back, in the little nest of seats between the connecting doors and the spot reserved for handicapped. The car was fairly empty, except for a group of college kids clumped in the middle. They completely ignored us, which was fine by me.

The train sped up, and I closed my eyes, exhaustion seeping into my bones.

"So that's your story?" Siobhan said. "A refugee from *The Walking Dead* kidnaps your sister to trade for a petrified egg, which you hocked to pay rent."

"Don't forgot the part where I stop time with my magic thumb."

"And the stalker/not-stalker the cops are chasing." Siobhan stretched out and yawned. She kicked an empty drink cup across the floor. "No wonder you've been acting so, so—"

"Weird."

"So shitbiscuit." She thought for a moment. "This has to do with Will Patrick's suicide and what's-his-face dying, right?"

I shrugged a yes and looked at my reflection in the scratched and foggy window of the train. I hardly recognized my own face.

"Kelly, too? Cause her mom's been texting mad crazy since the game, saying Kelly's gone missing." The gears turned in her head. "Is she dead, too?"

I remembered her crumpled up in the stairwell of the burned-out building. How could I explain that she was already dead when Siobhan had extinguished her? "Her, too."

She hugged me, and I hugged her back, and we both began to shake with exhaustion and grief. I clung to her like my father held on to my mother on those nights when he would come home empty-handed from a gig, and while I peeked around the corner, she would build a nest for his frustration. The door would close, and the sounds of crying wept through the door. All those times I thought it was Ma, but now I realized that it was my father.

Our friend was dead. She had drifted from us, and we had let the currents take her, but she had once been part of the Life Plan.

"How're we going to do this, Willie?" Siobhan whispered, sounding tired.

Maybe I was wrong to keep her out. Maybe I needed a goalie, at least for now. "The way the Life Plan says we make it through everything," I said. "Together."

"Jeezum H. Crowbar," Siobhan whispered, then, with a snap of her fingers made the connection. "The cemetery. Those three were futzing around with that tomb." She covered her mouth. "It was real. I thought Will Patrick was just nursing a wicked hangover and Kelly was being all drama queen about what's-his-face."

"Flanagan," I said and drew in a deep breath.

"Huh?"

"What's-his-face," I said as the tracks clacked and the train leaned into a turn. "His name was Flanagan."

"Flanagan. Yeah, Flanagan. *Nollaig shona duit!*" She raised an imaginary glass and let a moment pass out of respect, and I didn't have the heart to tell her she had just wished him a Merry Christmas. "Enough with the emotional claptrap, let's see it."

"See what?"

"The thumb. I've never seen a magic thumb before. Is it sparkly like fairy dust?"

"It's not sparkly."

"Want me to believe your wild ass story?" she said and picked up the cup she'd been kicking. She crushed it and shoved it under the seat. "Then I need some physical evidence, so get your head outta your ass, Conning."

"Be careful what you wish for."

I showed her my thumb. In the train's flickering lights it looked swollen and hot, with a hard knot of pus in the middle. A thick filament of gossamer peeked out, shimmering in the train's fluorescent lights.

"That's not magic," Siobhan said. "You've got gangrene."

"I wish."

"That could be a staph infection. A really, really nasty staph infection. One requiring amputation."

"Want it to get better?" I stuck the thumb in her face. "Give it a kiss."

"Gah!" She threw her hands up. "Get that nasty thing away from me!"

"Magic isn't something you shake out of Tinkerbell's ass."

"That thumb smells like ass," Siobhan said. "Which proves nothing to this doubting Thomasina. I'll buy our friends getting caught up in some crazy rituals because this is Boston, but magic?"

I opened my coat and pulled Dad's letter from the inside pocket. "Read this."

"Read what?" she said, squinting. "It's blank."

"To you it's blank. To me it's a letter from my dad."

"Nah."

"*To my darling daughter on the occasion of her sixteenth birthday,*" I began. Then I read her the whole letter, front and back, even the poem.

"Wicked creepy." She rubbed the goose bumps from her arms. "But you write poetry. Maybe you made it up."

"And recited it all from memory?"

"Says the girl who won the Scrabble championship three years running."

"Fine. Write a word on your palm," I said and tucked the letter back in my coat. "I'll do a glimpse, and the word will appear on the window behind you."

"If it doesn't?"

"I'll be the happiest girl on Earth."

"Then we can take your ass thumb to an emergency room."

"Write."

Siobhan scribbled on her palm. "Ready, Betty."

I pressed my thumb to my lips and pulled out a short bit of gossamer. *Please let it work. I need someone to believe me, or I may lose my mind.*

The train froze, and I opened Siobhan's palm. A smiley face stared back at me. The fate of the world was hanging in the balance, and she was drawing a smiley face.

With my house key, I scratched the image on the window behind her, then broke the thread.

The train surged forward.

"So?" Siobhan said. "When's this shiz going down?"

I pointed at the window. "Already has."

"Busted! There's no—" Siobhan turned around. "Smiley . . . face. Oh hell. Oh hell hell. Oh hell that hell! That means . . . you're a . . . oh hell."

"My thoughts exactly."

"Do you know what this means?" Siobhan jumped into my lap, smothering me with kisses. "You're a freaking goddess. My best friend is a goddess!"

People deal with death in different ways. Ma goes dark, I keep everything inside, and Siobhan, she goes full Jack Russell terrier. We were like Neapolitan-flavored PTSD.

"Siobhan, calm your crap," I said. "This is serious. Malleus is a murderous hag who kills innocent people, and she still has my sister."

"Sorry, sorry, sorry." Siobhan jumped to her feet. "It's just . . . just . . . My brain is about to explode, but if you can handle it, Willie, then I can, too. Let's go kick some zombie bitch ass!"

I laughed for the first time in forever. "How could I ever say no to that?"

CHAPTER FIFTY-EIGHT

WHEN we got off the T at the JFK/UMass station, the clock on the wall read 10:54.

"How long have we got?" Siobhan asked me.

"Till midnight, the witching hour."

"We can make it. Don't give up."

"I won't." Hell would freeze and thaw twice over before that happened. "Promise."

A block from the station we turned toward an orange and green neon sign flashing DINER. We waited for a car to pass, then jogged across the rain-peppered streets to the parking lot. There were just a few cars parked in the spaces. The cars were empty except for a Chevy with three guys in it. They looked like losers, so we took a wide circle and gave them plenty of room.

The driver spotted us and whistled. "Hey baby, wanna get lucky?"

"Since three kinds of STDs is your definition of lucky," Siobhan yelled, "I'll pass."

The losers whooped and applauded.

"Talk dirty to me, baby!" the driver yelled.

Siobhan put up a middle finger. "Here's some sign language for you!"

"We don't have time for this crap," I said and dragged her inside.

The diner was warm and drier. Streaks of condensation ran down the windows, and the noise from the kitchen drowned out the big-screen TVs on the walls. A reporter was broadcasting from the sidewalk in front of my triple-decker. A bad composite sketch of Harken flashed up. The SVU in cooperation with the Boston Police Department was expanding its manhunt. That was the good news. Harken had escaped, but had he found my sticky note and would he show?

I pointed to the TV. "That's him."

"He's way cuter when he's not knocked out," Siobhan

whispered. "Talk about fairy dust! He could sample my cinnamon roll anytime."

"Siobhan! Don't be gross."

"Willie, that kid is anything but gross."

We slid into a booth. I ordered coffee, and Siobhan asked for a double chocolate milk shake with jimmies.

"What's the plan?" Siobhan asked and unpeeled her straw.

"Plan?"

"For getting Devon back."

"It's still not fully formed in my brain."

"Meaning you don't have one."

"I have one." I just couldn't tell her that she wasn't part of it. She was my only friend untouched by Malleus. I planned to keep it that way.

"Call me Obvious Girl, but how about, y'know, using your magic? Just go back in time and snatch Devon before she gets kidnapped."

"It's not technically magic, so it doesn't work that way. I don't travel in time. Just stop it and rewind it a little."

"Rewind how much?"

"A little. Harken says it'll kill me if I go back too far." No, not kill me, make me Unmade. Like Malleus.

"Do you believe him? He's like the grand poobah of time-turning powers?"

The waitress put the milk shake and coffee on the table. She didn't bother to ask if we wanted anything else.

"Nature calls," Siobhan said after she took a taste of the shake. "Don't run out on me, okay? I'm not done with the third degree yet, convict."

Convict? It felt so strange to be called that again. AP English seemed like a whole lifetime ago. My memories of this morning were shopworn recollections. If only life was as simple as wiping lunch tables. I would take that life back in less time than it takes for a hummingbird's heart to beat.

The familiar restaurant sights and sounds warmed me up: the clatter of plates in the dish bins, the sound of the cash register on the counter, the smell of fried onion rings—Dad's favorites. I felt the warm heat on my face. I heard the bright clink of flatware, bright whispers of conversation, the resonating shine of chrome-lined counters and stools.

"More coffee?" the waitress asked when she came over.

"More coffee."

The coffee came hot. I decided against the cubes of sugar and the metal pitcher of cream. I would take it black and brightly steaming. I poured coffee into the small saucer to cool it, like Dad did, then sipped from the saucer until it was cool

"Interesting way to drink coffee," Harken said.

He passed the TV screen plastered with his handsome face and took the seat opposite me, looking a little worse for wear. His eyes were ragged, and even though he tried to smirk, it looked like a sad smile. Not being perfect didn't make me think less of him. It made him go up two notches in my eyes.

"I'm glad to see you," he said.

"I'm glad to see you," I said. Part of me believed he would show up, but a small part thought he had deserted us.

"That drawing doesn't remotely resemble me." He glanced back at the TV. "My chin is much stronger, and they overlooked my wry grin."

He did look hotter than the drawing, and I was surprised how relieved I was to see that wry grin. There was something different about it, though. Not so wry maybe, but still a grin.

"Thank you," Harken said and moved his hand so that our fingertips were barely touching. "For the help with the police."

"How do you know it was me?"

"When one is cuffed in the back of a police car but suddenly finds himself on the street, he puts two and two together. Unfortunately, I was unable to track Malleus."

"No worries."

"Don't be coy," he said and looked at me sideways. "What are you hiding?"

I took a slug of coffee to settle my nerves. "Nice sweater."

"This old thing? Just something I picked up along the way." He snatched my cup of coffee and took a deep swallow, and the old grin was back. "Sorry I'm late. It took a bit of maneuvering to slip past the police, and this diner is not an easy place to find."

"That's why I chose it. My dad used to bring me here every Sunday."

"Old times' sake and all that."

"My dad said that the old Irish Mafia hangs out here." I nodded at a couple of middle-aged guys in a corner booth. They were eating fries with gravy and talking in low voices. "Everybody minds their own business."

"How are you feeling?" he said out of the blue.

"Fine," I said. "Shouldn't I be?"

"There's something I—"

"Speaking of minding your own business." Siobhan slid into the booth next to me. She extended a hand to Harken. "I'm terrible at it. I'm Siobhan Ferro, Willow Jane's best friend. She's told me all about you."

"You don't say?" He turned to me. "Precisely how much does she mean by *all*?"

"Pretty much everything."

"This," he said, "is an unexpected wrinkle."

"Don't worry about me." Siobhan made a zipping motion across her lips. "I know how to keep a secret."

"That's all well and good, but—"

Siobhan put her arm through mine. "We're a package deal."

"You're a package deal," I said.

"High five!" Siobhan said. "You finally got how to do the joke!"

"The clock is ticking," Harken said.

"Dude," she said and wrinkled up her formidable eyebrows. "Chill. It's not the end of the world."

"I assure you," he said in a low voice, "it is."

"So anyway," I said. "I've found something interesting." I showed my cell phone photo. "This was written on the bathroom wall."

"It's spelled backwards," Siobhan said.

"Not when you're looking in a mirror."

"*When the witching hour begins to bell,*" Harken read slowly. "*Knock three time at the gates of hell.* It's a poem."

"Duh," Siobhan said. "She knows it's a poem, Captain Obvious."

"Not helping," I said.

"A poem," Harken said, "referring to the Hellesgate Hotel. Are you familiar with it?"

"Every kid in Boston's heard of Hell's Gate," Siobhan said. "Stories about ghosts, flying furniture, a dead woman hung from a rope over some chick's bed. Dead girl in an elevator shaft."

"They aren't just stories," he said. "That's where we'll make the trade. Her egg for your sister's life."

"Willie's egg, you mean," Siobhan said.

"Don't call me Willie."

"It's Malleus's egg." Harken leaned forward, his voice barely above a whisper. "Her soul was trapped when I stabbed it with the needle. She'd like it back. The soul, I mean."

"You're forgetting one minor little problem," I said. "The egg's still locked up in Louie's safe. I hope."

"As I said before," he said, "locks are made to be broken."

"Awesome!" Siobhan drummed her fingertips together. "I've always dreamed of doing a B and E!"

"Shh!" I said. "It's not just a B and E."

"Two," Harken said, "you are not going."

"The hell?" Siobhan said. "Willow Jane promised me some fun."

"Fun, yes," I said, regretting that I had asked Siobhan along. I had wanted my friend with me, but now, as I looked into Harken's eyes, I knew what he was thinking. Siobhan would walk through walls for me, and that didn't mean I should let her. "But not danger."

"I laugh in the face of danger." Siobhan cackled. "Ha! Ha! Ha! See? Laughing. Wait. Holy frickdoodles!"

"What?" I said.

"The egg," she said. "It contains that kid-snatching bitch's soul, right? What happens to her when you give it back?"

Harken raised his eyebrows in a question, and I started to ask the same thing, but he cut me off.

"Siobhan Ferro, I have your name." He took her hand, staring deep into her eyes and touching his neck. "There's something you must do for Willow Jane."

Chapter Fifty-Nine

"WHOA! It's so wicked freaking late!" Siobhan stood up abruptly. "I need to check on Willow Jane's ma!"

"Certainly," Harken said. "Give our regards to Mrs. Conning."

"I will," she said and pulled on her raincoat. "See you, bubs!"

I followed her to the door, then watched her run across the parking lot into the cold, wet night. The creeps didn't seem to see her. Good thing for them.

"She better be safe," I warned Harken when I got back to the booth. "What the hell did you do to her?"

"Vexed her," he said. "Put an idea into her head, that's

all. No harm will come to her. She won't even remember it."

She won't even remember it, I thought. Were there things I couldn't remember? "I know why you did it," I told him.

"Do you?" Harken dropped money on the table. "We need to hurry ourselves. Malleus isn't known for her patience—uh!" He grunted and pitched forward, a hand pressed to his ribs. "It seems as if," he said and showed me a bloody palm, "I've been wounded."

"And you've just been *sitting there*? Christ!" I took his hand and pulled him down the back hallway, past the storage closets and the kitchen, to the ladies' room. "This way!"

"The ladies' room?" he said.

"Cleaner than the men's."

Inside the restroom I parked him on the toilet seat and locked the door. "Let's see it."

He rested his head on the wall of the wooden stall and lifted his wet shirt.

My eyes followed a smear of blood to his armpit, where blood was seeping from a puncture wound. "Whoa! You're bleeding like crazy!"

"I am?" he said and I could hear the smirk. "I'm always the last to know."

"You total asshole!" I grabbed a maxi pad from the dispenser. "You were sitting at the table, bleeding the whole time. Why didn't you say something?"

"Because—" He winced and leaned against the stall. "—I've caused enough trouble."

I pressed the pad against the gash. "So who stabbed you?"

"The friendly Boston police," he said, "when I escaped. And it's a gunshot, not a stab."

"A freaking gunshot?" I pulled the paper back and took a closer look at the wound. It looked very deep, and the skin was an angry dark purple. In first-aid class they said puncture wounds were doubly dangerous because infection could start deep in the wound. "You've been searching for Malleus with a hole in your side?"

"It's just a flesh wound."

"Bullshit. There's a bullet in you!"

"My body can handle it."

"Like hell it will," I said. "We need a doctor,"

"No doctors. They call the police," he said. "And there are things about me that medical science can't explain."

"Like what?" I scoffed.

"For instance." Harken splayed out his hand. His

fingertips were smooth, and the skin was completely devoid of prints.

That wasn't creepy *at all.* "If you won't go to the doctor, then I'll have to do. Lucky for you, I'm not completely useless. There's a first-aid kit in the supply room. I'll be right back."

"You know this how?"

"Same way I know about the Irish Mafia in the corner. Don't go anywhere."

I ducked across the hallway to the supply room. The kit was on the wall above an eyewash station, both of which were coated in dust. So much for following OSHA guidelines for employee safety.

"I'm back," I said and opened the kit.

He grunted and gritted his teeth as I gently pulled off his shirt. His skin was a mess of caked blood and dried sweat. The shirt stank of both, an acrid odor like rotted cabbage. Harken might not be human, but he sure smelled like a teenage guy. It was the first time that I'd seen him without clothes obviously, and I was amazed to find that his chest, back, and arms were covered with tattoos. Not the average Allston tattoo parlor tats, either. They were arcane symbols and shapes like hieroglyphics.

"That's a lot of needlework," I said. "Who did your ink?"

He grimaced. "It is not ink."

"Looks like ink."

"Looks can be deceiving," he said. "If Puritans ruled Massachusetts, they'd call it a devil's mark and see me burned at the stake."

"Is it a devil's mark?"

He laughed and winced, sucking in air. "There's no devil, Willow Jane, except the one that lives within the human heart."

"Nietzsche said, *He who fights with monsters should look to it that he himself does not become a monster. And when you gaze long into an abyss the abyss also gazes into you.* My AP English teacher has it on his quote wall."

"That's an odd thing to say," he said.

"Nietzsche was an odd guy."

"Can't promise that I've never been the monster."

"It's not the monster that should worry you, my teacher says. Lift your arm." I tore open a thick gauze pad with my teeth and soaked it with antiseptic. I placed his hand on the pad so he could apply pressure. "You need stitches."

"Can you sew me up?"

"Daughter of a seamstress?" For a few seconds, my eyes lingered on his face. "More pressure. The bleeding's got to stop."

He grunted but kept pressing. "This hurts."

"Don't be a baby." I pushed on his hands to help. "I left a wick of gauze so it could drain."

"Thank you," he said. "I will be yet again in your debt."

"Again? I wasn't aware that you owed me anything."

"Owing is not what I meant." He sighed and smiled. "I misspoke?"

"Whatever." I covered the gauze with a sheet of transparent dressing. "We'll need to change the bandage soon. You're still bleeding."

Harken started to put his shirt back on. "I am honored to be patched up by an Uncanny."

"By Maggie Mae Conning's daughter, not by an Uncanny."

Harken gingerly tugged his shirt back on. "Before we go, I have a confession to make."

"Later." I showed him the time and pulled open the door. "The clock is ticking."

CHAPTER SIXTY

MINUTES later a cab dropped us in front of Louie's Pawnshop. I led Harken around back to a porch lit by a single bare bulb. The rear door was steel and thick, and the handle was sturdy, which I found out when I gave it a hard twist.

"Locked," I said.

"Imagine that," Harken said. "A lock that is locked. What miracles will they think of next?"

I stepped aside. "You're up, Houdini."

"Cover your eyes." Harken smashed the light above us. "Sorry for the glass."

"I thought the plan was to pick the lock, then crack the safe."

"It was," he said, "until I saw that door. Give me some light."

"Didn't you just break the light?" I said but shone my phone's flashlight on the handle. "It's late. We need to hurry."

"I am." Harken pulled out a leather case. He opened it and removed a blank key and a diamond file.

"Where did you get that?" I asked.

"Found it."

"Where?"

"Lying about." He inserted the blank into the lock and bore down with great force. He removed the blank and went at it with the file, notching out bits of metal. "I'm lucky like that."

"Can we hurry this up?" I tucked a strand of hair behind my ear. "What are you doing?"

"Isn't it obvious?" He blew metal shavings off and tested it again. "Making a key."

"Not a very good one."

"Patience." After a couple more notches he slid the key into the lock. "Voilà."

"Finally!" I pushed the door open. "Let's see you crack the safe."

The back hallway led to Louie's office. I shone my phone around till I found the light switch. The fluorescents flickered on, but there was no safe in sight. I pushed aside a painting of dogs playing poker and knocked on the paneling behind them.

"What're you doing?" Harken asked, picking up random objects from Louie's desk, then putting them back down. Probably "finding" other things to pocket.

"In the movies the safe is always behind artwork."

"The safe's almost never behind a painting, and I'd never refer to that as art. Try the floor. Or the closet."

I opened the only closet in the room. It was full of cheap suits and a few yellowed wedding dresses covered with that thin plastic.

"Nothing here but junk," I said. "It's getting really late. Maybe Louie lied about a safe."

"Found it." Harken's voice came from Louie's desk, followed by a loud slam. "Ouch! Damn it!"

"So much for stealth." I shone my light on the safe. It was a classic cube model, squat, hard, and heavy. "Just like Louie."

Harken pressed the buttons and tried the handle. "Locked."

"Imagine that." I didn't bother to hide my smirk. "A lock that's locked. What miracles will they think of next?"

"I was expecting a dial and tumbler," he said. "This lock is much more . . . modern."

"I can do it."

He raised an eyebrow and stepped aside. "You're up, Houdini."

I dialed 911 on Louie's desk phone. "I'd like to report a robbery in progress. Louie's Pawnshop on Broadway."

"A unit has been notified," the operator said. "Please identify yourself."

"I'm the owner!" I whispered. "Hurry up! Before they rob me blind!"

I hung up, then hit the speed dial button labeled "Home."

Louie's sleepy voice came over the line. "Who the hell is this?"

I gave it my best Southie accent. "Is this the owner of Louie's Pawn? This is Officer Rooney of the Boston Police Department. You better get down here. There's been a break-in, and your safe's been cracked. Right. Right. Does this sound like a joke to you? Yeah, I didn't think so."

I hung up, then grinned at Harken. "There you go. That's how you crack a safe."

"Someone forgot to tell the safe. It's still locked."

I patted his cheek, then checked the clock. "Watch and grow wise, grasshopper," I said. "Let's find a good seat for the show."

"Wait," he said and held my arm. "Do you know where Louie lives? What if it takes too long for—"

"He lives two blocks down Broadway. Everybody knows that. Now quit doubting my plan and come on. The clock is ticking."

Five minutes later, a squad car parked behind the pawnshop. Its lights were on, but not the siren. From our hiding place behind a Dumpster, we watched two cops walk to the porch. The female cop stepped on the broken pieces of the lightbulb and signaled her partner to draw his weapon.

Seconds later, a beat-up Mercedes pulled up behind the cop car. Louie kicked his car door open and swung his legs out.

"Stand where you are!" the female yelled.

"I'm the owner, officers!" he called out, and waddled over. "I got a call that my place was robbed."

The cops traded a quizzical look, and the male cop pushed past him. Louie started to follow, but the female cop put a hand up to stop him.

"Wait here, sir," she said and joined her partner inside.

Louie hung back for half a minute, stalking around and cursing at the shattered bulb. I could almost see the gears turning in his head and the curiosity building inside.

Seconds later Louie, obviously tired of waiting, went inside.

"This plan has no chance of working," Harken whispered.

I stuck my hand out. "Bet you twenty."

"Twenty what?"

"Twenty dollars."

Harken spat into his palm. "Agreed."

"I wouldn't shake spit hands for a hundred bucks." I wrinkled up my nose. "Wait. Here they come."

We ducked back behind the Dumpster, and I watched Louie lead the cops out. He patted both their backs, and the officers returned to their squad car.

"How much gossamer would I need for two minutes?" I whispered.

"Too much," he said. "You're not capable of a long glimpse."

"Theoretically speaking," I said. "A half inch? An inch?"

"Willow Jane, do not."

I caught a sliver of gossamer in my teeth and drew out an inch of silver filament, twisting it as I pulled. A wave of nausea hit my gut, and a cramp bent me in half. I cried out, the pain was so intense. Harken was right. I wasn't ready for such a long glimpse, and my body was delivering the message with pain. I fell to my knees, and the familiar red and blue triangles formed the rip across my vision.

The gap opened like a porthole into another world. It grew rapidly, and soon I was no longer seeing in full color. Even in the dim light the world had been rendered in sepia tone. I stared at Harken, frozen in place, his face like an old daguerreotype portrait.

With the back of my fingers, I touched his face.

It was warm.

Then his head turned toward me, and I scrambled backward, ready to scream but realizing that there was no need. His body moved awkwardly, with herky-jerky motions, like a DVR recording going backward.

Time was on rewind.

"Wicked," I said, because it was. The first time I'd glimpsed, I had somehow saved Devon from getting killed by a car, then blacked out. Now I could not only stop time, I could make it go in reverse.

I turned to the porch, where Louie and the cops were walking backward into the shop.

"Wait!" I yelled and chased after them. I had to reach Louie before he could get to the safe, or my whole plan would be ruined.

I caught them in Louie's office as they walked in reverse toward the desk. The cops moved to either side, and a red-faced Louie struggled to lower himself to his knees. He crawled backward, butt in the air. He reached for the safe.

"Hold on!"

I grabbed a notepad and pen, then squeezed my head under the desk. Louie's breath huffed out like a mix between rancid cheese and rotten sausage. I held my nose while Louie turned the handle, then pushed the buttons in opposite order. I scribbled down the combination.

Louie crawled out from under the desk. I scooted around the female cop and ducked into the closet between the wedding dresses. Then I pulled the closet shut, licked my thumb, and was sucked down the rabbit hole. It felt as if a meat hook had been driven through my side and then yanked hard, pulling my guts along with it. I struggled against the sensation, fighting to stay in the glimpse even though doing so was pulling me apart at the seams.

In the distance, like his voice was coming from a string phone, Louie said, "Sorry to waste your time, officers."

Nausea made me double over, and I had one final look at the cops and Louie leaving the room before I sank to my knees.

Then like that, it was over.

The nausea.

The vertigo.

All of it.

Outside, the car engines started. I crawled on hands and knees across the dirty shag carpet to the safe. My fingers danced over the dial to the tune of the numbers I had memorized. I said a little prayer, then pulled the handle.

The door swung open.

My egg lay inside atop a nest of twenties and fifties. There was enough cash to pay rent three times over. Yesterday I would've been like Tantalus beneath an apple tree, trying to grab it all. With no more landlord, there was no point in it. Like my dad always said, Connings weren't the most conventional people, but thieves we were not.

"Hallelujah," I said, picking up the egg.

The egg felt warmer than I remembered, and the surface seemed smoother and more delicate, almost translucent. I shone my cell phone LED on it and gasped when the light went straight through.

"So that's what evil looks like," I said, and with an eye roll to the heavens, I toppled over and hit the floor like a bird with broken wings.

CHAPTER SIXTY-ONE

I awoke in the back seat of a yellow taxi, feeling like I'd been punched. Harken was sitting beside me, and he patted my shoulder when the taxi stopped. I sat up, groggy, and stared out the rain-streaked window at the lights of the Harvard Bridge over the Charles River.

"Where are we?" I asked, exhausted. That glimpse had really done a number on me.

"Three seventy Helles Alley," the driver said. "That'll be forty bucks."

"Forty bucks?" I said, checking my nose to make sure it hadn't been bleeding. "Seriously?"

"Hey, sweetie," the driver said. "It ain't easy getting

from Southie to Back Bay in fifteen minutes. Your boy-friend said he'd make it worth my while."

Harken leaned forward and looked closely at the cab-bie's license. "Sorry, but I lied." He caught the guy's eye in the mirror. "Thank you for the ride, Robert Bickle. It's on the house. We should enjoy our night."

"Enjoy your night, kids," Bickle said. "This one's on the house."

"You'll be sharing your umbrella, too," Harken said.

"Sure thing." Bickle slid open the glass between the front and back seats. He passed his compact umbrella through. "Stay dry out there."

Harken swung the door open and held a hand out for me. I accepted not because he was gallant or anything but because the grogginess caused my head to spin as soon as I moved.

"Where's the egg?" I said, watching the taxi drive away.

Harken took it out of his back pocket for an instant, giving me a brief glance at it. Even in the streetlights, it looked as dull as before. "I picked it up in the pawnshop. After you blacked out."

"Can I keep it?" I said.

"Better it stays with me," he said. "Safer for you that way."

✕ ✕ ✕

We walked up Commonwealth toward the Hellesgate. Harken held an umbrella over us. I got as close as possible without touching him, exhausted from the long glimpse, feeling frayed at the edges. To our left the rain peppered a large drainage pond beneath the Mass Ave viaduct. Harken steered us across the street and turned right on Beacon, where the upscale street was lined with nice cars on both sides. During summer they were lined with shade trees, too, but the foul weather had chased the leaves away. The people, too. We were the only people on the block, if you didn't count drivers, and I didn't. They were nestled in toasty warm cars while we were dodging puddles and getting lashed by the wind. Harken and I were the only ones crazy enough to be out in the cold rain right before midnight.

Sickly streetlamps lit the sidewalk as we moved through the oases of light, the beams shining on our heads like halos, and our breath froze in the foggy night air. The wind was stinging my face, and I could feel my cheeks blooming from windburn.

"Thanks for rescuing me," I said. "I don't know what happened."

"An aftershock from the glimpse," he said, sounding cranky and a little worried, too. "Didn't I warn you not to go back too far? You're fortunate to be here."

"I feel more woozy—" My balance was shot, and my tongue felt too big for my mouth. "—than lucky. So what's our plan?"

"Plan?"

"To make the switch for Devon," I said and grabbed his sleeve. "We have to have a plan."

"Well, we go to the thirteenth floor. Find room thirteen thirteen. Give Malleus the egg and take your sister back."

"That easy?" I said. "A murderous magical death skeleton is just going to cooperate?"

"Malleus," he said. "always keeps her word, which is not necessarily a good thing. Here we are."

We stopped in front of the hotel entrance, a high marble arch with the name of the building carved in ornate Old English. All those horror stories Siobhan and I had heard and other ones I didn't like to think about, like a little girl falling to her death in an elevator shaft, but I never thought they were possible.

Until now.

I looked up through falling rain at the intimidating edifice. The hotel had been renovated, turned into condos, gentrified like the rest of this too quiet neighborhood. But under each window, lit by the glow of streetlights, almost as a reminder of the hotel's true purpose, were reliefs of gargoyles with open mouths and sharp fangs. A wild-haired gorgon held up a severed head over the arch of the main entrance, blood dripping into its hungry mouth.

"What kind of man built those?" I asked.

"You don't want to know," he said. "Trust me."

"I don't." Even though I was starting to really trust him. "Can't be people actually *live* here. Rich people?"

"There's no accounting for taste," he said, jimmying the front door with a penknife. "Especially among the wealthy."

"Where did you get the penknife?"

"Found it."

A rush of hot, stuffy air greeted us. The lobby entryway was straight out of the Gilded Age with ornate paintings, marble staircases, and fresco ceilings. An elevator sign pointed to an alcove on the right. We shook off the rain, and Harken tossed the umbrella into a corner.

"Stand by the elevator." He pointed to a desk in the

middle of the lobby where a man in a green uniform was snoozing. "I'll take care of the security guard."

"Don't—" I whispered.

"What?"

"—hurt him."

He winked.

I didn't wink back.

I slipped into the alcove, which housed the four elevators that serviced the old hotel. They were straight out of a black-and-white movie, with hand-controlled doors and an accordion gate cage. Above each elevator, old-fashioned arrows indicated the floors. I counted them, one through twelve, then fourteen. I couldn't believe these things still worked.

Wait. Where was the thirteenth floor?

Harken approached the guard. He chatted away, trying to meet the guy's eye but couldn't seem to manage it. His mouth tightened, then he passed a hundred-dollar bill across the desk. The guard stood and shook hands, but Harken gave the beefy mitt a sudden yank and jabbed his penknife into the man's fleshy hand.

"What the hell?" The guard pulled his revolver and aimed it at Harken's chest. "You're under arrest!"

Harken stepped back. "Willow Jane, can I get a hand?"

"Not again," I said, my stomach rolling at the thought of glimpsing again so soon.

I pricked my thumb with my teeth. A single drop of blood bubbled up, then, a few seconds later, it glimmered and turned silver, the bubble thinning until it formed a single strand. I bit down and drew out the thread. *Just a few millimeters*, I reminded myself, my knees shaking.

"I'll shoot you both!" the guard yelled, waving the weapon back and forth, then he stopped mid-threat.

The guard and Harken were suspended in time, then began to move backward, like they were rewinding. An electric chill went up my spine, and my tongue tasted like I had swallowed battery acid. The world began to swirl, turning all colors, then milky white as Harken and the guard morphed into statues carved from marble.

I walked slowly over to them, holding my chest because it was like breathing through a straw. I removed the gun from the guard's holster and hid it in the trash can beneath a pile of TastyKake wrappers.

"That should do it," I said, then returned to the elevators.

With a roar of sound and light, the glimpse ended, and

I leaned against the Italian marble wall. The stone felt so cool on my cheek I wanted to fall asleep right there.

Across the lobby Harken passed the hundred-dollar bill across the desk. The guard stood and shook hands. Harken gave the beefy mitt a sudden yank and jabbed the man's hand.

"What the hell?" the guard yelled and reached for his empty holster.

Harken grinned. "Looking for something?"

"My weapon!" the guard barked, then promptly passed out across the desk.

"Sorry about that." Harken grabbed the keys but left the hundred-dollar bill. "Aqua Tofana doesn't know her own strength."

When he joined me, he was noticeably agitated and carrying a fireplace poker on his shoulder. He put a round key in a lock by the elevator and pressed the call button.

"You couldn't vex him, could you?" I said.

He pressed the call button again. "Did you hurt him?" I said. "And where did the poker come from?"

"There's a lovely fireplace on the far side of the lobby," he said. "I didn't lay a finger on him."

"But you did stab him," I said. "Is he okay?"

"He'll wake up with a headache, but he'll live."

"What's Aqua Tofana?"

"You heard that?"

"I hear lots of things now," I said, rubbing a smear of blood from my thumb.

"It's a—" He paused, and I could hear a lie in the silence. "—sedative."

"For what? Elephants?"

He looked at me funny and started to say something as the elevator arrived. A bell pinged as the doors opened, eagerly inviting us to enter a cage made of dark mahogany panels and crisscrossed, gilded metal straps.

"Dammit, we have to take the stairs," I said wearily when I looked inside.

"To the thirteenth floor?" Harken pushed aside the old-fashioned accordion door, and we stepped aboard.

I pointed to the buttons on the panel. "In case you hadn't noticed, they skipped that floor. It goes from twelve to fourteen."

He pressed both ten and three at the same time. "You just have to know which buttons to push."

The elevator surged and began to move up. It rose with the creaking sound of metal on metal, and we watched the floor numbers light up, one after the other, until we passed the twelfth, then fourteenth floors.

Harken began tapping the stop button, but the lift kept rising. "Come on now," he said. "Do *not* make a liar out of me."

My heart began to pound. I could feel panic starting to tighten my chest, and my thumb started to itch seriously. At the top floor, number twenty-one, the elevator came to an abrupt stop. I reached for the cage to open it, but Harken pulled my hand back.

"Something's terribly wrong," he whispered.

CHAPTER SIXTY-TWO

THE lights went out, and we hung there like a spider clinging to its web. A booming clap of thunder seemed to shake the entire hotel, and I grabbed Harken's arm for support. He had just enough time to smile at me before the bottom dropped out. Air whooshed by, and the elevator free-fell so fast, it felt like the air was sucked out of my mouth, and Harken's eyes rolled back into his head. The cage shook violently, and I heard the noise of the accordion gate slamming against the shaft. Above us, the emergency brakes screamed but didn't slow our descent, the air stinking like brake shoes and me swearing to god we were being turned inside out. There was a loud, heavy clunk, and the floor indictor arrow swung wildly from the left to the right, then back, burying itself below the numeral one.

Another loud clunk, and my lungs found air and my voice caught up with me.

"Stop!" I yelled.

The lift stopped, as abruptly and violently as if it had hit bottom. I braced myself, legs wide and hips low, and broke my fall with my elbows and knees, but Harken wasn't so lucky. I heard him slam into the floor, and he lay silent for several seconds while I said a silent prayer.

Then he moaned and sat up slowly. "Welcome to the thirteenth floor."

"It's in the basement?"

"This isn't the basement," he said. "We didn't fall."

"The knot on my ass—" I pulled the gilded cage open and crawled outside. "—says different."

As soon as I cleared the lift, the cage slammed shut, capturing Harken inside. "No!" he yelled and leaped, but he was too slow. The accordion gate locked, almost slicing his fingers off. "Open up!"

He rammed the gate, then tried to pry it open with the poker, but it would not give. "It's too short. See if you can find a long pipe or something to help me wedge it open," he said. "Stay close. Make sure I can see you."

"And I'm the bossy pants?" I said and swept the area with my cell's light. All I found was empty metal shelves collecting a dust. "Maybe we can use one of the shelves if I can take them apart."

I took one step away from the elevator and heard a child's laughter. "Devon!" I said. "Harken! It's my sister! Devon, hang on!"

"No!" Harken yelled. "It's a trap!"

"It's Devon!" I said, sure of what I'd heard. "You have to find your own way out!"

"I said, do not leave!" he yelled.

"I am going," I yelled back, "to get my sister!"

Room 1313. Find it. Trade the egg. Rescue Devon. Head on a swivel. Stick on the ice. Control time and space. Get your head in the game, Conning. Then I remembered something and held out my hand to him. "Give me the egg."

"No. Wait for me to get out," he said. "If she takes it from you, you're both dead."

"Never mind! There's no time to argue." I turned heel and hurried away. "I'll find her myself!"

"Damned stubborn Connings! Wait!" he said and

pushed his hand through the gate. He held out his hand, and I shone my phone light on it. In his palm were a few mangled coins. They looked like old tokens for the T. His voice softened. "Take these, just in case."

"I need to *go*!" I said, but pocketed them. My cell's light danced along the floor until the beam found the outline of a door. It was a massive oak thing made of thick planks joined with rusted iron straps. The knob was a huge iron ring. I wrapped both hands around it, the rust dissolving in my palms, and pulled hard.

"Slow down!" Harken called. "You have no bloody idea what's waiting on the other side!"

"Do you know what's inside?" I swung my light back to him. His face was pressed against the accordion gate, and one hand was searching, as if he could reach me if he just strained hard enough. "Have you been here before?"

"I served her, remember? I know how she thinks!"

Maybe you still serve her, I thought darkly. "Knock three times on the gates of hell," I said and rapped on the planks.

With a dull clunk the lock gave way. The door swung open, revealing a hallway full of doors that stretched out past the beam of my light. They were painted sickly green and trimmed in yellowed white. They were out of place in the dank hallway that stank of mold and dead leaves, but they weren't the only thing off-kilter. The floors undulated and sloped hard to the left, and the walls and ceiling joined at wrong angles.

Boom! A clap of thunder shook the building so hard, debris fell from the ceiling. The dust danced like snow-flakes in the light beam until a second boom shook, and my light went out. I tapped my phone against the heel of my hand. The light brightened for a moment, then choked again.

A familiar singsong voice whispered, "Yesterday, upon the stair. I found a girl who was not there. A doll of paper she became. Oh, wish, oh, wish, the girl would hang."

I stood still as death. Waiting and holding my breath and praying that in the silent shadows I had only imagined the sound. My ears rang, filling with static until the air in my lungs was spent and it felt like I was creating a vacuum in my own chest.

"I like . . . ," the voice whispered. ". . . your thumbs."

"Devon?" I said and exhaled.

I was answered with a peal of laughter, followed by a thundering boom. It started on the far end of the hallway, a deep percussive thud that echoed through the wall. The hammering came closer, moving from door to door.

Closer.

Closer.

"Let me alone!" I screamed. "Get out of my goddamn head!"

The sound died, and the hallway fell silent.

"Jesus," I whispered, wishing that Harken were with me. *Should I go back for him?* I wondered.

Then came the footsteps, the padding of little feet like breath condensing on cold glass, moving across the floor. I heard the sounds of climbing, of soles on wooden steps, then another laugh before silence fell again.

"Devon?" I called. "Are you there?"

Then a clattering crash and a sound like rope being stretched. The air moved gently, like something—some*one*—was swinging in the wind. It was too much. The stretching sound was too much, and I couldn't bear to stand still another second.

Right behind me a door slammed, and suddenly I felt a hand pressing against my mouth, and a strong hand seized my coat. I screamed, "No!" I was not going to be caught this way!

"Willow Jane!" Harken said, and my phone light flickered to life. It shone onto his face. "Stop! It's me!"

"You asshole!" I punched his shoulder, then punched it again. "You scared me to death."

"Sorry," he said. "I didn't mean to frighten you."

"You asshole!" I hissed and would've slapped him if rusty hinges hadn't squeaked and a door hadn't scraped open. "Please tell me you heard that."

"I heard that."

Harken raised the poker. The nearest door, which had been closed seconds before, swung closed, as if someone had just darted into the room—someone laughing.

"It's my sister," I whispered.

"Wait," he said.

But I pushed the door open, crossed myself, and stepped inside.

Chapter Sixty-Three

A single bare bulb hung by a thread from the high ceiling, casting harsh light on the floors and walls. The room was empty. No furniture, no decorations, no Devon, and only a hint of rot in the air, but I couldn't escape the feeling that something was lurking in corners.

Reluctantly I backed out. "Which way now?" I said.

"Follow me."

Harken walked slowly into the blackness with the poker, then veered abruptly to the left. I snagged his coat and fought the urge to grab his hand. We cut to the right, then the left again, my shoes slipping on the dust-coated floor. Harken stopped short, and I plowed into him. My mouth hit his shoulder blade, and I felt something warm on my chin.

"What's wrong?" Harken said as he faced me.

I splayed out my fingers. "Blood."

A handkerchief appeared in his hand. "Wipe it off."

"I'm okay. It's just a little cut lip." I held the cloth to my mouth. "The bleeding's almost stopped."

"Good." He took the handkerchief, folded it carefully, and stuffed it back in his pocket. "Malleus shouldn't see your blood."

"Why not?" I said.

"The blood of the Uncanny drives—" He stopped as the sound of soft cawing drifted down the corridor. "Music."

"Where's it coming from?" I said.

"Your phone, please?" he said and held it up to illuminate the ceiling. There was only sagging wallpaper and decrepit plaster above, peeling from the ceiling like flecks of dead skin.

"It's not coming from the ceiling," I said.

"No, from the heating vents," he said. "Look at the walls."

"Oh my god," I said. The wallpaper was flayed open,

revealing jarring and disjointed red letters, all spelling out the same words hundreds of times: *BLOOD WILL HAVE BLOOD.* "Is that for us?"

"Malleus's idea of a welcome. Don't let it bother you."

Right, I thought. It was just wallpaper. That looked like skin. Flayed skin. "Still got the egg?" I asked. "Because I'm sick of being screwed with. It's time to do this."

"It's right here." Harken pulled it from his back pocket. "Remember, when the moment comes, we *must* give it to Malleus."

"The egg for Devon's life," I said angrily, "is a trade I'd make every day for eternity."

We made our way down the hall. We passed one, two, three doors. Harken tried each, only to find it locked, and none of them was numbered. With every step my eyes watered more, the tears occluding my vision, like I was swimming underwater in a murky pool. Malleus's stench grew stronger, and every breath stung my lungs, the fumes leaving a metallic flavor in my mouth.

"Shh!" Harken said sharply and pointed at a door, mouthing the word *Here.*

I heard the sound of flat chirps and caws, like an off-tune flute. The door was several inches narrower than the others and higher, too, with ornate carvings in the wood and etching on the crystal knob. It looked like the lid of a casket.

Harken tapped the door and then reached for the knob.

The door blew open, and a murder of crows burst forth, cawing and screeching, black wings beating the air, attacking us with beaks and claws, ripping at our flesh with ferocious anger. I threw my hands up to protect my face, stumbled backward, and slammed into the wall.

I rolled to the floor, swatting at the birds. "Get off me! Get off!"

They vanished.

As suddenly as we were attacked, the crows were gone. All that remained was a pile of rotting feathers on the ruined carpet, and inside the empty room Harken kicked mounds of feathers aside. No Devon. No furniture. Just an old, crumbling fireplace, stained walls, and rotted floors. He cursed and kicked again, then shut the door behind him.

"Not there, damn it," he said, sounding more agitated.

"Let's keep moving." Steading myself on the wall, I got to my feet, just as a wave of noxious odor seeped past me. "Jeezum, it smells like something died."

"She did." Harken held my phone light close to the wall, which was covered in paper that had been ripped to shreds, like huge claws had flayed it, and found a button switch. He punched it with a finger, and one after the other, three hanging bulbs started burning. "Malleus always leaves a trail of stench."

But it wasn't the Shadowless we smelled.

I bumped my head on something hard. I screamed and jumped back against the wall, then screamed louder. Harken raised a hand to calm me, but it was useless. My whole body shook as I pointed up. He followed my gaze with the phone light. The glow shone on a pair of dirty bare feet dangling at eye level. The broken toenails were painted dark purple, and though the polish was chipped, I recognized the shade. Siobhan and I had been seated next to her when the pedicurist applied it a week ago.

"Kelly," I cried. "Oh, Kelly." Her body rotated slowly, dirty hair hiding her face but not the rope digging into the bulging purple-black skin of her neck. "Please, cut her down."

"She's dead, poor thing," he replied and tried to hide the light. He reached out to comfort me. "And there's no time to help her."

"She was my friend!" I knocked his hand away, then

yanked the phone back . "Don't tell me not to help. Cut her down, or I will."

"I will," he said. "I need something to stand on. Wait here."

"Hurry," I said and raised the light again. It made my stomach turn to look at her, but I had to see it. I had to be witness to what Malleus had done. "Kelly, I'm so sorry."

Kelly's eyes popped open.

I screamed, "Harken!"

Laughter trickled heating vents, and Malleus stepped out of the shadows. "So kind of you to join the fun, Uncanny. Do you like the present we left you?"

"Oh, my effing god," I whispered as I saw her clearly for the first time.

She carried tailor's shears as long as her forearm. Her face looked like a mask: The flesh was mottled and pocked with deep scars, and the skin was so pale it seemed translucent. But it was the eyes that made me shiver—black as midnight, the irises reflecting the naked light. Hanging from her neck, like mummified ornaments, was a string of thumbs. There were dozens, the necklace long and looped.

"Do you like our thumbs?" Malleus licked her razor-thin lips. "Shall we add your sister's to our collection?"

CHAPTER SIXTY-FOUR

"NOT my sister, you bitch!" I yelled and lowered my shoulder. Square up. Stay low. Drive through the body. Check her hard. But before I could charge, Malleus seized my forearm.

"Give us the egg!" she demanded.

"Give back my sister first!" I yelled. "Harken!" Where *was* he?

Her bony fingers dug into my skin, and I could feel hard, swollen knuckles grinding into my muscles. She had an iron grip I couldn't break, even when I checked her, slamming a forearm to her shoulder. There was a sound of cracking bone, but Malleus held me tight.

"The price to be paid in flesh!" She pinned me to the wall with one hand and raised the shears above my head. "The price to be paid in blood!"

"No!" Harken said, swinging the poker and jamming it between the blades of the shears. He grabbed both ends of the steel shaft and shoved her back. She barely yielded, and they stood deadlocked, both of them towering over me, roaring and cursing, before Harken tore the poker free and swung wildly, making her dodge, forcing her farther away from me.

Eyes up! I told myself. Move! But I didn't. My feet stayed planted, like I was sinking into mud. Harken attacked again, using the poker like a gaff, stabbing Malleus in the chest. His eyes met mine. They were wild and silently screaming, Go! And yet I couldn't.

"You cannot kill." Malleus laughed and pulled the sharp tip out of her rib cage. "What is not dead."

Harken spun around and threw a roundhouse upper-cut that caught her chin. Crack! Her jawbone broke, and she howled. "Willow Jane!" he barked. "Wake up! Find your sister! I'll deal with Malleus."

"You have defiled us!" she screeched, then roared into Harken, slamming him against the wall. Her shears tore out chunks of plaster as she tried to stab him again and again as he barely got the poker up to block her. "Too slow!" Malleus said as she suddenly shoved him away. "Too weak! You cannot hurt us, familiar!"

Maybe he couldn't hurt her, but he could buy me time to find Devon, and that's what he was trying to do. Off your ass, Conning! I rolled away and jumped to my feet, shoving the phone in my pocket. I ducked back down the hallway, turned a corner, and found a stretch of rooms that went on forever.

I ran to the first door.

It was number 1313.

The clock ticks, Uncanny.

I kicked the door open. "Devon!"

The room was empty, the windows boarded up, the walls plastered with cobwebs, a thick carpet of dust on the floor. It looked like no one had been inside in decades.

I heard a child scream. "Devon!" I yelled and ran back into the hallway and to the next room down.

It was number 1313.

"What the hell?"

She wasn't there. Not in that room 1313, or the next 1313 or the next. Each time I burst in, it was the same boarded-up windows and empty, cobwebbed spaces until finally I reached the last door. *What if Devon isn't in there?* No, Devon had to be here. Malleus wanted the egg more than she wanted my sister. What good would it do her to trick us?

I twisted the knob.

Locked.

Open! I kicked the lock stile, and unlike the other flimsy doors, it held fast. I kicked it again. Something did not want me in the room, but by God, I was getting inside!

Then I heard flapping wings.

I tensed up to ram it with my shoulder, but the door swung open.

"Devon!"

A single bare bulb lit the room. The window was wasn't boarded up like the others, and cobwebs hung like sheets, In the middle of the room Devon lay on a stone table, a heavy wooden board pressing on her chest. Rooks were gathering pebbles from the floor and piling them on the board, adding to the growing mound, the weight ounce by ounce crushing my sister.

"More weight!" they cawed, mimicking a man's voice. "More weight!"

I stood in the threshold, not believing my eyes.

"Too late, too late!" they cawed. "More weight, more weight!"

Thunk!

Malleus buried her shears in the crossrail above my head. I screamed and ducked, but she wrapped a festering arm around my neck and held me while the birds piled more stones onto my sister's tiny body.

"Let me go!" I growled, but Malleus pulled me into the hallway as I fought back, yanking her arm off my throat. "I swear to God!"

"Leave her alone." Harken crawled toward us. His hands were bathed in blood, and a gash stretched across his forehead, blood trickling down his face. He collapsed onto his stomach, then reached out. "Please."

Laughing, Malleus stomped on his outstretched hand. "One of you will die now," she hissed in my ear and swung me around to face Harken. "Your sister or you. Choose."

"The hell I will!" I dropped to a knee and yanked her arm hard. "Choose this, bitch!"

Malleus flew over my shoulder and fell hard onto the hallway floor. I dived back into the room and kicked the door closed. Outside, Harken shouted something at

Malleus, but by then I had scrambled to my feet, my shoes slipping in the thick dust. I dived across the room, yelling and clapping my hands at the birds roosting on the thick board.

"Get off my sister!"

They were deaf to my cries, and they kept piling the stones, as if I were a ghost they couldn't see. With a sweep of my arm, I tried to scatter the rooks, but they bounced away and came right back, shrieking, "More weight! More weight!"

"Shut up, you goddamn birds!" I yelled. "Hold on, Devie! I'll get you out."

I tried to lift the board. My muscles strained, and I felt something pop in my back. All the blood rushed to my face, and little supernovas exploded in my eyes. The pebbles, though, began to shift. They rolled down the board and cascaded to the floor. The more I pushed, the lighter the board got until with one last heave I sent it flying.

"Devie!"

My sister lay like a corpse on the stone table. Her hair formed a halo around her head. I reached for her, and she sat bolt upright, eyes rolled back, and screamed, "Will and Kelly swinging from a tree, HA-NG-ING!"

I shook her shoulders. "Devon! Wake up!"

"WILL AND KELLY SWINGING FROM A TREE, HA-NG-ING!"

"Come on!" I slapped her cheek. "Snap out of it!"

Her head pivoted slowly toward me. Her eyes popped open, and she smiled. "The dead girl says hello." Then she went limp, her face drained of color, her body drained of life.

CHAPTER SIXTY-FIVE

I grabbed Devon's wrist to check for a pulse, but my own heart was beating too loud and fast to find one. I pressed my ear against her throat. A few seconds passed, then I heard it, the faint thump of a heartbeat.

"She's alive!" I yelled. "Thank God. Wake up, Devie. C'mon."

Devon's eyes stayed closed, no matter how much I shook her. She was alive, but for how long? We had to get to an emergency room. I checked my phone. No bars, no signal. I gathered her in my arms, kicked through the cawing rooks, and carried her to the door.

There I paused, an ear to the wood, listening for sounds of the fight.

Nothing.

Nothing but my own heartbeat.

If Malleus had beaten Harken, she would have the egg, and there would be no reason to spare our lives. I yanked open the door and stepped into the hallway. The way was clear both ways. No Malleus in sight, but no Harken, either.

I held Devon tight and headed for the elevator.

"Why do you hurry, little one?"

I looked up and wished to God I hadn't.

Malleus was suspended above the hallway, long, spindly arms and legs pressed against the walls. Before I could move, she dropped like a counterweight and slammed us to the floor. My ears rang like a shot had bounced off my skull, and Devon rolled out of my arms.

"We tire of the game." Malleus lifted Devon by the hair and pressed the tip of the shears against an eyelid. "Give us the egg, or we shall make the waif's flesh a pillow and stuff it with her pretty hair."

"Let go of her." I was woozy, my vision a blur, my equilibrium gone. The walls seemed ready to crash onto us. "It's me you want."

"We only desire the egg. What matters a weak-kneed girl?"

"She's lying!" Harken staggered toward us, a bloody hand pressed against his stomach. He held the poker in the other. "If any harm comes to them, I'll destroy your precious egg and your soul along with it."

"Destroy the egg," Malleus hissed, "and you destroy yourself."

"A small price to be rid of your stink." Harken stuck the poker under Malleus's chin. "Let go of the girl, or I'll break your jaw again."

Malleus laughed. "You cannot hurt us, only impede us. Pain is nothing."

"Say that after I rip your throat out." He pulled a shiny egg from his front pocket. "The egg for the girl, as agreed."

As agreed? I thought.

She eyed him suspiciously but then held out her hand. "Yes, the egg for the girl." Malleus let Devon slide to the ground. "You will pay dearly for this, familiar."

Harken moved between the Shadowless and us. "Willow Jane, take your sister," he said, keeping the egg raised.

I darted in and looped Devon under the arms, dragging her toward the elevators. "Come with us! You're wounded! You can't fight her now!"

"Do as I say!" he yelled, pocketing the egg. "No matter what you hear, don't look back!"

"Harken!" I couldn't desert him. "Come with us!"

But he wouldn't. He just flashed that annoying grin and bowed. Then with a deep feral growl he charged Malleus with the poker raised above his head. Ignoring the clash behind me, ignoring Harken's cries and Malleus's raging, and abandoning the guy who had just saved our lives, I pulled my sister toward the elevator and prayed that it would arrive fast enough.

CHAPTER SIXTY-SIX

HARKEN made a sweeping, low bow to the Shadowless. "How did you enjoy the performance?"

"We would have preferred more blood," Malleus said and pointed at the girl hanging from the noose. "Cut her down."

"Cut her down yourself," Harken snarled. "I'm done with your dirty work."

Malleus nudged Kelly's feet and set her body swinging. "Yet you continue to do it. Our egg?"

"We have a bargain, remember?"

"All magic has a price. Of all creatures doomed to walk this earth, you know that best of all. How will you pay for mine?"

Harken took the shiny stone from his front pocket and

wrapped it in his blood-soaked handkerchief. "With this. And the blood of the Uncanny."

"The price of that magic is BLOOD," Malleus screamed. "Not SOME blood. ALL THE BLOOD!"

"It's all you're going to get, *mistress*."

With speed that defied natural laws, she drove her shears into the meat of his thigh. Harken screamed and fell backward, Malleus collapsing on top of him, twisting the blades, then yanking them out. He only grunted when she plunged the sharp tips into his gut until he stopped trying to escape.

"Egg, egg," she said. "Who has the egg?"

Coughing up blood, Harken handed her the ensanguined handkerchief.

She held the egg up to Kelly. "Gaze upon it! Gaze upon the heart that will awaken the shadows." She spun Kelly's body again. "Even yours, wretched child, even yours."

She tucked the heart into her coat, grabbed Harken by the ankles. She dragged him to the end of the hallway.

"We made a bargain," Harken murmured.

"For the Uncanny's blood, and you aided her escape. So as you betray us, we betray you." She tossed him inside like an empty burlap bag. "But do not worry, familiar, the road will rise to meet you."

PART FIVE

A DIVINE AND SUPERNATURAL LIGHT

CHAPTER SIXTY-SEVEN

WHEN the elevator door opened, I summoned whatever strength I had left and swung Devon into a fireman's carry, evenly distributing her weight across my shoulders. For a little kid she weighed a ton, and I was so tired my knees buckled. I carried her across the lobby, past the snoring guard, and hit the door at full stride. I turned my hip to take the force, and the door flew open. I stumbled and almost slid down the rain-slicked steps. My hockey smarts took over, and I caught my balance.

"Sorry, Devie," I said. "It's going to be okay. I'm getting help."

The streets were more deserted than before. The rain

was coming down harder, and all the cars parked on the alley were dark. I spun in a circle bewildered, not sure what to do, until a horn sounded a block over.

"Hang on, Devie!" I yelled and ran toward the sound, my boots splashing through deep puddles, my chest tight from the struggle for air. Hang on yourself, I thought, and kept repeating it till I reached Beacon Street. "Thank God."

Beacon was busier. Much busier, with taxis and cars weaving through the night. Without even thinking about it, I stepped into the one-way street. A big SUV laid on its horn, but I didn't move—I was too freaking exhausted to. Headlights flashed, and the whole world filled up with their light. I dropped to my knees as the SUV skidded sideways, the brakes locking up, as it bumped the curb.

"What the hell?" A woman jumped out and came at us, just a silhouette in the headlights. "Are you *trying* to get run—holy Jeez! Are you okay?"

"Please, help me!" I was out of breath and struggling to hang on to Devon. "It's my sister! She needs an ambulance!"

The woman helped me lay Devon on the sidewalk, dialed 911 on her phone. "What happened to her?"

"She was taken!" My voice turned from angry to

frightened. My body started to shake. "It's on the news. The one who did it, she's upstairs in the hotel."

"We've got a little girl in bad shape here," the woman said when the 911 operator loudly asked for the nature of the emergency.

"Please tell them to hurry," I pleaded.

The driver nodded. She lifted Devon's wrist and closed her eyes, counting. "I got a pulse, but looks like she might be in shock? It's freezing out here."

But she'll be okay, I told myself. Shock could be treated with a blanket. That's what she needed, a blanket. Her skin was so cold, and she needed something warm.

Then above us, something crashed through a window, and seconds later broken glass rained down, followed by a weight that slammed into the sidewalk.

"Jesus," the woman whispered. "That guy jumped!"

"Jumped?" I said and followed the driver's eyes.

Harken's broken body lay on the pavement, arms and legs bent at the wrong angles, a puddle of blood forming around his head.

"No," I whispered. "No, no."

The driver stepped in front of me, blocking my view. "Don't look, don't look."

But I'd already looked, because I always looked. I'd seen everything from the instant the body had landed and then bounced. I'd seen the fractured face of a dead man, and I already knew what the driver was trying to keep me from witnessing.

Harken was dead.

I looked up at the hotel, where Malleus was leaning out a high window. She had the egg, and I had my sister. But Harken was dead, and that hadn't been part of the bargain. He wasn't supposed to die. A locust swarm of black spots clouded my vision. It felt like I was on the cusp of a terrible glimpse, but it never came.

"What a pity," Malleus called down, mocking me. "We have our heart's desire, and the girl has nothing but a paper doll."

She was cackling like a lunatic when I bit my thumb and pulled out a thread of gossamer, twisting it as I did. The world turned sepia, and everything ran in reverse.

Rain rose from the ground.

Glass flew into the air.

Harken's body was sucked from the pavement and pulled up, up into the window, and then the sheet of glass re-formed behind him.

"Stop!" I commanded, and the whole world did.

Gently, I set Devon on the sidewalk. Then I climbed behind the wheel of the woman's SUV and drove forward to the spot where Harken had landed just a few seconds before.

I returned to Devon and licked my thumb. "Please let it work," I begged.

The window broke above us, and broken glass rained down while I covered Devon's face with my body. With a deep thwack Harken's body landed on the SUV, collapsing the roof like a trampoline.

"Jesus!" the woman said. "That guy jumped! My car!"

"Please live," I prayed. "I need your help with Devon. I need *you*."

"He's breathing!" the driver yelled. "Lucky bastard! What're the odds?"

I stepped into the street and stared up into the night.

Malleus and the egg were gone.

CHAPTER SIXTY-EIGHT

MINUTES after Harken fell from the Hellesgate two EMTs unloaded Devon from the back of an ambulance. Like every cop/medical show I'd ever seen, they rolled her out past me and into the emergency room, calling out codes and vital signs to the nice people in scrubs who ran out to greet them. What was different from the shows was the way no one swooped down on me with a blanket and guided me inside, where they explained exactly what was wrong with my sister and how they were going to fix it. They left me standing beside the curb, shivering from the cold and working out how I was going to explain to Ma what had happened to her baby.

I sat on the curb, still alone, when a second ambulance pulled up. They unloaded Harken from the back and rolled him right past me, shouting about broken bones and contusions. No surprise that. That's what happens when you fall from a high building with a car for a pillow. The big shock was that he was still alive at all. With no one paying any attention to me, I borrowed a blanket from the back of the ambulance, wrapped it around my own shoulders, and wandered inside.

For fifteen minutes, I paced the hallway that connected the emergency room to the main lobby, looking at commemorative plaques. When my phone buzzed, I jumped, having forgotten that I had a phone.

Willie! Just saw the news on Twitter! He jumped? WTF? I mean, W! T! F!

That was Siobhan shorthand for Willie Jane, I have just seen the story of your sister's rescue on the news, and I would like to know her condition and how you are doing, and if it wouldn't be too inconvenient, an explanation of why I wasn't there.

At Boston Gen ER. Then I added: **I need a friend. ETA 30 seconds.**

I wanted to cry. So I did. I was still crying when I heard

the doors swish open, Siobhan walked in with my mother, and Ma called out my name.

"Willow Jane!" She came running across the lobby, arms thrown out wide like she used to when I was a kindergartner, and she swept me up, even though I was taller in my boots, and she had to stand on tiptoe to take me under her wing.

"Thank God you're safe."

That's when I really began to cry, letting loose every emotion pent up within me. I guess I needed my Ma, too.

More than I knew.

CHAPTER SIXTY-NINE

THE hours after we arrived at Boston Medical Center were like watching a Patriots game on fast forward: Ma in a chair beside Devie, holding her hand and resting her head on the mattress. Ma's eyes closing as Siobhan sang "Sweet Caroline" over and over again. Nurses and doctors rushing in and out, hooking up machines, inserting IVs, cocooning Devon in a thermal blanket, and checking and rechecking vitals so that they could hook up even more machines. Cops coming three times to get my story. Me ignoring their questions and Ma sending them away. The techs wheeling Devon out to run MRIs and ECGs and other tests with three-letter acronyms.

Then the fast forward would end, and I would be awakened in the deep windowsill, where I'd been sitting, praying for my sister to regain consciousness. Two points of light came from the twin fluorescents above Devon's bed, which imbued her skin with a bluish cast. Her black hair lay limp on her cheeks, and she was attached to an IV and monitors that displayed her heart rate and blood pressure in periodic beeping intervals.

Ma was curled up in a ball, a cardigan tucked under her chin like a comforter. Siobhan was splayed out, an arm over one side, a leg flowing over the other, sleeping like the dead.

"Willow Jane," Ma said, looking at me funny, "did your father visit your dreams?"

"Huh?"

"You were talking to him in your sleep. About the letter he left you."

"I was?" I could tell she was about to begin an inquisition, and that was a very bad idea. "Weird."

"Wicked weird." Siobhan sat up, yawning like she'd been asleep, but I knew she'd been on watch out for us. "How's the nap?"

"Balls." I worked my knotted neck. My back was so

stiff I could barely stand. "How long have I been snoozing this time?

"Not long," Siobhan said. "It's still dark out."

"Yeah, it is. How's Devie?"

"Doctors say there's nothing wrong with her, except hypothermia." Ma's voice sounded like she was reading from a script. "They think she'll be okay in a couple of days."

"A couple of days." I sighed and fiddled with my thumb. "So no brain damage or anything?"

Ma didn't answer. She fixated on my thumb, which was nicely hidden behind a Band-Aid that Siobhan had liberated for me. "What's wrong with your—"

"The doctors," Siobhan interrupted, "said it was too soon to tell."

Thanks, I mouthed to her. *I need to talk to you.*

Ma walked over and stood beside me. She looked like she'd had aged twenty years. "Willow Jane, you're hiding something. You've got to tell the doctors. You've got to tell me."

How could I tell her? There were two choices. Either I made up a lie on the spot, or I told the truth and watched Ma lose her mind.

"I just— It's a jumble," I said and tried to turn away. After everything she'd gone through, I just couldn't do it to her. "I can't make sense of it."

"Work on unjumbling it," Ma said with fire in her cheeks. "Start with that boy in ICU. The detective thinks you're protecting him."

"I'm not."

"She thinks he was an accomplice to the kidnapping."

"He wasn't."

"Then how did you find Devon?"

"I told you, from clues." How could I say, from writing carved into the bathroom wall? I pretended to look out at the city lights, hoping to short-circuit her.

"What kind of clues?" she said, pressing me. "It's that letter, isn't it? You've gotten mixed up in Michael's old troubles?"

The troubles started long before Dad, I thought, but I had to stop her questions, even if it meant pissing her off. "I found Devon because of a note."

"That boy left a note?"

"The *kidnapper* left a note. On the bathroom wall." I closed the blinds. The sky made me feel exposed and vulnerable. "It was directions to a hotel where Devon was held. *That boy* didn't take Devie. He helped rescue her, and he almost got killed doing it."

"You talk about him," Ma said, "like you care."

"Care about him? If I could get my hands on him," I said, "I'd care to wring his stupid neck."

"Somebody beat you to it," Siobhan said. "Just saying."

"Damn Michael Conning!" Ma said. "Sometimes, I curse the day I met that man." For a second she seemed wistful, then the fire came back to her eyes. "Young lady, I want answers, straight and true. What happened at that godforsaken hotel?"

"It's complicated," I said.

Ma cut a look that would break bricks. "Straight and true, Willow Jane."

"He got thrown out a window," I said after taking a deep breath. "Not that the cops care. They keep saying he jumped."

"If that's the truth, the police—"

"Ma," I said, "how many times did Dad say that cops don't care about the truth? How many times did they lock him up for no reason?"

"Sorry to butt in, Mrs. Conning," Siobhan said, "but that detective's a real ballbuster."

"I've had enough of your fresh mouth, Siobhan." Ma was about to give Siobhan the boot. "One more word."

"My throat's wicked parched!" I announced. "I need something to drink. Can I have a couple bucks?"

Ma started to argue, then her eyes met mine, and she softened. "Talking to you is like talking to your father. Might as well beat my head against a rock." She fished some dollars from her purse. "Get yourself a soda and come back ready to pay the piper."

"Let's go, Siobhan." I grabbed her before Ma could change her mind. "Ma, you okay to watch Devie?"

"I gave birth to this child," she said, and that was the end of it.

"Right," I said.

"Thanks for the soda, Mrs. Conning. Hug later? No?" Siobhan followed me out. "Wow, she's pissed! So where are we really going?"

"You sure you want to do this?"

"Hells yeah. Think I'm sitting this one out, after I missed Devon's rescue?" She pulled me down the hallway. "I know exactly where you're going."

Siobhan headed down to the elevators, following the signs that pointed to the snack bar, which we never reached.

"ICU, ICU." Siobhan ran a finger down the placard listing each floor. "Bingo! Third floor."

"How'd you know I was going to the ICU?" I said.

"Don't even try to lie."

"Lie about what?"

"Harken. You're totally into the guy, even if you do want to strangle him."

CHAPTER SEVENTY

THE third floor was much busier than Devon's. Visitors walked up and down talking on their cell phones. Most were grim faced and spoke in low, worried tones. I didn't make eye contact with any of them, and I swooped past the two full waiting rooms like I had important business to attend to.

"I am not totally into Harken," I said. "He's a total tool."

"Six feet? Black hair? Twinkling eyes? Little bit of a beard?"

"Beards are gross, and eyes don't twinkle."

"Yours do when you look at him, but okay, be that way.

You told me about your magic powers. Not a word about his. So spill."

He doesn't have any, I thought. But that wasn't true. Harken had some serious magic, and I had no idea what he could do. "Like I told Ma, it's complicated."

"Would this be any fun if it was simple?"

"This isn't my idea of fun."

"Maybe for the old Willow it wouldn't be," she said. "But the new you is loving it balls to the walls."

"You're so anatomically poetic."

"So rhyming body parts is my thing. Come on."

Up ahead two cops guarded a security door. It was thick and metal with a warning in huge red letters: NO VIS-ITORS. Maybe that's where the cops were keeping Harken. Now I just had to get to him. I took a quick look around and spotted the nurse's station.

"Hey," I said. "How about a distraction for your favorite defenseman?"

"Watch the master at work." Siobhan plucked an eye-brow hair. "Ow!" Then walked right up to the nurse's sta-tion, eyes leaking tears. "Excuse me? My grandmother's in ICU, and even though it's past visiting hours, I'd really like to see her. Please?"

"That was the worst acting I've ever seen," the nurse said, raising an eyebrow and cocking her head. "Girls, you better—" Her pocket buzzed, and she held up a finger to silence Siobhan. She checked the pager, then grabbed a chart. "I'm too busy for foolishness. You two better not be here when I get back."

Siobhan held her supplicant pose until the nurse was gone. She waited till the doors swung shut, then brazenly scooted behind the desk and snagged the nurse's sweater.

"Siobhan!" I whispered. "She didn't buy it."

"We'll be gone before she gets back." She draped the sweater over my shoulders like a cape and tried to push a patient chart into my hands. "Pretend you're talking on your cell."

"This is so not going to work." I gestured at my clothes. "I look like a truck ran over me."

She gave me a push. "Easy peasy lemon squeezy."

"I know a better way," I said.

I peeled the Band-Aid off my thumb and licked it.

Siobhan froze, along with everyone else. I returned the sweater and chart, then quickly entered the ICU. The patients were behind sliding glass doors, like experimental test subjects in a terrarium. Harken was to the left, his terrarium guarded by a cop who sat on a chair right next to a placard labeled "John Doe."

I ducked inside and ran over to Harken. Up close, his skin was pale and wan, and he was covered in cuts and bruises. They had stripped off his clothes—probably had to cut them off—and dressed him in a blue gown. His mouth was a rigid frown, and he had so many tubes and wires attached to his body, he looked like a Frankenstein monster. His head was tilted back so that his throat was exposed.

If Malleus was here, I thought, that throat would be cut.

His medical chart and a bag with his personal effects hung from the foot of the bed. For a second I almost read the chart, but no, I didn't really want to know how badly he was hurt this time. I buried my face into my cold hands, trying to push the dark thoughts out. When I looked away, my vision was all yellow and blue lights, so that it took a few seconds before I saw the dead girl standing at the foot of Harken's bed.

"How did you get in my glimpse?" I said.

She set a rotting finger to her lips and with the other hand bade me follow.

"No way," I said.

Yes, she nodded and pretended to lick her thumb. She walked into the light of the hallway. I followed her past the nurse's station to the exit, where she waited until I opened the door, then she scampered by me and downstairs to the next landing.

She pretended to lick her thumb again and pointed at mine.

"Wait," I said, but she didn't.

I licked my thumb, and she disappeared down the next flight of steps. I had to run to catch up, my boots squeaking on the slick concrete. When I reached the floor labeled "B" for basement, she was waiting again, her face hidden but her eyes shining blacker than even the shadows. I opened the door, afraid to speak this time, and she moved impossibly fast down the corridor. I hesitated, then followed, jogging to keep up. Her feet never seemed to move, and when she looked back at me, her expression hadn't changed. She was there, then there, then there ahead, at the corner where an arrow pointed left.

"Morgue?" I said when I read the sign.

I heard the rhythmic sound of dryer drums turning, faint at first but growing louder. The dead girl took another left and a metal staircase down. My feet rang on the stairs, deeper and deeper in the cramped and dark stairwell, and when my hand slid down the banister, it sounded like claws on the steel. Not claws—shears. I pulled my hand back and kept both of them close to my chest until I reached bottom, where I found only blackness.

I stopped to listen.

At first there was nothing, then I heard a pitiful sound like a frightened animal. A light came on. I snapped my head around, and there was the dead girl and the entrance to the morgue.

She was smiling.

And then, like a wisp of smoke, she was gone.

"I'm not going inside a stupid morgue," I said, but that's exactly what I did.

It felt damp inside the body holding area, and the light was barely strong enough to keep the blackness at bay. The room was full of stainless exam tables about seven feet long and three feet wide, the perfect size for a human body. There were tall trays of medical instruments to the left, a desk with an X-ray viewer in the corner, and a bank of cold chambers on the back wall.

I took a breath and smelled water and mold in the air.

I navigated by feel and had to walk slowly, too slowly. The strength seeped from my body. I took a deep breath, trying to keep my teeth from chattering.

"I see dead people," I said, but making jokes in an empty room was like tickling yourself.

Then I heard a sound, as if a pebble had bounced down a hole. It came from the cold chambers, where the dead were kept on ice. In the dim light I crept around an autopsy table to the series of square freezer doors. Each one was numbered, and under the number was a name tag.

There were four names written on the doors. I squinted to make out the letters.

Flanagan.

O'Brien.

Wilson.

And Haverhill.

People I knew—just kids, like me—were in the lockers. They had been brought here after Malleus killed them. Brought here to the hospital to be examined and then put away like lab specimens.

"Help me."

I jumped and spun around. "Hello?"

The room was empty, and the only sounds were my

panicked breathing and the squeak of my boots on the linoleum floor. It was just my imagination, the product of an overexcited nervous system. Who could blame me for a few hallucinations? What an awful place to be, caught inside a casket. There'd be no way to escape. The room was refrigerated, but that wasn't the reason I was shivering violently.

"If you think it's cold out there," the voice said, "you should feel it here."

I spun around again. "Stop screwing with me," I whispered.

Nobody was there.

"I'm not screwing with you, bubs," the voice said. "Get me out of here."

"Kelly?" I said.

"Open the door."

"Not such a good idea."

"It's about Devon," she said. "Open the effing door."

I opened the drawer marked "O'Brien."

I grasped the metal tray and rolled the body out. My friend lay naked on the slab. Her eyes were closed, and the blood had been washed from her body so that all her wounds were visible. The lacerations from the hanging rope were bloodless but still raw, like salt pork marinating in water. Tears dripped from my eyes, and I tried not to look at her, but it was impossible.

"This is all my fault," I said, starting to hiccup, the precursor to completely losing it.

Kelly's eyes popped open, but she lay still as death. Of course, she was still as death. She was dead. I looked into her eyes, black as tar and clouded with mist.

Then she grabbed my wrist with a cold, rubbery hand. "Come with me or your sister is lost."

CHAPTER SEVENTY-ONE

I took her hand and was no longer in the morgue, I was covered in fog, surrounded by it, like a dream sequence from *Nosferatu*. I expected Kelly to be waiting for me on the other side. Only fog awaited, fog so dense it clung to my face. It was dark ahead. A gas lamppost flickered in the darkness. Sounds were muffled and hushed, except for the swish of my sneakers on the cinder path. The steel resolve I had felt when I opened the cold locker was gone, replaced by the sensation that I was being watched by something that wanted to kill me.

Ahead an archway appeared—a huge oak door cut to match its shape. I knocked twice, then opened the peephole. I half expected Malleus to be staring back at me, but no one was there.

The door shut behind me as I entered. The mists faded, the last tendrils reaching under the door, clinging to my legs. I was glad to be inside, but my relief lasted only a few seconds. The cavernous room was lit by hundreds of tall candelabra, their lights flickering in the darkness.

The fog stank of sulfur, but the room was sickly sweet with the scent of human waste. I gagged and covered my mouth.

Then I found the source of the stench.

Beside each candelabrum, a corpse lay on the floor. They were covered with sheer shrouds that looked like cobwebs. Their feet were bare, their eyes closed, their mouths shut tight in thin lines. The room was too dark, the lights too dim, the smell too strong.

I looked straight ahead and walked. So many dead bodies! My heart pounded, and I could barely breathe. I took a deep breath of foul air and heard my sister cry out.

"Devon!" I yelled, but the only answer was the echo of my own voice. "Kelly?"

I took a few more tentative steps. If I didn't turn back

now, I would be lost in the caverns. I sobbed "Devon!" and turned back.

Then a strong hand, cold as steel, grabbed my ankle.

I screamed.

A pale hand reached out from the darkness. I screamed louder when I saw that the hand was thumbless and that it belonged to someone I knew.

Will Patrick lay on the ground, his skin the color of a mourning dove, his scalp covered in clumps of wispy hair. It couldn't be Will Patrick. He was dead. His mother had been on TV, her face puffy and bloated with grief, cursing and vowing to sue whoever had hurt her child. He was dead, and yet he was here.

"Willow Jane," he said, pleading. "Please help me. I am lost. I am lost. I am lost."

"Lost?" I said.

"In the Shadowlands," he said. "She has imprisoned us."

"Us?"

"Show yourselves," he whispered.

One by one, others came into the light. Their eyes were black as ink, their thumbs missing. I had to cover my mouth again. Their bodies were in a state of decay: Malleus had left them here to rot.

"Wait," I said.

"There is no time here," Will Patrick said. "Only pain."

"Only pain," Flanagan said and rose beside Will.

"Only pain," Kelly said and rose beside Flanagan.

"Only pain," Miss Haverhill said and rose behind them, followed by a janitor, a bus driver, and hundreds of others:

Only pain.

Only pain. Only pain.

Only pain. Only pain. Only pain.

Only pain. Only pain. Only pain. Only pain.

Only pain. Only pain. Only pain. Only pain. Only pain.

Only pain. Only pain. Only pain. Only pain.

Only pain. Only pain. Only pain.

Only pain. Only pain.

Only pain.

Only.

Pain.

This was what was waiting for my sister. "You're all dead," I said. "How can you be here?"

"Our lives were taken by the Shadowless," Will Patrick said.

"Our souls are locked out of time," Flanagan said.

"We can't rest," Kelly said, "unless you help us."

"There's hunger in my belly," Will Patrick said, "but I can't eat."

"I'm weary, but I can't sleep," Flanagan said.

"We're trapped," Kelly said. "Only you can set us free."

"I—I can't," I said. "My power doesn't—"

"You've got to," Kelly said. "There are others here. Some've been here a really long time. And the longer they're here, the more pain they feel."

"I'm so sorry," I said, shivering. "I can't imagine anything that horrible."

Kelly touched my arm. "You don't have to imagine."

As soon as our skin touched, I saw everything that she had seen. I heard the screams, and I felt the unquenchable thirst and the insatiable yearning and loss.

Tears rolled from my eyes, and I started to shake.

One by one, they touched me, saying, "You have my name." Kelly. Will Patrick. Flanagan. Even Miss Haverhill and two cops I'd never met. It felt like a glimpse, except there was no tug at my belly button, and time did not stand still. It ran faster, splintering, traveling down arteries of memory, through the hearts of their pasts. All of their emotions, thoughts, and recollections opened up in front of me.

I saw Kelly looking down on me as she swung from the ceiling in the hotel. I felt the gut-wrenching fear that paralyzed Will Patrick when Malleus drove her shears through the lock and lifted the trunk of his car. I heard Flanagan's screams, and I tasted the blood in Miss Haverhill's mouth. But there was more, memories not so vivid: birthdays, school days, last Christmases, first kisses, and happy birthdays. All of it was laid out before me in a million flickering images, sounds, and sensations. Their memories became mine, and I could no longer tell where my life ended and theirs began.

My knee was bent, my hair falling across my shoulders, and my head bowed like a supplicant. They had overwhelmed me, overshadowed who I was. The world had too much in it, and they had filled me to bursting.

I looked up, and the dead girl's face was inches from my own.

"Why did you do this to me?" I said, almost whimpering.

"Because only you can kill the Shadowless," the dead girl said, though her mouth didn't move and her black-ink eyes reflected no light. "And if you fail, your sister will join us."

"How am I supposed to kill her? No one knows how, not even Harken."

The dead girl whispered in my ear, "*To end the sleep of Shadowless, weave silver twixt her eyes, cut gossamer threads with sparks coalesced, then the Shadowless shall die.*"

She licked my thumb, and the world spun like a wobbling top. The spirits began to shimmer, and their bodies faded to black. When I opened my eyes, I was standing over Harken's bed, and the ICU nurse was right behind me.

"Get out," she said.

"But he . . . *sacrificed himself for us* . . . is my friend."

"Friends aren't family," she said and pointed toward the door. "I'm closing my eyes and counting to three. If you're still here when I open them, I'm telling the cops down the hall. One."

I was gone before she got to two.

CHAPTER SEVENTY-TWO

AFTER I escaped the ICU, Siobhan and I took the stairs back up to Devon's floor. Every step of the way Siobhan kept asking how the glimpse worked, how I'd saved Devon, why Harken wasn't dead.

"I'm not telling you," I said, pushing the door open, then freezing because Ma and Devon were not alone.

The attending physician, a tall woman dressed in a lab coat with navy blue scrubs underneath, glanced back at us. Her face puckered up. "As I was saying," she said, "Devon's still experiencing symptoms of shock, so we'd like to run more tests. Normally we don't see symptoms like this without a physiological cause."

"What kind of tests?" I said, butting in and puckering my own face. "What does 'symptoms like this' mean? Have you had cases like this before?"

"Don't be rude, Willow Jane," Ma said, shaking a disapproving finger. "Wait for the doctor to explain."

"Yeah. No." I was all done with waiting for adults. "What kinds of tests? You just said Devie was okay."

The doctor took off her glasses to clean them. "Rather, there's nothing *wrong* with her physically. It isn't quite the same—"

The lights blinked off and on.

"—thing?"

Then off.

"What's wrong with the lights?" Ma said.

"Nothing serious," the doctor said. "The hospital is undergoing a major renovation, and power outages are common. For us, it's business as usual."

"Don't be so sure." I rushed to the window and looked between the blinds. "I've seen this befo—oh, shit!"

Something heavy slammed into the window. Bits of safety glass tinkled to the sill, and I pulled up the blinds. The center of the glass was starred like a busted windshield. A dead crow lay on the outside sill. Blood trickled from empty sockets where its eyeballs had been. Its neck was bent at an impossible angle, and its beak was split in half, broken by the impact.

"What in fu—frickdoodles was that?" Siobhan said.

"A dead crow," I said. "One of hers."

Then the dead crow lifted its eyeless head and began to viciously peck the fractured glass. The TV turned on, filling the room with flickering static. The monitors attached to Devon started ringing, and the headboard erupted with warning lights.

Devon moaned. Her head jerked back and forth, and she flailed her arms. The IV whipped around and broke loose from her hand. She sat bolt upright, rigid as a board. Her mouth was wide open like Munch's *Scream*, and her eyes darted around manically. "Will she? Will she?" she sang. "Will Willow be hanging from the willow hanging tree?"

"Devon! No!" Ma threw her arms around her, and Devon sank her teeth into Ma's shoulder. Ma screamed, and blood bloomed under her shirt, but Ma wouldn't let go. "I won't lose my baby, too!"

Siobhan grabbed Devon and tried to pry open her jaws, but Ma's screams got louder and louder. The doctor pushed a knuckle into Devon's temporomandibular joint, and Devon jerked back, then let go.

"Security!" The doctor hit the call number and yelled, "I need a restraint team!"

"Holy shitburger on toast," Siobhan said.

"BLOOD!" Devon screamed. "BLOOD WILL HAVE BLOOD!"

Ma staggered away, and I caught her as the doctor and Siobhan tried to pin Devon's arms. She cussed and spit and tried to bite them, too.

Ma looked at me, a hand covering her wound. "Your father's letter," she said, her mouth set hard. "He knew this would happen."

"No way," I said. "The letter's more like a supernatural *Oh, the Places You'll Go.*"

Whap! Whap! Whap!

In quick succession, three more crows slammed into the window, and the glass cracked again, splintering like thin ice. One more attack, and the window would shatter.

Whap!

A raven hit the window like a cannon shot. Hunks of glass cascaded into the room, followed by rain and wind. The raven hopped past the shards and then fell to the floor.

Its neck was hanging by a thread, and its eye sockets were bleeding, but it beat its wings and began to croak, "Blood! Blood! Blood!"

"I think," the doctor said, "we should get Devon to safety."

"Ya *think*?" I said, unplugging the monitors. Ma and Siobhan pushed the bed by the side rails, and I got behind the headboard. "Did the talking crow give you a clue?"

The doctor stood watching the bird, shaking her head. "This can't be happening."

"THE SHADOWLESS IS HERE!" Devon screamed. "THIS IS WHERE THE DEAD GIRLS GO!"

"To hell with this!" the doctor yelled and ran from the room ahead of us, almost colliding with two nurses.

They looked at us, then Devon, then the squawking dead bird, frozen as they processed the scene.

"Help or move!" Ma barked, aiming the bed at them.

The nurses pulled on the bed and steered it into the hallway. Behind us black birds—starlings, crows, ravens, grackles, and jackdaws—flocked into Devon's room, clicking and cawing. Dozens, then hundreds, a swarm of iridescent feathers that clotted the window. They had come hunting, and their quarry was us. Then something, some sound, some signal, alerted them. For an instant they were silent, and their ocher eyes turned to me as one. I met their gaze, until a chill went up my spine, and I knew that Malleus was watching, and she was coming for us.

Then the birds took flight and blasted through the half-open door.

"Duck!" I yelled at Siobhan and Ma, and we hit the floor.

A black mass of wings and talons, the swarm swept right past Devon and attacked the nurses. They screamed, their voices lost in the cacophony, and fled toward the exit, the birds ripping at every bit of exposed flesh.

"What in God's name is going on?" Ma shouted from under the bed. "Willow Jane!"

"The kidnapper is back for Devon!" I yelled. "Siobhan, we've got to hide her!"

"Employees' lounge!" Siobhan pointed at a sign next to the nurses' station. "They'll have snacks!"

And the lounge door might lock. "Go!"

We jumped up and gave the bed a hard shove. It started rolling, gathering speed. We rammed through a crush of squalling jackdaws, then made a hard right toward the lounge.

"Clear the way, Mrs. C!" Siobhan yelled as we slid sideways.

Ma ran ahead and swung the door open. We pushed the bed inside, then Ma slammed the door and threw the lock, just before the birds started hitting it.

"Finally," Siobhan said over the rhythmic click of beaks pecking the wood, "it's over."

"It's a long way from over," I said, taking a breath and making sure the lounge was empty. "The Shadowless is just getting started."

"Wait! Did you say the Shadowless?" Ma said, her determination occluded by sudden fear. "Your father used to say a poem about the Shadowless. Another one of his fairy tales, I always thought."

"Ma," I said, shoving the sofa against the wall as Siobhan pushed Devon's bed to the center of the room. "He didn't make it up. The Shadowless is real."

"So effing real," Siobhan said and steered Ma to a chair.

"This Shadowless was the kidnapper?" Ma sat, not even cutting Siobhan a dirty look. "And she's still after Devon?"

"No, Ma. This time she's after me."

"But now the shitstorm's over," Siobhan said and

flopped on the couch. "We'll wait here till the cops come, right, guys? Right?"

Ma said nothing for what felt like an eternity. She looked at Devon, then at me. "Being a good Catholic girl, I always kept to the faith, but your father believed in witches and fairies and magic."

"Did you believe in them, too?" I said.

"I believed in him." Ma took me by the shoulders. "Now I believe in you."

Ma believed in me? Even in the crappiest moment ever, it made my heart soar. I also made it ten times harder to do what I had to do. "I'm sorry," I said and bit my thumb.

"Willow Jane!" Siobhan screamed. "You jerky-jerk jerkface! Don't go out there alone!"

"Siobhan," Ma said more quietly, "what just happened?"

What had happened was a glimpse, one involving a roll of white medical tape that secured Ma and Siobhan to Devon's bed, a bag of corn chips from the lounge cabinet, jackdaws covered with a borrowed sheet, and a door locked behind me.

"It's a long story, Mrs. Conning," Siobhan said with a resigned sigh. There would be plenty of time to tell it.

"Thanks for the snacks, Willie!"

"You're welcome," I called.

I bit my thumb again and, after skirting the sheet-shrouded birds, headed for the ICU. Even though I was running past nurses and orderlies like they were statues, my legs felt leaden and my boots were concrete bricks. Yesterday, I had no idea that glimpses existed, and now I was slipping into them like a pair of worn-out skates. It scared me that it was so easy, and I wondered what would happen when it got easier to glimpse than to deal with the consequences of my actions.

CHAPTER SEVENTY-THREE

I unplugged the machines and rolled Harken past the cop standing watch. When we reached the elevator, I ended the glimpse, then hit the call button again and again before giving Harken's shoulder a hard shake.

"Coast is clear!" I said. "Come on, come on. I know you're not dead."

"Don't be so sure," Harken said, opening his eyes. He tried to sit up but gasped and gave up. "I thought you would never come back."

The elevator opened, and I pushed his bed inside. "Which way?" I asked quickly. "Up or down?"

He winced. How could he move at all? His body looked

like it had been fed to a wood chipper, and the wound in his stomach was bleeding straight through the bandages. It killed me to harangue him, but every minute we wasted brought Malleus closer.

"Up or down?" I repeated. "We're sitting ducks here."

"Down. All the way down. Malleus is less powerful underground." His eyes actually twinkled, but then he frowned. "How close is she?"

"Those goddamn black birds found us. She can't be far behind."

"Your sister?"

"Hiding with Siobhan and Ma, but she's still—"

"Not herself. Nor will she be until we find a way to destroy Malleus."

Destroy her? How was he going that? He looked one step from death's door himself. "What about your wounds? They look really bad."

"I'll be cured soon enough," he said. "Death, they say, is the poor man's doctor."

"Yeah, not funny. It'll take Malleus's birds no time to find me, so stay alive."

"She won't need birds to find you. Where are my clothes?"

"Seriously?" I unhooked the plastic bag from the foot of the bed. "You want to get dressed *now*?"

He dumped the bag full of cut-up clothes, then fished something out of his back pants pocket. "Not when we still have this."

The elevator door opened, and I allowed myself a smile.

The elevator was at the end of a very long basement corridor. The walls were cinder block, covered with peeling green paint. It was more like a hidden path than a corridor. Above our heads was a network of wiring, plumbing, and air ducts. I half pulled Harken past two dark alcoves blocked with chain-link gates and covered with signs warning us of danger, high voltage, and death.

"How did you get the egg back?" I said. "You gave it to Malleus."

"I made a switch," Harken said. "A hunk of obsidian in my front pocket. The real egg in the back."

"Was that before or after she stabbed you?"

"During. Malleus so enjoys a good stabbing."

He staggered, so I pulled his arm over my shoulder to support his weight. He felt lighter than before. Probably adrenaline making me stronger. Behind us the elevator motor kicked in, and the shaft trembled as the car began climbing. We had to hide. If Malleus showed up now, we didn't stand a chance.

I checked behind us.

No Malleus.

So far.

We passed four doors secured with shiny padlocks, the nameplates painted over with fresh gray paint. All of them were plastered with the same sign: Facilities Closed for Renovation. Contact Environmental Services for Access.

"What should we do with the egg?" I asked, trying to pull him along faster. "Hide it?"

"No, she would only find it," he said, struggling to keep pace. "The egg has to be destroyed. *You* have to destroy it."

I fired it against the cement block wall. It bounced off, taking a chunk of paint and cement with it.

"The egg was formed by magic," he said.

"Not a scratch," I said, scooping it up and checking behind us again. We needed to move faster.

"So only magic can break it." He pointed at the iron needle in my lapel. "This needs to go through it."

I tried to jam the needle through the hole in the egg.

The tip bounced off, and I nearly lanced my hand.

"Without magic, you're wasting your time."

"And my skin. Ow." I put the bodkin back in my lapel. "How do I access this magic?"

"I'm puzzling it out." He leaned on me again, struggling to catch his breath. "If this walk is a very long walk, I might need a rest."

"Hang on," I said, trying to sound calm but thinking, *Hurry, hurry!* "Got to find a safe place."

Up ahead, beyond the laundry room, I saw two metal doors with old-fashioned brass panic bars, covered in the same peeling green paint. If we could make it that far, maybe I could give Harken time to puzzle out how to beat Malleus. But what about Devon? What if the Shadowless went for her instead?

"We have to kill Malleus?" I said, looking over my shoulder. "It's not enough to just bury her again."

He grunted, which I thought was an answer, but then his feet tangled with mine, and we both stumbled into the wall. Somehow I twisted enough to take the impact with my hip. I caught my balance, but only my use of leverage kept him upright. In the distance the elevator call button dinged, and the overhead lights blinked on and off.

On and off.

Oh, hell.

"Change of plans," I said. "Let's check out the laundry room."

"Lay on, Macduff," he whispered.

"That line was Macbeth inviting Macduff to attack," I said. "Macbeth gets beheaded in that attack."

"Point taken," he said. "Get it? *Point* taken?"

The door to the laundry was metal and thick. The posted hours said it was open 6:00 A.M.–6:00 P.M. MONDAY–SATURDAY. The door was just locked, not padlocked, and the glass pane in the center looked almost bulletproof. Was *almost* enough to stop the Shadowless?

"Wicked hilarious," I said and pulled Harken's penknife out of the bag. "Shut up and pick the lock."

As we entered, an automatic switch turned on the overhead fluorescents. I flinched, and Harken drew back like the vampyre facing the dawn. He hissed and covered his face. The ceiling was a swamp of huge in and out ducts, and chutes, handles, and overhead tracks to control the flow of laundry. Heavy hooks hung from the tracks, white duffels chained to the hooks, an assembly line for soiled linens.

Four clotheslines held oversize sheets, bolts of cloth as long as a wall that flapped as I pushed them aside.

To our left were a steam boiler and eight industrial washing machines, each of them big enough to stick a body inside. Beside the washers were twice as many dryers, even bulkier than the washers. I steered us through the middle of the room, which was lined with yellow barrels and red baskets full of soiled linens. A half dozen massive blue bins filled with clean sheets were parked next to a loom-shaped pressing machine that filled the far wall. The scariest machine in the room was some kind of automatic sheet folder on the right-hand wall, an array of tables and presses that looked like they could take an arm off at the nub.

I lowered Harken to the floor next to the sheet folder, then hit the light switches to make it dark again. My shirt was covered in blood, none of it mine.

"This body," he said, "yearns for the grave."

"Tell it to yearn for a cookie."

He laughed, and the laugh turned into a cough. Blood and spittle seeped between his lips. I was losing him. He was letting go, and I was losing him, and I didn't know how to stop it.

"Willow Jane—" His hard face softened. "—there's something I have to confess."

"I'm not a priest," I said, keeping watch on the door.

"Listen to me," he said. "When I first went searching for you, it wasn't to help, it was to . . ."

His voice trailed off. It didn't matter because his expression had told me everything. He had expected me to be another boy in an endless line of Conning boys, another boy he didn't want to serve.

"You planned to kill me," I said, watching the glass for signs of Malleus. I was sure the light through the frosted glass was growing more dim.

He turned away, and I saw the shame on his face. It should've made me angry—no, furious—but I was too tired, and he had saved my sister's life. Had saved mine, too, by facing the creature he feared most and sacrificing himself so we could survive.

Still, I was curious. "What changed your mind?' I asked.

"When I saw you, I realized that I'd done enough killing," he said softly, wincing. "The things I've done, Willow Jane. If only I could undo them. To have clean hands once more . . ."

I caught his eye, the way I'd seen him stare at Siobhan. "Give me your name."

"Harken."

"If you want my trust," I warned him, "you have to trust me, too."

He seemed taken aback at the command, but he answered anyway. "Edward Bruce Harken. After the last of the Irish high kings."

"Edward Bruce Harken," I said and touched his cheek, "I have your name."

A static charge danced from my fingertips, and my mind was alight with images of a little boy in the highlands snatched by a raven-haired woman with yellow eyes. Then the boy was a young man, and he stood beside a hooded executioner under a great oak tree and kicked the stool from beneath the convicted's feet. Then he was Harken as I knew him, carrying a flaxen-haired child from the dungeons of Salem, weeping as he buried her in a mass pauper's grave. Images of faces flew by, all of them ginger, all of them male, until he was running up the fire escape of Devon's school, terrified, but still swinging the door open and looking into the face of the same woman who had taken his family, his life, and his peace.

"I'm sorry," I said, opening my eyes. "None of this was your fault."

"No, it's *all* my fault. The Sisters made it my duty to bury Malleus. But she escaped, and I led her right to you."

"You say that like it's a bad thing."

Boom! A percussive wave shook the corridor, shaking the whole room. Boom! Above, the lights swung back and forth. The machines rattled, and Harken groaned. In the distance, a guttural voice sang, "Will she? Will she?" followed by the grinding of metal against stone. It was Malleus, and she had to be dragging the shears along the walls.

Closer.

Stronger.

"Will she? Will she?" she sang again, followed by a hammering boom! Boom! Boom!

The Shadowless was coming.

Coming for us.

CHAPTER SEVENTY-FOUR

I grabbed a pillowcase from the basket of dirty linen. I twisted it around the door's panic handles and tied it in a double granny knot. Then I rolled a cart to Harken.

"That will buy us some time," I said quietly. "Can you to get into this thing?"

"Watch me," he said, sucking in a deep breath and the strength to get to his feet. His face was ghostly white, and sweat poured from his brow, but he stood long enough to fall into the mound of linens. "Good God, that hurt."

"Sorry," I whispered. "If my plan's going to work, we have to move fast."

"Plan?"

"Shh," I said and grabbed a mop from the closet. I twisted off the head and hid behind the door, my ear next to the glass.

Listening.

Listening to the steel grind of the shears on the wall.

Watching.

Watching the hall lights all but die.

Eyes up.

Head on a swivel.

I could hear the click of her feet on the floor. My pulse quickened, and I felt the sudden urge to attack. I almost called her by name. No. Let her find me. Let her use her theatrics, the sound of the scissors scraping the wall that would've terrified me yesterday.

Now I would be the one waiting in the shadows.

As I crouched, ready with the mop handle, the frosted glass began to jangle. Malleus crossed by the window, shears raised, the points as long and sharp as fangs. The tips of the shears scraped the glass, slowly, agonizingly, two long strokes that sent shivers down my spine.

"Will she? Will she?" the Shadowless hissed. "Will Willow be hanging from the willow hanging tree?"

Shut up! I wanted to scream, but I bit a knuckle and

held my tongue. I gripped the mop handle tightly and held my breath, counting the seconds.

"Blood," she hissed again and inhaled. "Blood will have blood."

She threw herself against the door, a sudden, violent clash that pushed the door as wide as it would go. The pillowcase stretched out, straining against the fierce battering, then like a rubber band, contracted and slapped the door shut.

The next time, she would just cut the pillowcase, and she'd go for Harken first—blood will have blood. I raced to the steam boiler and scanned the controls. We had a machine like this in our triple-decker. A turn valve controlled the temperature gauge, and if you opened the valve too far, too much steam would build up, and bad things would happen.

I cranked the valve wide open. Flipped the switches to start the dryers. Threw the handle that made the ironing presses cough and wheeze, filling the room with more steam. Then I switched on the folding machine, its long rollers clacking and clanking so loud, I couldn't hear myself think. In a matter of seconds the laundry became a hell house of noise and steam, and I pulled Harken's cart behind the hanging sheets.

Waiting.

"What are we doing?" he said in a hoarse voice.

"Creating a diversion." I covered him with a fresh sheet. "You're not dying in a pile of dirty laundry, thank you very much."

"Door . . . won't hold forever."

"Forever never lasts forever," I said and watched the shears slide inside and cut the twisted pillowcase like tissue paper.

The outside air hit the laundry room, and the steam turned as thick as fog. The Shadowless stalked inside, head twisting this way and that, nose lifted to sniff for blood, eyes darting. Her head snapped—something caught her eye— and she slid between the hanging sheets, into the maze of billowing fabric, then disappeared.

I snuck away from the cart. Wary and checking over my shoulder. Where did she go? I slid around a linen cart, then stared into the maze of billowing whiteness. She was gone.

Get back, I told myself, she could be behind you. But the thought paralyzed me. What if I moved right into her? I waited another second, then ten more. Get the hell out of here, I thought, and turned back for Harken.

A scream. From Harken!

I ran to him, sneaking be damned, ducking through the maze. Found him and pulled back the sheet, his eyes popping open, surprised, wet hair plastered to his face, but okay. He was okay.

Another scream, then a laugh, high pitched and mocking from the maze. Tricked me. She'd tricked me, made me run, made me reveal myself.

I covered him again. "Be quiet," I whispered, not daring to look at him.

Mop handle in both hands, I moved quickly toward the sound, then stopped, waiting to hear it again. For several seconds, nothing . . . then a sharp ripple in the sheets to my left. I darted away, opposite, into the center of the room. Vulnerable here, ducking between the long metal folding tables stacked with clean linens, eyes scanning for shadows. No, movements, not shadows. She was the Shadowless.

No place to hide in the open, so I sidled up to the bank of dryers, clutching the handle, ready to strike, coming to the last dryer and finding . . .

Nothing.

She was here—hiding in the maze of steam and wet sheets, but here. Hunting me as I hunted her.

Now beside the presser. Huffing hot air, clacking and ratcheting, the machine hid my sounds in its own noise, Buttressed against it, my head throbbing and my eyes again scanning for movement. I could get away. I could. Malleus was lost in the maze, and I could see the door in the miasma of steam, the thick glass clouded with it. I could run upstairs and get the police and bring them back, and they could shoot this bitch, and if she was gone, then she was gone.

No.

There was no running. No leaving Harken, and if I tried to move him, she would catch us.

I slinked past the presser and hid behind the fifty-gallon laundry drums, where there was a clear view of the maze and a straight shot to a utility closet across the room. If I could draw her there, get her to chase me, and then lock her inside . . .

Another glance over my shoulder, and I decided to act.

I sprinted through the maze, screaming and slapping the sheets with my stick. I leaped over a folding table and crashed into the washers, slamming the doors and pounding on the sheet metal like it was a drum. *Come get me*, the noise was saying, and I hoped she would.

My heart was pounding, too, and the thick, hot air made it hard to catch a breath. The mop shook so hard in my hands, I gripped it like I was in a face-off, ready to sweep Malleus's feet when she showed up. She had to show up. The commotion had to draw her. She had to take the bait.

Seconds ticked away. My heart beat faster, but the sheets did not move. She wasn't coming for me. Dear God, no. She could've sneaked around me, could've found Harken. Where was she?

In the maze. Hiding in the maze. Waiting for me.

Find her.

I crept away from the washer so very quietly, my shoulder low, legs wide and ready to take a charge, my boots skating over the wet floor, mop handle waist high, ready to slap-shot the bitch. Into the open again, crossing behind the linen drums and curling around the edge of the maze, ever watching, head on a swivel.

Ready. Chin up. Eyes opened.

Then, in the all the rumble and shadows, I felt her.

Nearby.

I shoved a barrel into another, and ten feet away the sheets billowed up. There she is! I slipped around the folding table in the middle of the room, on hands and knees, and waited for the sheets to be still.

My head whipped around, in time to see the shears rip through the sheets. Not just rip, but shred like Malleus was trying to gut them. I screamed, ducked under the table, and crawled out behind the next clothesline.

I slid on the slick floor as Malleus laughed and tore down the sheets, one by one. She shoved aside a folding table like a child's toy as I fled to the rolling machine and its hungry mass of clattering rollers and bearings and gears. I jumped over a pile of linens, Malleus screaming and stabbing, right behind me. Turned and broke the mop handle on her head, knocking her off-balance, making her slip on the wet floor. She fell toward the folding machine and put out a hand to catch her herself.

"Bad move," I said.

A spinning roller caught the fringe of her bell sleeve, and the machine snapped it—and her arm—right up. Her head repeatedly smacked against the safety guard as inch by inch the rollers ate her and the fabric, trying to chew her whole arm off.

"Uncanny!" she screamed at me, eyes bulging with rage, not fear.

I wanted to stand and watch the machine chew her to bits, but I took off across the laundry room, tearing down the sheets as I ran. I grabbed Harken's cart and, slamming against the door, burst into the hallway, leaving Malleus behind to die.

The corridor ahead curved like a bend in a river. I pushed the cart around the corner toward the exit signs. But instead of an escape route, I found a dead end.

The hallway had been stripped of its plasterboard walls and drop-down tiles. Nothing of the building remained but naked columns and bare floors. The ceiling was clogged with loose wires that ran like arteries in a milieu of different directions, and the darkness was lit by a few bare bulbs hanging from those wires, which reminded me far too much of the Hellesgate Hotel.

Twenty yards ahead, the corridor stopped. No, it transformed. The smooth concrete floor became a brick path with half the bricks missing. The solid walls turned into arches, also made of bricks, many of which had fallen and were littering the ground. Now three large conduit pipes carried the current into the darkness, and a temporary ply-wood gate blocked the tunnel. It was covered with six strips of overlapping caution tape. As if that would stop anyone.

"An abundance of caution," I joked halfheartedly. "That must be where they're hiding the major construction."

Harken didn't answer. He lay in a crumpled ball, blood soaking the linens beneath him. His eyes were closed, and I couldn't tell if he was breathing. I looked behind me. Should I go back? Rush past the laundry to the elevators? Malleus had to be dead, right? But even as the thought coalesced in my mind, I knew it was false hope.

"Harken?" I shook his shoulder. "It's time to spill on how to kill your old boss."

His lips moved. I pressed my ear against his cold cheek and heard only one word: "Poem."

"What poem?" I said. "My dad's poem?"

He nodded and reached for my coat.

"Uncanny!" Malleus screamed. She came around the bend, all sound and fury. The sleeve of her robe was gone, exposing a gangrenous arm that was more sinew and bone than flesh. But the arm was still intact, and so was she.

There was murder in her eyes.

"You shall pay for that affront!" she bellowed.

"Oh, shit."

I tore the caution tape away and pushed the cart through the plywood gate. There was a bolt on the back side, so I threw it, laughing at how flimsy it was. I tipped the cart to its side and rolled Harken out. His eyes were fluttering when I dragged him to the only safe place I could see—a chain-link fence that housed an old-fashioned electric switchboard, with a dozen knife switches and open-link fuses, as well as six monitoring dials as big as a dinner plate. It was caked in dirt from years of neglect, and bundles of wire and lengths of conduit were piled inside the cage, along with outdated electrical boxes and switches. The power was still hooked up, though, and humming like a song.

"Some sanctuary, huh?" I said, nodding at the DANGER: DEATH sign.

"One man's poison," he managed to say, "is another man's cure."

I unlatched the chain–link gate, helped him inside, and placed him against the switchboard. I turned to go, and he caught my sleeve.

"Don't fight her," he said, wheezing. "Just protect . . . the egg."

"All I need," I said, grabbing a piece of steel conduit pipe, "is to bust some Shadowless ass."

I had just stepped outside the cage and closed the gate when behind me, bam! the plywood door blew open. With a rending screech, a monstrous crow ripped past me, its wings wide, talons out.

"Damn it!" I said, ducking. "Freaking birds! In a freaking *basement*! If I ever see another goddamn crow again, so help me."

"Do we frighten you?" Malleus stepped forward. Her body was covered with molted feathers, and her eyes were the color of vomit. "How lovely."

I held the pipe out like a sword. "It won't be so funny when I shove this pipe down your throat." I whirled and backed up, keeping it between us. "Want the egg back? You'll have to pry it from my cold, dead hands."

"The thought of your cold, dead hands thrills us in ways you cannot imagine."

I expected her to charge, but Malleus drew something dark around herself, and with a sound like flapping wings, she dissipated. "Now you will know why we are called the Shadowless."

Darkness fell like a smothering blanket, constricting

me, squeezing the air from my lungs. I pulled my phone out. Swung the light around, chasing sounds, making shadows. The light was too bright. It blinded me. Hid her from me. I don't like the shadows, I thought. They protect her and leave me naked. She could be anywhere. Beside me. Behind me. Or . . .

I flicked the light to the ceiling, remembering the hallway in the Hellesgate when she dropped like a spider from above. Nothing. Just mold-coated bricks and a steady drip of water.

"Willow!" Harken cried.

Sharp talons raked my neck, and I cried out, too, a hand going to the wound, stumbling away from the attack, away from the cage and Harken. Another flutter of wings, and something rammed my back, and I pitched forward, the phone clattering over the bricks, the light shining on the ceiling. Laughter now, echoing, and I crawled toward the phone, my neck stinging, hearing Harken calling my name, his voice weaker and weaker, the crumbling bricks chewing up the skin of my hands.

Another laugh, and another swoop of wings, and I dived, hand outstretched, grabbing the light and swinging it around, crazy spinning, trying to find her in the darkness. But it was shadows, all shadows, and she melted into them.

"Will she? Will she?" Her voice echoed, impossibly far away, "Will Willow be hanging from the willow hanging tree?"

I swept the light toward the sound. It found a wall, a solid brick wall so close I could reach out and touch it. How? Slowly, raising the pipe and turning, I cast the beam on the walls. Four walls. A room, not a tunnel. A rectangular room no bigger than a classroom, a ceiling so low I could almost touch it, smelling dank and moldy. How could she hide? How could she sound so far away?

"Foolish child," she whispered, breath on my neck, "the shadows go on forever."

I screamed and swung the light and the pipe, striking nothing but shadows, and she was laughing again, the voice behind me. Swinging again. Swinging and cursing and chasing her with the light, following the singsong, *Will she? Will she?* Running now. Running toward the sound. Running deeper into the shadows.

"Willow Jane," Harken whispered. "Don't follow . . ."

His voice trailed off, so far away now. Go back to him. Go back. But there was another sound, lilting and happy, a child's laughter. Devon? Wait! I ran toward the laughter, nothing but me and the familiar tug of a rope on my belly button, pulling me forward into a glimpse.

"Stop." The dead girl was there. She stood alone in the blackness, with her hands raised. "Stop," she said again. "Go no farther into the shadows lest you be lost. Go back. Go back. The familiar needs you."

I tried to brush past her, to keep running, but she was in front of me again, grabbing my light and shining it into my eyes. The beam blinded me for just a few seconds, and when my sight returned, I was facing the same brick wall, tears running down my face.

The first blow almost took my head off.

A fist or an elbow to my jaw. My head snapped, and I stumbled back. Raised the pipe but too late. Another blow, lower back. Another. Stomach. Doubling me over. Hard strikes so fast. So hard. My heart pounded. Head roared. Hand holding the pipe reaching into the dark, finding the wall. The wall. Fingers anchored to the bricks, nails digging into loose masonry. Back against it. If I stay against it, nothing can get behind me. Ears ringing. Chest sucking air. Too much noise. Too much breathing. Holy shitbiscuits! Can't see. Can't hear. Get your head in the game, Conning! She could be coming. She could be coming.

Down! I dropped down. A whoosh above me, grinding metal on bricks, sparks exploding where my throat had been. Crawl! Hands and knees on the floor. Low and fast and going for the corridor. Get into the light. How can it be so dark? So black the dark.

A swoop. A flutter. Down! I flattened myself, cheek on the ground, dirt in my mouth, crawling like a snake, shining my light on Harken. In the cage. Reach the cage. Get inside. Lock her out.

Another swoop in the shadows, and then she stepped out.

Between me and Harken.

Between me and the cage.

She flicked her shears. Inviting me. Daring me. "Save him"—she preened—"if you can."

Can I? Can I save him and myself? What could I do? Charge her? Attack and drive her back? Get inside the cage somehow and hold Harken as he took his last breath? And when he died in my arms, I'd be trapped with him, like a bird, in a cage.

"Will she? Will she?" she sang. "Will Willow be

hanging from the willow hanging tree?"

I turned off the light. Put the phone in my pocket. Raised the pipe, set my feet to take the hit, and waited.

In absolute darkness, I breathed in the dank of the room, whiffs of ammonia in the stale air. The charge of ozone from the switchboard. Heard the hum of electricity. The drip of water from the ceiling. Harken breathing, sharp, then quiet, unsteady. Felt the shadows wrap around me as everything went still.

Then I felt her reach for me.

Not with her hands but with shadow. She moved into my mind, and I could see myself through her eyes. She stood between me and the cage, barely moving. I was bright in her vision, a pulsing lantern. So small I was, so weak. No use to her except for my power, and soon, oh, soon, she would strip that from me, too. She would chop off my thumbs and hold them in front of Harken as she rammed her shears through his chest. Then she would have her vengeance. In the meantime there was nothing wrong with a little cat and mouse. So easy. It would be so easy to kill me now. She moved closer at the anticipation of it. Shears instead of a fist. Stabbing through the kidneys. Watch me bleed to death. She licked her lips. That she would enjoy. Oh. So much.

"Bitch!" I yelled and swung because I could see her now, see her as clearly as she saw me.

The clang of a pipe against a skull was sweet. Metal hit bone and vibrated all the way up my arm, and I did not give a shit. I hit her again and again, driving her back, away from the cage, away from Harken. Each blow stung my arms, and my ears were ringing with it, and I was screaming, not even words, just sounds of rage.

My next swing missed. Momentum carried me forward, and even as I realized that I hadn't missed, that she had dissipated again, I heard the cage door swing open. Then the sounds of struggle and a whistling noise. Her? Was it her? Had I put a hole in her deep enough to kill her?

The whistling turned to moaning, and I knew that I was wrong.

"Willow Jane," Harken gasped.

Malleus held him by the throat. Standing outside the cage, holding him in the air, a proud hunter showing off a fresh kill. "Such a pretty songbird." She shook him, a rag doll. "Would you still defend him if you knew he betrayed you, as he betrayed us?"

I inched toward her. Distract her, I thought, till you're

close enough. "Malleus the Deceiver, that's what the Sisters called you. Or was it undead ugly bitch? I get confused."

She looked at Harken, almost affectionately. "This is your hero?"

"He sacrificed himself to save my sister." Closer. The pipe tight against my leg. Closer. "If he did evil, it was for you."

"What would you know of evil?" Malleus dropped Harken, simply dropped him, and put her knee to his head. His skin had turned blue, and he was mouthing something as she pressed, hand on his throat, shears raised. "Any sins to confess, familiar?"

"Don't do it," I warned her. *This close.*

"Wish . . . I'd never . . . laid eyes . . . on you," Harken said, choking.

"If wishes were horses," Malleus said and plunged the shears into his gut.

"Harken! No!"

Harken was laughing. The shears had not missed—the blades were buried inside him—and he was laughing. "Want. Your. Precious heart?" With a jerk of his hand, he sent the egg rolling toward me. "Fetch."

The egg tumbled across the bricks like a malformed

obsidian marble. I scooped it up. It was warm, and I felt a heartbeat. My pulse? Or the egg?

She yanked the shears free and flew at me so fast I fell backward, and she was on me, reaching for my throat. I whacked her hand with the pipe, then drove my boots into her stomach. Rolled to my feet, but Harken was suddenly between us. His arms flew wide, right before the shears sank into his chest again. The tips emerged through his back. Malleus pulled them out, and his body crumpled.

"Harken!" I screamed and caught him as he fell, taking us both to the ground. I pushed the hair away from his face. "Please."

"Don't fret," he gasped, blood seeping from the corner of his mouth. "I've lived . . . too long already."

"You lived too long a coward," Malleus said, mocking him. "You die a fool, and your spirit is forever mine."

"Kill her," he said so softly. "Father . . . told you . . . how."

"It's just a freaking poem!"

"Willow Jane . . . Conning." He reached for me. "I have your . . . name."

He looked into my eyes one last time. Light wept out of him, shimmering and floating, even as Malleus yanked his body out of my grasp. The bronze torc slipped from his neck and clattered to the ground. His body seemed transparent, almost as if he were evaporating with each passing second. His spirit was moving from this world into the next. The only thing that seemed to hold it here was Malleus, who was gripping his thumbs so tightly.

"Please, no," I said, getting to my feet and limping toward her, carrying the egg in one hand and the pipe in the other. Harken had sacrificed himself for me, and I couldn't let Malleus take him. "Let his soul go free, and I'll give you the egg."

Malleus snapped the blades at his thumbs. "Too late! The familiar is bound for the Shadowlands."

Not if I could help it. "Come on, Malleus. Take the thing you yearn for." I raised the egg. "Let Harken go, and I'll give you what you offered me—eternity."

She cocked her head, eyes darting.

"Choose," I demanded.

"Why choose?" she said. "Together *we* can rule the past, the present, and the future. *We* can have control of life and death itself! *You* must only seize the power!"

Control of life and death? I saw my father lying on the popcorn and soda stained carpet in the movie theatre, the house lights reflecting in the dark blood blooming from his chest. I saw his eyes go wide and heard his teeth chatter. I held his hand and repeated, "Don't die, don't die, hang on, hang on." But he couldn't, and he died in pain and afraid with my fingers intertwined with his. My father's blood was on my hands. Bringing him back to life would change nothing. I thought about Harken's warning about raising the dead, of my sister in a coma, of Kelly hanging from the ceiling and smelling like a moldy newspaper. If I gave in to Malleus, their lives would be spent forever in the shadows.

Kill her, he had said. My father had told me how. Had he? I looked down at my coat where the iron needle was still safely tucked in my lapel. Why?

"Tempting, is it not?" she said, as if she knew my deepest yearning. "Give us the egg and step into the shadows, where you can truly live."

"Release him first," I said. "You destroyed his life. You can't take his soul, too."

"As you wish." Malleus released his hands and dropped her bloody shears. The last of Harken's body dissolved into light. The only thing that remained was the bronze torc resting on the ground. "Now ends his sleep of Shadowless."

"His what?" I said. *To end the sleep of Shadowless. Weave*

silver twixt her eyes. The poem! The needle! Yes! That was it! That's what Dad was trying to tell me!

"The egg," Malleus said.

"The egg," I said and, backing toward the switchboard cage, tossed it.

Malleus clawed the air frantically as the egg arced and fell toward her, as if it would never come. Her eyes went wide, so wide, and she cupped her hands to catch it. The fire behind her irises burned, and she licked her lips in anticipation as it fell softly into her palms.

She lifted the egg triumphantly, ecstatically.

A wave of electric darkness swept over her. She laughed, and her flesh began to regenerate around her bones. Patches of skin stretched tight over her face, and the straggling strands of silver hair that speckled her head grew thicker, longer, and darker.

"Spontaneous regeneration?" I said. "Seriously? What's next?"

"For you?" Malleus said. "Agony and death."

"That's funny," I said, biting my thumb and pulling a strand of gossamer long enough to maybe kill me. "'Cause death is what's next for you."

"Are you a fool, little one?" A thin, forked tongue

darted from Malleus's mouth, and her eyes narrowed, her regenerating body trembling with ecstasy. "Weaving gossamer in my presence?"

To end the sleep of Shadowless. "Want a taste?" I said, backing into the chain link. "Come get it."

She couldn't help herself. The gossamer was driving her mad with desire, and she shuffled after me, her face rapt, mesmerized by the glistening strand that clung to my thumb. Praying that this was what Harken had tried to tell me, I plucked the long bodkin needle from my coat and threaded the gossamer through its broad eye.

"The last time we ate gossamer," Malleus said, "your little dead girl died."

She laughed, and something inside me snapped. I forgot the gash on my neck, the pains in my back, the blows she had given me, and I rammed my left shoulder into her chest. She fell backward, but I grabbed her shroud and swung her around, pushing her back against the switchboard cage. I drove an elbow into her temple and snapped her head back. With the noise of metal threads shearing off, the chain-link gate swung inward, and Malleus fell hard against the row of knife switches.

"Get up," I said and followed her inside.

Her flesh was almost whole, her hair as wild and thorny as a blackberry bush. She was more ravishing than Harken had said, her beauty seemingly fed by the egg in her hand.

I paused there, perched between the cage and the tunnel. My head was pounding, and I heard ringing from far off, like a church bell. She smiled and started moving a hand to her rib cage—the hand with the heart.

"No!" I screamed, and before the heart reached her chest, I grabbed a handful of feathered hair and slammed her head against the box.

Again.

And again.

"Stop," she croaked. "Please."

And again. Until her eyes rolled back. Then I slapped her arm against the switchboard and stabbed her with the bodkin, piercing both her hand and the heart.

The obsidian cracked.

Malleus let out a low, deep moan and fought to free her hand, but she could not. She could not. *Weave silver twixt her eyes.* I wrapped the gossamer from her hand to her face. Watched it eat through her skin, a wick dipped in acid. Her new flesh began to molt, dripping like wax from her lovely face.

"My face," she moaned. "My beautiful face."

"Sucks to be you," I said. There was nothing left but to cut the thread. I picked up the tailor's shears.

"Stop! Do not cut the thread, we beg you," Malleus mewled. "You shall be damned to eternal life without kin, without a future, without hope."

"But you'll be dead, and I can live with that."

"Do not make this choice! You shall be Unmade!"

"No," I said, suddenly so weary I could hardly stand. "*You're* Unmade."

Cut gossamer threads with sparks coalesced. With a quiet snick, I cut the gossamer.

The whole switchboard hummed, and the hair on my arms stood straight up. As I jumped back, sparks flew through the air, and liquid steel poured through the gossamer.

Malleus became an inferno. Her shroud turned to ash, and the fire spread to her hair, then skin, as she began to melt like a tallow candle.

"Sister," Malleus rasped with her last breath as one eye rolled back into her head. "Have mercy."

"I'm so not your sister, bitch," I said and licked my thumb.

My hand jerked back as if I had grabbed a live wire. My spine arched, and I heard a sound like a train in a tunnel, and then for a few seconds the lights whipped around and around. With the familiar rush of sounds and color, I fell out of the glimpse.

And the Shadowless shall die.

CHAPTER SEVENTY-FIVE

ALL that that was left of Malleus was an ash-black skeleton.

"I never did like loose ends," I said, shaking from the glimpse, and picked up the bronze torc.

The metal felt cold in my hand. I started to put it around my own neck. To wear it like Harken had, when blood started pouring from my nose. I struggled to breathe as I staunched the flow with Harken's handkerchief. I'm coming Unmade, I thought. I had cut the gossamer, and now I would suffer the consequences. My life would be eternal. Maybe I could no longer glimpse, but my sister would live, and I had kept my promise to my father.

Rubbing the cold metal in my hands, I turned to go and gasped. Three tall women in white robes loomed over me. The hems of the robes reached the floor, and their sleeves covered their hands. Their faces were hidden by their hoods, but not their silver hair, which looked like gossamer.

"Sisters?" I whispered.

"Uncanny," they said in unison.

"I am Urth."

"I am Skuld."

"I am Verth."

"Um, I'm Willow Jane? The Uncanny, I guess," I said. "Are you here for Malleus?"

"The Shadowless is no more," Urth said.

"But," I said and held up the torc, "what about Harken?"

Skuld pointed at me. "To the family of the flaxen child he was yoked, spirit to sprit, until the day the Uncanny should return."

"The torc that bound him was removed," Verth said. "His soul has been reconciled."

"So it is written," the Sisters chanted. "So it is done."

"But that's not fair," I said. "He sacrificed himself for me and my sister. I wanted him . . . to live."

"Time and fate have no concern for your desires," Urth said, her voice cold and distant.

"Because I'm Unmade, right?" I said and made air quotes. "Damned to an eternal life, whatever the hell that means," I said. "What happens to me now?"

"A long life, perhaps, but not eternal," she scoffed. "The price you paid is losing your power." Then her demeanor changed, and her voice softened. "Yet we are not heartless ourselves. Name one boon of us, and it shall be done."

"A boon? Like a favor?"

They nodded, and their gossamer hair glistened in the light. It reminded me of my thumb and the power that I'd given away to beat Malleus. I could ask for it back. Having the power to manipulate time could come in handy, once I mastered it.

Or I could cut to the chase and ask for my birthday wish to be answered: My dad to be alive, to be father and husband again. To wake up in the morning and have him cooking breakfast, singing at the top of his lungs, to wrap his arms around me and make me safe again.

It was a sweet dream but impossible. My wish couldn't be selfish. If I'd learned one thing, it was that selfish wishes always went bad.

"The souls lost in the Shadowlands," I said. "Bring them back. Bring them all back."

The Sisters were silent. Some unseen breeze rippled their white gowns as they leaned close to one another. For a moment, I thought they would deny my wish and tell me to choose something more doable.

Then they all three bowed. "So it is written," they chanted. "So it is done."

The torc turned warm. Fireflies of lights danced from the metal, wrapping around my hand, and my fingertips spat light like sparklers. The sparks multiplied, gathered themselves like a swarm in the air. Then the swarm seemed to pulse. The light turned solid, then died out, leaving behind a human with a very familiar face.

"Harken," I whispered.

Harken smiled at me but didn't speak, so I nodded and smiled back. What could I say that meant more?

"Where's Devon?" I asked the Sisters.

"The child has returned to where she belongs," Urth said. "The rest must go onward."

"The rest?" I said. "And what do you mean, to where she belongs? Home?"

"The rest must go onward," Urth said again.

Sparks crackled again. From out of the veil stepped Will Patrick, Flanagan, and Kelly. None of them spoke, but they all opened their hands.

"What do they want?" I asked.

"Although you freed them," she said, "they cannot continue the journey yet."

"Can't go on? Why?"

"They must pay for their passage," she said.

Harken rubbed his fingers together, then opened his hand.

"Oh. Oh, yeah, of course, the tokens," I said. "Harken said I'd need these."

I dug in my pocket and produced the tokens that Harken had given me what felt like long ago. I placed one in each palm. Kelly's, then Will Patrick's, then Flanagan's, and finally, the dead girl's. As soon as they bowed and closed their hands, the sparks crackled and dissipated, leaving a sweet-smelling smoke behind them.

"Last but not least," I said and gave Harken a copper, letting the moment linger.

He rubbed the token with his fingers. For a few seconds it seemed as if his hand were flesh again, then I realized that it was just wishful thinking. He closed his fingers around the coin and began to disappear.

"Wait," I said, but Harken shook his head sadly.

There would be no waiting. Our time together had passed, and even for a girl who could control time, there was nothing to do about it. All that remained was an emptiness in my heart and one last copper token in my palm.

PART SIX

A TOKEN FOR CHILDREN

THE walls of our apartment were stripped bare, clean rectangles and squares marking the wallpaper where a lifetime of photos had been removed. The furniture had been carried downstairs to a waiting moving truck, and only a few cardboard boxes were left in the living room.

I was in the bathroom, brushing my teeth in the mirror. It was crazy, yes, wanting to complete this ritual on moving day, but owning my weirdness was the way I rolled now. I leaned down to spit in the sink, then looked up. Devon was behind me, hands raised like claws, white fangs jutting from her mouth.

"Jesus!" I yelped.

Devon popped the plastic teeth out and laughed maniacally, "Bwahaha! Made you jump, ya big ginge." She threw her arms around my waist and held on tight.

"Stop," I said, wiping my mouth. "You're squeezing my guts out."

We had a silly slap fight, and I found her tickle spots, too. Her dark hair bounced like a nest of slinky coils, and she laughed with abandon, the way only little kids can.

"I give!" she said. "Ma says to hurry. They're taking the last boxes."

"Be right there." I rinsed the toothbrush thoroughly and shook out the excess water. "Had to brush. Can't go to a new place with yucky teeth."

"Sure ya can. I do it all the time."

I dropped my toothbrush into the trash can and put the toothpaste and floss into my dad's old dopp kit. I tucked it into a box and handed it to Devon. "Carry this to Ma. I'll be right there."

Then she was rocketing down the hallway, sneakers echoing through the empty rooms. I heard the front door swing open and Ma greet Siobhan and her dad. He said something that made Ma laugh, a sound that still made me smile. The heavy plod of his work boots on the landing meant he was already going back downstairs. Ma followed him, calling for me to quit dawdling.

I closed the mirror and looked at the reflection. The repaired wallpaper behind me was smooth, except for a few air bubbles, almost like it had never been ripped open. After the apartment house had changed hands, Ma decided it was time for the Conning girls to get a new place, far away from the ghosts of the past. A change was as good as a rest, she said. Little did she know how true that was.

I wandered into my old room. The bed and dresser were gone, already loaded on the truck. My closet was empty, and the floors were swept clean. I had grown up in this room, had visited magical worlds in the back of that closet, and had cried myself to sleep next to the windows, not only for my father two years ago but for Kelly in the days after her funeral and for Will Patrick and Flanagan, too. So much sadness and grief here, all mixed in with happiness and joy. It was time to move on, and in doing so, I hoped to take the good things with me and leave the bad ones behind. One thing for sure, Harken was a memory I was keeping close to my heart.

"Hey, loser," Siobhan said, knocking on my door.

I wiped my face on my sleeve. "You're the loser."

Siobhan stood beside me. She put an arm over my shoulder, and we looked out at the street that had once been inundated with birds. Birds that had never returned.

"God, you're short," she said.

"In private, you can call me Willow Jane."

She held up a hand for a fist bump. "Good one, Conning."

"Thanks for giving us a place to," I said and gave her a bump. "Y'know."

"Hey, enough with the thank yous. We weren't using that half of the duplex anyway, and Dad's too cranky to let it out to strangers."

"Still, it's a big favor," I said.

Our new place was the other half of Siobhan's duplex. Her dad owned the whole thing, but he was a blue-collar guy who wanted to trust his neighbors. Siobhan said he'd always worried about us girls living alone after my dad died, and this was a way to help out. Once a Southie, always a Southie, I guess.

"Shut it," she said. "You know I've got your back. Okay, enough of this reminiscence crap. The truck's all loaded, and your ma sent me to get you."

"You go ahead." I sniffed. "I've got to lock up."

"Five minutes." She shook a finger at me. "Don't let me catch you sitting in the living room, bawling your eyes out."

"You won't."

"Won't what?"

"Catch me."

She smiled and squeezed my shoulder, then left the room. I listened for the silence, and when she was gone, I wandered into each room, checking to be sure the windows were latched, the closets were empty, and the lights were off.

Change was good. For the last month, Devon had slept through the night. You'd never know what she went through. Little kids really were that resilient. The show Ma was working on got extended, which meant a good, steady income for at least six more months and maybe a year. As for me, every day since the hospital, I had awakened, expecting to see the dead girl wrapped in rotting newspaper, but she, like Harken and all the others, was gone forever.

In the living room, I looked out the bay window one last time. I'd seen the same street corner every day of my life. Watched the neighborhood change bit by bit, while thinking that I never did. But it was me who was changing all along. There was no telling what the future would hold for me, but I knew that no matter what happened, the past would stay the same.

ACKNOWLEDGMENTS

Thanks to the bookmakers at Greenwillow, especially Virginia and Tim. Thanks, too, to the helpful readers who waded through drafts—Stacy Vandever Wells, Cheri Williams, Patti Holden, and Joy Pope. Many thanks to the patient and irreplaceable Rosemary Stimola. And to my family—Deb, Justin, Carolina, and Delaney—for putting up with the secret life inside my head.